THE AUKMONDI

SECRET OF THE YULULU BONE

H.D. HIGGINS

CITI OF BOOKS

CITIOFBOOKS, INC.
3736 Eubank NE Suite A1
Albuquerque, NM 87111-3579
www.citiofbooks.com

Hotline: 1 (877) 389-2759
Fax: 1 (505) 930-7244

Ordering Information:

Quantity sales. Special discounts are available on quantity purchases by corporations, associations, and others. For details, contact the publisher at the address above.

Printed in the United States of America.

ISBN-13:	Paperback	979-8-89391-677-5
	eBook	979-8-89391-678-2

Library of Congress Control Number: 2025908986

In *The Aukmondi: Secret of the Yululu Bone,* by H. D. Higgins, the time is the mid-eighteenth century – slave-hunting time. The setting is East Africa, where the village of the Chinchigwe tribe is overrun by the Batushi, slave hunters, who carry off thirty survivors and sell them to a colonial American slave trader named Oliver McIntyre.

When Captain McIntyre pays the Batushi with defective firearms, they return the affront by presenting McIntyre with a mysterious necklace – the Yululu Bone. As the Chinchigwe are driven, chained and shackled, to the African coast to begin the "middle passage" to America and a life of plantation slavery, they are put into makeshift pens to guard against escape. In one pen with them is Adaulah, an eight-year-old captive boy who claims to be a prince of the Aukmondi tribe. When the opportunity comes, Adaulah helps the Chinchigwe escape and, determined to find his home, he guides them to his people, who inhabit the lush and fruitful Aukmondi Valley. Here the Chinchigwe experience the high civilization and peacefulness of Aukmondi life. They also learn about their young benefactor Adaulah, who is the son of Ramuza Ncobba, the Aukmondi leader, or Mfalme.

Driven by greed, McIntyre follows them, with the Yululu Bone and the Batushi in tow. The Yululu Bone grants the power of a tribal chief to its possessor, and McIntyre uses it to order the Batushi to help recover his escaped slaves. But the Yululu Bone also carries with it a curse, and Ramuza must find the secret of the Yululu Bone in order to save not only the Chinchigwe but also the Aukmondi and their peaceful way of Life.

DEDICATION

To my mother, Edna Higgins North, who set me on solid ground; to my father, H. D. Higgins, Sr., and my grandmother, Pearlee Willis, who are the foundation of my most cherished childhood memories; and to all the rest of my family (present and ancestral).

CONTENTS

PROLOGUE

It is said that one of the things that makes a rose so beautiful is the knowledge that such beauty will not last forever. In time, it will wilt and die.

This, too, is the pattern of life. It will someday end; in most cases, it is an accepted fact. It is only a tragedy when a precious life ends untimely.

It is also said, if life exists in great abundance, then the unfit of life will find it more and more difficult to survive. The unfit must learn to survive, or die. This is nature's law, and it is irrevocable.

During the middle of the 18th century, the continent of Africa had an abundance of life. Throughout this so-called "dark continent," thousands upon thousands of life forms lived together. Life abounded from the Mediterranean coast of Algeria to the congestion of Cape Town, South Africa.

For example, the great and majestic African oaks grew awesomely big among the fragrant cedars on the plateaus of Morocco and Tunisia. Despite the heat and drought, tsama melons, jerboas, and hedgehogs thrived without a problem in the vast Sahara Desert. Elephants and rhinoceros, the gray giants of the Serengeti, roamed freely, devouring tons of shrubs and grasses. These giants left a devastating mark behind them. Yet, the shrubs and grasses recovered in time. In the tropical rainforests in the Congo River Basin, African teakwood and oil palms grew in huge clusters. In the jungles of West and Central Africa, lowland gorillas lived to protect their unique social groups and families. Over their heads, scores of birds hustled about from treetop to treetop as easily as the wind. Zebra and gnus, as if in some natural alliance, formed intermixed herds as they grazed the savannas and grasslands, and constantly watched for the lions and leopards that hunted them. And the Antelopes, giraffes, chimpanzees, and baboons moved in nomadic herds from one choice feeding ground to another.

Throughout this untamed land, in each of these vastly different places, and among all these diverse representatives of life, the "dark continent" questionably made room for yet one more animal, an animal that prided itself as the most ingenious and determined animal of them all, but yet, always at odds with most other indigenous life forms. It was truly unlike any of the others. This animal was called man.

African man carved out his life on the dry and dusty plateaus of the north. He made homes throughout the grasslands and in the tropical forest areas. He lived in the mountain ranges and the coastal areas. Truly more intelligent and adaptable than any other animal, African man sometimes made his home even in the sweltering deserts.

Anytime there is an abundance of life, such as this, there is a proportionate amount of death. Life and death go hand in hand. They are absolutely inseparable. Not only must every living thing eventually die, but a great majority of these life forms depend on the untimely deaths of others to continue living.

Fortunately, it is nature's brilliant design that the unfit of life be the first to die; that variety of African violet that can not endure the drought; that mindless rodent that hunts for food near the viper's lair; that feeble gnu or zebra that can not keep up with the herd when the leopard gives chase; or most tragically, that undetermined African native that can not outwit disease, famine, and all other natural threats to life.

But, if it is nature's law that the unfit die first, then it is assured that the strongest of life will have a better chance to survive and pass on to their young those qualities that made them stronger in the first place.

This is not to say that the unfit have less of a will to live and survive. On the contrary, the unfit want to live too, just as much as the fit do, if not more so. In angry defiance of nature's law, a dying lioness will defend herself and her kittens more viciously than a healthy lioness. A wounded eagle or a sickly dog will attack intruders without provocation. Even that intelligent animal called man will do things he has never considered doing to preserve his life.

In Africa, when life thrives in abundance, the survival instinct becomes the most valued instinct of all. Every living thing, plant or animal, fit or unfit, begins to rely on the survival instinct before any other.

As a result, some vegetation can seek moisture in the ground as if by conscious intelligence. The African beasts can out-maneuver their predators or fight them off savagely, exploiting every weakness a predator may have. And an African man, with intelligence unlike any other, can often master or avoid the things that threaten him.

None of these survival techniques is simple. They are extremely complex efforts that have been evolving toward perfection since their beginnings. Natural characteristics now cover many struggles, except where African man is concerned.

Unlike the vegetation and the beasts, which could rely greatly on nature's evolutionary help, African man could not. In addition to disease, famine, and natural disasters, African men had to contend with an unnatural enemy. He had to stay one step ahead of the ceaseless aggressions of other men; men who were, every bit, as crafty and as intelligent as himself.

For example, there were the ruthless, killer Wabanga people. These days, the Wabanga were the most merciless, the most barbaric, and the least predictable of all the aggressors. Very few facts were known about the Wabanga, except that they were bizarre, cunning, obsessively aggressive, and absolutely deadly. Somehow, their own twisted sense of survival demanded that they stalk and kill man and beast indiscriminately.

During this time, the slave trade to Colonial America reached its peak. Consequently, slave hunters were proving to be another very serious threat to African men.

Although the slave hunters were native themselves, they rejected the traditional native lifestyle. They were a parasitic people. They no longer lived off the land around them. They found the basic goods that Mother Nature provided to be insufficient, unreasonable, or unsatisfactory. Because of some aberrant sense of value, greed, or simply out of convenience, they only wanted the easily tradable good that the outside would have to offer.

Most slave hunters fed their families with supplements of food received from the outside world. They put clothes on their backs made from materials received from the outside world. Everything they got, including many things they didn't need, came from the outside world. And what did they give in return? They gave other natives, of course, the "faceless nobodies" conveniently found in abundance all over Africa.

And, as if the Wabanga and the slave hunters were not enough to contend with, an insurmountable mark against native survival was also made by the Asian, Arabian, European, and Colonial American salve merchants as well. As if the slave hunters and the Wabanga were not enough, the slave merchants infiltrated Africa like evil spirits from regions unknown. They competed with the Wabanga in open aggression. And they firmly established themselves as the corrupt and driving force behind the slave hunters.

Even though the merchants were not as bizarre as the Wabanga, they were much more alien in appearance. Though they were not as brutal and careless as the slave hunters sometimes were, most African natives would prefer to be in the hands of the hunters rather than the merchants. The hunters could be reasoned with. The merchants could not.

The slave merchants were so culturally different that the native mind could not imagine their potential horror. And every native knew that any association with these evil-spirited, man-like creatures would lead to a traumatic uprooting from home, land, family, and ancestors forever.

In the face of all these threats, African men had two choices for survival. He either resisted with his life, or he surrendered.

To offer resistance was the broader and more desirable of the two choices. Understandably, it was also the most costly. To offer resistance meant avoiding, discouraging, fighting, suppressing, controlling, or doing whatever was necessary to remain free of the aggressor. It took foresight and an inner strength that does not come naturally to the unprepared, especially the unfit.

As isolated as most African villages were, many natives were unaware of an aggressor's intent. And when they did find out, it was oftentimes too late. So when an aggressor attacked, the natives, individually or as a tribe, chose that second option – surrender. It was a very undesirable choice. It was a form of defeat. But strange as it seems, it did achieve a type of survival.

Only with the killer Wabanga was surrender an unwise choice. Obviously, with the Wabanga, it was either fighting or being killed. But with the slave hunters or the slave merchants, there was an understood guarantee that "if you did not resist, you might live to see another day".

1

THE CHINCHIGWE

In an East African wilderness, somewhere south of the great Lake Victoria and west of the great Serengeti Plains, the remaining members of the Chinchigwe tribe resisted their aggressors one more time. This time they ran.

Five days ago, slave hunters came into their village. The hunters were peaceful at first. But it was a tense situation from the very beginning. One of the tribe's people showed a minor show of resistance. The tension escalated, and the situation quickly grew violent. The slave hunters began to show no mercy as they destroyed the Chinchigwe village. In a madness beyond reason, the hunters began to burn the huts, raid the crops and livestock, and kill anyone who showed resistance.

Sadly, when the raid was over, only thirty Chinchigwe survived. Thirty men, women, and children found themselves captives of the brutal slave hunters. Unlike most of their family and friends, these so-called fortunate people had survived the hunter's attack that morning by submitting to the enemy. They essentially surrendered. And as a result, they would live to see another day.

But, for four days and three nights, the Chinchigwe suffered the seemingly endless and gruesome experience of living in total defeat. They endured inhumane brutalities as they were permanently uprooted from their land and homes. They endured the pains of hunger and physical degradations as they were driven from the comfort of their homes to the unfamiliar and unforgiving African terrain.

By that fourth day, they were led into a small encampment of a Colonial American slave merchant. Still chained and shackled together, they were held in a muddy and foul-smelling holding pen. There, they stood helplessly by as more of them died and their number dwindled from thirty to twenty-four.

It did not take the Chinchigwe long to realize their mistake. Living, after giving in to the slave hunters, was a completely intolerable situation. It was worse than they ever imagined. It was not truly survival. It seemed death with their family and friends would have been better after all. For four days and three nights, they began to wish for the death that somehow passed them by.

As that fourth night of captivity began, one more captive, a young African boy, was thrown into the holding pen with the Chinchigwe. He was a small, frail little thing. Nonetheless, the merchant needed to chain and shackle him with the rest of Chinchigwe. He was hungry, frightened, and just as helpless as the Chinchigwe. The Chinchigwe could not even offer him a single word of comfort. The young boy and the Chinchigwe could only sit silently and suffer through their mutual situation.

But by some strange twist of fate, the addition of that young boy in the holding pen set into motion a chance to live again. In his private struggle, the little boy managed to pull his tiny arms from the shackles on his wrists. Among the very last of their rapidly deteriorating abilities, and beneath their dying desire to do anything for themselves, the Chinchigwe realized the significance of this small accomplishment. It represented a very rare opportunity to escape.

Like magic, the chance of freedom rejuvenated them. A wave of energy washed over Chinchigwe, waking them from their slumber and apathy. Fortified with blind hope, they eventually became restless enough to break free from the merchant's pen. And when they did, despite their weakened condition, they ran. They disregarded all the consequences that they might have to face, including compounded injuries, continued hunger, and more deaths. Under the circumstances, none of that seemed to matter now. They felt their minds and bodies miraculously charged. They felt a reckless quest for life again as they threw all caution to the wind and took their chances in the African wilderness.

— 2 —

FOR THE SAKE OF OUR ANCESTORS

The Chinchigwe had lived in a small, remote village in the Mwanza region, in northern Tanganyika.[1] They regarded themselves as a people with a simple lifestyle; so simple in fact, that their daily tasks did not exceed the maintenance of their basic needs. Day after day, harvest after harvest, they enjoyed working their crops or tending their cattle and goats. Some spent their entire lives making various products to sell, trade, or wear, such as pottery, jewelry, sandals, and clothing. As for religion, they gave ample attention to their ancestors and several generally accepted spirits, praising the benevolent ones, and respectfully fearful of all the others.

Like most small villages, the Chinchigwe village had been raided several times. Needless to say, it suffered with each raid. Families were broken, and herds and crops were destroyed as slave hunters came and took what they wanted. Yet, the village would bounce back after each raid and over time. Through hard work, determination, and an instinct to survive, the people would regain some semblance of normalcy. They had to. The Chinchigwe needed to continue as a tribe and as a people.

Of course, there were times when the Chinchigwe tried to resist the hunters. They confronted the hunters in combat countless times, and they formed alliances with neighboring clans and tribes. But these pragmatic efforts always ended with the same basic results: too many costly deaths among the Chinchigwe people.

---

[1] Tanganyika is now called Tanzania after merging with the country of Zanzibar in 1964.

Lomani Usai, the Chinchigwe Mfalme, knew too painfully well that his tribe was never large enough to resist the overwhelming armies of the slave hunters. Throughout his lifelong reign, the fact haunted him, followed him like his own shadow. Before his own eyes, his people, his beloved tribe, grew smaller and smaller in number. And there was very little he could do to prevent it effectively. Lomani's only option, and his legacy as the last Chinchigwe Mfalme, was to retard the tragedy as best he could.

At first, whenever the hunters came, the Chinchigwe offered very little resistance to lessen the tragedy. They often tried to be forewarned of the coming hunters and hid whenever possible. But that feeble effort was the extent of their resistance. By limiting their behavior in this way, the losses, as tragic as they were, were kept at a minimum. The Chinchigwe pathetically allowed the hunters to select the best of their people like fruit from a tree.

Consequently, with so little resistance, the raids took an unexpected turn. They began to increase. The hunters came and went, almost at will, reducing the helpless Chinchigwe and their culture to almost nothing.

"No! No more!" Mfalme Lomani decreed. "Never again will we shame our ancestors so. It is clear to me now. The time has long passed. We must fight for our survival. If we must, we will resist the hunters until the last man, the last woman, and the last child among us is dead. If we can not finish what our ancestors have started, let us die strong, with pride and dignity, here and now."

As he spoke, his voice had as much fury as agony. With such an emotional decree, Mfalme Lomani Usai knew he was collectively speaking to his people for the last time. He knew that his decree would take down the last barrier against the complete genocide of his people. He knew that when the last of the Chinchigwe died, so would the life-force of all the Chinchigwe ancestors, the single element that defined and gave value to who they were.

The next time the Chinchigwe village was raided, the situation was not recoverable. There was no bouncing back this time. It wasn't meant to be. In the most brutal and merciless raids ever, the

Chinchigwe fought the slave hunters more desperately than in all their history.

Long before the slave hunters reached the village, the Chinchigwe had learned of their approach and were ready for them. In the darkness of early morning, Mfalme Lomani Usai led all two hundred of his brave warriors out into the dew-covered hills, outside the village. There, they silently took up hidden positions and they waited.

Almost one hundred slave hunters came openly up the pathway toward the Chinchigwe village. The vocal harmony of their hunting chant echoed throughout the hills and indicated that they expected this raid to be like all the other recent raids. They expected nothing unusual. They anticipated no resistance from the docile Chinchigwe. Their first indication of trouble was a startling thump in the darkness.

The hunters' harmonious chant stopped as one of the hunters fell to the ground, flat on his back; a Chinchigwe spear embedded in his stomach. He died within seconds. Two more hunters fell and died in the same manner before the rest of them realized what was happening.

That ambush, the first line of resistance by the Chinchigwe, was the best strategy employed throughout the battle that followed that morning. The enemy was being soundly defeated. More and more hunters fell. The hunters were too confused to retaliate. Almost a third of them were killed or seriously wounded before any of them could react. And when they did, it was a panicky retreat.

"Finish them!" Lomani shouted to his warriors from a nearby hilltop. He knew this would be the only chance that the Chinchigwe would ever have to strike fear in the enemy. He knew this would be the only battle where the Chinchigwe would have a decisive advantage over the hunters. "Never again will the Chinchigwe be as docile as sheep. Show them the lion in us. Give them no mercy. Finish them all, for our ancestors' sake!"

The faithful and encouraged Chinchigwe warriors emerged from concealment to attempt to defeat the hunters completely. They felt good, knowing that they were creating fear, chaos, and disorder in their enemy. The gap between the two armies closed as the Chinchigwe warriors charged.

The few moments it took the slave hunters to retreat gave them all the time they needed to reorganize themselves. The tactic also brought the Chinchigwe warriors out into the open. Almost as suddenly as the battle began, the hunters took advantage. They turned to fight the Chinchigwe, clashing with the warriors with their original evil ferocity. They began to answer the rain of traditional warrior spears with the terrible, alien thunder of gunfire. The acrid smell of gunpowder filled the air as fewer and fewer of the hunters fell.

Throughout the battle that morning, the Chinchigwe never learned that they fought for their survival against a regiment of the notorious Batushi tribe; a tribe of slave hunters whose army alone numbered into the thousands. Of all the tribes of salve hunters, the Chinchigwe encountered the Batushi by happenstance. From the very beginning, the Chinchigwe never really had a chance, even though they originally outnumbered their attackers two to one.

It was almost as if a tragic destiny was set for the Chinchigwe. Even if they had somehow won this battle, the victory would have been short-lived. The Batushi, a volatile people, would have been enraged and vengeful. Regardless of the outcome of this battle, the Batushi would have returned to destroy the Chinchigwe completely.

After the hunters had dropped back in panic and reorganized themselves that morning, the Chinchigwe began to lose their last firm hold on existence as a tribe. Their bravest and best fighters could not stand against the overwhelming force of the hunters' guns. Before the sun came up that morning, most of the Chinchigwe warriors were dead.

By dawn, the battle had been pushed back into the heart of the Chinchigwe village. By Mfalme Lomani's request, the second line of defense resisted the hunters. The farmers, herders, crafters, and their mates and children desperately fought the advancing hunters. In a pathetic, one-sided battle, each brave villager who did their best to support the decree of Mfalme Lomani Usai instantly died from a hunter's frenzied retaliation.

Mfalme Lomani Usai himself, dying from a gunshot wound in his side, ignored the pain that radiated throughout his body. He held his side as blood oozed through his fingers. He could barely stand. Each movement that he made took strength he no longer had. Still, he fought valiantly. From the strength that comes only from rage, he made deadly thrusts with his spear, bringing down several menacing hunters. He leaned heavily against a tree for all his support as he lashed out and killed whenever and wherever he could.

As Lomani began to slump lower against the tree, the last of his strength and life ebbing away, he noticed the apparent leader of the hunter regiment standing before him. Lomani forced himself to stand upright. He raised his spear to strike, but hesitated.

"Why must you do this?" Can you not see what you are doing?" Lomani fell back heavily against the tree again. "I beg you. Please, spare the rest of my people…please, for the sake of our ancestors."

For a moment, the slave hunter only stared at Mfalme Lomani. For a brief moment, he seemed to understand what the Chinchigwe Mfalme was asking. He looked around, surveying the destruction and bloodshed around him. "All this–it wasn't necessary." He turned back to the Mfalme, masking his understanding with anger. "You did this to yourselves. Why did you fight us?"

"We…we had to. We have our pride. We must live to love and honor those who have come before us."

"That pride, that love, and that honor are all dead now! You must face it. It is gone."

"Never!"

"We only wanted a few of you. You were a fool to fight us. Now, look what you have done. You have destroyed everything: your pride, love, honor, and existence!"

Mfalme Lomani smiled as he realized his final victory. "Our existence…ended long ago. Our pride, love, and honor…you can never touch."

Something about that statement touched a nerve in the hunter. He replaced his uncomfortable feeling with raw rage. He could say nothing. He raised his gun and shot the Chinchigwe Mfalme.

Lomani fell to the ground. He used the last of his strength to thrust his spear into the hunter's heart suddenly. Mfalme Lomani lived long enough to see the hunter die beside him. He also lived long enough to see one of his people, a young craftsman, approach him, kneel at his side, and try to comfort him.

"Twese? Twese Merende, my friend." Lomani could barely speak, as blood spilled from his mouth. "Mfalme Lomani. Please, do not leave us." There were tears in the young man's eyes. Usually, as a strong, single-minded person, Twese's determination never gave him a chance to yield to tearful weaknesses. But seeing his dying Mfalme seemed to symbolize a tragedy beyond his control. Twese felt more helpless and frightened than in all his past days. "What will we do if you leave us? We have lost everything!"

"No. Not…not everything." Lomani coughed. "A few of you … A few of you still live. The sacred link with our ancestors … it is not broken yet."

"What must we do? We need your guidance!"

"Lay down your weapons."

Twese looked at his dying Mfalme with confusion. Tears that welled up in his eyes kept him from seeing Lomani's face.

Lomani coughed again. Blood from the core of his body clogged his throat and spilled from the corner of his mouth. Sweat rolled down his face. He tried to talk, but his body stiffened with intense pain. Lomani forced the words from his mouth. "Lay down your weapons. Do not let the link be broken. If you do nothing else, for the sake of our ancestors, live…and remember your parents, your parents' parents, and all those who have come before us."

3

A POINT OF NO RETURN

As the hunters ended their overly motivated raid, Twese attempted to assess the damage that had been done. Through tearful eyes, he saw nothing substantial left of the Chinchigwe village. Property, which the hunters considered worthless or could not be carried off, was set afire. All the livestock was gone, either slaughtered or herded away. And the people? Twese sat huddled together with the only survivors.

On his left, Twese saw Ameh Jobabwe, the oldest and most well-known of the survivors. This wise, old farmer had been a strong and positive influence, a cornerstone throughout the Chinchigwe village. Understandably, he didn't seem so wise, strong, or positive now. A look of confusion masked his wrinkled old face. Even at his old age, his eyes had never been so tearfully red.

The usually talkative Embabi Tende sat on the ground on Twese's immediate left. She had been a close neighbor. Twese had known her most of his life. And in all that time, he had never seen Embabi so quiet. The faraway look in her reddened, tearless eyes was only a hint of how severely her spirit had been broken. Even when Twese repeatedly called her name, Embabi did not respond. She rocked back and forth, as if the gentle motion would soothe her pain.

On Twese's immediate right was another young woman, Lobarra Gendeyani. Unlike Embabi, Lobarra cried openly. Tears flowed freely down her face and dripped from her chin.

Lobarra was also pregnant. By the protective way she embraced her huge stomach, Twese assumed that her stomach had long ago become a hindrance. It was amazing that she survived the raid at all.

There was little doubt in Twese's mind that this woman, her unborn baby, or both would not survive the days ahead.

Farther to Twese's right was the physically big and strong Komu Ndizi. Twese had seen Komu forge raw and hot iron as flat as a cloth. His thick arms and fingers looked perfectly suitable for forging iron. But Twese saw a different revelation in Komu's face. This powerful young man sat silently crying now, like the big child that he was.

Twese saw no complete families here. Of all the faces, only the shy and soft-spoken young woman, Summarwe Bata, and her little brother, Jpuma, had each other as surviving relatives. Jpuma, who had just seen his tenth harvest, clung to his sister as if she were the last source of comfort. For everyone else, Twese realized, the tragedy was complete.

Including himself, Twese counted a total of thirty Chinchigwe who, somehow, managed to survive that tragic morning. Every one of them had just seen their neighbors, friends, and families killed. In less than a day, they had seen their way of life come to an unexpected end. It was enough to persuade them that nothing they did would serve any useful purpose. Nothing could be saved, not even the pride of resisting an enemy. It was time to yield to destiny now. It was time to accept whatever was to come.

In their battered and stunned condition, the Chinchigwe were forced to leave behind the land that had been their home. Under the scorching sun for three days, they were led across one hundred kilometers of merciless and unknown wilderness. Throughout this journey, they were given little water and no food.

They received rest, but only after each day's sun had set. And by the time the chilly nights came, they welcomed sleep, even though they slept on the bare ground with no cover or warmth of fire. Their only warmth and comfort came from the tight huddle of their bodies.

Most of the captured Chinchigwe successfully endured this journey. Three of them did not. Two had dropped dead in their tracks. A third one never woke from her sleep one morning. Exhaustion had been the final assault on their weakened bodies. When the slave hunters discovered these three, they were unchained and routinely discarded by the wayside, left as food for the hyenas and vultures.

On the third evening, the day's journey ended long before the sun sat. This was unusual. The Chinchigwe had apparently been taken to their destination. They found themselves deep in a wooded area, in an obscure encampment consisting of several old, abandoned grass huts. It looked to be an old village, long ago robbed of the people who had kept it alive.

In the center of the encampment was an alien campfire. It was built rather oddly, unlike any campfire the Chinchigwe had ever seen. Over the open flame, a whole boar, impaled on a stick, roasted slowly. A thick column of smoke rose from the flame and filled the air with the smell of wood and burnt flesh. The boar was someone's food. But despite their hunger, the Chinchigwe knew this food was not meant for them.

Deeper into camp, the Chinchigwe were led toward several holding pens. There were five of them. The pens had been recently built by the look of the freshly cut trees. Each appeared to be nine square meters in size, with walls about three meters high. Each was sturdy enough to contain an elephant. But the Chinchigwe could see no elephants in these pens through the narrow space between the upright logs. The first four pens held people; other captured natives. There were about twenty-five to thirty people in each pen. From behind the walls, sad, hopeless eyes stared back at the newcomers. The last pen was empty. Its door hung wide open, as if waiting for fresh occupants.

Because of these ominous-looking pens, the whole encampment began to take on a frightening significance. This place was more than just the destination for the day. The Chinchigwe had arrived at a major transition point in their journey. It was a point of no return.

Strategically centered in front of the five pens was a tall, wooden platform and watchtower. It was situated so that it offered an easy view down into each of the pens. The Chinchigwe barely noticed the platform and tower until they saw two imposing-looking men on the platform, looking down on them.

The first was a red-bearded white man. He was, probably, the first white man most of the Chinchigwe had ever seen. A rather tall and burly-looking man, he stood defiantly on the edge of the platform. In his right hand, he held one of those deadly thunder sticks. He held the handle and coils of a stiff, untested leather whip in his left hand. All eyes and minds of the defeated people helplessly volleyed from the thunder stick, to the frightening whip, and back to the face of this terrible, man-like creature.

He watched the Chinchigwe as they huddled at the base of the platform. He frowned, as if displeased with what he saw beneath him.

"Would you just look at this sorry lot, chief?" He spoke to the other man on the platform, an obese slave hunter who sat on the edge of the platform with his legs dangling over the side. "Where, in hell's fire, did your hunters find these folk?"

The slave hunter did not bother to answer. He chuckled, sending several ripples across the fat on his chest and stomach. He held a liquid-filled gourd in his hand. He put it to his mouth and took a long drink. Some liquid spilled past the corners of his mouth and onto his stomach.

The white man tucked his thunder stick and whip under one arm and turned to a ladder on the side of the platform. He began to climb down, never once taking his eyes off the Chinchigwe. When he reached the ground, he slowly began to circle them, looking them up and down. "You reckon I'm some kind o' fool, don't you, chief?"

The slave hunter's chuckling turned into outright laughter. He took another long drink from the gourd. When he finished, he wiped his mouth with his hand. He looked down at the white man, smiling broadly. He wasn't disturbed by the white man's anger. The drink seemed to mellow his mood. The smile hid his contempt. "My warriors have brought you what you asked for, merchant. You will accept what I gave you because you are no fool."

"You fat bastard! You promised me thirty bodies a pen. Looks to me, you owe me three more to fill this 'ere pen. And what, in hell's fire, is this?" The merchant grabbed Ameh's frail arm, holding it up as an example. "This is god-awful, defective merchandise, chief. What am I s'pose to do with this? Half o' these sorry folk are agonna die on me afore I get 'em across the water."

The slave hunter looked away, his smile dissolving as his tolerance of the merchant wore thin.

Getting no response from the slave hunter, the merchant released Ameh's arm and turned his attention back to the inspection of the other Chinchigwe. He continued to mumble to himself, speaking a recognizable Swahili dialect. His command of the language was very good. But it was peppered with unnecessary obscenities.

With brutal hands, the merchant poked and prodded at the Chinchigwe. He pried into their ears and mouths. He randomly selected some to count their teeth, holding back their tongues with his dirty, bitter-tasting fingers. He exposed their bodies as he checked for injuries, bone structure, or the presence of fat or muscle. He thoroughly humiliated them. And yet, just as the slave hunter had assumed, he spoke of them with great value. But to mask his satisfaction, he cursed the slave hunter and his warriors for battering "his merchandise".

The slave hunter was more amused by the merchant's cursing than anything else. He was confident that the merchant would take whatever was delivered to him. Rejecting any of these captured people would be out of the question. "You want them, or not?"

The merchant put his hand on Lobarra's stomach. "Look 'ere, chief. I'm agettin' two for the price o' one. Can you bring me a handful more like this one?"

"You will get enough to fill this pen, merchant. I will not promise you they will all be with child."

"Fare 'nough. These 'ere ain't no worse than the rest you brung me, so I reckon they'll do." The merchant looked up at the hunter. "Hoist yo' fat ass down 'ere. Let's go figure out what I owe you."

The slave hunter struggled against his weight as he got up from the edge of the platform, the gourd still in his hand. He went to the ladder and slowly climbed down, cautiously testing each rung before surrendering his full weight. His insolent chuckle never ceased. When he reached the ground, he took one last drink from the gourd and tossed it to the ground. He didn't even look at the Chinchigwe as he lumbered past them, following the merchant deeper into the encampment.

A sudden splash of water broke the Chinchigwe's attention away from the hunter and the merchant. Two more white men, obedient aides of the merchant, had come from nowhere. With buckets of cold water, they began to wash the "raw" natives down, washing away the sweat, the grime, and dried blood. When they finished, they herded the Chinchigwe into the empty holding pen. And, despite the impenetrable walls, the aides did not remove the heavy shackles and chains on the Chinchigwe's arms.

The Chinchigwe were left chained and shackled in the holding pen for two long nights and two miserable days. During that time, a couple of the Chinchigwe, including Twese, tried to communicate with the captured natives in the adjacent pen but got no response.

Twese learned the hard way that communication was forbidden. One of the merchant's aides was always on guard up in the watchtower on the platform. Any talking prompted a stinging lash from the aide's whip. Twese felt the whip twice before realizing that talking was not allowed.

Like the other captured natives, the Chinchigwe had no choice but to spend those two nights and two days in quiet solitude. During that time, rest was the first of two good things to come their way. The rest did them much good. They needed it. But to say it was any help in their recovery was not the truth – far from it.

During this time, the pathetic Chinchigwe began to accept their condition. Life in this holding pen was how things were meant to be. This was their entire world now. There was no hope for anything better.

As a result of their hopelessness, their health rapidly deteriorated. Within one day, two old men and a young woman died. The number of surviving Chinchigwe had shrunk again, from twenty-seven to twenty-four. The merchant was now six enslaved people short of the minimum he needed to fill that last holding pen.

Once put into the pen, the Chinchigwe never saw the merchant. They heard him often enough, talking with his aides or talking with more of the slave hunters who came to visit his camp. But they never saw him. The merchant's two aides tended to the Chinchigwe, bringing them their food and water rations. It wasn't until the morning of that second day that the Chinchigwe finally saw the merchant again.

For the first time, he came into the holding pen. He stood guard while his two aides removed the bodies of the two old men and the young woman who had died. He stood there, watching the Chinchigwe, frightening them with his appearance alone. His piercing gray eyes seemed unreal. His uneven, unkempt, red beard bobbed unnaturally as he chewed on something continuously. A small trickle of brown juice drooled from the corner of his mouth into his beard.

"Be quick about it!" He growled to his aides. "It's foul as hell's outhouse in 'ere. Me belly is amakin' cartwheels."

The aides unchained the three bodies and dragged them, one by one, from the pen. After the third body was removed, the aides returned, to the surprise of the Chinchigwe, with a small boy. They pushed him into the pen, untied him, and locked his tiny wrists into a set of shackles where one of the old men had been.

"Now leave 'im be". The merchant told his aides. He spat the wad of whatever he was chewing onto the ground and wiped his mouth with his sleeve. "This 'ere boy replaces one o' them that died. The hunters promised to fetch me five more by early morn'. That's when we break camp. And so 'elp me, if another one of these 'ere folk dies afore then, I'm agonna put one o' you in its place. Am I amakin' meself clear to you?"

"It wasn't our fault they died." Samuel Dawby, the younger of the two aides, mumbled under his breath.

"Say what?"

"Capt'n McIntyre, you ought to blame them drunkin' hunters you hired," Sam spoke more openly.

"Shut yo' mouth, boy. I'll handle business how I see fit, 'n I'll tolerate no disrespect from you."

"But, Capt'n…"

Before Sam could finish his statement, the merchant hit Sam squarely in the face with his fist. Sam fell back to the ground, knocking over a trough of water. The merchant glared down at Sam, daring him to get up or say another word. "I don't give a damn whose fault it was. Am I amakin' meself clear to you this time?"

Sam dabbed at a trickle of blood at his cracked lip. "Aye, Capt'n."

The merchant turned and stormed out of the pen. "Simple-minded fool. Now, get off your ass and give these folk some more drinkin' water. And don't forget to bar the pen behind you when you come out."

After the merchant had left, Peter Rexley, the other aide, came over to help Sam off the ground. "You alright, lad?"

"I'm fine, Mr. Rexley."

"How many times must I tell you to mind your tongue with that son of a bitch?"

"But…"

"But, nothing. Captain McIntyre has been doing business with these hunters for a long time." Pete Rexley helped Sam set the water trough upright. "Betwixt you and me, his business practices are rather questionable, but he's been doing it a long time, and he seems to know what he's doing."

"I reckon." Sam left the pen briefly and returned with a fresh bucket of water. He poured the water into the trough as he looked around at the Chinchigwe. "Mr. Rexley, I ain't got no doubt 'bout how Capt'n McIntyre is handling his business. You know that. It's just that, I mean, did you take a good look at these folk? Did we come all the way to Africa for this?"

"I know. It don't sit right with me neither. But this," Pete pointed at the Chinchigwe, "this is what the Captain wants. Let's just earn our pay and go home."

Sam followed Pete out of the holding pen. He closed the gate behind him. As he and Pete set the last of three cross-bar logs on the gate, he glanced through the gate at the Chinchigwe. They only stared back at him with blank looks on their faces. They were all pathetic-looking people, including that little boy just added to the pen.

That small boy was the other good thing to come to the Chinchigwe. As it turned out, he was the beginning of their escape. Just after dusk that evening, the merchant and his aides celebrated their accomplishment. The celebration started up in the watchtower. But the three men got so careless in their merrymaking that they climbed down from the platform and eventually left the holding pens unguarded.

At about that same time, the little boy was wrestling with his tragedy and fears. In desperation, he twisted and pulled at the chains and shackles on his wrists. He ignored the apathy that had developed in the Chinchigwe who had, long ago, given up trying to free themselves. The little boy continued to twist and pull until, somehow, one hand popped out.

It surprised him. The little boy looked back and forth between his hand and the shackle, not believing, at first, that his hand was free. He wasn't the only one surprised. Almost all the Chinchigwe noticed this freakish, but very significant event. With a common mind, they began to stir from their apathy. They became visibly restless.

Instinctively, the Chinchigwe assisted the little boy as he pulled at the shackle on his other arm. With their help, the little boy's hand slipped through the shackle more easily than the first. The Chinchigwe, almost noisily, cheered the little boy's success – their success.

With forethought, Ameh Jobabwe quickly silenced the jubilant people. He peeped through a crack in the wall to see if the slave merchant had heard them. No one had. Even the aide who had returned to the watchtower was oblivious to what was happening. He sat unmoved, passed out in a drunken stupor.

Ameh turned back to the people in the pen. Without a word, he pointed at the little boy and then to the top of the wall. It was instantly clear to everyone what he meant.

Quietly, the Chinchigwe gathered around the little boy. The little boy surrendered his body in complete cooperation as the Chinchigwe gently lifted him off his feet. With a sudden jerk, the Chinchigwe tossed him over the wall to his freedom.

The little boy hit the ground hard, but he recovered quickly. He immediately began removing the huge logs that barred the holding pen. He managed to remove two of them. By then, the merchant and his two aides had heard the commotion at the pen. They came quickly to investigate. As drunk as they were, they were unprepared for what they found. They saw the little native boy struggling to remove the last of the three logs that barred the pen door. The merchant took out his pistol, yelling for the boy to stop. He fired at the boy but missed. By then, it was too late to do anything else.

The Chinchigwe had gathered themselves up and stormed from the pen. Thoughtfully, they dislodged the logs on the neighboring holding pen. The other captives there also poured out. Yet another pen was opened, and more captives poured out. In mass, all the captives from the third, fourth, and fifth pens attacked the merchant and his aides. In an uncontrolled frenzy, they beat the three, already drunken men, to unconsciousness. They would have killed them had not their strongest instinct been to run free.

As they shuffled past the last two holding pens, Ameh, Twese, and the powerful Komu took a moment to dislodge the logs that barred the doors. All the captured people, the merchants' "merchandise", instantly scattered into the surrounding woods. The Chinchigwe and their newfound friend ran off into the night in a reckless quest to secure their stolen freedom.

— **4** —

THE SPIRIT TO LIVE

It was early morning on the sixth day now. The warm African sun had just come up over the horizon. In its huge red splendor, it melted away the chill of the night. The dew evaporated, rapidly forming a thick and fragrant land fog. The rising temperature sent many nocturnal creatures back toward their dens and burrows to begin a day of sleep. And the birds' and monkeys' fresh and cheerful sounds grew ever stronger with the morning light.

The Chinchigwe had been on the move all night long. Their progress was extremely slow in the darkness, and they were still chained together. They had to feel their way between the bushes, vines, and trees as they made their way through the unfamiliar territory.

These handicaps and the shock of their miraculous escape made them proceed through the wilderness in tense and whispered silence. It wasn't until they experienced the relaxing effect of the warming sun and the light of day that they finally felt secure enough to discuss what they had done and realize its impact.

For Ameh Jobabwe, the fresh new morning was almost like waking up from a bad dream. Since the raid on the village and the loss of his only son, his mind and thinking were somewhat foggy. His mind had been recessed and protected somewhere deep inside himself. As the morning cleared, so did the clarity of his mind.

Ameh, the oldest and most respected of the surviving Chinchigwe, lost almost everything when the hunters came. He and his only living relative, his son Mahjani, had fought the advancing hunters with more relentless effort than they ever expected of themselves.

Still, Ameh's hut, the place where he had lived for most of his adult life, was destroyed by a senseless fire. All the valuables inside the hut were either taken away by the hunters or destroyed. Precious and irreplaceable relics of his lifelong mate, who had died only three harvests ago, were destroyed, never to be seen again. Even the center of his current wealth, his three prized zebu, were slaughtered for no good reason.

Ameh would have lost his very life had he not been blessed with a presence of mind and an old man's wisdom. Despite the tragedies of that day, Ameh eventually realized that the slave hunters, as violent and brutal as they were, were not killing those who did not fight back. So against all urges to resist the hunters, he stopped fighting. He convinced Mahjani to stop resisting. The two men were spared a sure death and were taken captive.

But as they were led away from their burning home, Ameh and Mahjani happened to witness the brutal death of their neighbor, Whanu Gendeyani. Whanu instinctively fought the hunters and was promptly killed. Whanu's mate, Lobarra Gendeyani, who was due to bear the couple a child soon, also witnessed the killing. Unlike Ameh and Mahjani, Lobarra reacted in a hysterical and rebellious rage.

Lobarra grabbed a discarded scythe from the ground and ran screaming toward the hunter who had just killed her mate. She held the scythe high over her head, ready to strike a deadly blow. She was prepared to kill or be killed.

Of course, death would have been her fate had not Mahjani caught her. He held her tightly to contain her rage. He reached up to take the scythe from his hand.

"No, Lobarra! Put it down. The hunters are killing only those who fight them."

Ameh looked on as Mahjani continued to restrain Lobarra. As he watched, the two seemed frozen in time, the scythe still held high overhead. Ameh saw how Lobarra looked up into Mahjani's face as if searching for reassurance. For a fleeting moment, Ameh also saw something between the two that should not have been there under the circumstances.

Lobarra slowly lowered the scythe to her side. She allowed Mahjani to gently slip it from her grip and drop it to the ground. Then she collapsed into Mahjani's arms and surrendered to a torrent of crying.

As Mahjani did his best to comfort Lobarra, two hunters tore the two apart. One hunter pushed Mahjani ahead as the other swung Lobarra around to look at her child-filled stomach. He ripped open her garment to get a better view. A repulsive smile showed his approval.

This single sequence of heartless brutality inspired about the same rebellious rage in Mahjani as Lobarra had felt only moments earlier. Mahjani impulsively lunged at the hunter who stood gawking at Lobarra. He caught him by the neck and began to choke the life from his body.

"Mahjani! No!" Ameh shouted.

Mahjani held both his hands around the hunter's neck in a death grip. With teeth clenched and his face distorted, Mahjani squeezed with all his might. Possessed by rage, he did not hear his father.

"Mahjani!" Ameh rushed over to gain his son's attention forcefully. But he wasn't quick enough. Before he had covered half the distance, Ameh saw another slave hunter intervene. Ameh helplessly watched as his only son was fatally knifed in the back.

Ameh and Lobarra suffered separate, yet common losses. They embraced each other in tears, giving and receiving whatever comfort was between them.

Five days later, chained together with the twenty-three other surviving Chinchigwe and fleeing a ruthless slave merchant, all that Ameh had left now was his life, an old man's wisdom, and thankfully, a presence of mind still intact.

Ameh felt fortunate, in a sense. At least now, he could begin to think about the welfare of his fellow tribe members who had gone through no less than he had. Thinking about them seemed to take his mind off his losses.

Walking with the aid of a two-meter staff, found and originally used as a weapon during the Chinchigwe escape last night, Ameh surveyed the surviving Chinchigwe. All morning long, as the morning light became brighter, Ameh wondered about the chances of survival of his fellow tribe members. He had been trying to put into perspective all their needs, trying to see which needs should be sacrificed, which needs had priority, and which ones would truly secure their survival in light of their new situation.

During his study, Ameh noticed Twese growing increasingly restless with the light of day. He maneuvered himself next to the young man, hoping to find out if he could somehow help.

"Twese Merende, what is wrong? Besides all that has befallen us, what else troubles you?"

Of course, a lot troubled Twese. Since hearing the last words of the dying Mfalme Lomani Usai, he had wanted the Chinchigwe people, as a whole, to live more than anything else. The desire was prominent in his heart and on his mind. To him, it was more than just a matter of choosing life over death. It was the life or death of the whole Chinchigwe culture, a whole clan. And now, strangely enough, Twese felt their sudden freedom jeopardized this desire.

Possibly more so than the rest of the Chinchigwe, Twese was acutely aware that death was imminent in this wilderness. They were on their own and defenseless. He knew that, if help was not found soon, they were sure to die.

Over and over again, throughout the early morning, Twese kept trying to make thoughts of returning to the Chinchigwe village sound rational. It was like triggering a nightmare. Thoughts of the village brought back floods of memories of the bloody raid by the slave hunters. Twese was forced to accept that returning to the Chinchigwe village would waste time. Over and over, he kept coming to the same unwanted conclusion that the village, the people, and all that was home were not there anymore.

Twese and the rest of the Chinchigwe also had the opportunity to go with the escapees from the other holding pens. But Ameh reluctantly thought it best if the Chinchigwe followed the little native boy who had freed them instead.

Just after the escape last night, the Chinchigwe finally learned that most of the people in the other pens were from the Dwakuni tribe. Slave hunters had come and raided their village only a few days earlier. What was left of the Dwakuni was now led by a charismatic young tribesman named Juumbopo.

Juumbopo had asked Twese, Ameh, and the rest of the Chinchigwe to return to his village with him. It was initially a very tempting offer. But the images of the decimated Chinchigwe village were still very clear in Twese's head. Twese eventually asked Juumbopo if the Dwakuni village was still there. Juumbopo, himself, had doubts that it was. Twese tried to tell Juumbopo that returning to a village that offered no safe haven would be pointless.

At that point, the heroic little native boy gave the Chinchigwe, Juumbopo, and his people an alternative offer. The little boy confidently said there was help in his Aukmondi village. He argued that his village was not far away and, since it was not raided, it was still there. Under the circumstances, it was a better offer. Unfortunately, when Juumbopo asked the little Aukmondi boy where his village was located, he did not have a convincing answer.

"Should we go to find a village that may not be there anymore, only to have the slave hunters come and take us again?" Twese spoke mostly to himself. "Or should we follow the boy who may lead us in circles in the wilderness? Either choice will lead to certain death."

"That is not for certain." Ameh finally spoke up. "But whatever choice we make, we must decide quickly. It will be daylight soon."

Juumbopo turned to leave. "My people and I must return home. If we do not survive, we will die in our village. Please, come with us."

"No. It is not death that we seek." Twese turned to Ameh. "There must be another answer."

When Ameh was only at a loss for words, Juumbopo walked away. That was the last Twese and the rest of the Chinchigwe saw of the Dwakuni. Twese wondered if the Chinchigwe had made the right decision.

"What do you suppose has happened to Juumbopo and his people?"

"I do not know."

"Ameh, many of them were in worse shape than we are. Even if they did manage to return to their village, they are still as helpless as we are."

"I know. But I hear something else in your voice, my young friend. What are you saying?"

"For all we know, they may all be dead by now."

"Is that all that your pessimism is telling you?"

For a forgotten number of times, Twese considered and tried to accept what the Aukmondi boy had told them last night: that help was available in the Aukmondi village.

According to the little boy, the Aukmondi village was only a day away. But neither the little boy nor the Chinchigwe knew exactly where they were. Finding the Aukmondi village would not be so simple. With the light of day, all that the little boy had as reference points were the position of the sun and a distant mountain range.

None of this was reassuring to Twese, who glanced behind the group one more time. "Like the Dwakuni, I think our flight is ending. We are wasting what little strength we have left."

"There is no doubt, Twese. All of us agree that we are living in the very shadow of death now."

"I think I know what we must do. As strange as it may seem, I think, for our own good, we should surrender to the slave merchant."

Ameh had assumed himself the leader of the twenty-four survivors. At his age, he had grown accustomed to having his opinion and advice respected. His leadership, so far, had not been rejected or questioned.

"Twese," he said, "you make no sense. Juumbopo offered us refuge, and you rejected it. Now, you say, we must give ourselves up to the merchant?"

"Juumbopo could not guarantee our survival. As strange as it may seem, the merchant can."

"I know you to be a very persistent person sometimes. You were so focused since you were a small boy that few people could make pottery better or faster than you. Such a quality of mind can be of great value to us now. But then, there is your pessimistic side, refusing to make pots when the sky only threatens rain for fear that the rain would come and destroy your precious work. That quality, we can do without. Surely, you can not be serious about giving up ourselves to that merchant. It would be foolish. It is not what we want."

"Then, you do not agree that returning to the merchant would keep the Chinchigwe alive?"

"No. I do not." Ameh did not hesitate to answer that question. "You are being naïve, Twese. You are trying to act on desperate thoughts. The Aukmondi boy has given us our freedom. All that we have to do now is keep it. He says there is help for us in his village. I think it is best that we help him find it."

Ameh and Twese looked at the boy who walked independently ahead of the group.

"The Aukmondi boy does not know where he is."

"We can, at least, trust him for now. He seems reliable enough for our purpose."

Last night, Twese and the other Chinchigwe learned that the Aukmondi boy's name was Adaulah Azinti Ncobba. He had seen his eighth harvest and turned out to be exceptionally friendly. Given the right conditions, he had the potential to be somewhat talkative and inquisitive.

According to Adaulah's story, he was on his way to visit the Village of Teachers in northern Kenya when the slave hunters ambushed him and four Aukmondi warriors. In defense, two of the warriors were killed immediately. The other two eventually died in a subsequent and desperate attempt to free Adaulah.

Because the slave merchant needed more natives to fill his fifth pen, Adaulah was captured. No one suspected that his addition to the group was the beginning of a miraculous escape for him and everyone else.

Twese was one of the first to admit that the escape was a rare twist of fate. He was still the only one to admit that the escape and the decision to follow the Aukmondi boy were also a step closer toward certain death for all the Chinchigwe.

"Ameh," he pleaded with the old man. "Forgive me, but I must speak my mind. Our freedom makes no difference if it leads directly to our death. Adaulah is a young and imaginative boy. Honestly, I can not find the comfort I need in his words. Juumbopo may have been right. In truth, the boy's village may be nowhere near here. If we do not give ourselves up to the merchant soon, we will surely die out here, the very last of our people. We are without weapons. The merchant's chain and shackles still bind us together. We are prey for any beast that desires us. And we are helpless against the savage, killer Wabanga people."

Ameh looked around, allowing his failing eyes to cover the horizon as best they could, searching for signs of such dangers. "Twese, you are right in every respect. Still, you have said nothing that would make me want to return to that merchant's camp. At the moment, the cause of our death is not certain. Can we not find comfort and hope in that?"

"Hope does not guarantee our security."

"Hope will sustain us until we are secure. If a merciful spirit is still with us, we may not encounter any of those dangers you mentioned. After all, we have journeyed through the night and have come this far. Hope can take us just a little farther."

"Relying on hope can get us all killed, Ameh."

"That is not for certain. What is for certain, Twese, and what motivates me the most, is the slave merchant himself. You and the rest of us know that his plans for us are not good. I, for one, would rather take my chances out here than face him again."

"Then why did you not go with Juumbopo? Our chances would have been better. Do you not agree?"

"As you have said, it probably would not have made any difference whether we are out here or in Juumbopo's village. The merchant and his aides probably do all they can to recapture us. The truth is, there is no reason for you or any of us to help him. Undoubtedly, they will catch us long before we succumb to anything out here."

"Maybe." Twese glanced at Adaulah and the unfamiliar territory ahead.

"Let us continue. Let us use the strength and time we have left to better our situation. There is that one worthwhile chance that we just might succeed."

"Does it not bother you that we are the very last of our people, Ameh? We are in no condition to stumble about at death's feet. We are tired, weak, and hungry. And that is only the beginning. Look at us! Look there, at Jpuma." Twese pointed to the little boy who limped behind him. "His injured leg grows worse with each step he takes. Soon, we will have to carry him.

"And what about Lobarra Gendeyani, the weakest of us all? Her mate is dead. Your son, Mahjani, died so that she might live. Who speaks for her now? At least, these things will be treated in the merchant's camp. We will be cared for until we are strong enough to care for ourselves."

"Care for ourselves, Twese? In the hands of the merchant? Such a day will never come."

"But the pressure would be off of us. We could take our time. We could plan what must be done for ourselves. We…"

"How much planning did you do in the merchant's pen? You had three long nights of solitude, Twese. How much planning did you do?" Ameh was visibly angry. He jabbed the end of his staff into the ground and stopped walking. He turned toward the young Chinchigwe. Because the merchant's chain linked everyone together, they had to stop walking too. They had no choice but to listen to Ameh's rebuke. "You have spoken your mind. And I have heard enough. You will speak no more of this!"

For a moment, Twese only stood, staring back into Ameh's face. He lowered his eyes. "Forgive me, Ameh. I mean no disrespect."

Ameh forced the tension from his body and dismissed his anger. His next words were softer as he appealed to Twese. "Do you want to go back to the merchant's camp? Have you forgotten what it was like in that pen? Do you realize that we would probably be in our village now if the merchant and others like him had not sent the hunters after us? No. The merchant is the cause of our problem. He is not the solution. We can do without him. We will do without him."

Twese was silent for a moment more. He understood all that Ameh was telling him. He could, very well, remember what it was like in the merchant's pen. He knew that the merchant's plans for the Chinchigwe were not good. Still, he wanted Ameh to understand that he was only trying to choose life, any life, over certain and total death.

"Ameh, I was with Mfalme Lomani Usai when he died. He died in my arms. He had ordered us to fight the slave hunters because none of us could bear our end to come, and we did nothing about it. He thought it was the only strong and proud thing to do. But in the end, his heart was different when he realized fighting was futile. Lomani wanted his people, who consist only of us now, to live. It was his dying wish that the last of the Chinchigwe find a way to survive, whatever it takes. Out here, as we are, every last one of us will die."

"Sometimes, the clearest way may not be the best way, Twese."

"I am not concerned with the best way. At this point, I want our people to escape certain death."

Twese was extremely stubborn. Ameh sighed, almost exasperated. "If you wish to live, then do not be so concerned with death. You would not recognize death if it stared you in the face. It is said, my friend, that many of those who have come before us have walked this land, ignorantly putting one foot before the other, no realizing that they are no more among the living."

"You speak of stories and legends now. This is different."

"No. Not that much different. Life with the merchant will be a living death. Believe me. It is a spiritual death, a death just as final as any death that we may encounter out here. With the merchant, you too, would live your days, putting one foot before the other, not realizing that you are already dead."

"I understand, life with the merchant would not be a life we desire, but…"

"Twese, please! Listen to me! Those days and nights that we spent in the merchant's pen, we were dying. Little by little, we were all dying. True, we may not survive out here. Our end may still come." Ameh paused as he dismissed the thought. "If it does, then so be it. The Chinchigwe people were meant to die. At least, since the triumphant moment when the Aukmondi boy freed us, we have not been dying."

"We have been lucky."

"Call it what you wish. We have the spirit to live now. I believe that even Mbona, Kishamo, and the young woman, Nana, would be alive now if their will to live had not been broken in that merchant's pen. At least we have the will to fight death out here, even if we can not win. We have the will to run from death, even though some of us can barely walk. It makes a difference. Do you understand what I am saying?"

Twese nodded. "Yes."

"Good. Never again allow desperation to keep you from seeing that there is more to living than simply staying alive. Even in our case, the knowledge makes a difference that works to our advantage." Seeing that Twese had no more to say, Ameh dropped the subject himself. "Now come. Let us follow Adaulah and find the Aukmondi village."

— 5 —

CAPTAIN MCINTYRE

Oliver Reginald William McIntyre stood 196 centimeters tall. He was a big, red-bearded, tobacco-chewing man. At first glance, he impressed most people as a successful plantation owner and a precursor to what eventually became known as a southern gentleman. He usually wore all white, though not always immaculately. And he was seldom seen without a black string tie about his neck and a large sun hat on his head.

People who knew Oliver better would quickly say this first impression was deceiving. To be precise, Oliver R. W. McIntyre's manners and morals were more like a pirate's than anything else. He was dishonest. He was selfish. He disrespected or disregarded anything or anybody that did not promote his interests. And most of his victims did not learn, until it was too late, that he was an insidious thief.

McIntyre once owned a 130-acre tobacco plantation just south of Norfolk in the Virginia Colony. He inherited it, so to speak, from his only relative, his young brother, Joseph Lawrence McIntyre.

Joseph died as a result of injuries he received during a tavern brawl that got out of hand. On his deathbed, he was constantly visited by his brother Oliver, whom he had seldom seen before the accident. The two talked about the good old times they used to have when they were young; how Joseph would be sorely missed if he did not recover; and how wise it would be to keep "McIntyre" property in the family. Before he died, Joseph called in his barrister to change his will. All his property was legally deeded over to brother Oliver upon his death.

After all the hard work, convincing his brother to deed him the plantation, and convincing the courts that Joseph was of "sound mind", McIntyre did not care for most of what he had gained. He got a thrill out of giving impossible orders to the slaves who worked the plantation. He enjoyed hiring and firing the unfortunate white folk, the indentured servants, who needed the work. But he couldn't care less for raising tobacco.

"It's not in me blood," he often told James Allsbury, his plantation overseer. "There's not a wee bit of challenge in it. Not nary a bit."

"I beg to differ with you, sir." James would often respond. "There's plenty of challenge, but not enough to suit your fancy." The two men would share an unspoken secret with a glance and then laugh loud and hard.

James Allsbury hated Oliver. He loved the plantation. He had loved it since he started working for Joseph ten years ago. But he hated Oliver. The only reason he tolerated the man and asked to stay on after Joseph died was because he had no place else to go and because this scoundrel didn't know a damned thing about raising tobacco.

"A man should devote at least part of his life to something he truly enjoys doing," James told McIntyre one evening as the two sat drinking ale in a local tavern. "And sir, might I remind you, you're not getting any younger."

"Truer words were never spoken, friend James. People need friends like you who can see and speak the truth plainly."

"In that case, I know you to be a pirate at heart. This plantation is no place for you. A man like you, sir, belongs to the open sea."

"James, I'm your kindly lord. It's me own bidding that you do so dedicatedly about the plantation and I thank you for it. But, hell's fire, man, I know I'm more of a hindrance than a help to you. Could it be, you're trying to get rid o' me?"

"Well, if the truth be known, sir, I'd love to get you out of me hair for a while."

Again, the two men would share an understanding and force a laugh behind it. If James had upset this delicate relationship with his employer, he quickly refilled McIntyre's glass of ale and offered a toast.

"Here's to you, sir. May you enjoy all the little pleasures in life you so desire."

Once, McIntyre did take James's advice. He left the plantation in James's full charge and signed up as a crewmember with the "East Wind", a slave ship. The long voyage to the "dark continent", around through the West Indies, and back to home port in the Virginia Colony was ideal. It was one of the most enjoyable experiences of his life. Much to James's delight, he signed up for another voyage, and then another after that.

That adventurous beginning started over fifteen years ago. From that time, things could not have gone better for McIntyre. He eventually joined the Royal African Company, a slave import business. With his experiences, knowledge, and numerous circuitous efforts, he rose rapidly to captain his "Tidewater" vessel. Luck was with him every step of the way, until one day, when he was discovered embezzling Company earnings.

McIntyre was guilty. He and everyone else knew it. He stood to be convicted, which, in those days, meant a sentence of death. Desperately, cunningly, and with nothing to lose, McIntyre approached his accuser, the Colonial representative of the Company, Sir Stanley Warfield. He found Sir Warfield working late one evening in his Portsmouth office.

"It's so kind o' you to see me, gov'nor," said McIntyre, faking the utmost respect.

"Yes, Captain McIntyre. It is, indeed. I'm quite busy. What do you want?" Sir Warfield never looked up from his paperwork.

"I come to admit me wrong, sir. I want to apologize for the despicable thing I've done."

"Any apology I hear from you will be before his lordship."

"Beggin' your pardon, sir?" McIntyre acted surprised. "But you'll be awantin' justice, won't you, gov'nor?"

"Of course. Nothing less."

"Well, with all due respect to his lordship, sir, you'll not be agettin' justice. Not before the bench, you won't."

Sir Warfield stopped his work and looked up at McIntyre over the rim of his spectacles. The oil lamp burning brightly on his desk did not eliminate the grimy shadows on his face. "What are you saying, Captain?"

"What I mean, sir, if all that you want is what I took from the Company and a noose about me neck, then dismiss me now and I'll be on me way. But before you do, please consider that I'm more than willin' to pay for all the trouble and expenses I've generated." McIntyre paused to study Sir Warfield's expression, to see if his point was clear. "All in all, sir, if me figurin' is correct, it comes to double what I'm due you."

The point was exceedingly clear. It hit the respectable Sir Warfield like a direct slap in the face. Sir Warfield angrily threw a stack of papers on his desk and stood up. "Your reputation precedes you, Captain. You are, indeed, as deceitful as they say you are. After what you've already done, you dare come to me with such an illegal notion? You're dismissed, Captain McIntyre. Good night!"

"As you wish, sir." McIntyre headed for the door. "But, if you will, think about me offer. You only need to agree to it to make it legal-like. Tell the Company that you were wrong. You mistallied your figures, or something of that nature. Drop the charges, sir. We'll settle this nasty little matter betwixt the two of us."

"Get out, Captain!"

"Judgin' by the looks o' things, such a transaction will cut that there paperwork in half, if you know what I mean."

Before Sir Warfield could react, McIntyre left the office. When no one came to arrest him, McIntyre knew that Sir Warfield had reconsidered his offer. There was no doubt about it. The charges against him had been mysteriously dropped. McIntyre's gifted tongue for bargaining had saved his life and left him merely in debt to Sir Warfield.

To pay his debt, McIntyre had to sell his tobacco plantation. He didn't care about losing it. James Allsbury, the overseer, cared considerably more than McIntyre did. Probably, one of the kindest things McIntyre ever did in his entire life was to give James the first claim to buy the plantation. And one of the unkindest things McIntyre ever did was sell the plantation to someone else while James was still trying to raise the money.

The money that McIntyre got for the plantation was more than enough to pay his doubled debt to Sir Warfield. With the profit and the money he got for selling off his slaves and the rest of the estate, McIntyre went shopping for a fresh new start. He spent almost every copper piece he had left to buy the "Maiden's Hand", a 300-man slave ship. Oliver R. W. McIntyre was starting his own slave import business. He had to do only two other things to launch his ingenious recovery.

First, he had to find a crew for the "Maiden's Hand". This would be relatively easy. It was a matter of canvassing the men who were commonplace about the local Virginia ports and docks. McIntyre selected fifty of them. He could afford no more than that. As he selected them, he certified them on the spot as experienced and seaworthy.

The second and most difficult thing McIntyre had to do was borrow enough money to buy a tradable item to barter with the African slave hunters. Unemployed and unable to reference his last employer, McIntyre found it almost impossible. Then, too, there was that dishonest trait about him that made even the most lenient of sources wary of him. Even McIntyre's talent for bargaining was no help. He managed to pool together only a modest amount. It wasn't enough to buy anything worthwhile.

McIntyre had been refused credit by his last potential source when Peter Rexley, one of the dockworkers he had hired as a crewmember, heard of his problem. In confidence, Pete told McIntyre about a British soldier, no name given, who was secretly selling muskets and flintlocks to the colonists. After McIntyre showed interest and promised to keep the matter quiet, Pete instructed McIntyre where, when, and exactly how to approach the soldier.

McIntyre followed Pete's instructions to the letter. He found the soldier, late one night, sitting alone in a small booth in a Portsmouth tavern, just as Pete said he would be. McIntyre learned that, outwardly, the soldier was typical of all the British soldiers throughout the Colonies, dedicated to the service of King George II. Privately, he was a gun merchant who did relatively inexpensive business with carefully selected customers.

"Who sent you to me?" The soldier asked suspiciously. His red eyes narrowed as he studied McIntyre's face and listened for the right answer.

Of course, Pete had told McIntyre how to respond. Otherwise, the soldier wouldn't give McIntyre the time of day.

"Me name is McIntyre. Pete Rexley, of Norfolk, sent me to see you. He works for me."

"Oh, does he now? The lad scouts enough business for me, 'tis a wonder he works at all." The soldier welcomed McIntyre to a seat in his booth. He took a drink from his glass of ale and sat back smiling. "Tell me, Mr. McIntyre, what be your cause? Are you part of this crazy westward migration, like the rest of the colonists?"

"No. There's only Indians and wilderness out west. Nothin' that interests me. I'm aheadin' east."

"East? Why do you need me help to move east?"

"When I say east, I mean the dark continent, me friend. I'm a merchant in slaves. I need your merchandise to barter with the slave hunters there."

The soldier leaned closer to McIntyre with a look of confusion on his face. He spoke in a whisper. "Guns? You're takin' guns to Africa? Why not sugar or tobacco, like everybody else?"

"I can buy more with one gun than all the sugar and tobacco in the Indies. The slave hunters will trade their very souls for a gun. I've been there. I know what I'm adoin'."

The soldier drained the last of his ale from his glass. "Nevertheless, you'll need a good number of guns then – fifteen, maybe twenty score. I'm afraid, Mr. McIntyre, I can't supply that many."

"Hell's fire, man! I wouldn't have come to you if I could afford that many." McIntyre's burst of anger had disturbed several of the other people in the tavern. He looked around at the faces staring in his direction. He suppressed his temper. He leaned in closer to the soldier and lowered his voice. "I'll only need three score and fifteen, thereabouts."

"Is that all?"

"That's all."

"You're going all the way to Africa with only seventy-five guns? Who are you doing business with?"

"That there is me own business. Can you help me?"

The soldier scratched the underside of his chin. "I think I have exactly what you want, Mr. McIntyre. Give me two or three minutes' lead, then follow me."

McIntyre started to protest, but the soldier cut him off. "Don't fret none, Mr. McIntyre. I'll see that you don't lose me." The soldier dropped a small gratuity on the table as he left.

McIntyre did as he was told. He sat alone in the tavern for two minutes, nursing the last of his ale. After carefully surveying the other patrons in the tavern, McIntyre pocketed the soldier's gratuity. He casually got up and slowly walked toward the tavern's exit. He left the tavern as if in no hurry to go anywhere. Just as the soldier had promised, McIntyre caught a glimpse of the soldier's red coat at the end of the street. McIntyre immediately headed in that direction.

After several minutes of walking along the dark streets of Portsmouth, McIntyre was eventually led down a dark alley and up to the rear door of a gunsmith shop. The proprietor's name on the sign over the doorway said "Stuart Wakes". McIntyre didn't know Stuart Wakes, but he was sure the British soldier wasn't him. He assumed this was a black-market operation with "Wakes" as a cover and getting a percentage of the income. No questions were asked. McIntyre didn't care. He followed the soldier into a large repair and storage room.

The soldier went directly over to the far corner of the room and turned up the light on a lantern. He pulled the dusty canvas covering from fifteen neatly stacked wooden crates. He smiled proudly as he knocked the dust and smudges from his red tunic. "I think this lot is just what you need, Mr. McIntyre."

McIntyre looked expectantly from the soldier to the crates and then back to the soldier again. "Well? Break one open. I want to see what I'm agettin'."

The smile on the soldier's face faltered and then disappeared altogether. After a moment of hesitancy, he took a long metal wedge from a tool table and slowly began to pry the lid from one of the crates. He lifted the lid slowly and peeped inside. In the dim light, the lid on the crate still not fully open, the soldier studied the five flintlocks inside, neatly packed on a bed of straw. He was looking for something he did not want McIntyre to see.

To the soldier's surprise, McIntyre grabbed the lid and threw it back. McIntyre reached over the soldier's shoulder into the crate and randomly selected one of the guns. He examined it like a person who knew what to look for. It took him only a moment to find the lock that held the hammer and flint back was missing. McIntyre looked into the crate at the other guns. Even in the dim lantern light, he could see that at least three guns in the crate had the same defect.

"Hell's fire, man!" McIntyre threw the gun back into the crate. "These things are worthless."

The soldier shrugged. "Most of them. Not all of them. About four out of five have a missing hammer, a missing flint stone, misaligned lock – something of that nature."

"And you intend to sell these to me? What kind o' fool do you take me to be?"

"You're a slave merchant, hoping to do business with a bunch of wayward wild folk in Africa. Me business is here. I can't be depriving the colonists of me best merchandise. This lot here is the best I can do for you. You can take them or leave them. It's your choice."

McIntyre was so angry, he turned to leave. The soldier caught his arm. "Let me give you a word of advice, Mr. McIntyre. If you choose to walk out yonder door without my guns, I had better not see your face in Portsmouth again. It would be bad for business."

The soldier had the authority to cause a lot of unnecessary trouble. McIntyre took the guns. He did not have a choice. He eventually talked the soldier into lowering his price for them, but the savings were still insufficient to repair all the guns. When McIntyre finally loaded the guns on board the Maiden's Hand, a third were still worthless scrap iron. Of course, McIntyre fully intended to trade every one of them to the slave hunters anyway. He only hoped now that the slave hunters would not notice.

McIntyre knew he couldn't get many slaves on his maiden voyage, not with a small crew and few trading goods. He expected only about 125 to 150, hardly worth the trip. A cargo of only 150 slaves was only half the capacity of the Maiden's Hand. But the principle that mattered to McIntyre was the beauty of his independence. With all his preparations completed, he considered himself ready.

6

THE AFRICAN VOYAGE

On one of the most glorious mornings of his life, McIntyre stood on the command deck of the Maiden's Hand, his hands traditionally folded behind his back. He proudly bellowed the series of orders to launch her. With an exhilarating sense of freedom, he was finally on his way to Africa.

McIntyre and his crew were lucky enough to miss most of the headwinds across the Atlantic. They made the trip in only five months. The whole time, the crew had little to do but keep the Maiden's Hand seaworthy by day, and exchange stories of past adventures by night. Captain McIntyre pitched in here and there with some of the work. And he was always the center of attention as he mingled with his crew.

Morale was high across the Atlantic. Captain McIntyre gained his crew's respect and loyalty just like he had always dreamed. Morale did not falter until a day or two after the Maiden's Hand had docked on the west coast of Africa at Port Harcourt in Biafra.

Captain McIntyre had gone into the city to conduct business. He had left the Maiden's Hand under the charge of his first mate, Mr. O'Connor. It was a beautiful, tropical morning. Mr. O'Connor stood, resting against the ship's port rail as he watched the crew shuttle food and water on board the Maiden's Hand. This morning, the docks were busy with people coming and going. But despite the crowd, Mr. O'Connor could easily see Captain McIntyre in the distance, barreling his way through the crowd with strong, angry strides.

"A storm is coming," Mr. O'Connor said to himself.

When the captain reached the Maiden's Hand, he started up the gangplank behind one of the crew members who was carrying a barrel of water on his back. Captain McIntyre pushed the young man aside. He said nothing until he heard the young man stumble and drop the barrel, breaking it open.

Captain McIntyre turned to the young man. "Boy, you'd best sap up every drop, 'cause that water is your ration for the next couple of months." McIntyre turned and boarded the Maiden's Hand.

Mr. O'Connor pushed himself off the railing. "Captain on board," he announced to the crew, as if it wasn't obvious. He rushed behind McIntyre, trying to match the captain's angry pace. He followed the captain below deck, hoping to discover the reason for the captain's behavior. He finally caught up with the captain just as he entered his quarters and slammed the door behind him.

Mr. O'Connor gently knocked on the door. "Captain? May I have a word with you, sir?"

"Now is not a good time, O'Connor. Go away."

Mr. O'Connor started to open the cabin door anyway, but thought better of it. "Sir, is there anything I can do?"

"Hell's fire, man. Mind your own business."

Mr. O'Connor stepped backward when he heard a bottle break against the door, glass raining down onto the deck. O'Connor took the liberty of slowly opening the captain's door anyway. He stepped inside. Glass crunched under his feet as the strong smell of rum assaulted his nose.

"I am minding my business, sir." Mr. O'Connor found the captain sitting behind his desk, taking a long drink from another rum bottle. "I take it, business did not go well?"

"Whatever gave you that notion?" McIntyre turned to a cabinet behind him and pulled out another bottle of rum. He shoved it across his desk to Mr. O'Connor. He sat back and took another drink from his own bottle. "We've been 'ere, what, two 'r three days now? I haven't had one successful bid yet."

The acquisition of raw slaves here in West Africa is simple. Merchants come into any one of hundreds of slave warehouses and fortresses up and down the west coast of Africa, from Senegal in the north, to Angola in the south. Slave hunters capture natives from inland regions and bring them into these fortresses to be auctioned off in groups by slave brokers who acted as middlemen between the slave hunters and the merchants. Merchants place sealed bids on various groups based on what they can afford and the size and condition of the groups. The brokers periodically announce the highest bid on each group.

"Times have changed, Captain." Mr. O'Connor took a sip from his bottle. "When was the last time you were here in Africa? Business is not as easy as it used to be."

"What can I buy with only fifteen crates of flintlocks? These brokers look at my bid and laugh like it's some joke."

"Was it that bad, sir?"

"There was this one group of raw slaves, eight of them, to be exact. They looked like they hadn't eaten in several months. You could count every rib in their chest – scrawny, sorry-looking creatures. Every one of 'em had running sores all over their bodies. Mr. O'Connor, I was still the lowest bid on the bunch."

"Why did you make a bid on such a lot? None of them would have made it across the middle passage."

"Hell's fire, I think I must 'ave been feelin' a wee bit desperate."

"Sir, have you thought about trying somewhere else?"

"You mean, Ghana? The Gold Coast? Cameroon? I came 'ere to Biafra, 'cause I thought the competition wouldn't be so strong. I wouldn't stand a chance any place else."

Captain McIntyre and his first mate sat in silence for a moment. They nursed their rum bottles, McIntyre drinking heavily, O'Connor only sipping. McIntyre finally noticed that his first mate was lost in thought.

"Speak your mind, O'Connor. You reckon I should o' made me living raising tobacco?"

"No, sir. I was thinking, maybe you should try the East Coast."

"The East Coast? The east coast of what?"

"Africa, sir. I understand the slave business is done a bit differently over there."

"How so, Mr. O'Connor?"

"Well, sir, you work directly with the slave hunters. There are no middlemen. You make an offer to the hunters, and they will bring you raw salves based on your offer. There is no competition. And you, with your gifted tongue, you should be able to make a deal to get exactly what you want with the price you're willing to pay."

"You make it sound so easy. Is it that simple?"

"As far as I know. I mean, I've never been to the East Coast. But, from what I hear, that is basically how it works. The biggest drawback is that you may have to get in the good graces of some Arab sultan to do business in his region. And of course, you have no choice in the raw slaves that the hunters finally bring you."

"But I do me own negotiatin?"

"Aye."

Captain McIntyre sat back smiling. He put his feet up on his desk. "I can live with that." But then his smile disappeared. "Do we 'ave enough provisions to make the trip around southern Africa and back? The crew is 'bout tired of flour, beans, rice, and water."

"We may have to make another port call or two. And don't worry about the crew, sir. You have a loyal following. You can keep most of them happy with a taste of rum here, a piece of meat there. We can make it."

Captain McIntyre and his crew spent an additional four months at sea, sailing from Port Harcourt down toward the Cape of Good Hope and up the east coast of Africa. Morale was not as high as before since there was more work and less rum to drink.

Morale reached its lowest point after the crew weathered a raging storm off the coast of Algoa Bay. Two crewmen were lost in a desperate struggle to keep the Maiden's Hand under control. One man fell from the main mast to the deck and broke his neck. The other fell overboard and was never seen again. Both were very well-liked men. The crew took it hard and never really recovered.

Captain McIntyre endured the extra time it took to sail around South Africa, the loss of the two crewmen, the low morale, and the rising complaints. He considered these minor sacrifices. His mission had taken an unexpected detour, but now, he saw his way back on track.

Two brief ports of call were made. The first was soon after the storm, in the Natal settlement. Captain McIntyre gave the crew three good days to try and recover from their ordeal, repair the Maiden's Hand, and load fresh mangroves to supplement their food supply.

The second port of call was in Stone Town, on the island of Unguja, Zanzibar. There, Captain McIntyre used his gifted tongue to gain free passage in the territory of the Sultan of Oman. The Sultan's governor, Nasr ibn Abdallah al-Mazru'i tried to establish a partnership with Captain McIntyre. This was the standard procedure for most slave ships. But Captain McIntyre insisted on direct negotiations with the slave hunters in the region. Governor al-Mazru'i had no objections. As long as Captain McIntyre made port in Mombasa and paid the slave hunters for their services, the captain had the freedom to come and go as he pleased.

Captain McIntyre and his crew spent one more day at sea, sailing up the African coast. As directed, they made their final stop in Mombasa, on the coast of Kenya. It was there that Captain McIntyre experienced most of his difficulties on this leg of his voyage. He and his first mate spent five good days searching for an independent tribe of slave hunters who could fulfill the captain's request. It wasn't that the slave hunters were not willing. All of them were busy with other mandates and too busy to accommodate Captain McIntyre.

On the morning of the sixth day, Captain McIntyre finally contacted a slave hunter who seemed only mildly enthusiastic about taking on a new mandate. McIntyre found out that the hunter was reluctant because a trip had to be made about 500 kilometers inland to secure the contract. The hunter wasn't sure if McIntyre was willing to do this.

After five wasted days, Captain McIntyre jumped at the chance. With arrangements quickly made, Captain McIntyre left the Maiden's Hand under the charge of Mr. O'Connor. He selected only two of his best crew members to accompany him and went eagerly with the slave hunter to push his deal through.

The trip deeper into Kenya wasn't as difficult as Captain McIntyre originally thought it might be. He learned that, if he was willing to pay for it, most of the trip could be made by rail, at least as far as Nairobi. The last 100 kilometers had to be made on foot.

With nearly the last of his carefully budgeted money, Captain McIntyre hired thirty-five local natives to carry the fifteen crates of flintlocks and other supplies he would need. Since cargo on the Kenyan rail service was less expensive than passengers, Captain McIntyre paid for the rail service to Nairobi by convincing the rail authorities that his entire entourage was all cargo.

The trip inland took almost two days, but Captain McIntyre felt good about it. For the slaves he so badly wanted, this inland trip was a small price. He knew that if he could get face-to-face with the leader of these slave hunters, he would get what he wanted. Confidence told him that there was even the possibility that he could leave Africa with the belly of the Maiden's Hand full of cargo.

— 7 —

DUE RESPECT TO THE CHIEF

Only two days after Captain McIntyre had talked with Chief Jagotta of the Batushi tribe, he was delivered one hundred fifty African natives. McIntyre accepted the natives, feeling very proud of himself.

The slave hunters had done their part. Now it was McIntyre's turn to uphold his end of the deal. After his aides had secured the last of the natives in the holding pen, McIntyre ordered out the fifteen crates of flintlocks. Knowing that Chief Jagotta would want to inspect the guns, he quickly indicated two particular crates to be opened first, two he had secretly marked, two he had repacked with the best guns.

To McIntyre's relief, Chief Jagotta was happier about the guns than McIntyre was about the fresh natives. The fat chief smiled broadly, examining several guns from the open crates. To McIntyre's greater relief, the chief ordered his warriors to gather up the other thirteen crates and carry them off without inspecting any of the contents. The chief continued smiling and holding on to one of the guns as he followed his warriors out of the merchant's camp.

That is when the first of two celebrations started. Captain McIntyre let out a loud yell of victory. He was finished with the slave hunters. If he remained lucky, further contact with them would be minimal. Before the hunters were completely out of sight, Captain McIntyre uncorked three bottles of rum, one for each of his aides, Sam and Pete, and one for himself. He joyously told Sam and Pete to drink up and celebrate.

The next morning, Sam went to the holding pen to feed and water the natives. He was hungover but happy. This was the morning that

Captain McIntyre had planned to break camp and begin their long trek back to the East Coast and the Maiden's Hand.

As Sam filled a trough with fresh water, he happened to notice one of the natives, a little girl, lying limply in the lap of another native. The girl was too limp to be asleep or unconscious. A sixth sense instantly told Sam that the little girl was dead.

Sam did not have to examine the girl to confirm his feelings thoroughly. The reddened, swollen eyes of the other natives told Sam there was much grief in this pen. Sam left the pen before discovering that there were two others in the pen who were also very near death.

When Captain McIntyre found out moments later, he was desperate and furious. It was too early for his merchandise to start dying off like this. He immediately sent Sam and Pete back into the pen to try to save the dead girl. It was like a personal insult when Sam came back out, only seconds later, and told him that the girl was already dead. Then Sam thoughtlessly compounded the insult by reporting that two old men in the pen were also dying.

Captain McIntyre flew into a rage. He grabbed Sam and hit him twice in the face with his fist. The second blow knocked Sam to the ground. Captain McIntyre then grabbed Pete and was about to give him the same punishment when he looked up and saw Chief Jagotta and two of his warriors coming through the trees.

"Oh bloody hell!" McIntyre released his hold on Pete and went quickly to strap on his holstered pistol. He knew exactly why Jagotta had come back.

"Captain, what are you doing?" Pete asked. He looked about in confusion, finally turning to see Chief Jagotta approaching. "What's going on? Why are your hunters coming back, Captain? I thought you said you were finished with them."

"Never you mind. Just go get your guns." There was a quiver of panic in Captain McIntyre's voice and his hands as he buckled his pistol around his waist. "You too, Sam! Go quickly now!"

While Sam and Pete went to do as they were told, Captain McIntyre physically checked his pistol to see if it was loaded and primed. He returned it to his holster but kept his hand securely on the butt. When the Batushi chief was within speaking range, Captain McIntyre forced a nervous smile on his face.

"Chief Jagotta, me old fat friend. Welcome back to me camp. This is a might bit unexpected. What, in hell's fire, do you want?"

Chief Jagotta said nothing. He stared without wavering into the eyes of the merchant. And just as the merchant had done, he too forced a smile on his face. Only his smile showed no sign of nervousness. His smile concealed a death sentence.

"I'm sure you came back 'ere to do more 'n just stand there agrinnin' at me like that." Captain McIntyre played innocent. "Me and me boys are sort of busy at the moment. We have a mighty full day ahead. What do you want?"

The Batushi chief reached into a pouch at his waist, never taking his eyes off the merchant. He removed a small trinket, a primitive-looking necklace. He stepped closer to the merchant, face to face. He grabbed the merchant's wrist and forced the necklace into his hand.

McIntyre looked at the necklace. He recognized it instantly. He threw it to the ground as if it were red hot. He took a step back.

"Ain't no cause for this, chief." McIntyre made a nervous attempt the push the necklace away with his foot. He managed to kick it back at the foot of the Batushi chief.

"It is a gift, merchant." Chief Jagotta picked the necklace up. He walked up to McIntyre again and stuffed the necklace into McIntyre's pocket. "It is yours. You are Yululu. You are Mfalme."

"Mfalme? That's like a chief or something, ain't it?" McIntyre fished the necklace out of his pocket and looked at it again. He held it delicately, between two fingers. He had just been given a special gift with no choice but to accept it. When he looked at Jagotta again, the Batushi chief and his warriors had turned to leave.

Captain McIntyre swallowed the lump in his throat. He suppressed his fear. He pushed it aside just enough to let his anger overtake him. "Is this a token of our friendship?" His voice got louder and louder as the Batushi chief walked away, and the adrenaline surged in his body. "With all due respect to the chief, you fat heathen snake, you owe me! Three of these worthless folk you brought me just died on me. You owe me replacements!"

At that moment, Sam and Pete had retrieved their pistols, muskets, and flintlocks and ran back toward Captain McIntyre. They returned just in time to see the captain's rage.

"Captain, are you alright?" Asked Pete.

Although his rage was subsiding, Captain McIntyre barely heard Pete's question. "They owe me! These three, plus the three slaves they already owe me, are six in total. And I'll have them, or that fat bastard will meet 'is heathen maker afore I do! I swear it!"

"What did they want?"

In truth, Captain McIntyre didn't know if he should take his chances, close his camp, and get out of Africa as fast as he could, or see if he could outsmart the Batushi chief. Unlike the trek inland, which was done mostly by rail, the long trek back to the east coast and the Maiden's Hand would have to be done on foot. It would be difficult enough with all his merchandise. The Batushi chief would eventually catch up to him. McIntyre knew he would have to confront the chief anyway. He had no choice but to try and beat the chief at his own game.

McIntyre finally realized Pete was talking to him. "Damn it all to bloody hell, Pete. Unpack your gear. Make yourself at home. We're agonna be 'ere another day 'r two."

"Why? I thought you said we were breaking camp this morning?"

"Never you mind what I said."

Pete was beginning to show impatience. "The Batushi chief returns unexpectedly, and everybody is ordered to arms. Then the chief leaves as quickly as he came. And now, you tell us we're staying another day or two. For what?"

"The Batushi will be abringin' me replacements for the darkies that prematurely died on me. We might as well wait 'ere for their return."

"For the love of Queen Anne, may she rest in peace, how did you manage that? What are you going to pay them for these replacements?"

"Nothing. I don't 'ave to pay them a damned thing. They are adoin' it because I asked them to." Captain McIntyre sighed heavily as he held the necklace tightly in his hand. "You see, I've just been made an honorary chief of the Batushi tribe."

Captain McIntyre did not seem too pleased with his new honor. He stuffed the necklace in his pocket and walked away from Sam and Pete, leaving them with their own confused thoughts on the matter.

Sam and Pete knew enough about the captain not to pursue the matter any further than he wanted to take it. The captain's temperament was volatile. Under the current circumstances, it wasn't wise to question him. Sam and Pete kept their distance from the captain for the rest of the day and all that night.

A day later, Batushi warriors delivered the little native boy to the merchant's camp. According to the Batushi warriors, they had initially captured five of the six natives the merchant had requested. But evidently, four had to be killed for one reason or another.

"I asked for six replacements, now didn't I?" Captain McIntyre stood nose to nose with the Batushi warrior. There was something different about the captain's behavior and confidence this morning. Once again, he was a changed man. "What, in hell's fire, am I supposed to do with one little feebleminded boy?"

"If this boy displeases you, merchant, we will kill him." The Batushi warrior spoke with respect. "We will find stronger natives if you wish."

"No. I will keep the boy. But, yes, you will fetch me the rest of me replacements. You promised 150 natives and I'll not leave with one head less."

"It will be done, merchant. You will have them before the sun rises tomorrow."

"Good. Now get your heathen asses out of me camp. And if you can't bring me what I ask for, don't bother to come back." Captain McIntyre watched as the Batushi warriors left. He finally turned to Sam and Pete. "Come on, lads. We got a lot of celebratin' and much work to do."

That is when the second of the two celebrations began. Captain McIntyre was himself again. As usual, he uncorked bottles of rum and began drinking heavily. He knew that his accomplishments, this time, were somewhat precarious. He still felt confident enough to know that he could be more successful with a little strategy than ever before.

8

EGO, GREED, AND REVENGE

But things still didn't go exactly as planned. Captain McIntyre and his aides unintentionally celebrated well into the night, drinking and sharing recent and past adventures. As usual, it was the captain and Pete exchanging stories. Sam was the awestruck listener. When the captain noticed Sam nodding during one of his stories, he called an end to the celebration. After all, the men needed their rest, and much work would be done tomorrow.

The three men always took two-hour shifts in the guard tower to watch over the slaves. Since Pete seemed to be the drunkest, McIntyre told him to go ahead and get some sleep first. A couple of hours of sleep should be all he needed before taking the second shift. Sam, on the other hand, was told to wake his lazy ass up and take the first watch.

Captain McIntyre and Pete made themselves comfortable right where they were. That was all it took for them to fall promptly asleep. They were asleep before Sam could finish gathering his jacket, musket, and bottle of rum. When Sam realized no one was listening to his grumbles and complaints, he yawned and shuffled out of the captain's tent.

Sam was tired too. The night air was refreshing but wasn't enough to clear his head or rejuvenate his overworked body. He walked slowly across the camp to the platform and the holding pens. With his musket securely tucked under his arm and a half-empty bottle of rum in his hand, he climbed up the ladder to his post in the guard tower.

Sam had the sincerest intent to watch over the slaves for the next two hours. After all, it was his turn, and he would do it dutifully.

Unfortunately, he made the mistake of finishing most of his rum. Shortly after shifting himself to a more comfortable position and a few more swallows of rum, Sam also fell soundly asleep. Even when the bottle slipped from his fingers and shattered on the ground below, the sound failed to wake him.

All three men, Captain McIntyre, Pete, and Sam, enjoyed the peace of rum-induced sleep for the next two hours. It was the captain who woke up first. The snore that caught in his throat jolted him awake. He rolled over and thought to check his timepiece. Only a couple more minutes remained before it was time to wake Pete up for his shift in the guard tower. He made himself comfortable again. As he settled back down to resume his sleep, he heard a loud thump outside. It sounded as though something heavy had fallen. In his groggy state of mind, the captain initially dismissed the noise. He was mistakenly confident that Sam would alert him if it were anything serious. But moments later, he heard an unusual restlessness from the holding pens. It didn't sound right at all.

Captain McIntyre sat upright, intently listening for more unusual noises. He peeped outside his tent and looked out across camp toward the pens. Because of the darkness, he could not see very well. Even the light of the waxing moon and the amber glow from the smoldering embers of the central campfire were no help. The captain could barely make out what appeared to be a wild dog or some other small, antelope-size animal rustling about near the door of the fifth holding pen.

He vigorously wiped his face and focused his eyes, forcing his vision to gather more details. He suddenly realized that what he was looking at was no little animal. It was the little native boy who had just been delivered. At that very moment, the third log on the door fell to the ground with a resounding thump. The door of the pen flew wide open.

"Oh, bloody hell! Sam!" Captain McIntyre yelled. He scrambled to his feet. "Sam, you son of a bitch! They are abreakin' out!" He turned in a panic to wake Pete up.

In the guard tower, Sam was awakened by Captain McIntyre's voice calling his name. He woke with a spasmodic jump. He was so startled that his musket flew from his arms and, like the rum bottle, fell to the ground. When he looked down and saw the slaves pouring from the holding pen, he jumped up and rushed toward the ladder. He had to stop the escaping slaves. Instinctively, he knew that, at this point, he needed the compelling force of his gun to do so.

In his haste, his first step down the ladder was misjudged. Sam slipped and tumbled to the ground. The impact twisted his ankle and threw him backward. His head hit the ground hard. Sam felt a sharp pain radiate up his leg. He tried to massage his ankle to quell the pain but quickly lost consciousness.

By this time, Captain McIntyre and Pete had made it halfway across camp toward the holding pens. Pete was yelling and waving his hands over his head, as if the erratic behavior would stop the escaping slaves or frighten them back into the pen.

Right on Pete's heels, Captain McIntyre pushed Pete out of the way. He had a better, more forceful plan in mind. Captain McIntyre had his pistol drawn and was getting ready to use it. He was running too hard to check if it was primed. There wasn't enough time. He only stopped running when he took a moment to refine his aim and fire.

A plume of flame and smoke exploded from the pistol barrel in the darkness. The sharp clap echoed in the surrounding woods. It was a frightening show of force. But when the smoke cleared, Captain McIntyre saw that the shot was wasted. The pellet had lodged in a log, just above the little native boy's head.

"Oh, damn it to hell! This can't be happening!" Captain McIntyre angrily flung the useless pistol aside. Without a second thought, he grabbed the pistol from the holster that Pete wore at his side. Before he could even pull the hammer back and aim, he saw the doors on the third and fourth pens fly open. And by the time he was ready to fire the commandeered pistol, he was slammed in the face by a wooden pole. Ameh had grabbed a two-meter limb from the ground. Six centimeters in diameter, the pole was sturdy enough to lay the merchant on his back. The last thing the merchant remembered was a horde of frenzied, heathen natives piling on top of him.

It was two hours before dawn before McIntyre, Pete, or Sam stirred again. Sam had fallen unconscious. Captain McIntyre and Pete had both been trampled and beaten to unconsciousness. The residual effects of the rum kept them that way most of the night. Captain McIntyre was the last one to regain consciousness. Pete and Sam were leaning over him. Pete was pouring water on his face.

"Capt'n? Capt'n, are you alright?"

"No. I ain't alright." Captain McIntyre angrily knocked the water cup from Pete's hand. He tried to sit up but grabbed his head in pain. The instant recollections of what happened last night made him suppress his pain. He sat up anyway. He looked toward the holding pens. The doors to all five of the pens were wide open. "This can't be! Please, tell me I'm adreamin'. Where're me damned slaves, Pete?"

Pete slowly stood up and stepped back. He knew better than to be this close to the captain when the truth came out. He gently tugged at Sam's shoulder to do the same.

Sam, on the other hand, was not as insightful. Sam felt it was his fault that the slaves got away. He was about to apologize when Pete forcefully pulled at his shoulder. Sam looked up at Pete.

"Not now, lad." Pete stepped protectively in front of Sam and addressed the captain. "Sir, what do you want us to do?"

"Damn it, Pete. What, in hell's fire, do you think? We gotta fetch 'em back! Quickly now, gather your things. Get your muskets, pistols, and flintlocks. And be sure to bring plenty o' water." Captain McIntyre forced himself up. He continued to spew a series of frantic orders to his aides as he hurried off to gather his gear.

"Ah, Capt'n." Pete hurried in behind McIntyre. He addressed the captain several times to no avail. He had to grab McIntyre's arm to get his attention. He pointed toward the edge of the campsite. "What about him?"

Captain McIntyre turned and focused his eyes in the direction Pete was pointing. He saw nothing at first. But as his vision cleared, he finally saw a Batushi slave hunter, standing as still as a tree in the darkness.

"Well, I'll be tarred and feathered." McIntyre only stared at the ghostly hunter for a while, trying to convince himself that he was not hallucinating. He finally beckoned to the hunter to come closer. He was pleased to see the hunter obediently walk out of the darkness into the campfire's light.

As the hunter approached, Captain McIntyre's face showed a hint of a smile. He thoughtfully reached into his pocket and retrieved the necklace that the Batushi chief had given him. He hung it around his neck and adjusted it so the hunter could see it.

"How long you be astandin' there?" McIntyre asked the hunter.

At first, the hunter said nothing. When he did speak, he asked the captain, "How long have you been, Yululu?"

There was now a broad smile on Captain McIntyre's face. He found humor in the hunter's question. "I should've known. It's only fittin'. You been awatching me."

"You are Yululu."

"Yeah, well, lucky me. I reckon, you saw everything that's been going on 'ere?" The hunter said nothing. But the unwavering stare told the merchant what he wanted to hear. "Which way did me slaves go?"

The slave hunter pointed to the left with a spear that he carried. "Most of them, from the first four pens, went that way, toward the great lake." The hunter then pointed to the right with his hand. "The rest, from the fifth pen, went toward the Serengeti."

"Well, alright then. I do believe we have a salvageable situation 'ere." The merchant took a thoughtful moment, looking first toward the great lake and then toward Kilimanjaro. "I want me slaves back."

Sam, still feeling apologetic, limped closer to McIntyre. He made a feeble attempt to be helpful. "Capt'n, your slaves went in two different directions. Are we splittin' up?"

McIntyre turned angrily toward Sam. He held a warning finger in Sam's face. "You take one more step near be boy 'n, so help me, I'll split your head wide open. Go get your damned guns 'n things, like I told ya!"

McIntyre watched Sam limp away before he turned back to the hunter. He took an arrogant stance, almost nose to nose with the hunter. "Tell your, fat ass, Chief Jagotta, I want him to fetch me slaves back. You reckon, you can do that?"

"It will be done, merchant."

"I want Jagotta to fetch the lot that headed toward the lake. Bring 'em back 'ere to me camp. Wait 'ere 'til I return. Me and me boys will go after the ones that went toward the plains. Now git!"

The slave hunter turned to follow the merchant's instructions. He immediately adopted a strong trot as he headed out of the merchant's camp, quickly disappearing into the forest's darkness.

McIntyre thoughtfully removed the necklace from around his neck and stuffed it back into his pocket. He seemed to realize its power as he resumed walking over to gather his guns and other gear. The thoughts brought a smile to his face, and he was still smiling when he finally joined Sam and Pete.

"Come on, lads. Hasten up. I want to make it at least halfway to the plains afore sunrise."

Both Sam and Pete were completely baffled by what had just happened. They turned to each other with questioning looks on their faces. There were no obvious answers. They had no choice but to dismiss it for now and finish gathering their gear.

Captain McIntyre and his aides gathered food, water, guns, and torches within half an hour. With travel packs on their backs in the early morning darkness, they began pushing their way through the surrounding forest.

******

Despite their freedom to move about and the light from their torches, their progress was only relatively better than that of the runaway slaves. Captain McIntyre and Pete still suffered from the unexpected beating the slaves had given them. Sam limped on a sprained and swollen ankle. All three of them suffered the discomforts of rum hangovers. The main reason they kept moving at all was because of the captain's drive to get his slaves back.

Because of his ankle, Sam brought up the rear. He was lagging farther and farther behind. Sam had been a reliable dockworker most of his adult life. Before Captain McIntyre came along, he was used to long hours and hard work. Under the right conditions, he could carry his workload just as well as the next man, if not more. But his hangover, the swollen ankle, the dark forest, the heavy pack on his back, and the captain's persistence were not the right conditions. Just before sunrise, he finally succumbed to the pressures and stopped walking.

"Capt'n McIntyre," he almost whined with discomfort. "I simply must rest a bit. It seems we've been stumbling through this god-forsaken jungle half the morning. I can't go another step."

Sam took the liberty of sitting down on a log. He slipped the pack from his back and casually drank water from his canteen. He looked up just in time to see Captain McIntyre power-walking in his direction.

Without a warning, McIntyre knocked Sam's canteen away, spilling most of the water inside. He caught the young aide by the jacket, pulled him up, and struck him hard. When Sam fell back over the log, McIntyre came after him and grabbed him by his jacket again. He would have struck him again if Pete had not rushed up and caught his arm.

"Leave 'im be, Captain."

"The hell I will! None o' this would be happenin' if it wasn't for his sorry ass."

"It's not all his fault, Captain. All three of us were drunk. We're all at fault here, and you know it. Blaming Sam ain't gonna get your slaves back."

Captain McIntyre reluctantly dropped Sam to the ground and angrily pushed Pete away. He looked down at Sam. Of all the losers he had hired as crewmembers, he couldn't believe this simple idiot was one of his hardest workers. "I'll be damned if I don't blame somebody."

"Well, you just do that. But not right now. Let's concentrate on getting your slaves back." Pete delighted in getting the captain to listen to reason. "You somehow talked Jagotta and his jungle-bunnies into fetching most of them for you. The hard part is halfway done. And the handful of folks we're chasing can't be more'n six or seven kilometers ahead of us now. Let's not waste time here by laying blame."

Captain McIntyre settled himself down. He dusted himself off and readjusted the pack on his back. He stared at Sam. "Get yourself up. If you don't care to keep up, you can lie there 'til the fire in hell burns out, for all I care. It'll make profits just that much easier to divvy up." He turned and stormed ahead to emphasize what he said, leaving Sam and Pete where they stood.

Pete watched the captain leave and then turned to Sam. "This is getting to be a habit. Are you alright, lad?"

"Aye. I'm fine, Mr. Rexley." Sam picked up his backpack and half-empty canteen and limped beside Pete. "Why is he so, so...."

"Desperate? The truth is, Captain McIntyre has invested his whole future in these slaves. I was with him years ago when he started this business. He stands to lose more than you'll ever know. The very idea of losing a single one is something he can not tolerate."

"But he's a merchant. He should be used to losing slaves."

"No. Not Capt'n McIntyre and not these slaves. They are all he's got."

"A lot of them will die anyway, Mr. Rexley. I'll be surprised if half of them make it during the middle passage voyage."

"Aye. You know it. I know it. And most of all, the captain knows it. At least one in five will die from one thing or another. That is why it pains the captain to start losing them now."

"That is not our fault either."

"No, it's not." Pete took Sam by the arm. "Let me give you a bit of advice. It's for your own good. Just don't ever again give him the impression that you don't care about those slaves. If you do, I'll lay odds, he just might kill you for it."

"But I do care! You know that, Mr. Rexley."

"I don't doubt that you do, lad. You don't have to convince me of anything. It's him that needs convincing."

Sam wanted nothing more than to please his employer. He had always been like that. A hard, dedicated worker was always the right of a credible and respectful employer, or so he thought. Maybe he was just now waking up to something the other crewmembers had learned long ago.

"You know, Mr. Rexley. He's more than just desperate. I think he is just downright evil."

"Now you're learning, lad. And don't tear yourself up none because of him. Convince him if you can, for your own sake. Just don't expect any results. That man is about as appreciative as a domestic boar. And like the boar, he cares nothing about the hand that feeds him. Think of it this way, and rightly speaking, too. Those slaves are just as much ours as they are his."

"Are they now?"

"You'd best believe it. If Capt'n McIntyre doesn't get a good lot of them to the Indies, he won't get paid. And if he doesn't get paid, we won't get what's due us."

"I never thought of it that way."

"It's about time you did, lad."

It was, more or less, the truth. Captain McIntyre would get a small profit from selling the raw salves. Most of it would go to pay off his loan for the flintlocks. The rest would go to his crew. McIntyre, himself, would get almost nothing. The completed mission would be his pay. It would be a personal victory. Despite all the things that had happened to him, he would finally come out on top of things with a clean bill, a "legitimate" business, and good credit.

When Sam and Pete finally caught up with Captain McIntyre, they found him somewhat calmer but still fuming. He was mumbling under his breath, expressing all the things he was going to do once he caught up with his slaves.

"When I get me hands on 'em this time," he said, a fresh wad of tobacco in his mouth, his cheek bulging, "I'm agonna chain 'em together by the leg, the arm, and the neck. Hell, I'll be damned if I don't pair 'em up and yoke 'em, like it suppose to be done. Then let's see 'em run away. Those folk are agonna learn to stay where I put 'em or, so 'elp me, it'll be the last time they run away from anybody."

When Captain McIntyre heard his aides closing behind him, he looked back only briefly. "You are probably right, Pete. Maybe all of us were a little to blame. But you know, now that I think about it, you know where the real blame is?"

Pete winked at Sam but answered the captain, "Let me guess. Was it that Batushi hunter who just stood by and let it happen?"

"No. It was that little bastard native boy who opened me pen. I saw 'im with me own eyes, I did. What, in hell's fire, did he think he was doing? I have to discourage that kind o' behavior."

"What are you saying, Capt'n?"

"I'm saying, I'm agonna kill 'em. I swear to you, on King George's grave, so 'elp me, I'm agonna kill 'em. I'm agonna cut his throat so damned wide he'll be agrinnin' his way into hell from under his chin."

"You think that's the right thing to do?" Pete initially was toying with Captain McIntyre, for Sam's sake. After the short lecture he had just given Sam, something in the captain's voice didn't sound right. "Are you serious?"

"I'll tolerate no disrespect like that, Pete."

"But Capt'n, you can't do that."

"I can do, damn well, anything I want."

Since leaving the coast, Pete had thought of himself as the most level-headed of the three men. In most cases, he even felt he was Captain McIntyre's superior, but he was wise enough to keep that fact to himself. According to himself, his only mistake was signing up with such a ridiculously small slaving crew. He didn't need the money. He did it for the adventure. And now, the captain seemed driven by ego, greed, and revenge. He was turning this adventure into a very bad and very profitless experience.

"Capt'n, you need all the slaves you can get. You can't afford to lose a single one. If I were you, I'd be more riled up over the way your slave hunters handled their raids. I hear tell, they destroyed a whole village to fetch you a handful of slaves."

"That there is their business, Pete. They did what they had to, to bring me what I asked for. Just you never mind about me hunters. That there native boy is me concern now. He's bad merchandise. I'd be better off if I kill 'im.'"

"Sounds to me like your mind is made up?'

"He's a trouble-maker, Pete. He's truly bad merchandise. Nobody will buy 'im.'"

"So what? No one knows he's a troublemaker if you don't tell. Sell him anyway. Besides, he's still wild. He hasn't been domesticated yet. When they get through training him in the Indies, be it a house-boy or field hand, he'll bring in a healthy sum. A boy that young is worth more than a full-grown male."

"I'm atellin' you, Pete, nobody will buy him. Take me word for it. He's worthless in me book. If I don't kill 'im, I got this terrible gut feelin', we may not get the lot of 'em off this continent, let alone to the Indies."

Captain McIntyre stopped walking. "We're awastin' good time like this. Let's split up 'ere. Day is breaking and its agonna get hot around here pretty fast. Pete, you go that way. Sam, you head out toward the clearing, up yonder way. I'll take the middle 'ere. Now hasten up! Find me slaves! We'll meet back here."

The captain watched his two aides veer off in separate directions as he spit and wiped another trickle of tobacco juice from his beard.

9

SOMETHING QUITE DIFFERENT

The Chinchigwe had gone without a decent rest since their village was raided over five days ago. It was beginning to show now. Jpuma walked with a painful limp. His swollen ankle was getting worse. Two of his fellow tribe members, who staggered under his weight, supported him. Lobarra Gendeyani was supported in the same manner. Shear fatigue was her greatest and most immediate concern. She faithfully allowed her two supporters to lead her on as she held her stomach and struggled to keep her eyes open. And the healthier ones of the group, including Twese and Komu, sweated profusely from the African humidity and stifling heat.

To rest now was out of the question. It meant stopping. The Chinchigwe could not afford to stop. Their escape was not guaranteed. They knew that the merchant and his aides would come after them as soon as they recovered. In their condition, they could be easily overtaken and recaptured. If there was any hope of ever finding Adaulah's village, they had to continue moving, no matter what.

To compound their fatigue, the Chinchigwe had also gone with decent food. The last nourishing food they had was in their village. They had tried eating the unrecognizable foodstuff given to them in the merchant's pen. That food, whatever it was, did more damage than good. The smell of it alone put their stomachs in constant chaos, causing some of them to lose everything they successfully swallowed.

Although the Chinchigwe were free now, the prospect of securing anything better had not improved yet. Several people, including Adaulah, tried to make bows and arrows from small branches and vines. They intended to hunt small games with them. Unfortunately, the weapons were so crude that the arrows often skewed from or fell short of the target. And to make matters worse, the hunted game would hear the jingle and clinking of the chains on the Chinchigwe's arms and would flee.

Adaulah, the Aukmondi boy, was the only one free enough to hunt properly. The problem here was that he came from a tribe of people who were not hunters. He had no hunting experience at all. Despite his sincere efforts to secure food for himself and the others, he was no more successful than the rest.

Not long after the darkness and the night had dissolved away, the Chinchigwe and Adaulah were fortunate enough to eventually find a small pond in the center of a cluster of trees. With unusually clear water, the pond was surrounded by a large family of baboons. The baboons freely abandoned the pond when they saw the people approaching.

The water in the pond was not provided by a stream or river and had the potential to be stagnant. But judging from the baboons, it appeared relatively safe enough to drink. Adaulah and the Chinchigwe took their chances. They rushed toward the water. They remained there only long enough to appease their thirst. After a few precious handfuls of water, they surrendered the pond to the baboons and continued.

It wasn't until mid-morning that something food-wise was finally found. They flushed out a large, wild hare by sheer chance and cornered it. Everyone who had a bow and arrow aimed at the creature.

This was the first time that Adaulah had ever done anything like this. He had never deliberately killed anything larger than a fish in his life. If he and the Chinchigwe had not needed the food, it would have been difficult for him to hold such a deadly aim on the creature. "If you can not kill it, do not eat it," Adaulah recalled something he had once overheard an Aukmondi warrior say. Adaulah fully intended to secure food for himself and the others, so he held his aim. He also held his breath as he painstakingly tried to decide when to release his arrow, if at all.

The pathetic hare had taken refuge in the cavity of a large acacia tree stump. Despite its unbelievably rapid breathing, it was trying to sit as still as possible, trying to blend in with its background. Only a twitch, now and then, indicated that the hare was ready to dart from the cavity at the first opportunity and seek a safer refuge.

Suddenly, with the swiftness of a lightning bolt, an arrow appeared in the hare's neck. The furry creature darted from the cavity as if to make its escape. The instant its forepaws touched the ground, its legs buckled as if boneless. The helpless creature somersaulted twice from its own weight and initial speed. It kicked several times and died.

Adaulah still held his unsteady aim. He was so stunned by the hare's desperate behavior that he failed to realize that his aim was no longer necessary. It wasn't until after the Chinchigwe gathered around the dead animal that the young Aukmondi dropped his aim and began to breathe again. As he watched Twese Merende hold the creature up, he realized, for the first time, that Twese had killed it.

Without a word, the Chinchigwe quickly began to prepare the hare. There was no time to waste. Ameh Jobabwe skinned and gutted the creature as best he could with a sharp-edged stone. Twese and Embabi Tende started a fire by ingeniously using a bowstring, a sturdy stick, and a stone. The rest of the able-bodied Chinchigwe, within their limited reach, gathered dried grass and sticks for the fire. Adaulah watched all this with fascination.

While the hare was cooking over a strong fire, everyone took the opportunity to rest in their chosen manner. Komu Ndizi insisted on tending the hare while Ameh, who had started to do it, was forced to rest. Jpuma took the time to dress his swollen ankle. He sacrificed a small strip from the sleeve of his garment to wrap his ankle. Lobarra and several of the others relaxed to the point of sleep. And Twese stood guard for everyone, watching the surrounding area for signs of danger.

Adaulah watched the hare cook. Coming from a tribe not used to eating meat, he was amazed by how the purplish-pink flesh turned dark brown. He wondered the whole time if he could eat any of it.

After Komu declared the hare done, Ameh quickly broke off twenty-five pieces as best he could. He ensured everyone had a piece, then ordered everyone to their feet again. Under the circumstances, they would have to eat on the move.

Adaulah was given a small rib section. He nibbled slowly and cautiously at his piece. The flesh was dry and tough. The strange taste was almost overwhelming as it seemed to coat the whole inside of his mouth. The food, however, was remarkably good. Adaulah ate it well until he remembered how the hare had twitched and kicked as it died. *"If you can not kill it, do not eat it,"* the warrior's voice echoed in his mind. He felt slightly uneasy. He kindly offered the remainder of his portion to Lobarra. Although Adaulah was still a little hungry, he felt better watching Lobarra clean the tiny rib section to the bone.

Not long after Adaulah and the Chinchigwe began moving again, they came to a reprieve in the forest area and entered a clearing. Overhead, the morning sun was already intense. The land fog had burned off long ago, and very few trees blocked the sun's heat. The people started across the clearing with only a mild reluctance. They dreaded the heat but knew they had no choice but to continue.

The clearing was a relatively small stretch, about four or five kilometers wide. It was full of knee-deep grass, parched brown by the relentless heat. Here and there, small clusters of bushes or stunted trees broke up the consistency. The other side of the clearing merged into another forest area, which could be seen through the shimmering quicksilver.

The group endured the heat and headed for the opposite forest. They waded uneventfully through the grass for almost three hours, looking closely for another wild hare, lizards, snakes, or any other creature that might inhabit such a place. Any one of such creatures would be considered an acceptable food source.

Their search was so intense that the escapees did not see, only fifty meters to the left of them, behind a patch of tall bushes, a huge black rhinoceros grazing in the grass. They did not know the creature was there until they heard it snorting restlessly. They looked around for the noise. Embabi was the first to see it. She pointed it out to the rest of the group. They were all chilled by what they saw.

Awesomely bigger in reality than ever imagined, the rhinoceros was an unbelievably frightening animal. It stood 150 centimeters high at the shoulders and almost three and a half meters long. Its hide looked like thick armor, making it plain that he was indestructible. And, more frightening than anything, the beast was agitated by the escapees' intrusion. It was ready to use its superior advantages to the fullest.

The rhinoceros's eyesight was naturally poor. It did not see the escapees. Its sense of smell, however, was amazingly sharp. By smell alone, it was confident that something had entered its territory somewhere. With its head held high, it gracefully trotted off several meters in one direction and suddenly stopped to sniff the air. It stood inanimately still. Only its tiny ears wiggled momentarily.

After a moment, it trotted off in the opposite direction, more disturbed this time. Again, it froze to test the scented air, looking for the unseen invaders. Then suddenly, as if the rhinoceros had pinpointed the exact location of the escapees, it charged directly toward them. It grunted loudly with each powerful gallop.

Clamors of terror came from Adaulah and the Chinchigwe as they turned to run, fortunately in the same direction they had been initially traveling. Panic-stricken, they ran as fast and as hard as they possibly could. But virtually weaponless, chained together, and laden with handicaps, they were doomed people. They felt the ground under their feet vibrate harder and harder as the beast thundered closer and closer. There was no way they could get away. Their movement was uselessly slow.

Under the sudden stress, the pregnant Lobarra fainted. The whole group, of course, had to stop when she did. Komu, the largest and strongest in the group, tried to get in a position where he could lift and carry her. His relative position in the chain's linkage made the task almost impossible.

The rhinoceros continued its fierce charge.

Only Adaulah was free enough to act. He was as frightened as any child would be in such a situation. But his nature and upbringing would not let him stand there and allow this to happen. He had to do something. He had to use his freedom to the advantage of everyone.

Adaulah bravely ran out to intercept the rhinoceros. It was a dangerous, thoughtless, and reckless thing to do. Four Green Warriors died to save his life. Was it wise to throw his life away so carelessly? Adaulah hoped to distract the beast and take the pressure off the Chinchigwe. It worked frightfully well. Before fully preparing to react, Adaulah saw the rhinoceros turn and charge him with surprising agility. Adaulah tried to turn as well. His agility failed him. Adaulah slipped and fell. The rhinoceros was only ten meters behind him when he was on his feet again.

In the meantime, the Chinchigwe were free enough to find safe cover now. None of them dared to look back until they reached the opposite forest edge. Twese was the first to take the dare. When he did, he saw something he did not expect at all.

In the distance and through the quicksilver, Twese saw the rhinoceros galloping off in the direction Adaulah had led it. He saw the creature gradually slow down to a brisk walk, and eventually to a standstill. Then he saw a woman standing calmly within arm's reach of the rhinoceros.

As much as he could see through the shimmer of heat, she was a very lovely woman, one of the most natural and beautiful he had ever seen. She wore colorful, simple, native clothing, contrasting with her rich, dark skin. Her hair was attractively short. Twese was too far away to distinguish any other features. The fact that she was standing there at all was enough to demand his full concentration.

But who was she? Where did she come from? What was she doing out there, so close to such a deadly animal?

Twese felt that he had to be seeing things. There was no other acceptable explanation. It was much easier to believe that his mind was playing tricks on him. Twese turned to the others in the group to see if any of the others saw the woman. Everyone else was tending to Lobarra, Jpuma, or other urgent needs. He looked back out over the clearing. The woman was still out there.

Before Twese could demand someone else's attention, the woman and the rhinoceros turned and walked away. The beast began to graze peacefully in the grass again, as if nothing unusual had happened. Just as peacefully, the woman walked into the shimmer of quicksilver, into obscurity.

Twese pulled himself together. He forced himself to believe that he had made a mistake, that there was nothing out there except the rhinoceros. It was just an illusion. He tried to dismiss what he thought he had seen as he focused his attention back on the group's welfare. He was still quite shaken as he approached Ameh.

"Ameh, are you alright?"

"I will be fine." Ameh was breathless. His lungs ached for air. He was lucky to be so healthy at his age. The many years of tilling the farmland in his village were paying off in ways he never expected. With blurred vision, he noticed Twese looking at him strangely. "What is wrong? Do I not look well?"

Although Twese looked directly into Ameh's face, he was unaware that Ameh was talking to him. "Yes. You …, you look well."

"Then what is wrong? Why do you stare at me so half-mindedly?"

Twese looked back toward the clearing. "Did you see that woman? There was a woman out there."

"A woman?" Ameh looked at Twese questionably. "Twese, my friend, everyone else saw something quite different."

"No! Believe me, there was a woman out there. I saw her. She was standing next to the rhinoceros. She was standing there. She was…"

"The lack of air to your head has made you see spirits, Twese." Ameh moved over. "Here. Sit down and rest before you collapse."

Twese did not argue his point. He couldn't. Maybe he did see a spirit of some kind. Once again, he sat down next to Ameh and tried to dismiss his confusion.

At this point, Komu looked back out across the clearing himself. He had overheard the exchange between Twese and Ameh. He had his own opinion about what Twese had seen. He searched the clearing with an increasing alarm. "The Aukmondi boy! Where is he?"

No one had noticed, until now, that Adaulah was missing. Ameh, using his staff – the newfound, merchant-battering pole, forced his tired body to his feet. The horrible thought that the rhinoceros had caught Adaulah flashed across his mind.

"Adaulah!" Ameh called out across the clearing. He cupped his mouth with his hands and called out twice more. The open grassland swallowed his voice. Something within him told him that his voice would not be heard. "We have to go get him." He made an impulsive motion to do so. Twese held him back.

"Ameh, wait! You do not intend to go back out there, do you? The rhinoceros is still out there. We got away once. We may not be so lucky a second time."

"But Adaulah is still out there, too. If he is not dead, then he is surely hurt."

"We can do nothing for him in either case, Ameh." Twese scanned the clearing. "Besides, something tells me he got away."

"How can you say that?"

The vision of the woman somehow reassured Twese. But rather than explain it to Ameh, he groped for a more reasonable answer. "He had no chain on his arms. He was free. He had a better chance than any of us to get away. He probably escaped by running in a different direction."

"What are you saying? Surely you cannot leave it at that. I would feel better if we knew for sure."

Twese held on to Ameh's arm. "Listen to me. We cannot go back out there. We can not afford to go through what we have already gone through."

Ameh stood thinking, feeling painfully helpless. Because of the chain, if one of them went out there, all of them would have to go. In their condition, it couldn't be done. Unfortunately, Twese was right. It would be suicide to go back out there for any reason. He looked at the chain on his arms and shook them as if to free them.

"We need Adaulah," Ameh said, not expressing his true concern for the boy. "How ... how will we find his village?"

"I do not know. As you well know, it was my feeling that we would not find it anyway."

Ameh felt the pressures of leadership. He realized that his decisions now meant life or death for someone; Adaulah, the Chinchigwe, or both. He looked into the faces of the people around him. Most of them stared back at him expectantly. What were they to do? Only halfway into the morning, their greatest hope was lost, and he could do nothing about it.

"We will wait a while here," he finally said. "If Adaulah is not hurt, he may come to us."

"Can we afford to wait? The merchant and the hunters are surely coming for us."

"Yes, we have to wait."

"Ameh, what if Adaulah is dead? Even if he is only hurt and can not come to us, we may be throwing our freedom away."

Ameh looked at Twese. "What is it, my pessimistic friend? Can you not at least hope that Adaulah is safe? Do not be so willing to pay for our freedom with someone else's life."

"I am only saying that the longer we wait here, the more it jeopardizes us. I do not mean to be insensitive about Adaulah. We owe him our lives. I am only being practical, for the sake of our people."

"Twese, believe me. I understand. But the situation is different. Let us do this. Adaulah deserves whatever we can do for him, even if it is only to wait for him to find us, to give him a little time to find us, if he can." Ameh sat down again and fixed his gaze across the clearing. "We will wait here for a while."

"So be it. We will wait." Although Twese felt differently, he surrendered to Ameh's leadership. He offered a compromise as he sat on the ground next to Ameh. "Let us wait until Lobarra has recovered enough to travel again. Agreed?"

Ameh glanced at Lobarra. Her head lay in Summarwe's lap. Summarwe was gently stroking her stomach to comfort her. Lobarra was either asleep or unconscious. "Agreed."

"And if there is no sign of Adaulah by then?"

Ameh had known the Aukmondi boy for only a few hours, but he had grown to like him very much. Losing him would be like losing his son again.

"What choice do we have? If there is no sign of Adaulah by then, we will continue… without him."

10

A THINKING CREATION

Adaulah ran hysterically from the charging rhinoceros. One sustained scream bellowed up from the pit of his stomach as if to amplify the energy he put into his strides. He ran with all the strength his legs could muster. Like the fastest cheetah, he forced the ground to flow beneath his feet in a blur. He couldn't stop. He didn't want to stop. He would have continued running, but a vine caught his foot. Adaulah tripped and tumbled hard to the ground.

The young Aukmondi lay rigidly on the ground, his arms protectively covering his head. He waited with no choice but to surrender to his fate. He listened for the thundering approach of the rhinoceros. He heard only the peaceful sounds of the birds and monkeys calling in the distance. He heard the tall grass rustling as it waved in the warm breeze about his head.

Adaulah raised his head. He sat up slowly. He wiped the tears that blurred his vision from his eyes. He searched all around the clearing for the creature. As far as he could see, the rhinoceros was nowhere in sight in every direction.

There was a fleeting moment of confusion and disbelief as Adaulah tried to understand what had happened. Where did the rhinoceros go? Did he outrun it? If so, how did he lose it so completely?

The young Aukmondi knew there had to be an explanation. There always is. But it was beyond his understanding, and he had no time to figure it out now. Instead, he simply accepted the development. He wiped the last tears from his face and forced himself to relax.

The energy still pumped through his body gradually transformed into a powerfully jubilant feeling. Adaulah sprang to his feet. He let loose with a healthy cry of victory, loud enough to frighten a flock of birds in a nearby tree. It was an expression of gratitude to the Supreme Spirit.

Adaulah ended the rhinoceros incident with a sigh of relief and a broad smile. He felt good. He had escaped death once again with only a small abrasion on his hand where he had fallen. He was free to return to the Chinchigwe now. He gathered up his crudely made bow and arrows and quickly headed back up the clearing. He could barely wait to see Ameh, Twese, and the others. He wanted to share this most recent escape with them, too.

Thinking more about his reunion with the Chinchigwe than about where he was going, Adaulah retraced what he thought were his steps. He walked as far back up the clearing as he thought he had come. But after several meters, he only found unfamiliar territory and no signs of the Chinchigwe. Just a little farther, he thought.

The farther he went, the more unfamiliar the surroundings he saw. With each step, he grew increasingly convinced that something was wrong. He stopped and turned, searching his surroundings again. Nothing looked familiar to him except the mountain range in the distance. The young Aukmondi finally realized that he was relatively lost.

Once again, he tried to recover his steps. This time, Adaulah looked for signs of the Chinchigwe in a more concentrated effort. He looked for traces of their original journey across the clearing toward his village. He even looked for signs of the rhinoceros that had once threatened his life. He saw nothing that would lead him toward a reunion with his friends.

Ever since the escape from the merchant's pen, Adaulah had felt somewhat responsible for getting the Chinchigwe to his village. He had promised them there would be help for them in his village. He knew that getting them there was their best hope of survival. The Chinchigwe needed him. Those unfortunate people were somewhere out here alone, with nowhere to go. Anything could happen to them now. Adaulah began to experience a terrible sensation of failure.

Adaulah wondered if he would ever see the Chinchigwe again. He thought of his family and friends in the Aukmondi Valley and how the Chinchigwe would have been welcomed there. He would have given anything to have witnessed the meeting between the Chinchigwe and his people.

But then, it occurred to Adaulah that he was alone in the wilderness, too. It had not occurred to him until now that he was in a dubious predicament. His chances of encountering danger had just increased significantly.

Everything was going wrong. He was losing control. The near-fatal threat of the rhinoceros, the anxiety of losing the Chinchigwe, and his sudden alienation gradually took on the form of an unshakeable hopelessness. It was one of the worst feelings Adaulah had ever experienced. Tears began to well up in his eyes again.

"Never give up hope." The stern voice of his father echoed in his head. *"A thinking Creation is never hopeless. If you can create new thoughts, those thoughts will lead to new possibilities. And with new possibilities, hopelessness can be worn away."*

Adaulah wiped away the new tears that trailed down his face. He began to think of himself as the honorary warrior that he was. He forced himself to act calmly about his situation, even if he wasn't. In the grassy clearing, the sun beaming directly over his head, Adaulah calmly sat down to think. He wouldn't get up until he had a decisive idea of what to do next.

There were several problems that he had to consider. First of all, it was obvious to him that he would have to find his village by himself now. He was only disoriented and not lost. So, this task would not be any more difficult. It was just a matter of continuing as before. After all, he was the one leading the others.

Adaulah realized that the truth of the matter and the part that concerned him the most was that he had lost the Chinchigwe. Those people were alone now. And, unlike him, they were truly lost. What would become of them? Would they survive? Could they find this village without him?

Their alternatives were limited. Since he and the Chinchigwe were not likely to find each other, they might decide to give themselves to that slave merchant. Adaulah had overheard Ameh and Twese discussing this before.

The sudden flight of a francolin falcon from the nearby grass startled Adaulah. It jerked his mind away from the Chinchigwe and brought it back to his most immediate problem: his own survival.

He looked to his left, then to his right, realizing that taking care of all threats to his life was completely up to him now. He thought of how secure he had felt with the Chinchigwe, not that they were significantly helpful in their condition. Still, Adaulah desired their company and the illusion of comfort that their presence had created.

Adaulah found himself clutching the unused bow and arrows that he carried. He studied the bow from tip to tip, looking at it for the first time. He selected one of the arrows and touched the crudely sharpened end. The dull point seemed ineffective for any purpose.

Adaulah wondered, from a disturbingly new perspective, if he would ever have to use the weapon defensively. He wondered if he could use it to wound or kill with. He remembered yesterday, when the slave hunters captured him; the day when four Aukmondi Green Warriors were killed before his eyes. Green Warriors were some of the most experienced warriors in the Aukmondi Army. Could he use his weapon as the warriors tried to use their weapons?

Adaulah was overwhelmed by the thought. Childishly, and with finality, he tossed the bow and arrows to the ground. How could he possibly defend himself when four Green Warriors could not?

Adaulah had already found hunting for food with the weapon extremely difficult. He recalled the image of the pathetic wild hare, the arrow through its neck, the useless struggle it gave for its life. Adaulah shuddered. No, he could not use the bow and arrows as a weapon.

Of all the random and pragmatic thoughts that formed in his head, Adaulah responded to one with growing excitement. He remembered how Twese and Embabi had ingeniously used the bow to create a fire. He could create a fire, too, or better yet, smoke. He could make a smoke signal. Maybe the Chinchigwe would see it. It was a jubilant idea. It was a breakthrough in the middle of a crisis.

Adaulah picked up the rejected bow and arrows. He selected one of the arrows again and broke it in half to make a pointed stick of suitable length. Next, he began to part the tall grass about him until he eventually found two large, flat stones. Adaulah piled these things together. Then he quickly went to gather an armload of semi-dried grass.

Adaulah was now ready to try something he had never done before. Just as he had seen Twese and Embabi do, Adaulah placed one stone on the ground. Then he twisted the bowstring around the stick. Finally, he braced the other end of the stick with the other stone and began to saw the bow string rapidly. The faster he sawed, the faster the stick turned against the stone. Friction caused the heat to build. The point between the stick and the stone got hotter and hotter.

Driven almost as much by curiosity as by his original objective, Adaulah held the stick up for inspection. He touched the point of the stick with his finger. The heat was unexpectedly intense. It burned his finger, forcing him to jerk his hand away.

Adaulah quickly placed a bunch of the dry grass next to the stone. The grass smoldered, but nothing else happened. As hot as the stone was, it still wasn't enough to ignite the grass. Adaulah tried again.

After several unsuccessful attempts, Adaulah finally mastered the trick. He smiled at the spiraling whiff of white smoke and the pungent smell of smoldering grass. With a minor adjustment and a couple of gentle but sustained blows of air from his breath, he finally got a strong fire burning.

Adaulah immediately piled his collected grass on top of the fire. The growing flames were suddenly transformed into a column of white smoke. Adaulah watched the thick smoke gently swirl upward toward the south. It was a strong enough signal for anyone to see.

When Adaulah felt satisfied that his signal had been received, he let the flame grow and burn down. He covered the smoldering ashes with plenty of dirt. The Aukmondi warriors had taught him how to extinguish a campfire responsibly.

Then he waited. He waited and waited. No one came. The young Aukmondi briefly considered the possibility that the Chinchigwe could not come to him. If this were the case, then his signal may prompt them to respond in a similar manner, giving him directions to travel. He searched the horizons for any similar columns of smoke. He was too optimistic to think that the Chinchigwe may have already given up on him and were forced by circumstances to move on. He waited a few more minutes and then prepared to repeat his signal.

As he collected the necessary grass for his next attempt, Adaulah saw something move, about ten meters ahead. He stopped everything to get a better look.

To his alarm, he saw a Wabanga sitting crouched, peeping through the tall grass, watching him. Adaulah could barely believe what he was seeing. The white camouflage markings painted boldly over the tribesman's face were unmistakable.

Adaulah knew enough about the Wabanga to know that his life was, once again, in very grave danger. There was no doubt in his mind that the Wabanga sitting out there was coming to kill him. So often, from the warriors of the Aukmondi Army, he had heard, *"No one lives after an encounter with a Wabanga!"* The words *"no one"* echoed like rolling thunder in his mind. His heart skipped and pounded. Fear lodged like a rock in his throat.

Adaulah quickly picked up his bow and one of the unbroken arrows. He looked at the weapon in terms of his defense. It was his only defense. As ineffective as it looked, under the circumstances, it had to do. He placed the arrow nock into the bowstring and drew it back. He was ready to defend himself. He looked out across the grass to where the Wabanga was sitting.

The Wabanga was gone. As if he had disappeared into thin air, the Wabanga was gone.

Adaulah wasn't fooled. This was no rhinoceros. This was a stalking tactic. The Wabanga were famous for ghostly movements such as this. Adaulah knew that the Wabanga was still around and dangerously closer to him by now. He searched the clearing with his eyes, trying to restrain the fear that shook his body. Sure enough, Adaulah found the Wabanga, standing openly only five meters behind him, as if he had been there all along.

Adaulah panicked. He was going to be killed. He brought up his bow again and aimed. Braced by his nervous, untrained fingers, the arrow lazily slipped and fell to the ground, as if by its own will. Adaulah picked it up, but realized he was no match for this experienced killer.

Once again, Adaulah turned and ran for his life.

11

SAMUEL DAWBY

Shortly after splitting up from Captain McIntyre and Pete, Sam emerged from the forest area and entered the clearing. He had reached the clearing sooner than he expected. Why did Captain McIntyre tell him to go toward the clearing when the clearing was only a few meters away? Sam peeled the heavy backpack from his back and dropped it to the ground. He limped over to a nearby log and sat down to rest and to think. What did Captain McIntyre expect of him? Was he expected to search the clearing too?

Sam looked out across the clearing. The four or five-kilometer stretch was covered by knee-deep grass. Only a tree or large bush, here and there, provided shading from the African sun overhead. Another forest area spanned the entire horizon, visible through a quicksilver shimmer on the other side. It looked larger and cooler than the forest Sam had just emerged from. But the clearing itself did not look inviting at all.

Sam was already tired, hot, and uncomfortably wet with sweat. His jaw still ached from the beating Captain McIntyre had given him. And his ankle did not seem to be getting any better. Sam pulled up his pant leg to look at his ankle. It did not appear to be swollen, but it hurt, nonetheless. Sam took out his bandana and wiped the sweat from his eyes. He looked out at the clearing again and dreaded what lay ahead. These moments made him wish he were back on the Virginia Colony loading docks.

Things would be different if only he and his best friend Thomas hadn't listened to Captain McIntyre. Sam had been a dock worker for most of his twenty-two years. He and Thomas started working the docks when they were nine years old. Nowadays, dock work is fast becoming slave labor. It never occurred to Sam and Thomas until Captain McIntyre came along and pointed out that subtle fact to them.

According to Captain McIntyre, Sam's dockside employer had been taking on more and more slaves. These slaves were doing the same work that Sam and Thomas had done. The only difference was that these slaves were doing it for a ration of food and community shelter. Sam and Thomas were paid meager wages and had to afford their own shelter. Given time, workers like Sam and Thomas were destined to become obsolete.

Maybe all of that was true. But Sam knew that if Captain McIntyre had not been so persuasive, he and Thomas would still be on the docks. They would be doing something they knew how to do or were good at. The two of them wouldn't have foolishly quit the docks and signed on as crewmembers of the Maiden's Hand.

Thomas tried to argue that they knew nothing about working on a slave ship. They had no idea what it was like to sail for months on the open seas. Even the little knowledge they had picked up from the merchants and seamen who came into port with all their wild stories and adventures wasn't enough.

But Captain McIntyre insisted that Sam and Thomas were strong and willing workers. Those qualities made them seaworthy enough for him. The food would be palatable. The wages would be better. And the wild stores and adventures would be priceless. Sam has been miserable since signing on with the Maiden's Hand. It cost poor old Thomas his life in that horrible storm off the coast of Algoa Bay.

Sam took a sip of water from his canteen and stood up. He limped back over to his backpack. As he slipped it on, he smiled at the pathetic irony of his predicament. If he hadn't listened to Captain McIntyre, he wouldn't be over here in this ungodly place, chasing runaway slaves who are meant to replace him in the first place.

It was mid-morning now. The sun was rapidly climbing overhead. The grassy clearing was already sweltering. The forest on the opposite side of the clearing seemed to dance in a quicksilver river as Sam caught a glimpse of it through the current of hot air. As he stood there, he seriously debated whether to make the crossing or not.

His instructions were simple. *"Go toward the clearing…"* As far as Sam was concerned, that meant going only as far as the clearing. If nothing is found, turn around and come back. That was what Sam originally intended to do. But he had reached the clearing in a relatively short time. Turning around and going back now didn't seem right, somehow.

Sam knew Captain McIntyre was already angry at him for falling asleep during his watch last night. Sam was not going to make matters worse. He wiped his face again and stuffed his bandana back into his pocket. He looked out across the clearing and forced himself to continue.

"For the love of King George!" Sam did not realize the intensity of the heat until he began walking in direct sunlight. Everything was uncomfortable. He reset his hat on his head to keep the sun out of his eyes. He shifted the weight of his backpack because the straps to his canteen and gunpowder horn were already cutting into his left shoulder. Even his musket, which he carried across his right shoulder, seemed to weigh more than it should.

Sam did have honest intentions to search for the runaways. From the moment he separated from Captain McIntyre and Pete, Sam knew that if he were the one to find the slaves, he would do his best to bring them back or, at least, tell Captain McIntyre which way they were going. But finding them was something he didn't expect to occur. And finding them was the least of his concerns right now.

Most of Sam's attention was centered on himself. His jaw still hurts. His leg still hurts. Hunger pains began to gnaw in his stomach. He was tired. He was hot. None of these conditions would probably improve soon. If nothing else, Sam considered himself overdue for a deserved rest.

Sam reasoned that under these circumstances, he would not be the one to find the runaway slaves anyway. Captain McIntyre and Pete were somewhere north of him. They were determined and responsible men, doing their best to locate the slaves. The odds were in their favor. Why should he overexert himself? Besides, if he did not take a restful break soon, he would become a useless burden to himself and Captain McIntyre.

"To hell with Capt'n McIntyre!" Sam was irritated and feeling rebellious. It was time to put first concerns first. He had made up his mind to cross the clearing. But he would also find a cool shade tree and take a rest. What would it hurt? If McIntyre wanted to accuse him of doing a half-hearted job, the time it took to cross the clearing and then re-cross it later would support the thoroughness of his apparent search.

But not long after starting, Sam realized a flaw in his plan. The heat of the sun was making the crossing unbearable. His bandana, again in his hand, hung uselessly wet through his fingers as he, himself, dripped with sweat. The pungent smells of parched grass and animal odors stung his nostrils with each hot air intake. He had practically emptied his canteen into his agitated stomach only to become nauseous. And the worst thing of all, feeling the way he was, Sam realized that he could have, just as easily, rested before crossing the clearing.

Faulty thinking was another one of Sam's acquired traits. Even his best friend Thomas had often accused Sam of being a faulty thinker; never seeing the whole scope of anything; seldom considering all the consequences. But who could? Maybe he was somewhat of a faulty thinker. Nobody's perfect. He was still a hard worker and earning his keep. And, unlike Thomas, his faulty thinking had not gotten him killed yet. Whatever situation he found himself in, Sam's so-called faulty thinking had gotten him out of it, one way or another.

Sam turned around, wondering if he should go back or continue. From where he stood, both forests appeared to be equally close. He had come halfway and could go either way. If he continued, he would have to come back across the clearing to find Captain McIntyre and Pete after resting. On the other hand, if he went back, Sam realized the captain might just beat him for returning so soon. And matters would be especially worse if he were caught resting back there. Sam decided to complete the crossing. The progress would look good in the captain's eyes.

The closer Sam got to the opposite forest, the cooler and more inviting it looked. There was less quicksilver distorting his view now. The forest was clearer. It was thicker and greener with plenty of shade. Even the sky over the forest was bluer and full of immaculately white clouds.

Sam's haphazard view of a lazy, anomalously low cloud of smoke toward his southwest was quickly stolen away by a huge shadow that suddenly sailed over his shoulder from back to front. Sam glanced skyward to see a black vulture lazily circling just a few meters above his head. The bird was so amazingly close that Sam got the impulsive urge to shoot at it, just for fun.

Instead of putting the stock of his musket to his shoulder, Sam took his pistol from his side holster. Like his musket, it was also a flintlock. He checked the powder in the powder pan. It was dry. He locked the flint back, aimed the sight at the bird, and pulled the trigger. The pistol only clicked. It did not fire. The flint hammer fell but did not ignite the gunpowder.

"Useless bastard!" Sam cursed the pistol. He wasn't as angry as he let on. He halfway expected the pistol only to click. He habitually rechecked the flint and the powder. Both were still in good firing condition, in his opinion. Still, the pistol had failed to fire – nothing unusual.

By the time Sam was ready to aim and fire again, the vulture had circled too far out of range. Sam re-holstered his pistol and watched the bird gracefully glide southward toward a flock of other vultures, circling the sky.

Something's dead, Sam thought. Probably the remains of a zebra, antelope, or something like that. Sam tried to see, but the tall grass and the quicksilver obscured his vision. He wasn't too concerned about this either. It was too hot to be concerned about anything like that now. All he wanted was to get to the other side of the clearing, the forest edge where he could rest.

The more Sam walked, the hotter the air seemed to get, and the cooler and more inviting the opposite forest area looked. Sam could already see himself stretched out under a tree, maybe napping. He dwelled on that thought, mindless of his surroundings. Had he been more observant, he would have noticed a handful of the crudely made arrows lying in the grass, less than a meter from his foot.

As it turned out, Sam didn't see much of anything until he had finished crossing the clearing. That unattractive stretch of land behind him was pushed from his mind. He was determined not to think about it again until it was time to re-cross it.

Immediately after reaching the forest edge, Sam found a large oak tree. It was one with low-hanging limbs and cast a cool, dark shadow. He quickly inspected the area for safety as he removed his backpack. He leaned his musket against the tree trunk and removed his canteen and power horn from his shoulder. He untied his semi-useless pistol from around his waist to ensure his comfort and dropped it beside his backpack. Finally, he slumped against the tree himself. With a slight smile, he slid down to the comfortable position he had longed for.

Sam's body tingled with fatigue. He could feel his muscles relaxing. Savoring the moment, he reached for his canteen to take the last swallows of lukewarm water. As he expected, the water ran out before his thirst was quenched. He tossed the canteen aside, refusing to be discouraged by anything.

Sam knew he was tired, but had underestimated the magnitude of his fatigue. Unaware that it was happening, Sam's consciousness gradually gave way to sound sleep.

12

ON THIS DAY, YOU DIE

As Sam's body recovered, Sam lay dreaming.

Sam's most vivid dream was that of a hunting safari. He was the leader of that safari. He took great pride knowing he had planned everything from beginning to end. He led a selected team of the bravest African natives into an obscure part of Africa, into a part of Africa where a legend lived.

Sam was on the trail of a great lion. This lion was a frightening beast, known to all as *"The King's King"*. This lion was a killer. According to the legend, *"The King's King"* was an immortal force, virtually unstoppable. Many had hunted *"The King's King"*, but no one could bring him down. Sam hunted this vicious slaughterer of livestock, this blood-thirsty man-killer, when everyone else had given up. Sam was determined to be the one who finally defeated *"The King's King"*.

During Sam's flawless hunt, the moment was finally approaching when Sam would have *"The King's King"* cornered. Sam had strategically sent the natives ahead to flush him out of hiding and drive him back toward a showdown. Now, from over a grassy hill, Sam could hear the brave natives singing their hunting chant and rhythmically pounding on their drums. The harmonious sounds grew louder and louder as the natives approached. Sam knew that somewhere between him and the natives was *"The King's King"*.

As planned, Sam stood alone, waiting calmly. He held his musket ready, aiming toward the crest of the hill. It was a flawless plan.

"The King's King" pranced up to its summit from the other side of the hill. He stopped so that Sam and everyone else could see all

his majesty. He seemed to realize that Sam would be waiting for him at the foot of the hill. He welcomed Sam, used to the idea of taking on all challengers. The beast seemed to announce his presence with a snarl and a roar that shook the ground. He stared at Sam. There was murder in his yellow eyes. Fresh blood from its latest victim stained his oversized teeth.

Sam intended to shoot the moment *"The King's King"* appeared. That was the plan. That was the way it had to be done. Sam knew that he had to strike first when he came face to face with this killer. He would not get a second chance.

But the unbelievable size of the lion stunned Sam. Never, in his life, had he ever seen a lion so impressively big. This lion cannot be real! Sam dropped his aim briefly as he stared in awe. Like so many others, Sam had been ambushed by the sheer presence of *"The King's King"*.

"No! It's not going to be this way. You'll not kill again, my friend. On this day, you die!" Sam refined his aim, crosshairs on the heart. Sam fired.

"The King's King" leaped as if fighting an unseen attacker. Dark red blood began to stain its majestic mane as it fell. *"The King's King"* roared and struggled fitfully against the deadly force that was taking its life. He refused to be taken so easily. In his fight, he disappeared from view over the hill's summit.

Sam was the hero. He could hear the native's hunting chant as it became a song of victory. *"The King's King"* was dead. Sam's victory cry was loud enough to be heard all over Africa. Because of Sam, not another man's blood would stain the teeth of *"The King's King"*.

Sam rushed up the hillside to the summit. Spattered drops of blood trailed over the summit to the other side. Sam followed the trail toward a huge gathering of his native hunters crowding around his glorious kill. As he approached, the crowd parted, exposing a shocking revelation.

Sam had not killed *"The King's King"* by some strange circumstance. He had not killed a lion at all. To his surprise and horror, he had killed a man. On the ground lay the body of a man, clad in all white and a black string tie around his neck. Sam had killed Captain McIntyre.

Sam's team of selected native hunters was silent now. There was no singing. There were no rhythmic drums. The natives were all pointing accusingly at Sam.

Sam turned to run.

Sam moaned in his dream as well as vocally. The sound from his mouth jolted him awake and back into reality. He woke feeling both disturbed and very relieved. He had never killed anyone before. His heart was racing from the dream of having done so. On the other hand, he was so very glad that it was only a dream.

Sam's mouth was dry. His tongue stuck to the roof of his mouth. He reached for his canteen again, hoping enough water was left to quench his thirst. There was only enough to wet his lips.

As Sam held the canteen up, begging the last drop of water to come out, he wondered how long he had been asleep. It felt like hours. He was groggy. The shadow of the tree had grown by almost two meters. Sam realized that he had slept past noon. He had been so worried about returning to Captain McIntyre too soon. Now, Captain McIntyre was probably wondering where he was.

Sam looked back out across the clearing. The task of re-crossing it was just beginning to demand his attention when he happened to notice two natives out there. He saw two ghostly figures staring back at him through the shimmering heat. Two natives, in their crouched positions, about 40 meters away, seemed to be waiting for Sam to wake up and take notice of them.

"Wild men!" Sam dropped his canteen and got quickly to his feet.

When Sam stood up, one of the wild men stood up, too. He slowly came to a flexible, poised attack position.

From one nightmare into a real one, Sam grabbed his musket. He quickly checked the flint and the powder. Captain McIntyre had told him there were wild men around here. Sam had not thought much of it. He did not expect to see any. Now, there were two of them out there. One of them was preparing to attack him. Sam knew he had to defend himself.

When Sam looked up from his gun, the wild man who had gotten up was still in his attack position, but he had also begun his unusual approach. Sam watched him take a few rapid steps toward him, and then he stopped as if frozen. After a few seconds, he slowly swayed from side to side, as if mechanically. The wild man repeated this approach several times as he drew closer and closer.

Sam had never seen anything like it. Just as he had been awed by the lion in his dream, he was awed by the wild man. As the wild man got closer, Sam saw a chalky white mask painted across the wild man's eyes and bridge of his nose. Polka-dot spots of white covered the rest of his face, neck, shoulders, and chest. On his head, he wore a grass-woven headband. Two boneless, dried, and decaying lion's tails hung on each side of the headband. Four feathered bracelets were worn around the wild man's wrists and ankles. Around his waist was a very scant frontal loincloth.

The wild man was truly bizarre-looking. But what frightened Sam the most was what he held in his right hand. A knife, about 25 centimeters long and sharpened on both edges, was held ready to be used.

Sam had never killed before. The dream he had only moments ago was not enough to emotionally prepare him for what he knew he had to do here. He raised the stock of his musket to his shoulder. With some hesitancy, he aimed. Down the sight of the musket, he saw the wild man in a full charge now. Undeterred by the gun pointing at him, the wild man was completely ignorant of what was about to happen to him.

Sam closed one eye to refine his aim, held his breath, and fired. To his utter dismay, he heard a familiar click. Panic hit him with a solid impact. The musket was usually more reliable than this. Now there was nothing he could do.

The wild man was only ten meters away and still coming. It was too late to re-check the flint and powder, pull the hammer back, and fire again. It was too late to even go for his pistol. Sam felt like his whole body was doused in icy water in the African heat.

In desperation, Sam turned the musket around and prepared to use it like a club. He would knock the living hell out of him if he couldn't shoot the wild man. Sam held his breath again. With precise timing, he swung the musket with all his strength. He hit the wild man squarely across the left upper arm. He felt the wild man's bone crack as he knocked him to the ground.

Panic had caused Sam to hit the wild man harder than expected. The wooden stock of his musket shattered and flew off in several pieces. Sam was left holding only the lock and barrel. The flint jaws on the lock were bent to a useless position.

Instead of beating the wild man with the lock and barrel, Sam tossed it aside. Now was the time to go for his pistol. If he could get it ready in time, he could count on it to be a much more deadly weapon. With two quick steps, he rushed over to where his pistol lay on the ground and pulled it out of its holster. He quickly checked the flint and powder and turned to face the wild man.

The wild man was gone. The other wild man was still out in the clearing, unmoved in his original crouched position. But the wild man who had attacked him was gone.

"What is this?" Common sense told Sam that, under the circumstances, the wild man had left in the most open and direct route possible. But there was no sign of him. He didn't even hear him leave. Sam ran back over to the very spot where the wild man had fallen. He searched in every direction. The wild man had disappeared into thin air. "This is bloody impossible!"

Sam stood there wondering how the wild man, in his battered condition, had gotten away so quickly. His thoughts were interrupted when a small drop of blood fell on the side of his face. Sam did not recognize it as blood until another drop fell on his shoulder. He looked up just as the tuft end of a lion's tail fell into his eyes. Sam jumped back, frightened, and fell to the ground.

In the tree, the wild man hung from a limb by his legs. His broken and bloody arm was curved grotesquely across his chest. A piece of bone protruded through muscle and flesh. The wild man was looking down on Sam with bloodshot, horrifying eyes. In the hand of his good arm, he held his knife ready. His intent to kill Sam was as strong as ever.

From where he lay on the ground, Sam raised his pistol. Without aiming or hesitating, he fired. There was no click this time. With a resounding bang and a puff of acrid smoke, a pellet was discharged. Sam rolled over out of the way just as the wild man fell from the tree, dead. Sam had shot him squarely in the chest.

Sam slowly got to his feet. He studied the wild man, nudging him with his foot. The wild man was dead. Sam had shot him, though accidentally, in the heart. Sam stepped back, trying to wrap his mind around what he had just done. At that moment, he remembered the other wild man in the clearing. Sam wheeled around to see the other wild man, already up and approaching in his strange, ritualistic manner.

Sam scrambled for his powder horn and pellets. He had to reload his pistol. With his musket destroyed, the pistol was his only chance against these killer wild men. Trying to control his panic, he opened his power horn with shaking hands. Sam looked toward the clearing to see the second wildman coming at him in a full charge. Sam froze. With the unloaded pistol in his right hand and the power horn and pellet in his left hand, Sam turned and ran for cover, deeper into the forest.

13

THE WABANGA

Ameh sat thinking about Adaulah Azinti Ncobba of the Aukmondi tribe. The name "Ncobba" and the Aukmondi tribe sounded vaguely familiar to Ameh. As he and the others waited in the shade of a huge African oak and the silence of their own thoughts, Ameh tried to recall the significance of those names. Since the Aukmondi boy told the Chinchigwe who he was and where he was from, Ameh knew he had heard of the name and tribe.

When Ameh asked Adaulah to tell him more, he had heard variations of the same responses from Adaulah. He had heard Adaulah describe, with a child's values, the "likes" and "dislikes" about the Aukmondi Valley and the Aukmondi people. Several times, during Adaulah's descriptions and stories, Ameh heard the boy proudly say, *"The name Ncobba is my father's, the Aukmondi Mfalme. When we find my village, my father will help you."*

"If your father is Mfalme," Ameh had teased the boy, not fully believing him initially, "then you are a prince."

"I am," Adaulah had quickly responded, and he wasn't joking. *"I am an honorary Black Warrior. Someday I, too, will be Mfalme."*

Ameh had said the Chinchigwe would wait for Adaulah until Lobarra was strong enough to travel again. About an hour after they began waiting, Lobarra regained consciousness. She felt tired and hungry, but she was ready to continue on. When she learned everyone was waiting for Adaulah, she suddenly wanted to rest a little longer.

The Chinchigwe waited for another hour. At that time, Ameh never learned what was so familiar about the Ncobba and the Aukmondi tribe. However, he realized he had developed a strong fondness and admiration for the little Aukmondi boy due to his thinking. Adaulah spoke with such sincerity and innocence that Ameh eventually began to believe that the little boy was some prince and that his father was a good and great Mfalme.

Whether or not Adaulah's descriptions and stories about his father and his people were true, it did not matter now. To Ameh and the Chinchigwe, Adaulah was simply a godsend. He was a blessing, dropped briefly among the last of some helpless people. He had come to do his great deed for them, but now he was gone. Ameh closed his eyes, holding back his grief. It is widely believed that an old man has no tears – not true.

At that moment, Twese happened to look out over the clearing. In the distance toward the southwestern horizon, he saw a large flock of vultures circling the sky. He quickly got Ameh's attention. "What do you suppose it means?"

Ameh forced his stiff old body to his feet. At first, he saw nothing. He cleared the water from his eyes with his hand and focused his vision. When he saw the vultures, he could not suppress his fear. "It is Adaulah. He must be hurt!"

By this time, all the rest of the Chinchigwe were on their feet, including Lobarra. Every one of them saw the flock of scavengers as Adaulah's fate. They huddled around Ameh for his comfort and his leadership.

"The distance is not far," Ameh said. "We must go to him."

"Can we?" Despite his question, Twese had no objection in his voice. It sounded more like a request.

Ameh considered the possibility of the group changing their flight into a search and rescue. Were they physically capable of doing it? Ameh looked over the group around him. It would be most difficult for Lobarra and Jpuma.

When Lobarra saw Ameh looking at her, she stepped forward to show her willingness. Jpuma did the same with a painful limp. Ameh understood the young boy's willingness, but Jpuma was not capable.

Komu, who stood behind Jpuma, touched Jpuma's shoulder. "Ameh, I will carry him."

"Then, let us go." Ameh turned in the direction of the vultures and began walking. He added more instructions as he led the Chinchigwe down the clearing. "Let us pace ourselves. We will hasten our steps, for Adaulah's sake. But we must also be mindful of our limits. I see no sign of the rhinoceros, but we will remain close to the forest if we need to seek cover."

Ameh and the Chinchigwe walked almost half a kilometer without incident. Lobarra held her stomach constantly as she walked, but she kept up the pace with no problem. As planned, Komu carried Jpuma on his back in a piggyback position. Despite his great strength, Komu struggled, but he did not complain.

Because the Chinchigwe kept close to the forest edge, the African heat was only a minor problem. They made good progress. Although the group was much closer to the vultures, they still could not see what the birds were circling over.

Suddenly, the Chinchigwe heard a loud bang. The sound echoed across the clearing like a thunderclap. It frightened the Chinchigwe. They stopped walking.

"What was that?" Twese asked.

Ameh slowly stooped down as if to conceal himself in the knee-deep grass. All the other Chinchigwe instinctively mimicked his behavior. Ameh began to look out across the cleaning area anxiously, searching. "Such an unnatural noise," he whispered. "It sounded like one of those thunder sticks, carried by the merchant."

"We knew all along that he was coming. Now we know, he is close." Twese searched the clearing too. "What are we going to do now?"

Ameh looked toward the circling vultures again. Whatever they did, he did not want to abandon the attempt to rescue the Aukmondi boy. "We must do what we can for Adaulah."

Just before Ameh cautiously rose back up to continue the journey toward the vultures, Twese caught his arm. "Wait a moment, Ameh. I want to help Adaulah as well. And I do not doubt that we heard the noise of the merchant's thunder stick. But I am puzzled."

"About what?"

"What was the merchant shooting at?"

Ameh resettled into his concealed position. It was a good question. He had no answer for Twese. He and everyone else began to search the clearing again, trying to locate the reason. Jpuma, who had climbed off Komu's back and hid in the grass, suddenly scrambled to his original piggyback position. "There!" He pointed toward an obscure spot in the middle of the clearing.

Through the tall grass, all the Chinchigwe witnessed a Wabanga, squatting in the middle of the clearing. The Wabanga was stalking something farther down the clearing. They saw him slowly rise to his flexible attack position and sway from side to side.

"What is he doing?"

"He is preparing to kill something. Fortunately, it is not us yet." Ameh glanced at the circling vultures in the distance. The Wabanga was between the Chinchigwe and the vultures. The relative positions made Ameh feel helpless. He knew that if the vultures circled Adaulah, there was no way the Chinchigwe could get to him now.

With just a touch of anger and frustration in his inability to help, Ameh slowly rose from concealment. He reluctantly turned away from the clearing. "Come. Let us go into the forest."

"You wish to abandon, Adaulah?"

"If the Wabanga sees us, he will kill us all. We have no other choice now. We will find help for Adaulah in his village." With this, Ameh and the Chinchigwe slowly receded into the forest. At one point or another, each of them looked by toward the clearing, not to see if the Wabanga had spotted them, but in hopes of seeing Adaulah.

******

This forest area was a lot more pleasing to walk through than the previous forest area had been. The temperature was much cooler. Millions of green leaves filtered the heat and glare of the noon sun. A rich collage of plants and animal scents filled the air. And even though the forest was denser with trees, bushes, and vines, it had a network of unobstructed pathways to walk on.

After walking several hurried kilometers, the Chinchigwe had made their way deep into a virtual paradise. The thick foliage created a serene beauty enhanced by slanted rays of hazy sunlight. Birds of various colorful types darted from tree to tree, calling and screaming, seemingly for the fun of it. Monkeys competed with the birds with their noises and daredevil moments. The forest was unlike any other that the Chinchigwe had ever seen.

The Chinchigwe were so impressed by what they saw, the sparkling greenery and the restless panorama overhead, that most of their recent misfortunes had been temporarily pushed toward the back of their minds. Thoughts of forever being homeless, of lost loved ones, and of Adaulah's loss, were suppressed.

The Chinchigwe began to forget about the pursuit by the slave merchant, their lack of food or water, rest, and about their injuries and handicaps. The beauties of this forest area even made them forget about their immediate exposure to danger – until danger began to haunt them.

As if some evil spirit had taken a special interest in them, the Chinchigwe began to feel uneasy and threatened. Each of them gradually began to sense an ever-growing presence around them. They felt watched. Something or someone was watching them. They had abandoned their quest to help Adaulah because of the Wabanga threat. Now they were experiencing the same eerie type of feeling one gets when being stalked by those savage killers.

The Wabanga, with their odd appearance and strange rituals and behaviors, came from somewhere outside central Africa. No one knew exactly where their tribe was located. In fact, it was not known if they had a single tribal location at all. They were just a scattered lineage of wild, madmen.

No female Wabanga has ever been seen, only males. They were scattered throughout the central and northeastern portions of Africa. Though they were usually seen in groups of three to five, it was not uncommon to find one by himself, on a premeditated, relentless killing spree.

The sole purpose of a Wabanga seemed to be to stalk and kill both man and beast. There was no discretion. They would stalk their prey as if their own lives depended on it. Then they would kill, seemingly for the sport of it, leaving the corpse where it fell, for the vultures, hyenas, and other scavengers.

By anyone's definition, the Wabanga were madmen. Their outward behavior was unmistakably insane. To begin with, they seem to have only one fear. For some unknown reason, they religiously avoid fire. They won't come within fifty meters of the smallest flame. A simple campfire has unintentionally saved thousands of lives in the past, right in the heart of Wabanga territory.

Very few people know that fire has such an effect on the killer Wabanga. This was probably because it wasn't a fear of fire at all. It was more like an unusually strong respect for it, rooted in some primitive belief of theirs. When these madmen came upon a fire, it didn't frighten them away. They patiently waited, hiding until the fire was gone. Once the fire was gone, they would come out of hiding to kill. If a fire was started in their presence, they left immediately, only to return after the fire was out.

In truth, the Wabanga are driven by such a violent and savage nature that they had no true fears. They feared absolutely nothing, not even imminent death. Wabanga have been known to deliberately attack wild dogs, ill-tempered water buffalos, and even lions and leopards, barehanded. Lone tribe members have willfully initiated attacks on whole African armies without the slightest hesitation.

And, as if a complete lack of fear was not enough, the Wabanga also lack the sensation of pain. These savage killers continue murderous assaults, suffering pains that would incapacitate the ordinary man. If a Wabanga's arm, leg, or rib were broken, he would continue his attack. If a Wabanga were only wounded with an arrow, a knife, a spear, or a gun, without showing so much as a flinch on his painted face, he would do his skillful best to continue his murderous attack.

Nothing short of death stops a Wabanga. Fire will hold him off, but that is all. Once he begins to stalk a prey, if it takes him forever, he will keep coming until his prey dies. The only way to stop him is to kill him first.

Covering their presence with an almost supernatural-like skill, the Wabanga can stalk their chosen prey, sometimes for days at a time, without being seen. They become visible only when they want to be seen. They can quietly and suddenly appear in places where no one was only moments earlier. And they will continue this "here, gone, here again, gone again" stalking, producing terror in their prey, until a precise moment known only to them. Then they would attack. Very few people have lived to tell of an encounter with a Wabanga.

The deeper into the forest the Chinchigwe went, the more they felt that they were being watched. Even the birds and the monkeys became noticeably silent, adding to the terror of the situation. The Chinchigwe reached a point when they were afraid to take another step.

"I feel the Wabanga is stalking us," Twese finally admitted.

"As do I." Ameh looked at the bow and arrows in his hand. He had almost forgotten that he was carrying them. They were meant to hunt for food. As a weapon, they looked so inadequate.

Trying to think like a Wabanga, Ameh searched in every direction, including up in the trees. He was the first to notice, for a fact, that someone was watching them. Up ahead were two large trees on either side of the pathway. Ameh saw the ends of spears protruding from behind one of the trees. He pointed. A paralyzing fear kept him and the Chinchigwe from doing anything, except standing where they were.

"Good and Great Spirits," Ameh said in desperation, "If this is our end, please let it be swift."

As if on cue, a large group of native warriors suddenly sprang up all around the Chinchigwe, who were surrounded, trapped, and totally helpless.

14

RAMUZA KONEHENI NCOBBA

With its own surprising impact, no end came.

From behind the two large trees, three native warriors came out and blocked the pathway. One of the three warriors, the one in the middle, looked impressively big. His sleek, 204 cm frame was solidly built. The muscles of his arms, legs, and entire body appeared to be as powerful as they were obvious. His piercing eyes were full of confidence as he studied the Chinchigwe.

For a while, the powerful warrior only stood, watching the Chinchigwe, as if daring the Chinchigwe to challenge him. But then, he realized that the people before him were not who he expected. He moved toward them and began to inspect each one of them.

None of the Chinchigwe moved or said a word. Though they were not attacked, as expected, they were still too afraid to speak. They still assumed that one sound might provoke a deadly reaction.

The warrior reached for a shackle that held Embabi's arm. He examined it, apparently trying to determine how strong the metal was or how securely it fitted. He studied Embabi's arm, noting the abrasions and the swelling. His expression showed concern as he looked into Embabi's face and slowly released her arm.

The warrior continued in this manner down the chain's linkage. He inspected three more of the trembling Chinchigwe until he approached the pregnant Lobarra. He studied her longer than any others before her, probably because she was pregnant. Her condition seemed to demand more of his attention. At one point, he boldly and firmly put his hand on Lobarra's bare stomach.

Already wet with sweat and trembling uncontrollably, Lobarra tensely submitted to the warrior's examination. She did not realize that she was holding her breath. When the warrior touched her stomach, she suddenly felt dizzy. The whole forest began to spin.

The observant warrior could tell that Lobarra was beginning to faint long before he started to examine her. When her eyes began to flutter, he caught her and gently eased her to the ground.

At this point, Jpuma's sister, Summarwe, let out a short, muffled scream. She could not contain the fear that had welled up inside her. It was the first sound that anyone had made since the encounter. Somehow, it also gave Ameh the courage to speak up finally.

"Please! Please, do not harm us! We are without weapons. You see these bows and arrows only for securing food. We are a peaceful people. You will find no sport in killing us."

The warrior shifted Lobarra to a comfortable position. At first, he seemed not to pay any attention to Ameh's pleas. When Lobarra appeared to be comfortable, he finally spoke to Ameh.

"You have no reason to fear us. We are not like the Wabanga." The warrior's voice was deep and distinguished. It was filled with confidence and authority. He rose to his feet, faced Ameh, and introduced himself. "I am Ramuza Koneheni Ncobba, Mfalme of the Aukmondi. Who are you?"

Ameh took a step back and looked up into the warrior's face. He looked around at the estimated 150 to 200 warriors surrounding the Chinchigwe. As he did, what he had been trying to remember finally came into focus in his mind. Like a dream suddenly recalled, his memory became crystal clear. It was all triggered by the impressive man standing before him.

According to an obscure legend, a legend that Ameh had never given serious thought to, there existed, somewhere in East Africa, an army of warriors known as "rainbow" warriors. They were so-called because their lower ranks were signified by one of several rainbow colors (*See Appendix II: Echelons of the Aukmondi Army*). These proud and notable warriors had miraculously maintained security and peace for their people for over 100 harvests. And the last eighteen of those harvests, they had been led by a man who was more legendary than his warriors.

Ameh suddenly realized that the legend was true. A visible relief showed on his face as he looked at Ramuza again. If this was truly the man of that legend, he knew the Chinchigwe were safe. Ameh bowed his head in submissive respect for the Aukmondi Mfalme.

But just as rapidly as the joy had come, Ameh began to show sorrow. At such a great moment, when he was face to face with a great legend, he regretted the news he felt obligated to tell.

Ameh raised his head. "Mfalme Ncobba, please, you must hurry. Your son may be in great danger."

"You know my son?"

"Yes. He was a captive with us. But he is the reason that we are free and here now. We are deeply indebted to him. So please hurry out to the clearing. We were separated from him there when a rhinoceros charged us."

Since Adaulah left for the Village of Teacher, Ramuza feared the journey would not go smoothly. He was reluctant to let him go, but it was necessary. Adaulah was special, to him and all the Aukmondi people.

The Supreme Spirit has blessed Ramuza with three honored mates. All of them are strong and fertile women. After nine harvests, these three mates have borne Ramuza ten children. But, by some grand design, known only to the Supreme Spirit of Life, only one mate has given Ramuza a son, Adaulah, the only prince of the Aukmondi people.

Ramuza studied the face of the old man who stood before him, not seeing him. His thoughts were on his son. Ameh had not mentioned the four Green Warriors who had accompanied Adaulah. Because of their loyalty, experience, and dedication, Ramuza already knew something disastrous had happened to them. The muscles of his jaw were visibly flexing with tension. For a moment, all his other reactions were calmly contained.

Ramuza gestured toward one of the two warriors who had flanked him earlier. After the warrior came and stood at his side, Ramuza spoke to Ameh again. "When did this happen?"

"It happened only this morning, just as we were halfway across the clearing in the wilderness." Ameh dreaded making his next statement. He swallowed and forced himself to make it because the Aukmondi Mfalme had a right to know. "Mfalme Ncobba, I would not be totally honest if I did not say that we suspect the worst has already come."

Ramuza was experiencing one of his worst fears. He momentarily stepped away from Ameh and wiped his face as if to smooth away his frustrations. He turned back to Ameh, maintaining his self-control. "Tell me more. I must know all that you know."

"After the rhinoceros separated us, it stood its ground. That, along with our handicaps and an enemy that pursues us, prevented us from searching for Adaulah. We waited, Mfalme. We waited and waited, hoping that Adaulah would find us. But he never came. Later, when we had the opportunity and a direction to search, we encountered Wabanga. That is when we fled into the forest, hoping to find you before it was too late."

Ramuza quickly assessed Ameh's story and turned to the warrior standing beside him. Quazzi, take five warriors here and escort these people into the valley. I will take the rest and lead a search … "

"No, Great Creation." The Brown Warrior Quazzi knew his Mfalme and friend well. He anticipated his request. "Please allow me to begin the search for Adaulah. May I suggest you return to the valley and better prepare yourself for a more prolonged and thorough search. Most warriors here, and I will use the time well before you rejoin us."

Ramuza was a strong leader who knew when to rely on the wisdom of his advisors. None of the warriors out here were prepared for a lengthy time in the wilderness. Despite his urgency, Ramuza understood and accepted Quazzi's suggestion.

"So be it. Go out to the grassland clearing and begin the search. Do not return until you have found Adaulah, or until I have come with other warriors to replace you. Understood?"

"All is understood, Great Creation. Do you think only five warriors here will be sufficient protection against the Wabanga we have been trailing?"

Ramuza made a quick scan of the area. "We are close enough to the valley to be relatively safe. At least, between here and the valley seems clear. But do not worry about us. Find my son. I will be returning as soon as possible with the replacements."

Ameh could not help but overhear the mention of Wabanga. After Quazzi and most of the warriors had departed, he addressed the Aukmondi Mfalme. "Then our suspicions were true. Were Wabanga stalking us?"

"We have seen none since last night, but they are here."

"It appears we are extremely lucky to be alive."

"Yes. You are." There was a subtle, sarcastic tone in Ramuza's voice. He was hoping that his son could be just as lucky.

At that moment, Lobarra, still lying on the ground, began to stir. She opened her eyes. She first saw the huge, unfamiliar native standing over her. The residue of her original fear caused her to try to sit up and back away.

"It is alright, Lobarra." Ameh kneeled at her side, gently placing his hand on her shoulder. "We are safe now."

Ramuza assured her by kneeling and wiping away some of the sweat from her forehead. As he did, he spoke to Ameh. "Once again, I ask, who are you people?"

"Mfalme Ncobba, we are all that is left of the Chinchigwe people. Our village was raided and destroyed by slave hunters about four or five days ago. We, who you see here, are the only survivors. We need help if you can give it to us. We need food, water, freedom from these chains, and most importantly, protection from those who still wish to harm us. Your brave son has directed us to you."

Ramuza considered the requests. He again gave the impression that he was not going to answer Ameh. After looking over the twenty-four desperate people again, he finally spoke decisively: "I will give you the food, water, freedom from the chains, and the rest and treatment you need."

The relief felt by all the Chinchigwe was centrally reflected in Ameh's face. The grateful expression lasted only until Ameh realized Ramuza had not acknowledged all of the requests. Ameh's expression slowly turned into concern.

"Mfalme, what about protection from our enemies?" Ameh asked. "You must understand, we are the last of our people. And we are defenseless."

"I do not know your enemies. If I give you protection, your enemies become my enemies. I must consider it at length before I can promise you protection."

Hearing this, Twese knelt where Ramuza and Ameh were talking. "Mfalme Ncobba, if Adaulah is still alive, our enemies are already your enemies. There is a slave merchant who pursues us. He pursues your son as well. You can not help your son without helping us."

Ramuza looked at Twese so directly that Twese slowly stood up and stepped backward. The young Chinchigwe seemed to realize he had overstepped a boundary that should not have been crossed.

"Who is this?" Ramuza asked Ameh as he waved a gesture toward Twese. "Does he speak for the Chinchigwe too?"

"He is Twese Merende," said Ameh. "Since our captivity and escape, his assistance to me has been greatly appreciated and valued. But I will speak for the Chinchigwe."

"Please accept my apology, Ameh." Twese gave Ameh his due respect. He took another step back.

Ramuza rose to his feet and addressed Twese. "Great Creation, I have my people to consider. I will not jeopardize their safety by inviting a new enemy upon them. That limit will bind my actions between you and your enemy."

"I understand, Mfalme Ncobba." Twese bowed his head. "My apology is to you as well."

Seeing that Twese had no more to say, Ramuza kneeled again to lift Lobarra into his powerful arms. Two Aukmondi warriors took the initiative to support Jpuma.

"Come," said Ramuza in a more cordial tone. "We have a short distance to travel. The Aukmondi Valley is this way."

15

THE RIGHT PLACE AT THE RIGHT TIME

After killing the first wild man, Sam ran from the second one in near panic. He was virtually defenseless. He had only a horn of pellets and gunpowder in one hand, and an unloaded pistol in the other. Sam's only immediate protection was to seek cover in the forest. He needed only a moment's refuge to load his pistol. If he could load his pistol, he could take care of this wild man, like he did the first one.

For almost an hour, Sam evaded his relentless pursuer. Initially, he followed the forest pathways. He occasionally increased his pace as fast as possible to lose that frightening killer behind him. When he got tired, he deliberately deviated from the pathways, crashing through tangled bushes and vines, in an equally desperate attempt to disappear. He hoped to beat the wild man at his own game.

Once, when Sam stumbled and fell, he looked back to see that no one was chasing him. Not a living soul could be seen behind him. Sam got up and frantically looked around for the wild man. He turned in a circle twice, trying to locate some sign of him. There was nothing. The wild man was gone.

By now, Sam knew better. He was used to the wild man's tricks. He remembered the disappearance of the first wild man, only to find him a moment later, directly over his head. Sam looked up. He saw only an intense glare of the afternoon sun beaming through the trees. He saw several birds screaming at his intrusion. The wild man was gone this time.

This was Sam's moment. He could load his pistol now. He tried to end his labored breathing by taking one last gulp of air into his lungs. He slumped against a tree, wiped sweat from his face with his sleeve, and cursed his predicament.

Faulty thing – that's what it was. Faulty thinking had gotten him into this mess. Sam admitted, maybe he was somewhat of a faulty thinker sometimes. But he wasn't unlucky either. No one had ever considered him unlucky. In fact, throughout his life, Sam has usually managed to be in the right place at the right time. It was like a god-given gift, a compensation for being such a faulty thinker. But considering his circumstances, Sam realized this could be the day his luck ran out.

With shaking and sweaty hands, Sam quickly poured gunpowder into the powder pan of his pistol and packed it. Then, he stuffed a pellet into the barrel. "There! Loaded." Sam locked the hammer back. He held the pistol ready as he looked round again for the wild man. There was still no sign of him.

Sam took another moment to check his reserve of pellets and gunpowder. There wasn't much left, just enough for a half dozen more shots. Just then, as Sam was putting his powder horn away, he saw a knife thrust toward his stomach. The tip of the blade stopped just before touching him. Within seconds, before Sam could look up, the tip of the blade came up toward his face. The front of Sam's bush jacket and shirt were cut open. The strap to his powder horn was also cut and hung by a thread. A thin, bloodless scratch trailed across the right side of Sam's exposed chest.

Sam looked up into the painted face of the wild man. Deadly, excited, insane eyes stared back at him. Sam was astonished to see the wild man standing less than 60 centimeters before him. Sam raised his pistol to shoot, but the wild man, with that ever-present knife, deflected Sam's attempt. Sam's sleeve was ripped open. A painful cut was left on his arm. Sam's pistol and powder horn were skillfully dislodged from his hand and sent tumbling several meters away.

Gripped with fear, Sam had a sudden sinking feeling. He had felt like this only once before. During that storm off the coast of Algoa Bay, he and his friend, Thomas, were taking down a sail on the Maiden's Hand. A windswept boom knocked both over the ship's starboard rail. Both men managed to catch the railing.

Against the wind and torrents of rain, Sam struggled to pull himself back on deck. Before he or anyone else could come to Thomas's aid, Thomas's wet and raw hands failed him. Thomas slipped into the turbulent black water below. The raging wind and water seemed comparatively quiet, almost silent, as Sam stood, looking over the rail. For endless seconds, Sam hoped that Thomas would surface. Time seemed to stop as Sam waited. Thomas never surfaced.

Sam stepped back. The tree blocked his retreat behind him. The wild man made a murderous lunge. His knife stuck soundly in the tree as Sam rolled out of the way.

The wild man needed considerable effort to remove the knife from the tree. It gave Sam enough time to put the tree between him and the wild man, but only that. The wild man stood ready to lunge again.

If only I had me pistol, Sam thought. If he had his pistol, he could end this madness suddenly. Unfortunately, his pistol lay on the ground behind the wild man.

While Sam desperately eyed his pistol, the wild man repeated an unusual, ritual-like movement. He peeped out from one side of the tree at Sam. He slowly closed his eyes and withdrew behind the tree, as if to hide. He would peep out from the tree's opposite side a moment later. Again, he would slowly close his eyes and withdraw behind the tree. The lion's tails on each side of the wild man's head were the last things to disappear each time the wild man withdrew.

It was a strange, eerie behavior. It made no sense at all to Sam. He had never in his life seen anything like it. Sam found himself spellbound. He watched in awe despite the situation. It was as if the wild man was playing a game with him. But the more Sam realized this was no game, the more mesmerized he was, the more frightening the ritual became. Sam wanted to run as a cold chill enveloped him.

But he didn't run. Instead, Sam waited until the wild man closed his eyes again. At a carefully timed moment, Sam grabbed one of the lion's tails and jerked it as hard as possible. Sam pulled the wild man's head into the tree with a resounding thump.

The sound of the thump alone was enough to boost Sam's confidence. He stepped from behind the tree, hitting the semi-conscious wild man on the jaw with his fist. Sam knocked him to the ground.

Astonishingly, the wild man had remarkable endurance. Even in his semiconscious and disoriented condition, he still made wild and deadly slashes with his knife. One of those slashes put a small rip in Sam's trousers.

Sam jumped back; his confidence shaken again. He eyed his pistol once more. In an attempt to get it, he leaped over the wild man but unexpectedly fell short of his goal. The wild man had caught him by the leg in mid-air and tripped him to the ground.

Sam rolled over on his back and began kicking his attacker in the face. Three solid thrusts with the heel of his boot finally dislodged the wild man. Sam managed to get up before the wild man recovered. Instead of going for his pistol, Sam went toward the wild man. In a rage unlike himself, he stumped hard on the wild man's right hand, the hand that held the deadly knife. Sam was sure that at least three of the wild man's figures were broken under his weight. He could hear the bones snap.

Any normal human being would have buckled and screamed in pain. But no, the wild man didn't even flinch. He sprang to his feet and picked the knife up with his left hand. He swung the knife toward Sam's face, missing by only a centimeter.

Sam fell back to the ground. His rage suddenly dissolved into panic. He desperately scrambled for his pistol without considering his chances of reaching it. All that mattered in the world was getting his hands on that pistol. It was his only chance. As he crawled on his hands and knees, Sam expected to be stabbed in the back at any second.

By sheer luck, Sam made it to his pistol. He grabbed it with both hands and flipped over on his back. The wild man stood directly over him, the knife held high over his head. Sam pulled the trigger without refining his aim.

Click … The pistol did not fire.

This was it. After 22 years, this was how his life would end – on his back, in some unheard-of African forest. It did not seem right somehow. All those burdensome worries that he had carried around all his life; all that hard work to impress the people he worked for; all that effort to do the right thing – what was it all for?

Sam was about to throw the pistol at the wild man when he suddenly looked up and froze. He had heard or seen something, so he instantly turned and ran.

Sam watched him until he disappeared among the trees. But what was it that ran him off? Sam quickly got up to see for himself. At first, he neither heard nor saw anything. Then he spotted, in the distance, an army of colorfully cloaked, native warriors weaving through the trees toward him.

A hundred meters off to Sam's left, about 150 to 200 warriors were seen, rapidly approaching, apparently headed toward the clearing. Sam didn't know if they were hostile or friendly. They could be as deadly as the wild man. He wasn't about to take any chances. Like the wild man, Sam went into hiding. As an added precaution, he began to make ready his unreliable pistol.

The warrior army only came within 75 meters of Sam, much to his relief. Yet, it was close enough for him to get a pretty good look at them.

Their apparent leader was an impressive, middle-aged native who wore a brown cloak. The rest of the warriors who trailed behind him were cloaked in either natural green, gold, or one of several other colors. All of them were armed with long spears and a shield to match their respective colored cloaks.

Because of their uniformity, Sam sensed they were a well-organized army and could be deadly. Sam was pleased with his decision to hide. On the other hand, he was also pleased that they had come along when they did. They had sent the wild man into hiding, not a second too soon. The warrior army had indirectly saved his life.

Sam smiled. His luck had not run out after all. Maybe Thomas was right about him. He was a person who was constantly in the right place at the right time. "And only a person like Sam," Thomas often said, "could be caught in the very act of thievery by the constable, and then lucky enough to have the charges dismissed on the spot by the proprietor."

After the warrior army had passed, Sam took a few minutes to catch his breath and to reconsider his fate. He was grateful for the luck he had. It was truly a gift. But he often wondered how long it would last. Sam thought about the past few weeks. He had been almost killed more times in the past few weeks than in all his life. And each time, sheer luck had saved him. One of these days, he will rely on luck, and there won't be any.

While he had the opportunity, Sam took the time to carefully treat the fresh cuts and scratches that the wild man had given him. He took his shirt sleeve, which was already shredded anyway, and made bandages for his wounds. There was nothing he could do to sterilize or clean them. His only practical recourse was to use the new bandages to prevent more infections.

Sam removed his boot to examine his sprained ankle. It still hurt, but there was no swelling. He massaged the ankle and put his boot back on.

After Sam felt rested and relatively safe, he came out of hiding. He made a quick search of the local area for the wild man. He saw no sign of him. But, of course, that meant nothing. He wasn't going to relax his vigilance for a second.

Sam slowly worked his way over by the tree where the wild man had caused him to drop his powder horn. He began to pick up as many of the pellets as he could find, for all the good they would do him now. He had no gunpowder. The gunpowder from his powder horn was hopelessly scattered. There was no way he could recover it. This meant all the gunpowder he had left was the single measure already packed in his pistol. And that single measure had failed to fire the last time he had tried to use it.

Sam cursed and hoped that the failure was only a matter of dampness. If luck were still with him, it would be dry the next time he needs it. He dismissed this concern for now. Sam wasn't going to let this minor setback worry him. Decisively, he turned his attention to what he thought was his next biggest concern. A gnawing hunger pain turned all his thoughts toward food.

Sam realized he was very hungry. He had eaten very little since last night. Honestly, he did not know where his next meal would come from. He had already nibbled away all the dried food he had managed to grab after Captain McIntyre ordered this hasty search.

His backup plan was to shoot a hare, bird, or some other small game. But now that he was down to his last shot, that plan was out of the question. As hungry as he was, Sam decided to try to hold out until he rejoined Captain McIntyre and Pete.

Luckily, on his way back toward the clearing, Sam spotted a small crop of wild nutgrass just before the area where he had abandoned his backpack. Captain McIntyre had told him and Pete how to recognize it and that part of it was edible. But, like the captain, he didn't bother to say which part was edible.

Sam veered over to the crop and began to examine the grass-like plant. He was driven as much by curiosity as by hunger. He broke off one of the triple stems and cautiously tasted it, wondering if it was supposed to be cooked or if he could die from eating the wrong part. It tasted sweet, but not as palatable as Sam would have liked. He spit it out and pulled up another plant, root and all.

There, hanging near the ends of the roots, were several small pear-shaped tubers. Sam broke one off and cleaned the dirt away with his fingers. "Am I really this hungry?" He asked himself. He popped the tuber into his mouth and slowly began to chew it.

There was a tough rind that Sam was unable to chew. The core, however, was starchy, sweet, and somewhat nutty tasting. It was good, particularly for a hungry man. Sam spit out the rind and began to harvest several plants, averaging about a dozen tubers per plant. He didn't bother to clean away the dirt. He could do that later. He broke the tubers off and loaded the pockets of his jacket.

Just when Sam felt that he had collected enough, he noticed an unusual movement in the grass a few meters away. He didn't have to wonder what it was. He knew.

Sam dropped the bunch of grass in his hand and fumbled for his pistol. As he was doing so, he saw the wild man slowly and ceremoniously rising from concealment.

"You heathen bastard!" Sam cursed. He aimed his pistol carefully and immediately pulled the trigger. In the next few seconds, Sam's feelings were tossed like a ship on a stormy sea; dashed when his pistol clicked; soared when a hardy shot finally rang out and the wild man collapsed to the ground; dashed again when the smoke cleared, and the wild man ceremoniously rose from the grass again.

"But I shot him!" Sam protested. "I shot him! I know I shot him!"

It was true. Sam did shoot him. A messy gunshot wound was visible in the chest, near the right shoulder. It wasn't necessarily a vital area, but the wild man was severely wounded. Blood trailed from the wild man's shoulder, down his chest, and stomach. Sam could not believe that the wild man was on his feet again and still willing to kill.

Sam was terrified when the wild man began to sway in his usual ritualistic manner. He knew that an attack was imminent. Once again, Sam turned and ran for his life. Instead of running toward the clearing, Sam retreated deeper into the forest. In the forest, there were more places to hide.

The wild man's pursuit was not strong this time. Occasionally, Sam was pleased to see that the wild man stumbled badly, a good sign. Sam also realized that the wild man had not disappeared once but popped up much closer moments later—another good sign. The wild man was growing weaker from the gunshot wound.

Sam's confidence began to return. The longer he ran, the more convinced he became that a confrontation with the wild man would end in his favor. Sam smiled. He stopped running. He turned to face the wild man.

As the wild man stumbled closer, Sam noticed a dying tree nearby. One of the branches, which angled out about 10 centimeters above his reach, was just thick enough to make an excellent club.

To ensure his victory, Sam went after the branch. He jumped up and hung on it to break it off. It resisted at first, but then, it broke off with a dry and unexpected snap. Sam fell flat on his back, hitting his head hard.

Sam quickly struggled to his feet. He was shaken up badly by the fall. Pain was felt throughout his back and head. Still, he held the branch ready, waiting for the wild man to get closer. Despite how he felt, he still felt fully capable of taking complete control of the situation.

"Aye. Keep acomin', you crazy bastard." Sam intended to bash the wild man like he had done the first one.

But no, the forest began to spin faster and faster. Pressure seemed to build in Sam's head. The whole forest seemed to move as Sam's vision tunneled. Things were growing darker.

Sam wanted to cry out in horror when he realized he was passing out and could do nothing to stop it. He shook his head vigorously as if to clear the darkness. It didn't work. His friend Thomas was wrong. No one has a monopoly on luck. As darkness swallowed him, the last thing that Sam remembered was falling with a helpless thud at the wild man's feet.

16

THE BROWN AND THE WHITE WARRIORS

The Great Creation Quazzi Kuuza Gembali was a Brown Warrior. He was the only Brown Warrior in the Aukmondi Army. His brown cloak clearly distinguished him, among all the other warriors, as the Aukmondi Army's Foremost Lieutenant. And except for Mfalme Ramuza Ncobba and Kharaambi, the leader of the Aukmondi Army, no single person has more tribal authority than Quazzi. In the absence of Ramuza or Kharaambi, Quazzi becomes an indisputable spokesman for all the Aukmondi people.

Besides the fact that Quazzi was one of Ramuza's closest friends, experience, dedication, and a mature and sharp mind are only a few qualities that have qualified Quazzi for the position of Brown Warrior. Quazzi grew up with the simple attitude of someday being an honorable warrior. He did not set out to be the Foremost Lieutenant. He had no compelling desire to lead a regiment. Nor did he aim for the Royal cloak and his independent army.

He would have been satisfied with the green cloak of the Sentinels and other specialists as long as he could fulfill his dream of being an honorable warrior. But his qualifications forced him higher through the ranks. When Kharaambi needed someone to wear the brown cloak, no one else was more qualified and capable than Quazzi.

It was one of Quazzi's daily responsibilities to select one of the twenty independent armies to go out and scout the north and south regions: the regions north and south of the Aukmondi Valley. These regions were not part of the Aukmondi domain, but the Aukmondi take an interest in them. Any adverse development in these regions could indirectly affect the valley and its people.

Scouting them was considered a necessary job, which Quazzi supervised very efficiently. After eleven harvests as the Brown Warrior, the job was routine.

Today's reconnaissance ventures, however, were given more than the usual concerns. All last night, the vigilant Aukmondi Sentinels had made frequent sightings of Wabanga tribe members ghosting about in the north region. The sightings were promptly reported to Kharaambi. Kharaambi declared that, in addition to the usual early pre-dawn scouting, another special scouting would be made of each region during midday.

In the north region, Ramuza accompanied Quazzi and the Bendabe Regiment of the Nionu Hemboga Vogama Army. Kharaambi, Nionu himself, and the other half of his army, the Dabete Ehkili Regiment, scouted the south region.

During this special midday scouting of the north region, Ramuza and Quazzi discovered the Chinchigwe and that Adaulah was in danger. This scouting developed into the desperate search for Ramuza's only son.

Quazzi led this search with all the skill and thoroughness possible. He searched like he knew Ramuza would have wanted. After Ramuza took the Chinchigwe into the valley and then returned with other warriors, Quazzi did not want it necessary for Ramuza to recover ground that was supposed to have already been covered.

It took Quazzi and the Bendabe Regiment just over one hour to reach the forest edge and the clearing. So far, they have uncovered no clues about where Adaulah could be. It was still too early in the search to expect any strong trails. Still, Quazzi saw to it that no warrior showed any negligence. Though such an order was unnecessary, each warrior had been told to put forth their best efforts. After all, they were looking for the son of the Mfalme.

The grassy clearing was where the search intensified. Quazzi dispersed the warriors out to span almost one and a half kilometers. Like grazing animals, they moved slowly southward from the trail on which the Chinchigwe were found. Nothing went by unnoticed. Even some of the most insignificant things were scrutinized.

The closest warrior to Quazzi's right was a young female. Her uncommonly smooth and dark skin stood out against the brilliant white of garments and shield, the primary color of her rank. Her name was Upenda.

Upenda was a White Warrior, indicating that she had practically no experience as a warrior. She was still in the early training phase of her career, so she had a long way to go and a lot to learn.

Quazzi happened to notice her searching technique. It was extremely good for a warrior with so little experience, which aroused his admiration and curiosity.

"Sacred Woman," he said, "do you know what signs you are looking for?"

Upenda was momentarily startled that someone was talking to her. Without seeming disrespectful, she gave Quazzi only a moment's glance and continued her search as she responded to the Brown Warrior.

"Yes, Great Creation. I am looking for broken or bent grass, freshly overturned stones, and grass creatures headed in the same general direction. I am looking for anything unnatural that might indicate Adaulah was here."

"You answer like an experienced warrior." Quazzi was more than satisfied with her response. "You have learned well. In no time, you will wear the cloak and carry the shield of a Red Warrior. Who is your trainer?"

Upenda did not know whether to give Quazzi the official answer or the answer that was closest to the truth. There was a difference. She thought a moment, then gave Quazzi the name of the warrior who had spent more time than any other teaching her what she must learn as a warrior. "The Great Creation Nionu."

Quazzi was a little surprised by this answer. He expected the name of one of the Gold Warriors, the official trainers in the Aukmondi Army. The vast duties and responsibilities of warriors above the gold cloak did not usually allow them time to act as trainers. Nionu was a Royal Warrior and the commander of this particular independent army.

"How did you get Nionu as your trainer?"

This time, Upenda interrupted her search long enough to look Quazzi directly in his eyes. She shrugged with a coy smile on her face. "I asked him."

There was no more to be said. Quazzi understood. He knew Upenda to be one of the most amorous and unfettered women in the Aukmondi tribe. Only the general attitude of the Aukmondi kept her life and behavior uncontroversial.

Quazzi smiled back at Upenda. "Continue your search, Sacred Woman."

The first positive clue that the warriors found was the area where Adaulah's smoke signal had been. Discarded arrows lay in a pile not far from a small circle of dirt and ashes. And footprints, unmistakably Adaulah's, were all about. The warrior who found them quickly called Quazzi over.

Quazzi studied where the fire had been extinguished and pushed back some of the dirt with the end of his spear, exposing more of the black ashes. He kneeled and cautiously touched them. The ashes were only as warm as the soil exposed to the sun.

"It has been some time since Adaulah was here," Quazzi said. "At least we know now that the rhinoceros did not trample him as the Chinchigwe suspected."

Quazzi rose to his feet and searched for Upenda in the crowd around him. He found her eclipsed by two taller warriors. He beckoned her closer. "Tell me, Sacred Woman, which way do we go from here?"

A trainer must instruct, demonstrate, and constantly test their trainee. Upenda's unofficial trainer, Nionu, had gone with Kharaambi to assist in scouting the south region. Quazzi realized this. Upenda was developing into an honorable warrior, but she still wore the cloak of a White Warrior. Her training should not be relaxed just yet.

Upenda knew what Quazzi was doing and dutifully cooperated. She took a moment to study the ashes and dirt. She pointed southward with her spear. "That direction, Great Creation. The spacing of Adaulah's footprints here suggests he left in a hurry, probably running."

"Again, a good warrior's answer." Quazzi raised his voice slightly so that everyone could hear him. "Let us spread out again and proceed."

As Quazzi instructed, the warriors continued their search southward down the clearing. They knew that they were on Adaulah's trail now. The second clue was found only minutes later. Quazzi found the bow and the single arrow Adaulah had dropped or lost. There was some doubt that the weapon belonged to the young Aukmondi. But the arrows matched the other arrow found. The bow was also like the ones carried by the Chinchigwe. It had to be Adaulah's.

Quazzi was extremely worried now. There was mounting evidence that Adaulah was in trouble, something other than the threat of the rhinoceros or alienation.

Adaulah had left his signal fire area, "probably running," to quote Upenda. A few minutes later, his bow and an arrow were found. Even though Adaulah was an Aukmondi, he would not have deliberately discarded the weapon out here. It was still intact and, unfortunately, still necessary. And worst of all, there were more signs of Wabanga in the area.

Fragmented trails crisscrossed all through the clearing. Most of them, however, were too old to be of any significance. They faded or led to dead ends. Still, such trails were very typical of Wabanga movements.

There was yet another trail that inspired more than the usual attention. This trail indicated that a single individual crossed the grassland from forest to forest. The warriors ruled out the possibility that it was the trail of a Wabanga. It was much too definite and direct.

For a moment, Upenda and several other junior warriors thought it was Adaulah's trail because it was where the young Aukmondi's bow and arrow were found. Quazzi quickly disproved that idea. The trail only momentarily paralleled Adaulah's suspected course and did not intersect with the area where Adaulah's smoke signal had been. This trail disappeared on both sides of the clearing into each forest. Since it wasn't Adaulah's, it wasn't deemed important. For now, it was left as a mystery.

Upenda began to consider the chances of finding Adaulah alive. With so many dangers about, the chances didn't seem favorable. She wondered if anyone else felt as she did. She came within speaking distance of Quazzi. "Great Creation, do you believe we will find him? Alive, I mean."

"I can not say."

Upenda was about to ask Quazzi what he expected the consequences would be if Adaulah weren't found or if he were found dead. Her wonder was cut short when she noticed Quazzi's preoccupied behavior. He was intently scanning the horizon and the forest lines.

"What is it?" Upenda asked. "What is wrong?"

"Quiet, please!" Quazzi spoke just above a whisper. He continued his visual search, looking for something very close by. His attention now seemed to be on the nearby grass and how it waved in the gentle breeze.

Upenda also began to study the nearby grass's movement, though she didn't know exactly for what. She felt somewhat inadequate when she noticed most other experienced warriors were also looking for something other than Adaulah. Upenda looked at Quazzi again, trying to get some idea as to what was going on.

Suddenly, Quazzi stopped walking and listened intently. Everyone else who noticed him followed his example. Finally, he spoke to Upenda, still in a whisper. "Wabanga are very close by, watching us, studying us."

Upenda made a quick search herself. She saw nothing. "How can you tell?"

"The creatures of the grassland can not be blinded, not even by the Wabanga. Listen. Have you not noticed, in recent moments, we stirred no birds? Something has frightened them all away already."

Upenda listened. At first, she thought it was solely the presence of the Aukmondi that had caused the birds to become so silent. But there was an unusual numbness everywhere. The birds that usually inhabit the grass were already gone. The profound silence suggested that some intruders had frightened them off long before the warriors.

With a wave of his arms, Quazzi signaled the other warriors to close in for strategic safety. Outwardly, he behaved as if he suspected nothing. Quazzi knew that if the Wabanga were nearby, he could delay their inevitable attack by showing ignorance of their presence. One weakness of the Wabanga was the pleasure of stalking prey.

The Aukmondi warriors proceeded down the clearing wordlessly and without incident. Upenda, who was still astonished by the significance of the birdless environment, was the first to see the vultures circling ahead on the southern horizon. Instinctively, she knew they did not circle over the remains of some dead animal. She strongly suspected that it had to be Adaulah. "Quazzi, Great Creation. Look!"

As soon as Quazzi saw the vultures, his cautious pace became a run. The other warriors followed him toward the ominous birds.

Adaulah was found lying in the tall grass, sprawled out in an unnatural position, as if dead. Many of the warriors quickly surrounded the young Aukmondi. They found blood streaming down one side of his face and staining the ground under his head.

"Is he alive?" Asked Upenda.

"If he were dead, the vultures would be upon him already." Quazzi quickly examined Adaulah's lifeless body. "He is alive. It seems he fell and hit his head. He needs help, but he is alive. Let us try to get him back to the valley as quickly as possible."

Upenda looked about apprehensively. The vultures overhead were already beginning to disperse. The unseen Wabanga, Upenda knew, was another matter. "It is a blessing by the Supreme Spirit that Adaulah was not killed with the Wabanga so near."

"He was probably not killed because he fell helpless. The Wabanga are not so quick to attack things that can not give them a challenge or flee in fear. But make no mistake. The Wabanga will kill anything alive. Adaulah's moment was coming."

"What about our moment? Why have they not attacked us yet? We are not helpless. We offer a great challenge, for we certainly will not flee in fear."

"I can not truthfully answer that, Sacred Woman." Quazzi lifted Adaulah into his arms as he looked around. "I suspect that there is but one or two of them, requiring a longer time to study us. Otherwise, they would have attacked already, without hesitation. They are probably stalking us, trying to determine the best way to attack and kill such a number as we. Let us hope we can get to the valley rim before they foolishly decide that our number makes no difference."

17

THE VALLEY RIM

Ramuza continued to carry Lobarra effortlessly in his powerful arms. His pace was strong, causing a gentle rocking motion. Lobarra had grown so accustomed to the movement that she relaxed to the point of sleep. Her head rested comfortably against Ramuza's shoulder.

The rest of the Chinchigwe trailed behind Ramuza, with great effort. Despite their fatigue, they pushed themselves to keep up with the Aukmondi Mfalme. It wasn't easy, but none of them complained. They were grateful for Ramuza's help and understood why his pace was so strong.

After the initial barrage of questions and answers, everyone became quiet. Ramuza was preoccupied with thoughts of his son, and the Chinchigwe, devoting most of their energy to keeping pace, were preoccupied with thoughts of Ramuza and the help he offered.

When the journey toward the valley began, Ramuza had initially bombarded the Chinchigwe with questions. As a concerned father, he wanted to know all that had happened to his son. Learning all the details seemed to help him keep his worry and anxiety at bay.

"When did you first see Adaulah?" He had asked, reconstructing the events in his mind. "What condition was he in? Were there any Aukmondi warriors with him at the time? Did Adaulah say when and where the slave hunters captured him?"

Through his questioning, the Aukmondi Mfalme eventually determined that his son had encountered at least two life-threatening situations within the past two days. Neither situation was anticipated.

When Adaulah began his journey, Ramuza had assumed that four protective warriors would be sufficient.

The first situation was the attack by the slave hunters. Incidents of kidnappings and raids by slave hunters in this area were rare. Of all the possible things that could happen, Ramuza considered an attack by slave hunters one of the least likely. In hindsight, if Ramuza had suspected such an attack, Adaulah would not have left the valley. He wished now that an entire warrior army had accompanied Adaulah.

Since Adaulah was reported to have led the Chinchigwe toward the valley, he had come through the situation with no major physical injuries. Ramuza felt a tremendous gratitude toward the four Green Warriors who did accompany Adaulah. A great and life-long memorial was due to the families and friends of those warriors.

Even though death had resulted in this situation, Ramuza did not dwell on it as long as the second one, concerning the rhinoceros. He still did not know the outcome. The Aukmondi Mfalme could not learn enough information to dismiss his worst fear—the death of his son.

"What happened when the rhinoceros started chasing you?" Ramuza had asked the Chinchigwe. "What did Adaulah do when the beast charged you? Why did you not see the rhinoceros before the attack? When was the last time you saw Adaulah? Did you see any sign of Adaulah after the attack?"

Ramuza had asked the Chinchigwe question after question and listened carefully to their responses. He eventually had a good idea of what had happened to Adaulah, from when he left the valley to when the rhinoceros was encountered. Beyond that, Ramuza could not learn any new details. When the Chinchigwe's answers became repetitive, Ramuza stopped his inquiries and lapsed into silence. He began to ask questions in his mind and speculate on the answers.

As for the Chinchigwe, their impression of Ramuza, after that initial shock wore off, was one of instant admiration. He was called "Mfalme" with good reason. Through his concerns, they began to suspect he was a strong and confident leader. Although he seemed accustomed to having absolute cooperation from his people, this extraordinary amenity was not demanded. Instead, it was given to him out of earned respect and love from his people.

Mfalme Ncobba seemed to be a powerful, authoritative figure who ruled, not with fear, but with wisdom and compassion. And lucky are the people dear to him. For more reasons than one, the Chinchigwe felt good to be in his presence.

When Ramuza asked his questions, the Chinchigwe, through Ameh, did their best to answer him. They understood this father's worry for his son. They wanted to help, and did so by giving him, to the best of their memories, the most complete and credible answers possible.

Unfortunately, throughout the reconstruction of events, the Chinchigwe respectfully answered only Ramuza's questions. No one mentioned the time the slave merchant fired his thunder stick at Adaulah during the escape. And for the sake of credibility, no one said anything about Twese's vivid hallucination of the strange woman he saw standing next to the docile rhinoceros.

When Ramuza finally lapsed into silence, the Chinchigwe respectfully did so too. They did not want to disturb his thoughts. Consequently, as they waited for Ramuza's next question, their attention was drawn elsewhere.

The pressures that had developed from their tragedies were still present but, for the moment, had begun to ebb again. The desperate people were finally able to take notice of their surroundings for the sheer pleasure of it.

This portion of the forest, which Mfalme Ncobba had referred to as the Valley Rim, was cool and thick with vegetation. Wood lilies, asters, and other wildflowers grew in random places. The Chinchigwe even saw one or two fig trees growing among the bushes and trees. Honeybees and swallowtail butterflies commuted among the flowers. And, of course, various birds and monkeys darted overhead from tree to tree. The whole busy environment was a very beautiful and interesting place.

It was hard to believe that such a place could still have its share of dangers. The Chinchigwe were reminded of this fact rather unexpectedly. Fifteen meters to the right of the pathway where Ramuza and the Chinchigwe walked, an unseen elephant raised its trunk and gave a frightening blare, drawing attention to itself.

There were three gray giants. They had been standing in the cool forest, quietly feeding on tender leaves and twigs, when the sound of the approaching people frightened them. After the lead elephant blasted its warning, the three elephants turned and quickly walked away from the intruders, toward the valley.

Even in the tranquil atmosphere of the forest, everyone was still somewhat jumpy. The moment the elephant trumpeted, Lobarra stiffened in Ramuza's arms. The rest of the Chinchigwe suddenly stopped walking. A few of them instinctively dropped to their knees in panic. It did not ease the situation much when the two warriors who carried Jpuma almost dropped him as they scrambled to defensive postures. Ramuza himself stopped his strong pace to see exactly what was going on.

As it turned out, the frightened elephants were not a threat to Ramuza and the Chinchigwe. However, in their flight, they were a potential threat to the valley. Their mindless flight toward the populated area would have to be stopped.

Realizing this, one of the five warriors flung his orange cloak away from his spear arm and addressed Ramuza. "Should we try to avert them, Great Creation?"

Only fifty meters remained before reaching the valley's slope and the protective Aukmondi Sentinels who stood guard there. Ramuza did not want to relinquish the five warriors' protection until the slope was in sight. This was an added precaution against the Wabanga, who could not be trusted, even when security was immediate.

"No, Wema," said Ramuza. "Stay with us. The Sentinels will take care of the elephants."

Overhearing this, Ameh became curious. He watched the movement of the elephants, hoping to see just how the huge beast would be stopped. He was about to ask Ramuza about the Sentinels when he saw Aukmondi warriors coming out of the forest ahead.

In the distance, through the trees, and across a 30-meter clearing, Ameh saw two, then three, then five, eight warriors standing defiantly in the path of the three elephants. More warriors were coming out of the forest. From the far right and the far left, more and more warriors were coming to join them. At first, Ameh and the rest of the Chinchigwe had not seen any of these warriors. But now they were seen forming a human barrier in defense of the valley.

"The warriors that you see are the Aukmondi Sentinels," Ramuza could see the surprise on their faces. They will stop the elephants."

The warriors were dressed like typical warriors of the Aukmondi tribe, except they all wore the color-rank green. The cloaks that they wore were subdued but natural shades of green. The shields that each carried were also predominantly green. Many of the shields were decorated or camouflaged to look like growing grass. The warriors were so well camouflaged with the color that, after the elephants were driven away, most of them disappeared into the forest again, as if they were never there.

"Very impressive, Mfalme Ncobba," said Ameh. "How many of these Sentinels do you have hidden out here?"

Ramuza smiled. He was proud of his warriors. "There are two regiments, or a complete Sentinel army, out here on the north rim. We have one regiment stretched along the mountainous south rim of the valley. All together, there are up to 500 warriors at any given moment. They surround the entire populated portion of the valley."

"Admirable! It is a very ingenious way to protect your people. More of the Chinchigwe would probably be alive today if we had taken such precautions about our village."

Since Ramuza had encountered the Chinchigwe and was told about Adaulah, most of his thoughts had been on his son. His primary concern was to get the Chinchigwe to aid and comfort as quickly as possible so that he could return to the wilderness to lead the search for his son. Only now did he realize that there was more to the Chinchigwe tragic story.

"When you have been given the attention that you need and I have returned from the wilderness, you must tell me more about the Chinchigwe."

"Have no doubts, Mfalme Ncobba," Twese said impulsively. I sincerely believe you are bound to hear much more about us."

That was the second time that this Chinchigwe had spoken so tactlessly. Ramuza glanced at Twese. Certain insinuations in his words were debatable, but Ramuza maturely restrained himself and said nothing. He knew there was still a lot that he and all the Chinchigwe had to learn. Only time would bring it all out.

Twese and his insinuations were forgotten as Ramuza called the Orange Warrior back to him. "Wema."

"Yes, Great Creation."

"We are close enough to the valley now. Preparations must be made to receive the Chinchigwe. Listen carefully and do exactly as I instruct. Go ahead of us. Tell the Great Creation Kon-Shambique and the Sacred Woman Tongda to be ready at their hut. Tell them their knowledge and skills will be needed. Also, I summon my mate, Rwuva, and the crafter, Tanake, with his tools to Kon-Shambique's kraal. After you have done these things, tell the Royal Warrior Ratuzu to assemble his army immediately in the Pahoma Garden. Have him wait for me there and be ready to journey long and far. Understood?"

"All will be done, Great Creation."

"And Wema," Ramuza paused. "Tell no one that Adaulah may be in danger. If necessary, I will handle that task myself."

"As you wish, Great Creation."

"That is all. Go quickly now."

The Orange Warrior hurried along the pathway with these instructions, almost running. He weaved through the forest, across the clearing, and finally disappeared in the far forest, down the valley slope.

Several minutes later, Ramuza and the Chinchigwe were on the valley slope. They could see across most of the valley that was the Aukmondi domain.

What the Chinchigwe saw by the early afternoon sunlight was breathtaking. Trees in various shades of green seemed to carpet both the north and south slopes. Short segments of a sparkling blue river could be seen in the distance at the bottom of the valley. A flock of Demoiselle cranes winged lazily over the treetops, their bright color enhanced by the sunlight and contrasting trees.

From the valley rim, Ramuza led the Chinchigwe downward into the land of the Aukmondi people.

18

THE LAW OF THE LAND

Back at the point where Captain McIntyre, Pete, and Sam had initially split up in their search for the escaped slaves, the captain paced restlessly. He was inwardly fuming over Sam's prolonged absence, and his back-and-forth moments were only a small reflection of his frustration.

Pete sat quietly, slumped against a tree. He had pulled his hat down to just above his eyes to limit his field of view. He wanted to close his eyes and catch a nap. Instead, he watched the captain's pace and stayed clear of the captain's anger.

According to the captain, each of them had already wasted "a good hour or more" in pursuit of the escaped slaves. When they realized that they were not on the slaves' trail, they doubled back to meet up with Sam. The captain and Pete converged at the designated point as planned. They began waiting for Sam's return and wasted another good hour.

Sam still had not shown up. Captain McIntyre was getting angrier by the minute, and his pacing was becoming more frantic.

Pete saw the captain as a volcano about to blow its top. If all that anger got loose, it would be no good for anyone. Pete shifted his hat from his eyes and sat up. "You know, Capt'n, you didn't give Sam a time to meet us back here."

"I didn't give you a time either. Now did I?" Captain McIntyre did not wait for Pete to respond. "Any fool with half o' mind knows not to venture out too far alone around 'ere."

McIntyre pulled a twist of tobacco from his pocket and angrily bit off a huge piece. His jaw bulged grotesquely as he continued to talk.

"You know, I could tell Sam Dawby wasn't too bright the moment I laid eyes on him."

"Then why did you hire him?"

"Hell's fire! He was ahangin' on to the coattail of this other lad. Thomas, I believe 'is name was. He was the lad who fell overboard comin' over. You remember 'im, don't you?"

"Aye, I remember. A hard worker, he was."

"That, he was. Anyway, the fact of the matter was, I couldn't hire Thomas without taking on Sam too. At the time, I wasn't too objectionable. Hell, I was atryin' to get me a crew together. I took them both on, gladly." McIntyre thought about that storm and how he almost lost the Maiden's Hand. He felt lucky that only two lives were lost. "Yet and still, when Thomas and Sam went over that there railing, the wrong lad climbed back on board me ship that day."

Pete removed his hat and wiped sweat from his brow with his arm. He knew Captain McIntyre was ruthless. He could accept that. After all, Pete had known people almost as cruel in his life. You must be a little ruthless to survive in this world. But what irritated Pete the most about the captain was that he was also one of the most self-centered bastards he had ever known.

"Capt'n, I know you still blame Sam for falling asleep during his watch. That could have been any one of us. We were all drunk. Give the lad a break. Sam's a pretty hard worker."

"Keep your opinions to yourself, Pete."

"I've yet to see Sam carry less than his fair share of the load. You just have to let him know exactly what's expected of him sometimes. He's a bit slow and careless sometimes, but a decent and likable lad. He'll pull through for you. Just give him a little time."

"I'll give 'im hell! Mark me word. Matter of fact, I'll not waste another minute on 'im either. Get your gear together. We're aheading back to camp."

Pete hesitated before beginning to gather his flintlocks and canteen. He was ready to leave but had reservations about abandoning Sam and returning to camp. "Shouldn't we check the clearing? I mean, suppose Sam found something? We all went in three different directions. The two of us didn't find anything. It would be within reason to expect that maybe Sam did."

McIntyre considered that thought for a moment. His original plan was to return to camp and order the Batushi slave hunters to retrieve these slaves, too. But Pete was right.

McIntyre looked toward the clearing. "If Sam found me slaves, he's probably not capable of herdin' 'em back this way by himself. I reckon, we'd best go take a look-see."

Pete finally got up from where he was sitting. So far, he has been considering only the positive possibilities. There was a negative line of thought that Pete held in reserve until now.

"What if something has happened to him?"

"I should be so damned lucky." Captain McIntyre spat tobacco juice and started toward the clearing. "I'll tell you this much. If I've lost me slaves on account o' him, something will happen to 'im for sure."

Captain McIntyre and Pete reached the clearing only after a few minutes. Like Sam, they had reached the clearing too soon to turn back already. And the very idea that Sam just might have found something was enough to keep Captain McIntyre moving out across the clearing. On the other hand, Pete was more than ready to turn around or, at least, wait a few more minutes on the edge of the clearing. Only his concern for Sam's safety prevented him from objecting to the captain's venture across.

Not a word was spoken by the two men during most of the trek across the clearing. The afternoon sun was beaming down hard. It was too hot for idle conversation. Pete's immediate concern was getting out of the heat as he followed behind Captain McIntyre, who maintained a steady pace despite the heat.

The heat was only a secondary concern of the captain. His mind was preoccupied with the likelihood that Sam had found his slaves. He had tried to dismiss the idea when Pete brought it up. But now, it seemed like a likely occurrence. He was driven by it. He was beginning to feel that he was getting close. At this point, he noticed that a lot of the knee-deep grass was bent unnaturally southward.

"Somebody's been 'ere," he said. "And not too very long ago either."

"Oh?" Pete's disinterest was lost to the captain. There was a long pause before he finally asked. "How can you tell?"

"Why, there're trails in the grass. Look ahere. They're all over the place."

Pete didn't bother to look. "Probably a herd of wildebeest and zebra or something like that."

"Wildebeest, hell! I know the signs of people when I see 'em. These 'ere are the marks of people, a whole mass of 'em. They went right up the middle of the clearing 'ere."

Pete finally wiped the sweat from his eyes and looked down at the grass. He wasn't an experienced tracker, but he could tell himself someone had come through the grass. "You think it was your runaways?"

McIntyre studied some of the trails and spit tobacco juice again. "No. It looks more like other natives, a group of nomads, or a hunting party. It wasn't me slaves."

During Pete's reassessment of the bent grass, he looked up and down the clearing to see how far the bent grass stretched. He spotted a horde of vultures up ahead, circling on the northwest horizon. The first thing to come to his mind was "Sam". He pushed the thought aside and pointed at the huge birds for the captain.

"Come on! Let's hasten up." Captain McIntyre adjusted his backpack and musket on his shoulder. "I've a funny feeling it's not the carcass of some animal they are acirclin'."

Pete was disturbed more than he cared to admit when he learned that the captain's suspicions were like his own. Pete didn't know Sam that well. They were shipmates who had been through a lot together in the past few weeks. He knew that Sam had pulled through some tough moments. The poor lad was not tough enough to make it alone in this environment.

Except for the sight of vultures lazily circling ahead, the rest of the way across the clearing went uneventfully. Even the sun's intense heat was forgotten as the two men hurried along faster than was healthy.

Captain McIntyre and Pete saw that less than half of the vultures circled overhead as they approached their destination. The bulk of the filthy creatures, about twenty to thirty of them, were already on the ground in a feeding frenzy, squawking, fighting, and tearing over something as yet unidentified.

Captain McIntyre had to shoot his musket in the air to frighten the birds away. After the birds scrambled skyward, only the captain had the stomach to approach what was left on the ground.

Pete voluntarily stayed back. "Well?"

"It's human, alright. Or, might I say, it was human."

"Sam?"

"No. It wasn't Sam." Captain McIntyre took a closer look. "From the looks o' things, it might have been a native they were afeastin' on."

Pete experienced both repulsion and relief. After his stomach settled, he moved a little closer. He intentionally averted his eyes from the mangled body. In doing so, he recognized something in the grass and picked it up.

"Capt'n, look at this! This canteen is Sam's. I'm sure of it."

"Aye. I don't doubt you. Look over 'ere at what I've found." Captain McIntyre held Sam's musket's battered lock and barrel in his hand. He could tell that the gun had been used in a way it wasn't meant to be used. "Sam's been here alright. And I'd say it was Sam who killed this 'ere native."

"What? Sam?" Pete couldn't believe it. It just didn't seem like it was something Sam could do. "Are you sure?"

"No doubt about it." Captain McIntyre took a closer look at the mess on the ground. There was a look of repulsion on his face now. "Don't be none too surprised, Pete. Your boy, Sam, really didn't have much choice in the matter."

"What do you mean?"

"Remember me atellin' you about the wild men in these parts? Well, I do believe this here is one o' 'em. Sam got 'is fool self caught up in the law of the land – kill or be killed."

Pete forced himself to come closer. He looked down at the native's body. He thought he saw a lion's tail entangled in the bloody mess. He turned away before he became more confused.

"Where do you suppose Sam is now?"

Captain McIntyre briefly looked the area over once again. He found Sam's backpack lying against a large shade tree. He knew that even the simple-minded Sam would not have intentionally left it there. "He's probably ahidin' out in this 'ere forest someplace, for all the good it'll do 'im. We'd best find him fast. If he's not already dead, he soon will be." "Why do you say that?"

"These 'ere wild men hunt in groups of two or three. And I'll tell you something. Neither man nor beast is left standing in their wake."

19

WELCOME TO THE AUKMONDI VALLEY

From the Valley Rim and past the Aukmondi Sentinels, Ramuza led the Chinchigwe down into the valley. The pathway on which they walked was well-used. It meandered through the trees down a gentle decline. The Chinchigwe were grateful. It made the pace that Ramuza set much easier to maintain.

A tributary of the Mara River created the beautiful Aukmondi Valley. This tributary, the Aukmondi River, flowed westward from the mountain ranges northwest of Lake Natron. Its outlet on the Mara River is located on the northwest corner of the great Serengeti Plain, where the waters rush across the great migration routes of gnu, zebra, and gazelle toward Great Lake Victoria.

Through clusters of trees and shrubs, the Chinchigwe caught glimpses of the sparkling blue water of the Aukmondi River two or three kilometers below. At first, it seemed that Ramuza was leading them down the valley slope directly to the river, but after several meters, the pathway forked. Ramuza took the branch that turned eastward.

The Chinchigwe eventually emerged from the cluster of trees and shrubs and found themselves in another grassy clearing. They walked parallel to the river now. The assistance the Chinchigwe had received from the gentle slope decline was gone. It was becoming difficult again to maintain Ramuza's strong pace.

Being one of the oldest among the Chinchigwe, Ameh was thoroughly exhausted. His two-meter staff worked overtime supporting his pace as he walked behind Ramuza. His fatigue finally forced him to move closer to the Aukmondi Mfalme with a special request – a moment's rest. But just as he was within speaking range, Ameh was distracted by the first sight of an Aukmondi community.

Up ahead, on the other side of a broad stream and on the edge of a large clearing, was a kraal of family-size, mud-grass huts. There were about fifteen or twenty huts in all. They were simple and cozy-looking, made of clay and stones. They were round in shape with dome-shaped, grass roofs. The huts were built like the huts the Chinchigwe had lived in.

As the Chinchigwe got closer to the kraal, they could see that several small vegetable and flower gardens were scattered among the huts. To the left were also several orchards. And to the right and out back was a sizable corral of dairy cattle.

The Chinchigwe were so busy taking in their first impressions of an Aukmondi settlement that they almost didn't notice the unusual movements of the people there. In mass, most villagers were coming out of their huts and gardens. They were all heading toward the main exit of the kraal. About twenty or thirty men, women, and children converged onto the pathway ahead. Some were carrying baskets or bowls full of fruits and flowers. Others carried gourds of water and other beverages. Once on the pathway, they turned toward Ramuza and the Chinchigwe.

Instead of asking Ramuza for a moment's rest, Ameh's request was overshadowed by his curiosity. "Mfalme Ncobba, what are your people doing? Do they come to greet us?"

"No, Great Creation. Few people know that you are coming. Certainly, none from this kraal." Ramuza studied the approaching people. At first, he was just as curious as the Chinchigwe, but then he remembered.

Every evening, just after sunset, in a large open area on the bank of the Aukmondi River, the Aukmondi people traditionally hold an informal, free-spirited gathering. This gathering lasts well into the night and is simply called "The Celebration". Each day, a different kraal community prepares for "The Celebration". Today's responsibility just happened to belong to this kraal community. This was where these villagers were going. Their massive approach toward Ramuza and the Chinchigwe was only coincidental.

"No welcome was intended here," Ramuza added. "Nevertheless, you may still receive one."

When the villagers saw Ramuza, a wave of excitement was obvious in their behavior. In his excitement, one little boy seemed to think it was his responsibility to alert everyone as he ran up and down the group, yelling "Mfalme! Mfalme! Mfalme!" As Ramuza drew nearer, the rest of the villagers respectfully surrendered the pathway to him. They gave casual but warm greetings to their Mfalme, suppressing their unending awe of him.

Ramuza returned the casual and warm greetings as he led the Chinchigwe through the parted crowd. His pace did not slow at all until one Aukmondi woman stepped onto the pathway behind Ramuza. She stood directly facing Ameh. Ramuza stopped walking. He turned to see what was going on. For the first time since his encounter with the Chinchigwe, he finally eased Lobarra to her feet.

The woman who blocked Ameh's path held a large basket of fresh figs in her arms. Without a word, she set the basket down and reached inside. She came up with a warm smile and three figs in her hand. She gave the figs to Ameh.

"Thank you." Ameh accepted the figs.

"The people of the Pogobi Kraal welcome you to the Aukmondi Valley, " the woman said, her smile broadening.

The other villagers who saw this exchange began to follow the woman's example. All of the villagers were fully aware of the Chinchigwe's battered conditions and the heavy chains and shackles on their arms. But they were not distracted. They responded to people in need. They began to give away small portions of whatever they carried, including some of the flowers. Those villagers who carried the gourds of water and other beverages began distributing dish-sized portions to the Chinchigwe.

"Your people are most kind, Mfalme Ncobba," Ameh said. He had three figs, a coconut chip, two daisies, and a dozen peanuts.

Ramuza acknowledged the compliment with a cordial nod. "When you are ready, we must continue. We have another kilometer to go and a small hill to climb."

None of the Chinchigwe were ready to continue, especially after hearing that a small hill was ahead. But Ameh understood Ramuza's urgency. He and the Chinchigwe thanked the villagers and quickly prepared to resume their trek along the pathway. Even Lobarra, willing to try and walk the rest of the way, made herself ready. Ameh gave Ramuza a nod of readiness. He and the other Chinchigwe stepped behind Ramuza, eating as they walked.

The pathway they traveled was relatively straight now. It went through another cluster of trees and emerged at the foot of a noticeable hillside. From there, as Ramuza had said, the pathway began to wind up and around the right side of a moderately steep climb.

It was a very uncomfortable walk. In fact, the Chinchigwe began to lag farther and farther behind Ramuza. At one point, Ramuza finally doubled back toward the Chinchigwe. He seemed to realize that the least he could do was resume carrying Lobarra.

The only rewarding part of the walk up the hillside was the magnificent view. Almost the whole eastern stretch of the valley was visible, including an unbroken view of the Aukmondi River and a lake directly below. Three colorful flower gardens stood out attractively on the south slope of the valley.

Several neatly arranged kraal communities, like the one the Chinchigwe had passed, were situated just beyond the lake to the east. High on the south slope, several kilometers in the distance, and behind one of the flower gardens, the Chinchigwe saw what appeared to be a pair of huge golden doors built directly into the slope itself.

Ramuza did not take the Chinchigwe all the way up the hillside. The Chinchigwe were thankful. Most of them never would have made it. They were tapping the very last of their strength. Ramuza took them up only about halfway, to a kraal just off the pathway.

This kraal was not like the other kraals that the Chinchigwe had seen. The Chinchigwe noticed several unique characteristics instantly. In the first place, the kraal was occupied by only one large hut. Hanging on the walls outside the hut were several gourds, calabashes, grinding stones, and large stirring spoons. The hut was bound on both sides by gardens, not vegetables and fruit, but herbs and other medicinal plants. Out in front of the hut, an aromatic concoction was brewed in a large black caldron that hung over an open fire. An unmistakable mystique emanated throughout the whole kraal.

Ameh and Twese looked at each other. Not a word was spoken. Their thoughts were mutually understood. This kraal and hut had to be the exclusive domain of the tribe's medicine man. Nothing else could explain the unique surroundings.

Once they entered the kraal, the Chinchigwe saw ten people waiting. There was the Orange Warrior Wema and two White Warriors. They stood just inside the kraal entrance. An old man, about Ameh's age, sat on a tree stump by the hut's doorway. He was deep in conversation with a young man and woman who sat on the ground to his right. Off to the left, near the entrance to one of the herb gardens, four youths – a boy and three girls - stood talking. None of the ten people looked like a typical practitioner of tribal medicine.

When the people in the kraal saw Ramuza, as expected, all attention was drawn toward him. The four youths and the warriors gathered around. The young man and woman assisted the old man to his feet.

"Tanake, Great Creation," Ramuza addressed the old man as he gently placed Lobarra on her feet. "I see you made it up the hillside without problems."

"Then you see wrong, Mfalme." Tanake, the Craftsman, was not disrespectful, although his words seemed to snap as loudly as his old bones as he stood erect. "You know how I hate walking up that hill. Why could you not have summoned everyone to my hut?"

"I am sure the climb had done you good, my friend."

"You have summoned me up here. There must be a very good reason."

"I have several requests that can best be fulfilled here at the hut of the Favored Tribesman." With this said, Ramuza quickly introduced the Chinchigwe to the rest of his people. Just as quickly, he explained to his people who the Chinchigwe were and what they needed.

The Chinchigwe eventually learned that this kraal and hut belonged to the young man that Tanake had been talking to earlier.

He was the mysterious medicine man. Although he looked too young to be a medicine man, there was a reassuring look of maturity and wisdom in his face and his manners. He was referred to as Kon-Shambique, the Favored Tribesman. His friend and closest aide was the young woman, Tongda. The four youths were all aides to the craftsman, Tanake.

The Chinchigwe were unaware that all of Ramuza's summoned people were there except one. Ramuza noticed it the moment he entered the kraal. After he had made his introductions and imparted his instructions, he stepped aside and beckoned the Orange Warrior over.

"Wema, where is Rwuva?"

"The Sacred Woman will be here directly, Great Creation. When I gave her your instructions, she was deeply involved with some of the preparations for The Celebration. All else has been done as you requested."

Ramuza thanked Wema and dismissed him. Then, without a word, he left the Chinchigwe in the hands of Kon-Shambique, Tongda, Tanake, and their youthful aides. Ramuza exited the kraal. His strong strides took him quickly down the hillside and beyond sight before anyone knew he was gone.

— **20** —

STORIES TOLD AND STORIES UNTOLD

"**W**hich of you speaks for the Chinchigwe?" Tanake asked the group as he approached them.

"I am called Ameh Jobabwe. For now, I speak for the Chinchigwe."

"Ameh, Great Creation, you have probably heard it before, but once again, welcome. Come. Let us begin to remove those chains." Tanake took Ameh's arm and led the Chinchigwe over to a nearby worktable. He directed the people to be seated comfortably on the ground as one of his youthful aides began laying various work tools on the table.

"I feel we should reintroduce ourselves," Tanake continued. "Mfalme Ncobba has done such a poor job of introductions. Only the Supreme Spirit knows what drives him in such haste this time."

The Chinchigwe liked Tanake instantly. The old man, Tanake Tayabo Kanti, had a pleasing familiarity about him. He was exceptionally friendly and very talkative. Although he had a full head of white hair and wrinkles across his brow, he was physically only slightly older than Ameh.

One of the first mannerisms the Chinchigwe noticed about Tanake was his tendency to talk while working. He sorted through the tools that his aides had laid out for him. Then he turned to the chains and shackles on the Chinchigwe's arms as he continued to talk. "The Mfalme is a very Head-strong Creation. He is a great leader, one of the greatest of his bloodline, but sometimes, I believe, he thinks with a ram's head. One of these days, I fear, he will put his head to something that will not give."

Tanake just happened to start on the chain link between Ameh and Twese. In doing so, he examined Twese's hand and arm. He looked briefly into Twese's face. "Great Creation, you are a craftsman."

"Yes." Twese was surprised at Tanake's insight. "Yes, I am. In my village, I made pottery. How did you know?"

"You are a Kindred Spirit. I can see the gift in your hands." Tanake selected a hammer and a large chisel from his tool table. "I am the senior craftsman in the Aukmondi tribe. I am considered the mentor to all the other artists and crafters here. I can recognize another craftsman when I see one."

"Then, your gift honors you."

"I have not done much in my time, but the Supreme Spirit has let it be known that my descendants will always remember me. When my heart gives out from climbing mountain-sides, my descendants will tell you about me. That is all the honor I need."

"Tanake, Great Creation. Please!" The young man called Kon-Shambique walked up just in time to hear Tanake's sarcastic reintroduction of himself. He set the tools of his trade, a collection of medicinal herbs and a water bowl, on Tanake's worktable. "After all these people appear to have gone through, I am sure they are not interested in hearing all about you."

"Oh, please continue!" Ameh insisted. He and the rest of the Chinchigwe were already captivated.

Unfortunately, Tanake did not continue where he left off. After pounding the wedged end of his chisel into one of the shackles, he indicated the young man who had just walked up. "This Young Creation is called Kon-Shambique Isi Bwenu. Listen to him, for he knows everything. And I do not say this in jest. The elephant will sail upon the wind like a falcon on the day Kon-Shambique is dumbfounded by anything."

"Then protect your heads. That very day has come." Kon-Shambique mumbled just loud enough for everyone to hear. After Tanake had pried the shackle open, freeing Twese's arm, Kon-Shambique began treating the bruises, cuts, and scratches.

Tanake had already moved on to the shackle on Ameh's arm. His talking never stopped. "No. In all seriousness, Kon-Shambique is a remarkably Wise Creation. I have lived over fifty harvests longer than Kon-Shambique, yet the Young Creation often enlightens me. Not a day has passed since Kon-Shambique has not amazed someone with some insight or wisdom. At his youthful age, he is our healer. He is our philosopher. He is our spiritual teacher. All the Aukmondi people, including that ram, Mfalme Ncobba, often come to him for advice, counseling, guidance, and treatments. Personally, I would come more often if he didn't live up here on this awful mountain."

"I must admit," Ameh glanced at Twese and smiled apologetically, "when we first entered this kraal, some of us suspected that the dweller of this hut was the tribe's witchdoctor."

Kon-Shambique smiled at Ameh's comment.

"Witchdoctor?" Tanake laughed out loud. "If you refer to him as that, I am sure it would not offend him. Depends on how you look at it, he fulfills that function."

"Kon-Shambique," Twese spoke up. "You are a healer, a philosopher, a spiritual teacher. What do you call yourself?"

Kon-Shambique opened his mouth to answer Twese, but Tanake responded first. "We prefer to call him the Favored Tribesman. And there is an interesting reason for this. Allow me to explain."

"It never ends," Kon-Shambique mumbled almost inaudibly this time.

"Yes, please explain." Ameh understood by now that Tanake was about to explain anyway. There was no stopping him. Ameh smiled at Kon-Shambique and shrugged.

"It is an interesting story." Tanake ignored the silent exchange between Ameh and Kon-Shambique. He moved down the line of people and began working on the chain link between Summarwe and Jpuma. "You see, the Aukmondi people believe Kon-Shambique's insights, wisdom, and skills come from a very close association with the Supreme Being."

"Being?"

"You heard me correctly, Great Creation. Supreme Being. You may know Her and call Her by some other name. When she walks among us, we call Her the Sacred Woman Eledah, Creator of all existence. Rumors say that She comes to visit with Kon-Shambique often. They sit and talk for great lengths of time. No one knows what they talk about, possibly the secrets of life itself. But that is another story, and besides the point here,"

"Another story at another time, perhaps," Kon-Shambique mumbled again.

"Anyway," continued Tanake, "whatever the subject, the rumors are persistent. And they are so well accepted and believed that Kon-Shambique is popularly known as the Favored Tribesman."

"Kon-Shambique, you, of course, deny these rumors?" Ameh wanted to know.

Again, Tanake responded before Kon-Shambique. "Do not ask him. Of course, he denies them. But, you see, he is not the one to ask. The Sacred Woman there, Tongda Sameah Leng, is the one you should ask."

Ameh and the rest of the Chinchigwe shifted their attention to the attractive woman who had come over to assist Kon-Shambique. Tonga stood about 179 centimeters tall. Her skin was unusually fair for an Aukmondi. Her hair was noticeably straight and black. Most of her features were slightly Asian in appearance.

Tongda carried the ancestral family name of Sameah, the name of the 34th Tribal Mother *(See Appendix I: Aukmondi Family Names)*. Her immediate family name, Leng, was compassionately given by her grandfather, Leng Chou-Li, an immigrant from China.

Tongda smiled but tried her best to ignore Tanake and his endless talk.

"Please explain." Ameh addressed Tanake. "Why ask Tongda?"

"Because, just like the Sacred Woman Eledah, the Sacred Woman Tongda will only speak the truth. Tongda will not deny the rumor. Go ahead. Ask her yourself and listen to her answer. Remember that if the Sacred Woman Eledah speaks, by Her sacred nature, there will be only truth in Her words."

"There are stories told, and stories untold." Tongda finally spoke up in her defense. "Just as the Great Creation Tanake delights in telling you stories, there are other stories that he does not tell. What he is failing to tell you is that I have chosen, for a long time, to ignore these rumors. There is a chance that someday, these stories may all die away. But it seems this strategy is not working very well."

Twese sat forward. He was fascinated. He turned to Tongda. "What difference does it make? Whether or not the rumors die, this is a very bold accusation. If what Tanake is saying is true, then people must see you as … "

Tanake cut Twese off too. He pointed at Twese with the hammer in his hand. "Now you are beginning to understand, Great Creation. Tongda is the other half of these so-called rumors. Anyone can see that she is a caring and compassionate woman. She easily wins the heart of anyone who knows her. However, she is quiet and does not talk as much as I do; she is naturally adventurous and outgoing. Describe Tongda, and you could be describing the Sacred Woman Eledah. But, to walk among us without causing too many distractions, she takes the guise of Kon-Shambique's apprentice. She works as his closest assistant."

"Such a close association with the tribe's healer and Spiritual teacher would explain some things, but … "

"You have not heard the rest, Great Creation." Tanake was enjoying himself. "She is his greatest love and the unquestionable source of his strength. The two are inseparable. You have never seen a more perfect example of young love. They live in an unannounced union, but there is no question that the day will come. The way these two carry on is probably the only thing that will make you doubt that the Sacred Woman Tongda is the incarnated Supreme Spirit."

Most of the Chinchigwe found Tanake's stories fascinating, whether they believed him or not. Tanake seemed to be a man who thoroughly enjoyed mixing truths and legends.

Of all the Chinchigwe, Twese was the most skeptical. He needed more convincing facts. He found himself staring at Tongda. He could easily accept that Tongda was a woman with a beautiful mind and heart. Her physical beauty was obvious. He recalled the image of the woman he thought he saw in the clearing. He tried to figure out if there was a connection. Tongda looked nothing like the woman he remembered seeing.

Twese sat back. He decided to dismiss the rumor, for now. "Tanake, you must forgive me. You cannot be as serious as you sound."

"Then go ahead, Great Creation. Ask Tongda to deny the rumors. I have been trying for the longest time."

When Twese looked once again at Tongda, she smiled back at him. Her beautiful liquid-amber eyes reflected something very special. But there was a warning look on her face. "I just met you, Great Creation. I would hate to begin ignoring you already."

"Tanake, you have successfully spread deathless rumors." Kon-Shambique finally stood up from his work. He had just finished putting a splint and palm-leaf bandage on Jpuma's leg and moved over to give Lobarra full attention. He addressed Ameh as he did. "Great Creation, I believe the only way to stop Tanake is for you to tell us more about the Chinchigwe."

"I am afraid that the story of the Chinchigwe is not as pleasing to hear as Tanake's stories."

"Tanake's only purpose was to pry these chains from your arms and put you and your people at ease. He is doing those things, I think. Now tell us about the Chinchigwe. We want to know."

"Where shall I begin?" Ameh reviewed the past few days and searched for an appropriate starting place. He began by telling Kon-Shambique, Tongda, and Tanake who the Chinchigwe were; their life and hopes of so long ago; and their greatly simplified life and hopes now. He described the ever-increasing raids that had taken place in their village and the dwindling number of Chinchigwe people. Ameh went into great detail about the final battle against the slave hunters; the battle to live or die, to save the honor and respect of their ancestors. He told about their failure and the subsequent capture by the hunters. Ameh described the horrors of the red-bearded slave merchant, his two aides, and the quality of life that the merchant had provided in his holding pens.

Details were given in almost every case until Ameh told about the escape. From that point, remembering Ramuza's special instructions to the Orange Warrior Wema, he gave a brief, edited version of what had happened. He told about the flight from the merchant's camp, the dangerous journey across the wilderness, and finally, their encounter with and desperate request to Ramuza. Ameh did not refer Adaulah.

Ameh concluded the recent history of the Chinchigwe by reintroducing, by name, the only survivors of the entire Chinchigwe tribe: Lobarra Gendeyani, Twese Merende, Summarwe Bata, and her brother Jpuma, Embabi Tende, Komu Ndizi, and seventeen others.

Just as Ameh finished up, everyone noticed several people entering Kon-Shambique's kraal. Ameh let his account trail off to silence as all eyes were drawn to the approaching people.

There were two Red Warriors, one in front of the group and one in the rear. In the center of the group were five women. Four women were girls slightly on one side or the other of full womanhood. The fifth woman, however, was more mature and had a radiant majesty about her. She was someone very important.

When Kon-Shambique saw her, he stood and welcomed her to his kraal. He introduced her to the Chinchigwe as the Sacred Woman, Rwuva Azinti Ncobba, the Principal Mate of Mfalme Ncobba. The four young women at her side were their daughters: Omari, Yejide, Kunto, and Audi.

After Kon-Shambique made introductions, Ameh quickly realized that this woman was also Adaulah's mother. The woman, her four daughters, and Adaulah had a strong family resemblance.

The Sacred Woman Rwuva was elegant and attractively mature, with dark, velvety, soft-looking skin. Her bright red, wrap-around garment made her skin appear richer and her large eyes brighter.

"When I was told we were having visitors," Rwuva began, "I did not expect this many."

Kon-Shambique escorted Rwuva closer to the group and completed his introductions. "Sacred Woman, these are the Chinchigwe people."

"Please accept my apology for not being here when you arrived," Rwuva said. "As Official Hostess, I officially welcome you to the Aukmondi Valley. Please, consider this welcome and greeting from all the Aukmondi people."

"Thank you. We are most grateful for all the hospitality your people have given us." Ameh tried to reflect as much of the warmth as he received.

"After the Great Creation, Kon-Shambique has treated you, Zhanguta here," Rwuva indicated one of the Red Warriors who stood behind her, "will take you to an area where fresh water awaits your complete refreshment. You will then be taken to where food awaits your nourishment."

"Again, thank you."

"If there is anything else that you need for your comfort, anything at all, please let me know. I will try to see that you get it. May your stay here with us be among your best memories."

With this said, Rwuva and her four daughters began exchanging a few cordial words with Kon-Shambique, Tongda, and Tanake. The women watched the three continue to work as they also took the opportunity to mingle among the Chinchigwe, getting to know many of them individually.

All the while, Rwuva was hoping to speak with Kon-Shambique privately. She did not want to appear rude, so she did not pull the Favored Tribesman aside. Instead, she continued her brief conversations with one person after the next as she waited for the right moment. When she noticed Kon-Shambique walking away to empty a large water bowl, she quickly followed him.

"Great Creation, the Orange Warrior Wema told me Ramuza would be here. Where did he go so quickly?"

"I do not know, Sacred Woman. The Mfalme left in a hurry. There was urgency in his behavior. I thought it was unusual, but I did not get to talk with him about it."

Rwuva gave the matter a little thought, then tried to push the matter aside. She glanced back at the Chinchigwe. "I counted twenty-four. That is a number of people to treat at one time. You seem to have your hands full."

"No, not really. Mainly, there is only one sprained ankle and one pregnancy. There are a few blistered feet, swollen wrists, bruises, and minor cuts. None of these is a problem. These poor people suffer mostly from their experiences of the past few days and the lack of food and water."

"The food and water are no problems either. Food is being gathered and prepared for them as we speak. After they have eaten, they can rest for as long as they please."

"Then, if anyone's hands are full, I would say, it is Ramuza's. These people are asking him for aid against a slave merchant who is yet pursuing them."

"Surely Ramuza is going to help them. Do you suppose his quick departure has something to do with the Chinchigwe request?"

"It would seem so, but I cannot say for sure. The situation is a little more complicated than simply giving them aid. As they told me of their escape and flight, I was aware of something they deliberately chose not to mention. I do not know what it is and did not pry for it. Whatever it is, I think it may make all the difference."

Rwuva looked at the Chinchigwe again. Tanake had finished removing all the chains and shackles. Some Aukmondi aides were now helping the Chinchigwe gather up after their treatment. Tongda was leading Lobarra into Kon-Shambique's hut for additional treatment.

Rwuva thanked Kon-Shambique. She walked over to say her parting words to Tongda, Tanake, and the Chinchigwe. After giving the Red Warrior Zhanguta some final instructions, Rwuva gathered her daughters and left the kraal.

21

THE BLACK WARRIOR

The Royal Kraal was located at the very center of the valley. It covered almost 3,750 square kilometers, proportionally one of the largest kraals in the Aukmondi Valley. Its single entrance was only a stone's throw from the north bank of the Aukmondi River. Almost 750 meters from the entrance and recessed in the very rear of the kraal was Ramuza's hut.

Ramuza's hut was only one of four huts in the whole kraal. Each of the four huts was atypically large and about 85 meters apart in a thick cove of trees at the base of the north slope. Ramuza's hut was one of the middle huts, with two huts to his right and one to the left. These three huts belonged to his three wives. The hut to the immediate right of Ramuza's belonged to Rwuva, the Principal Mate.

Out in front, in that 750-meter stretch between the huts and the entrance of the kraal, was a special dirt clearing that the Aukmondi call the celebration area. In this clearing, before the homes of the Ncobbas, people from all over the valley, from every other kraal, come together every evening. They come, as they say, to celebrate life. They produce rhythmic music, sing, dance, laugh, talk, and play as they pass the time and pay tributes to the passing day.

Ramuza entered the kraal and hurried across the celebration area toward his hut. He could see that the area was relatively bare, but not quite as bare as he preferred. The people from the Pogobi Kraal, whom he and the Chinchigwe had met earlier on the north slope, were here, preparing for this evening's celebration. Ramuza knew that some would rush over to ask him questions as soon as they saw him. He had no time to answer questions.

The Mfalme hastened his already strong pace. He avoided contact with everyone. He hoped the direct approach across the clearing would show his intent and urgency to anyone who saw him. Respectfully, and to his relief, no one in the clearing stopped him.

Ramuza's next concern was meeting his wives. He was not yet ready to explain the situation concerning Adaulah. Ramuza was an Honest, Forthright Creation. He would provide explanations or answers if asked. And rightfully speaking, any of his wives had the right to know. He just felt that now was not the right time. He wanted to lead a thorough search for his son first. Then, if tragedy occurred, he would return and tell them and the rest of the Aukmondi people the bad news.

Ramuza realized that, at this time of day, the Sacred Women Rwuva and Kharaambi should not be in the Royal Kraal anyway. He did not see Rwuva out front, helping with preparations for tonight's celebration. This meant that she was, no doubt, still meeting with the Chinchigwe in Kon-Shambique's kraal. Kharaambi, on the other hand, had gone with the Royal Warrior Nionu and his Ehkili Regiment on the reconnaissance venture on the south rim. There is still time before she is due to return. Ramuza glanced at their respective huts as he walked by.

His most likely encounter would be the Sacred Woman Olabisi Sheetswa, his second mate. Ramuza was unaware of any task that Olabisi would be involved with now. He rushed past her hut, hoping that he would not be seen.

When Ramuza reached his hut, he quickly disappeared inside. There was no way to tell how long the search for Adaulah would take. A supply of food and water is likely necessary. Ramuza knew that most of the water and food would be provided by the warriors of the Royal Warrior Ratuzu's army. Ramuza decided to take only a small amount of water for his convenience. He quickly filled a small water pouch from a freshwater barrel.

Next, Ramuza went to the rear of the hut's main chamber, where a large cloth tarpaulin hung on the wall. Ramuza tugged on a rope at one end, and the cloth tarpaulin fell to the ground. All of his warrior gear hung neatly on the wall. Ramuza stood back, surveying the knives, spears, shields, and all the other warrior accessories.

As he was deciding what he should take, Ramuza heard a noise behind him. He turned to see the Sacred Woman Olabisi standing just inside the doorway.

"Great Creation, you have returned." She did not expect Ramuza to return from the north rim so soon. Her concern was in her voice.

"Yes, Sacred Woman." Ramuza walked back across the chamber and tenderly embraced his wife. This was wife number two and the mother of his fifth, sixth, eighth, and ninth child. Unlike the Sacred Woman Rwuva, who had given him four beautiful daughters and a son, one at a time, Olabisi Sheetswa had given him two sets of twins – all females.

Ramuza's embrace was long and affectionate, but it was different. Olabisi sensed it instantly. She glanced at the warrior gear on the wall and looked into Ramuza's eyes. "What is wrong, Great Creation?"

"The Brown Warrior and I encountered a problem in the wilderness."

"The people from the Pogobi Kraal say that we have visitors. Does it have anything to do with them?"

Ramuza smiled. He should have known that news of the visitors would reach the Royal Kraal long before he did. Some news cannot be suppressed. "No, Sacred Woman. They are related, but they are not the problem."

"Then what requires the Mfalme to don the gear of the Black Warrior?"

Ramuza released his embrace of Olabisi and went back toward the back wall. "I have learned that Adaulah did not make it to the Village of Teachers. The Ratuzu Army and I will return to the wilderness to search for him."

The fact that Mfalme Ramuza Koneheni Ncobba has only one son was profoundly significant. If the Ncobbas and all the Aukmondi people did not look upon the predicament as the Supreme Spirit's design, it would be a tragedy. In the beginning, Ramuza and the

Sacred Woman Rwuva knew that a natural male heir was only a matter of time. But after the first four daughters, the concerns began.

Ramuza currently has three wives. After eleven harvests, the three women gave him ten beautiful children. It was the Supreme Spirit's design that, after all that time and with the loving support of three strong women, the next Aukmondi Mfalme would not appear until the tenth child—a rare and special jewel.

When Ramuza turned to face Olabisi again, he saw her suppressing the horror she felt. Adaulah was not Olabisi's natural son. He was Rwuva's son. But Olabisi had bonded with the Young Creation as strongly as any mother. She stood strong, but her eyes had already welled up with tears.

To fortify her strength, Olabisi went to stand at Ramuza's side. She studied the warrior's gear on the wall. She forced her voice to reflect the strength that was failing her. "Allow me to help prepare the Black Warrior for what must be done."

In the next few minutes, Ramuza and Olabisi did not speak. No words were necessary. Olabisi, almost ceremoniously, selected a belted knife from the wall. With tears rolling down her face, she tied the belt around Ramuza's waist. After some consideration, she selected a thick black cloak and tossed it across Ramuza's left shoulder. The cloak freely hung down the calves of Ramuza's legs. Olabisi then selected one of the spears. She checked it for balance and straightness before placing it in Ramuza's right hand. Finally, she unhooked a huge black shield. The shield stood almost as tall as she was. It eclipsed her as she fitted on Ramuza's left forearm.

At this point, Olabisi stood back. She was aware that Ramuza was not dressing for a ceremonial performance. The decorative headgear, beads, bracelets, and anklets were not necessary. Ramuza was not fully dressed as the Black Warrior but was ready for a practical mission.

"Great Creation," Olabisi began, "the instant you step from the hut, there will be questions. What must I say?"

"As always, you must speak your heart, Sacred Woman. But I would prefer not to alarm the people just yet. Let the people know that all their questions will be answered upon my return."

Olabisi smiled. Holding back the masses would not be easy. She gave Ramuza a final embrace. "May the Supreme Spirit guide you."

With her tears wiped away and her face refreshed, Olabisi was the first to step from Ramuza's hut. She knew what was about to happen when Ramuza exited. She stood directly in front of the doorway, staring across the celebration area at the people there. She stood tall and proud. The fact that she was the Mfalme's second wife was enough to draw all the attention. But there was more to come. Olabisi stepped aside, realizing there was no way to avoid what was coming.

Ramuza stepped from the hut. The Mfalme dressed in the garments of the Black Warrior was a rare sight. As expected, the whispers and excitement started instantly. People began to move toward him. Ramuza had no time to explain his appearance or what he was doing. He began his strong strides across the celebration area to exit the Royal Kraal. As before, his direct mannerism strongly suggested that others stay clear of him. Consequently, the crowd respectfully gave way. The people gathered around Olabisi instead.

— **22** —

A PROBLEM WHERE IT DOES NOT BELONG

Ramuza exited the Royal Kraal and circled it to head back up the north slope. Because of his pace, he quickly disappeared through the trees. He took one of the pathways leading him to the Pahoma Garden, where the Royal Warrior Ratuzu and his double-regimented army would await him.

Since learning about Adaulah's situation from the Chinchigwe, Ramuza felt a nagging regret. Initially, he felt it was not a good idea to let Adaulah go to the Village of Teachers so soon. Adaulah was much too young. Adaulah would not understand the significance of what the Teachers had to offer. Yet, out of pride in his only son's maturity, Ramuza promised Adaulah that he could soon visit the Teachers.

Like all proud fathers, Ramuza wanted his son to grow up knowledgeable and wise. Ramuza loved his son dearly and, naturally, wanted to provide him with the best opportunities to grow knowledgeable and wise. After all, Ramuza's second daughter, the Sacred Woman, Yejide, had successfully visited the Village of Teachers several harvests ago. She had benefited greatly from the visit. Ramuza never regretted it. Now it was Adaulah's turn.

This propensity of Ramuza's was not only for Adaulah's own sake. It was for the sake of the Aukmondi people, too. Ramuza knew that, unlike Yejide, Adaulah would someday be Mfalme to all the Aukmondi people.

Adaulah would inherit the leadership of the Aukmondi in a time when things would be much different than the present. Ramuza understood that there was an alien world beyond the bounds of the valley; a world with many alien things, good and bad. This alien world was growing every day. And with all its good and bad, it will eventually spill into the valley, bringing influences that only strong hearts, strong minds, and wise leadership could survive.

Ramuza wanted Adaulah to be well prepared for those inevitable days and the tremendous responsibilities they would need. Such preparation, Ramuza knew, begins with knowledge. So Ramuza solemnly promised Adaulah that he could visit the Village of Teachers, but only after Adaulah had seen his eighth harvest. At the time, the eighth harvest seemed like a proper future time.

Adaulah's eighth harvest came much too soon. Ramuza regretted ever making the promise. He wished that he could have, at least, postponed its fulfillment just a little farther.

This regret of Ramuza's first appeared in the subtle form of doubt. Since Adaulah was told he could someday go to the Village, Ramuza has seen a growing enthusiasm for his son's desire. It became so strong that Ramuza doubted if Adaulah truly understood what he was asking for.

"But I do understand," the young Aukmondi had insisted to his father. "I know the purpose of the Village. I have heard you and Yejide talk of it many times. I can learn about other tribes, other peoples. I can learn how they live and better understand my own people."

For some reason, Ramuza was never fully convinced. He found it easier to believe that Adaulah was too young to appreciate the importance of his journey. He could not shake his reluctance to let him go, not now!

But then, there was that promise he had made. When Ramuza went to talk with Kon-Shambique about the problem, the Favored Tribesman led Ramuza toward a telling revelation.

"Mfalme, Adaulah's age is not the problem," Kon-Shambique had explained. "When a mind and heart such as his are motivated to learn something, there is no better time."

"Yes, but you do not understand, Great Creation. The knowledge given by the teachers of the Village must not be taken lightly, particularly by someone who will someday be Mfalme."

"Ramuza, neither age nor subject has much to do with a mind ready to learn. I feel your reluctance is born out of something else. It seems you have put a problem where it does not belong."

"What do you mean?"

"I will answer that question with two questions of my own." Kon-Shambique took a moment to prepare his strategy mentally. Then he presented the Mfalme with his first question: "At what age should Adaulah visit the Village of Teachers?"

Ramuza thought a moment, searching his mind for his most honest opinion. "I suppose, there is no specific age, but older than he is now. The Sacred Woman Yejide did not go until after her fifteenth harvest."

"I see," Kon-Shambique smiled. Then, what if the Village was right here in the valley?"

Ramuza could suddenly see where his problem lay. If the Village were here in the valley, Adaulah would have been exposed to it long ago. His reluctance was due to the difficult task of getting Adaulah safely to the village and back. It was a matter of adequate protection for his son, which Ramuza felt could never be enough.

The Sacred Woman Yejide made a successful trip to the Village with only two warrior escorts. In hindsight, she was very lucky. Adaulah, prince of the Aukmondi, was understandably special. The element of luck had to be practically guaranteed.

Two days before Adaulah's departure, Ramuza and Kharaambi summoned four of the tribe's elite specialists to the Royal Kraal. Like the Sentinels, these were Green Warriors. These warriors have come up through the ranks, eventually obtaining talents, skills, or abilities unmatched by anyone else.

There was the Green Warrior Modano. He was a scout and tracker. He had the amazing ability to find a village he had never visited or heard of before. His observation skills were so acute that he could follow the trail of the smallest creature over amazing distances.

There was the Green Warrior Thula. This sensitive and brilliant drummer could speak the language of signal drums and his own tongue. He could listen to the drums of unfamiliar tribes and interpret the meanings almost precisely.

Finally, there were the Green Warriors Lupwa and Wazhomo. Both of them were combat strategists. There was no question that these warriors were destined to ascend to the rank of Blue or Royal Warriors. Upon his return, Lupwa was due to take charge of his own regiment, becoming a Blue Warrior.

Both Ramuza and Kharaambi spent several hours with these four warriors. They planned the journey to and from the Village of Teachers and developed contingencies for every phase.

On the morning of Adaulah's departure, a small crowd gathered to see the five travelers off. Adaulah and the four warriors would be gone for five full cycles of the moon, a long time to hope that nothing goes wrong when so many adversities were possible.

Ramuza stood at the head of the crowd. Behind him were his three wives: Rwuva, the principal wife; Olabisi, the second wife; and Kharaambi, the third wife. Behind them were all nine of Adaulah's sisters. And behind them were all the other Aukmondi who had come to see Adaulah off. Ramuza wondered if he was the only one in the crowd who felt strongly uncomfortable about Adaulah's departure.

A day and a half later, Ramuza learned that his discomfort was not without reason. The five travelers' journey had been tragically unsuccessful. He did not know exactly what had happened. He only hoped that the tragedy was not as complete as it seemed.

The sun had already descended into the west when Ramuza reached the Pahoma Garden. He found Ratuzu and his army waiting as ordered. He greeted the Royal Warrior and took ultimate charge of his warriors.

There wasn't a moment to lose. Ramuza let the warriors know this by telling them who they were going after and what the situation was. They set out at once on the long search that would not end until Adaulah was found. As Ramuza led the way out of the Garden, over the north rim, out of the valley, and into the wilderness, he relayed to them all that he knew about Adaulah's whereabouts.

Ramuza walked with his usual strong, broad steps. His black cloak, signifying his ultimate rank, hung loosely over his shoulder and swayed rhythmically with each step. He easily set the urgent pace for the column of warriors trailing behind him.

******

Once in the wilderness, they did not have to go very far. In the forest area, approximately where Ramuza found the Chinchigwe, the Brown Warrior Quazzi, and the Bendabe Regiment could be seen coming.

Quazzi's instructions were not to return until other warriors had been sent to replace him or until Adaulah was found. Adaulah had been found. The question now was whether or not Adaulah had been found alive.

Ramuza took a deep breath and mentally prepared himself for the worst. His pace turned into a run as he hurried to meet Quazzi. His first spark of relief came when he noticed the casual, unconcerned mood of the Bendabe warriors, and finally, Adaulah riding piggyback on Quazzi's back.

"You found him, Great Creation! How is he?"

Adaulah was sound asleep. Quazzi allowed Ramuza to lift Adaulah from his back. "I think his most serious injury is a bump on the head, Mfalme. The cut there is not as bad as it looks. Other than that, I think he is only exhausted."

"Yes. After all that he had gone through, I would assume so."

"When we found him, he was soundly asleep in the clearing between the Langinzi and Bongii Forests. He has not awakened fully yet. We forced him to drink a little water. He may still be quite thirsty."

"Thank you, Quazzi, my friend. You have done well."

When Quazzi transferred Adaulah to Ramuza's arms, Adaulah became fully awake for the first time. The young Aukmondi was extremely happy to see his father instead of the frightening Wabanga. He embraced Ramuza tightly—a flood of emotions too overwhelming for him to say anything.

Ramuza returned the warm embrace, also extremely happy and relieved to have his son back. He wondered what he would have done had he lost his son. It was truly frightening to have come so close to losing someone so close to him and so important to a whole tribe of people.

"Tell me, Adaulah, what happened?"

Adaulah wiped the tears from his face before he spoke. "We were attacked by slave hunters, Mfalme. There were so many of them. And it happened so quickly. The warriors Modano and Wazhomo were killed during the attack. The warriors Thula, Lupwa, and I were taken captive. But the Green Warriors were killed too, when we tried to escape. The slave hunters took me away. I was put in an animal pen with … "

Adaulah's tearful account was interrupted by the voice of the White Warrior Upenda. She and several other warriors were strategically scattered about the local area, looking for any sign of danger. Upenda, positioned only 25 meters from Adaulah and Ramuza, was the first to meet a definite sign of danger – a Wabanga.

As if by magic, the Wabanga swooped down out of a tree, just two meters in front of Upenda. Truly frightened, Upenda's warning was more of a scream.

The Wabanga was unbelievable. He stood crouched before Upenda, with a menacing knife held ready. He stared at Upenda with an undetermined expression on his face. He looked as if he had already been in one bloody massacre and was ready to delve into another one.

Before Upenda could get complete control of her voice or prepare to defend herself, she was attacked. By sheer luck, she blocked a wide, graceful swing of the Wabanga's knife with her shield. She stumbled back from the force of the attack. She fell hard to the ground. Only the reflexive nature of her warrior training brought her quickly to her feet again. But by then, the Wabanga was gone.

"Sacred Woman!" An Orange Warrior had finally rushed over to aid the White Warrior. "Are you alright?"

"I am fine." Upenda brushed debris from his arms and picked up her spear off the ground. "Did you get him?"

"Get whom? We heard you scream, but … "

Upenda looked at the warrior with astonishment. "You mean, you did not see him?"

The warrior looked around. He looked into the faces of other warriors who had also rushed over. They all showed a complete lack of knowledge about what had just happened. "We saw no one, Sacred Woman."

"Please tell me, you are not serious." Upenda could barely believe it. She was almost killed, and no one saw the Wabanga except her. She bent down to pick up her shield. The shield had an unmistakable, jagged cut over half a meter long.

Although the other warriors did not see the Wabanga, they did not doubt Upenda's claim. Experienced had made them accept Upenda's words as fact. They relayed to Quazzi that everything was alright, but that danger was immediately present. Quazzi, in turn, told the Mfalme.

"The Wabanga's blood-lust has become rampant, Great Creation. I suggest we return to the valley."

Everyone who had heard Quazzi's suggestion agreed, except Adaulah. He suddenly objected. "No! Wait! We must not leave now. There are others out here. My friends are out here. They need help!"

"You must be referring to the Chinchigwe," said Ramuza. "We have them, Young Creation. They are safely in the valley already."

Adaulah's face seemed to brighten. His spirit was rekindled. "You found the Chinchigwe? The Great Creation Ameh? And Twese? And the Sacred Woman Lobarra?"

"Yes. We have them all. They are safe. Come. Let us go and get you treated. Then we will sit and talk with your friends."

— 23 —

IF YOU KNEW WHAT I KNOW

The last thing that Sam remembered was standing ready to beat the living hell out of that wild man. Then he passed out at the wild man's feet. By all accounts, Sam should be dead. But he wasn't. Instead, he was carried rather precariously across the wild man's shoulder.

"What the hell!" Sam began to struggle after returning to full consciousness. "Put me down!"

The wild man dropped Sam to the ground. He jerked out his knife from his twine belt and held it ready. He seemed to have been waiting for Sam to regain consciousness. Now, he was ready to resume his challenge, pick up where he left off, and finish his kill.

While Sam was lying on the ground, he immediately noticed two things in his favor. One was the fact that the wild man was still bleeding from the gunshot wound. Blood streamed copiously down the wild man's chest, down his side, and dripped from his thigh. Sam couldn't tell how much blood the wild man had lost or how far the wild man had carried him. But, from it all, the wild man had to be considerably weaker.

The second thing that Sam noticed was that he still had his pistol, of all things. The wild man was too ignorant to know what a pistol could do. Even after witnessing the shooting of his companion and after being shot himself, the wild man had not bothered to remove Sam's pistol. Surely he couldn't know only one potentially good measure of gunpowder was left in the pistol. Possibly, thought Sam, the wild man got a greater thrill when he knew his subject had a fighting chance. Sam decided to give this heathen bastard his last thrill.

"You should have killed me when you had the chance. You will not get another." Sam drew his pistol and scrambled to stand. He pulled the hammer back on the pistol and aimed. But then, the wild man suddenly turned and ran for cover. The evasive act caught Sam completely by surprise.

Sam knew that there could only be one reason for this behavior. He had seen it before. Someone or something was coming. Sam instinctively bent down low himself. He quickly looked about, trying to cover the whole area at once. Through the trees, he eventually spotted two warrior armies, about fifty meters apart, heading toward each other.

One army of warriors on his left turned out to be the same one he had seen earlier. This army was evidently on its return trip. He recognized the lead warrior with the brown cloak. This brown-cloaked warrior was carrying someone, a small boy, on his back. Sam couldn't tell, but the boy looked like the same little boy who opened the holding pen and freed Captain McIntyre's slaves.

The other army, coming from the opposite direction and toward the clearing, was one Sam had not seen before. It was obviously from the same tribe because the two warrior armies were dressed similarly.

That second army was led by one of the most impressive natives Sam had ever seen. He wore a black cloak and carried an ominous-looking black shield. Everything about him told Sam he must have been a very important warrior.

Sam watched the two armies come together from his hidden position and gradually spread out over the local area. He watched the brown-cloaked warrior surrender the boy to the black-cloaked warrior, who embraced him tightly. Then, out of the corner of his eye, he saw something else that demanded his full attention.

Not too far away, the wild man, the very same one he had shot, was in a tree, preparing to pounce down on an unsuspecting female warrior. Sam almost absent-mindedly got up to cry out a warning, but thought better of it. Instead, he remained concealed and allowed the incident to run its course. After all, why should he warn what might be a tribe of cannibals of an attacking wild man?

Sam saw the wild man swing squarely from the tree to the ground in front of the female warrior. Despite the broken fingers and the gunshot wound in his shoulder, the wild man was still as graceful as a chimpanzee. He swung his knife at the warrior and, in an instant, vaulted over a bush out of sight.

The female warrior was frightened. She almost screamed when she saw the wild man pop up out of nowhere in front of her. She was so unprepared or inexperienced that she could barely block the wild man's attack.

Other warriors rushed over to aid the woman warrior, but apparently, none of them saw the wild man hiding behind the bush. Only Sam saw the wild man slip away, like a cockroach, to another hiding place.

This incident must have convinced the warrior armies to move on immediately. Sam watched the armies regroup and move off deeper into the forest.

Before they got too far out of view, however, Sam made a special effort to get a good look at the little boy. He almost came out of hiding as he did so.

Sam was still not sure about the boy. He could not find anything about the boy that convinced him one way or the other of the boy's identity. A strong feeling tells Sam that this is the same boy who had freed the captain's slaves. This was the boy that Captain McIntyre wanted so badly. Sam smiled proudly at this conclusion and the valuable information he had learned.

Once he felt safe, Sam tucked his pistol away and emerged from hiding. He looked around briefly to get his relative bearing. The walk ahead of him, out of the forest area and back across the clearing, would be long. Sam knew that the sooner he got started, the better.

Sam felt good, considering the situation. For the first time in a long time, Sam felt he had accomplished something that someone else would appreciate. Captain McIntyre would be very pleased to know what he had just learned. He couldn't wait to tell him.

Just then, the wild man sprang out on the pathway before Sam. He was unbelievably persistent in his intent to kill. He slowly swayed as he waved his knife menacingly in Sam's face.

"You bleeding bastard! You are nothing but a show now." Sam didn't feel threatened at all.

The gruesome man-creature standing before Sam was in no shape to kill anybody. Several fingers on his right hand were broken. His whole right arm hung uselessly at his side. Even the hand that held the knife was shaking from severe weakness. Sam believed one good battering would finish him off for good. The fact that the wild man still stood there full of the will to fight amazed Sam more.

With surprising speed, the wild man suddenly lunged at Sam. His knife ripped through Sam's left sleeve and cut Sam's shoulder. Blood, Sam's blood, was visible on the wild man's knife.

Sam was jolted back into reality and a full sense of caution. He realized with a shock that the wild man was still quite capable of killing him.

Sam started for his pistol again, but found it easier to hit the wild man as hard as he could in the stomach. Sam thought he saw surprise on the wild man's face for the first time. Sam hit him again before the wild man recovered, placing an unreserved blow to the side of the face. The wild man spun around and fell to the ground on his stomach. Sam rushed over, grabbed him by the shoulder, and flipped him over on his back. He drew back to hit him once more, but realized lifeless, bloodshot eyes stared back at him. The wild man was dead, his own knife lodged in his stomach.

Sam stood up and stepped back as he looked down at the wild man. The sudden death surprised him. As the event took root in his head, Sam found himself smiling. Contrary to what anybody might say about him, Sam knew he was a survivor now. He could take care of himself. Here was proof of it. In less than three or four hours, he had succeeded in killing, not one, but two of the craftiest, most deadly creatures in the African forest. Sam was very proud of himself.

Before Sam resumed his walk back toward the clearing, he took a moment to treat the new wound on his shoulder. He took off his ragged jacket and ripped the remaining sleeve of his shirt. He quickly made several new bandages, one for his shoulder and the rest for his old injuries.

Sam was grabbed from behind just as he was putting the finishing touches on his work. He did not see it coming. Strong, forceful hands slammed him hard against a nearby tree. Sam's fragile confidence shattered like glass when he saw Captain McIntyre's angry face only inches before him.

"Where, in hell's fire, 'ave you been?" The captain's sour tobacco breath poured across Sam's face. "Answer me or, I swear, I'll break every worthless bone in your feeble body!"

Sam had enough trouble controlling the wave of nausea that suddenly gripped him. Giving Captain McIntyre an answer was only a secondary objective. Sam was relieved when Pete interrupted the Captain's interrogation by pointing out the lifeless body of the wild man lying nearby.

"Sam, did you do this?"

"Aye, Mr. Rexley." Sam's voice was a knot in his throat. "I did it."

McIntyre looked around to see what Pete was talking about. With his anger set aside for the moment, he released his hold on Sam. He went over to take a closer look at the body on the ground.

"And with 'is own knife, too." McIntyre pulled the knife from the wild man's stomach. He looked up at Sam. "If George ain't king, I'll be damned. This 'ere was a daring thing you done. Frankly, I never thought you had the guts."

"I had no choice, Capt'n." Sam finally stood away from the tree. "These wild men are mad. They are obsessed with killing. I have never seen anything like it. And it matters not what you do to them, they keep coming at you, and coming at you, and coming at you. You have to kill them to stop them. There was another one out at the clearing. I almost broke his arm off, and he still came at me. I finally shot him."

"Aye. We saw 'im, or what was left of 'im anyway."

Pete moved away from the wild man's body and stood beside Sam. "This one looks like he's been shot, too. Which did you do first? I mean, what finally killed him?"

"I shot him first. But he, too, kept coming at me. You should have seen it, Mr. Rexley. This one was worse than the first one. The knife there is what killed him. He fell on it after I hit him."

Pete was looking closely at Sam for the first time. "You look as though you've been through hell yourself. Are you alright, lad?"

"I'm fine. Just a few cuts and bruises here and there. Nothing a little rum won't cure."

"Tell me somethin', Sam." McIntyre wiped blood from the wild man's knife on the ground and stood up. "Why didn't you finish this one off with your pistol? Has all this killin' and swashbucklin' gone to your head? You reckon you're some Sir Galahad or something?"

"No, Capt'n. Honestly, I've never been more frightened in all my life." Sam explained to the captain why he did not use his pistol. He recapped almost every important thing he had done since starting across the clearing.

It was his story, his adventure. He told it in his own, carefully chosen words. He tried to let the captain know he was not as simple as he had assumed. He mentioned his laborious trek across the clearing, all for the sake of locating Captain McIntyre's slaves. He omitted his short nap, which he promised himself he would never do again. He gave selected details about his battle with the first wild man, the pursuit by the second one, and the battle that had just ended.

Then, for Captain McIntyre's strategic benefit, Sam told as much as he could remember about the two warrior armies he saw. He estimated their combined strength. He emphasized how well-organized the armies had appeared. He highlighted the impressive leadership of the armies. He tried to make Captain McIntyre understand that those armies could be serious obstacles if confronted.

But Sam saved the best for last. He finally described the little native boy who was transferred between the armies. As he told his story, he grew more and more confident in his facts. He unnecessarily repeated some details as he was delighted to hold the captain's undivided attention.

"About that native boy," McIntyre asked, "are you sure it was the one that belongs to me?"

"Aye, Capt'n. I am pretty sure of it. He was the same size, about the same age. And he looked like one of your runaways."

"What about the other darkies that were with 'im? Did you see any o' them?"

"I've seen neither hide nor hair of any of them, Capt'n. If you ask me, I think they are probably halfway back to wherever the Batushi found them by now."

"Now what did I tell you about your worthless opinion?" McIntyre's disposition changed instantly. "I don't want to hear it."

Sam's self-esteem was shattered again. Sam stared at the captain. He was surprised that he had not gained the captain's respect.

"Me darkies can't be too far," McIntyre spoke to no one in particular. He stared off in the direction that Sam had indicated. "And, with me chains still on 'em, they can't move that fast. They 'ave to be nearby."

"Capt'n," Pete was seriously questioning the captain's sanity. "That is what you said last time, before we crossed the clearing. What's your plan now? Are you still going after them?"

McIntyre thought a moment. Whatever he was thinking, he was considering it very carefully. He finally turned to Sam. "How long ago was it when you saw these warrior armies?"

"About twenty or thirty minutes ago, I reckon."

"Aye. We're agoin' after that there darkie-boy. He's the key. He knows where the rest of me slaves are. And he's agonna tell us too."

"What? After what I just told you?" Sam couldn't help speaking up despite Captain McIntyre's previous instructions. He had to say something. "Capt'n, the Batushi are going after your other slaves. Why don't you send them after this handful, too?"

"'Cause they're right up yonder through those trees." McIntyre pointed angrily. "I mean, we're this close to 'em. I can feel it. Besides, I owe that little darkie-boy a lesson."

Sam looked desperately at Pete for support. He saw only a look of exasperation on Pete's face. He turned back to McIntyre. "Capt'n, if you knew what I know, you wouldn't do this."

"Lad, on the day you know anything worthwhile, that damned melon head o' yours will rot wide open." McIntyre stared directly into Sam's face, as if to convey his final warning. He finally turned and stormed ahead. "You acomin', Pete?"

$$— 24 —$$

THE YULULU BONE

Sam and Pete followed Captain McIntyre through the forest in the direction the warrior armies had gone. They lagged further behind the captain. A strong sense of danger affected the two men. Both knew that the captain was exercising poor judgment. What he was leading them into was not right.

"Mr. Rexley," Sam's voice was low. He did not want the captain to overhear. "This is all wrong. You must talk to the Capt'n. I think he's going to get us killed."

Pete agreed with Sam. He said nothing at first. He continued to walk with his head down, deep in thought. He had butt heads with the captain before. It was usually a losing situation. After a moment, he finally gave Sam a pat on the shoulder. "I'll see what I can do."

Sam and Pete took brisk steps to catch up with Captain McIntyre. Pete took that time to put the final touches on his cautious approach to the captain. When he finally caught up with the captain, he still wasn't sure what he would say. His only recourse was to tell the captain how he and Sam felt.

"Capt'n," Pete began, "you need to think this through a wee bit more."

"Think what through, Pete?"

"Has it occurred to you that you don't know what awaits you up ahead?"

"I reckon I know all I need to know. Speak your mind. What are you atryin' to say?"

"I can understand how anxious you are to get your slaves back. All of that's fine and dandy. Sam and me, we are behind you one hundred percent. We just think you are going about it all wrong. If you continue the way you're going, we want no part of it."

McIntyre stopped walking. He turned to face his aides and chuckled. "Sounds like I got meself a mutiny on me hands, Mr. Rexley?"

"Damn it, Capt'n, no one said anything about a mutiny." Pete's frustration was finally boiling to the top. "Would you just stop and listen to reason for a moment?"

There was a smirk on the captain's face. "I'm alistenin'."

"This boy that opened up your pen and got you so fired up; Sam just told you that he was right in the middle of two warrior armies. Suppose they have a village or tribe up ahead? I don't know about you, but I got the clearest impression that the boy found his people. We can't storm into a village just like that and expect to get what we want. There's no telling who they are. For all we know, they could be wild men, head-hunters, … "

"Aye, or cannibals," added Sam.

"And the three of us," continued Pete, "we certainly can't handle two warrior armies."

"I really wouldn't worry none about all that, Pete." The smirk on McIntyre's face would not leave. "We'll go in peaceful-like, get the boy, and come right back out."

"Capt'n, you know it ain't gonna be that easy." Pete took his hat off and scratched his head. He felt that McIntyre was still oversimplifying a very serious task. "You are a damned good haggler – one of the best I have ever seen. But, if you don't mind me saying so, you are not that good. What if these natives are violent? We would have to shoot our way free."

"It won't come to that, Pete. Take me word for it. Now, me mind is made up. There will be no talkin' me out of it. Let's just go in, take our chances, 'n see what 'appens."

Pete stepped away from McIntyre in total frustration. He glanced at Sam before he turned back to McIntyre. "If you think you can pull this off, Capt'n, I have to tell you, you are one arrogant son of a bitch."

McIntyre laughed out loud. Sam and Pete could only look at each other in confusion. As McIntyre regained control of his laughter, he removed his backpack. "I want you boys to just settle down. Let's take a break here." He pointed to a small grassy area just off the trail. "Here, sit down. Let me explain something to you."

Sam and Pete did as they were told. After they were comfortable, McIntyre took a seat on his backpack. He made himself comfortable as if he were preparing to tell another one of his adventure stories. "Hear me out, now. If these natives up ahead are wild, we'll learn that soon enough. We won't go into their village right away. I'll get help from the Batushi. I give you me word."

"Well, that's a relief." Sam didn't mean that to come out the way it sounded.

Pete quickly followed Sam's comment with a question. "Capt'n, what makes you so confident the Batushi will still help you? By now, they probably figured out what you did to them. They would love to get their hands on you about now."

All this was new to Sam. "Why? What did you do, Capt'n?"

"Those flintlocks that he gave the Batushi," Pete explained, "half of them were defective."

"Defective. What do you mean by defective?"

"As in worthless." Pete was talking to Sam, but he was looking at McIntyre. "I'm truly surprised the Batushi went after that other group that escaped. I would love to hear how you pulled that off."

"Well, I'm about to tell you." McIntyre reached into his jacket pocket and pulled out the necklace that Chief Jagotta had given him. He held the necklace up so that the center trinket, the dried bone, swung freely. "Either of you lads know what this is?"

"It's a necklace," said Sam, "with a dried-up, old bone in the middle."

McIntyre jerked the necklace down from display and glared at Sam. The smirk he held finally disappeared. "You know, I finally figured out what bothers me about you. You're just so god-awful simple. And you're so damned open about it. You'd think that anybody as simple as you would 'ave the decency to keep your mouth shut sometimes."

"Leave him be, Capt'n." Pete was still eying the necklace. "What is that exactly, if it ain't just a dried-up old bone?"

McIntyre held the trinket up again. The smirk crept back on his face. "It's an earmark of a sort. Because I hold this bone, I'm an honorary chief of the Batushi tribe. All I 'ave to do is tell 'em what I want, and it will be done."

"Just like that?"

"Just like that. And there's no limit. They will follow me very word to the letter or die tryin."

"How, on earth, did you receive such an honor?"

McIntyre chuckled again. "Let's just say, the Batushi think I deserve it."

"How do you know it works?"

"It's already been tested. Remember when I sent the Batushi back out to fetch me six more slaves to fill up me fifth pen? They tried. As I understand it, they captured five but had to kill four of 'em. That's how we ended up with that scrawny little darkie-boy. Anyways, that was the first test. Then, after the slaves escaped, I sent the Batushi after the bulk of 'em. They set out instantly, no questions asked. It works alright. With this bone, I hold as much authority over the Batushi tribe as Chief Jagotta himself."

"Let us suppose that you have stumbled on a magic lamp, a magic genie inside, and all that, Capt'n." Pete was beginning to have some disturbing suspicions. "Something is still not sitting right with me. I've heard of something like this before. What do you call that thing?"

"Pete, this 'ere is what you call a Yululu bone."

The instant Pete heard this, he scrambled to his feet. He instinctively tugged at Sam's shoulder, suggesting he should move away, too.

McIntyre's smirk turned into laughter after Pete's reaction. "I reckon you've heard of a Yululu bone?"

"Aye. I've heard some stories about them. I had no idea that a Yululu bone was real. And just like the genie in Aladdin's lamp, it ain't what you think it is. The genie is evil. He only grants your wishes because you freed him from the lamp. Don't you know? That thing is a death sentence. It will get you killed!"

By now, Sam was on his feet too. He followed Pete's example. He was still unaware of the bone's significance but was putting it all together. "Chief Jagotta returned to camp the other day to give you that necklace and make you an honorary chief." Sam giggled. "And he didn't bother to tell you it would kill you?"

"Of course not, Sam," Pete answered. "The Capt'n ain't supposed to know."

"Pete, Sam, let me put your minds at ease." McIntyre stuffed the Yululu bone into his pocket to suggest to Sam and Pete that it was all right to sit back down. "You're right, both of you. Jagotta does want me dead. And no, I ain't supposed to know that the bone is deadly. Hell's fire, that is why I say I'm a whole two or three steps ahead of that fat ignorant fool."

"There is no such thing as being two or three steps ahead of death. Dead is dead. That fat, ignorant fool is preparing to kill you." Pete resumed sitting on the ground, slightly farther away from the captain. "All the stories I heard about Yululu bones – none of them are pretty. Every single story ends with the death of whoever owns one of those bones."

"And do you know why? 'Cause each of the poor bastards never learned there's a secret to staying alive."

"A secret?" Sam's curiosity was piqued. "Do you know the secret, Capt'n?"

"Aye. It's quite simple." McIntyre fished around in his other pocket and pulled out a twist of tobacco. He bit off a piece. "All I 'ave to do is get rid of the bone before the next full moon rises."

Sam and Pete looked at each other. Pete turned to the captain. "Is that it? Are you sure?"

"That's too easy," added Sam.

"It's all part of the trap," McIntyre explained, his jaw bulging with tobacco. "In the first place, most folk who possess a Yululu bone only think the Batushi has given them a great honor. They are blinded by all o' that honor. They don't realize that they've been given a death sentence. That's where they make their big mistake and the main reason all owners of a Yululu bone end up dead."

Unlike himself, McIntyre began telling one of the many stories about a Yululu bone. He told a story about a Frenchman who was given a Yululu bone.

******

"He didn't know that his life had been marked, so he didn't worry about finding any secret.

He just knew that the natives had begun to give him boundless respect. For almost a month, he lived like a king. He ordered the natives to bring him precious gems. The natives went so far as to steal the gems to honor his request. He requested female companionship. The natives made sure he bedded down every night with no less than three beautiful ladies at his side.

"Over a fortnight, this Frenchman became pretty close to one of the women he had been given. According to the story, he fell in love with this woman. And it was that serious, sick love where he wouldn't let her out of sight. Just so happened one day, the woman got caught in a burning hut and couldn't get out. The Frenchman ordered one of the natives to go into the hut to fetch her out. The native did it without hesitation. He got the woman out, but he got badly burned doing it.

"A couple of days later, this native who was suffering from his burns and very near death, was visited by the grateful Frenchman.

They sat all day, talking with each other like two very close friends. Later that evening, the moon rose. When it did, the native casually rose from his deathbed and cut the Frenchman's gut open, just like that. No warning. No anger. I mean, the native killed the Frenchman as routinely as he had laughed and talked with him."

******

"And now, Capt'n," Pete began, "you're telling us that all the Frenchman had to do to stay alive was get rid of the bone?"

"That's exactly what I'm asayin."

"Is there no other way? Why don't you get rid of the bone right now, Capt'n?"

"Why make things difficult, Pete? With this bone, I can do a whole lot of things I couldn't normally do. I promise you, I'll get rid of the bone in due time. Trust me! Besides, the Batushi gave the bone to me. It's me own life that's in jeopardy 'ere, not yours."

"I truly hope you know what you are doing, for your own sake."

25

BORN SON OF THE MFALME

After Tanake had taken the chains and shackles from the Chinchigwe arms, and after Kon-Shambique and Tongda had treated the Chinchigwe, only one of them remained at Kon-Shambique's hut for more treatment – Lobarra Gendeyani. She would have to join the rest of the Chinchigwe later. Right now, behind the birthing curtain, in the rear chamber of Kon-Shambique's hut, she was preparing to give birth to her baby. The birth would occur at any moment.

With her feet planted firmly on the ground, Lobarra sat in a comfortable squat position. To withstand the contractions in her stomach and to keep from falling over, she held tightly to a tall, wooden pole directly in front of her. But at the moment, Lobarra felt that losing her balance was the least of her problems.

On her right, Lobarra allowed Tongda to dab away sweat from her forehead. For this, Lobarra was grateful. Lobarra also listened, half-heartedly, to Tongda's endless stream of words. The words were meant to keep the young Chinchigwe woman's mind relaxed and preoccupied. It wasn't working. Lobarra was much too distracted. For, on her left, was Kon-Shambique.

Kon-Shambique was working with two urns over an open flame. The larger urn was full of boiling water. The smaller urn held a mixture that created a thick fragrant smoke. The smoke and the fragrance filled the chamber. Whether or not these urns had anything to do with Lobarra's condition, Kon-Shambique did not seem to be in any hurry to finish what he was doing and leave.

Lobarra did not like it. She had always believed that childbirth was an affair taken care of strictly by women. Men had no place in it. All her life, she had accepted these beliefs without question. As her contractions became increasingly frequent, it was obvious to Lobarra that Kon-Shambique intended to stay on this side of the birthing curtain. It wasn't right.

Lobarra finally turned to Tongda. She had decided that whatever Tongda was talking about was irrelevant. Lobarra had more immediate concerns. She nodded toward Kon-Shambique and spoke to Tongda in a whisper. "Why is he here?"

Tongda was sensitive enough to understand how Lobarra felt. She anticipated Lobarra's reaction. Tongda was trying to put Lobarra's mind at ease about Kon-Shambique's presence. Lobarra never heard a word she was saying.

Tongda gave Lobarra a reassuring smile. "If you truly wish the Favored Tribesman to leave, he will leave. I will help you deliver your baby. But among the Aukmondi, Kon-Shambique's treatments are cherished."

"In childbirth, too?"

"Yes, in childbirth too." Tongda gave Lobarra a moment to think about it. She could see that Lobarra still had reservations. "Trust him. In his hands, the Supreme Spirit has placed remarkable medicines. Most women, who have given birth with Kon-Shambique's help, tell me that they would have it no other way."

Lobarra was about to continue her objection when one of the strongest contractions gripped her midsection. She closed her eyes tightly and gripped the pole in front of her. She wanted to scream as the pain tore at her inside. She took a deep gulp of air and held her breath.

"Sacred Woman, you must breathe."

Kon-Shambique's voice startled Lobarra. It was such an unexpected occurrence that Lobarra opened her eyes. She saw Kon-Shambique waving the small urn in front of her. The smoke from the urn enveloped her face. Lobarra fought the natural impulse to hold her breath and forced herself to breathe. When she did, the pain began to dissipate. It was a very unnatural sensation. The smoke from the urn seemed to melt the pain away.

"Such a wonderful aroma!" Lobarra tried to look into the urn, but the smoke was too thick. "What is that?"

"It is an herbal mixture. It is something my grandmother taught me."

Lobarra closed her eyes again. This time, she wasn't in pain. She was relaxing in a wave of euphoric pleasure.

"Now, Sacred Woman," Kon-Shambique handed the urn to Tonga. He moved to a kneeling position behind Lobarra. "If I am allowed to touch you, we will try to remove the rest of your pain."

Lobarra nodded her approval. Kon-Shambique began to massage Lobarra's back, near her shoulders, just below her ears. Like the magic imparted by a true witch doctor, a tremendous release washed over Lobarra, from her head to her toes. It was such a pleasurable sensation that Lobarra took her hands from the pole and wrapped her arms around herself.

"Did your grandmother teach this to you, too?"

"I am who I am because of my grandmother."

Tongda smiled knowingly. She leaned close to Lobarra's ear and whispered. "Can you keep a secret?"

Lobarra kept her eyes closed. She refused to let go of the sensation she felt. "You would be surprised how well I can keep a secret."

"Among the Aukmondi, I suspect that many women only have babies to have Kon-Shambique attend the delivery."

At this statement, Lobarra opened her eyes again. She looked directly into Tongda's face, but then realized Tongda was only joking. The broad smile across her face was cut short by another gentle contraction. Lobarra took a deep breath to recover the feeling she had. The feeling returned instantly.

"Kon-Shambique," Lobarra allowed the euphoria to envelope her again, "how long have you been doing this?"

"I do not know, Sacred Woman." He continued to massage her shoulders. "I do remember, my very first time helping with childbirth was when I was ten. I helped to deliver my cousin into the world."

"Seriously?"

"Yes. My mother's sister and I were working alone one day in the olive groves deep in the valley. Completely without warning, my aunt began to give birth. She stooped to the ground and tried sending me back to the village for help. But we were too far out. I knew that, even if I returned to the village, help would not be returned to my aunt in time. I did not feel comfortable leaving her alone out there. So, I stayed with her. I asked the Supreme Spirit to help me do what must be done. That evening, the two of us walked back to the village without a single olive. Instead, I carried my cousin in my arms."

Lobarra was rapidly becoming used to the idea of having Kon-Shambique nearby. His soft-spoken manner and gentleness were qualities Lobarra was beginning to accept and enjoy. His magical effect on her was of great value. She dropped all her original inhibitions.

At that point, someone could be heard on the other side of the birthing curtain, in the front chamber. At Kon-Shambique's nod, Tongda set the smoky urn down and went to see who could be so untimely.

When Tongda pulled back the curtain, she was surprised to see Ramuza and Adaulah in the front chamber. She was more surprised to see Adaulah's condition. She rushed to the young Aukmondi's aid.

"Sacred Spirit! What happened to him?" She asked Ramuza.

Ramuza set Adaulah down on the edge of a cot. "He fell and bumped his head. Will you help him?"

"Of course, Great Creation."

Tongda had worked with Kon-Shambique long enough to become skilled in many medical treatments. She looked briefly at the wound on Adaulah's left temple, assessed what needed to be done, and quickly went to several places around the chamber to gather the materials that she would need.

After Tongda settled again at Adaulah's side, she cleaned the wound on Adaulah's face. Ramuza looked on. Both of them were relieved to find that the wound was just a bloody abrasion.

"With a thorough cleaning, a bandage, and a few days healing, you will be as good as new." Tongda smiled at Adaulah.

"Thank you, Sacred Woman."

"You look tired. How do you feel?"

"I feel …," Adaulah searched for the words to describe best how he felt. "I feel unhappy. And I feel sleepy. The Chinchigwe and I walked through the forest most of the night."

"The Chinchigwe?" Tongda stopped doing what she was doing. She stared into Adaulah's face. She had heard Ameh's complete story. There was no mention of Adaulah. She had to confirm what she had just heard. "You were with the Chinchigwe?"

"Yes, Sacred Woman."

Tongda carefully wrapped a bandage around Adaulah's head. She glanced at Ramuza as she tied it off. It occurred to her that Ramuza knew Adaulah was in danger when he delivered the Chinchigwe. It was clear to her now why he left so quickly.

Tongda was also beginning to piece together the ordeal that Adaulah had just gone through. The Young Creation had survived a serious tragedy. "You did not reach the Village of Teachers. How did you meet the Chinchigwe?"

"On the way to the Village we were attacked by slave hunters. The Green Warriors Thula, Lupwa, Modano, and Wazhomo were all killed. I was taken captive and thrown into an animal pen. That is where I met the Chinchigwe."

Tongda knew the rest of the story from there. For the first time, she understood the enormity of Adaulah's condition and situation. She stopped her treatment. She could do nothing but listen to Adaulah's story.

"The deaths of those warriors," Adaulah was saying, "were unnecessary. They did not have to die. I did not have to go to the Village of Teachers. I could have waited. I could have waited until … until a later time. If I had waited, they would be alive right now."

"Maybe so, Little Creation. But you could not have waited long enough. Even if you were an Adult Creation, you still would have needed warriors to escort you safely to the Village and back."

"Even so, four warriors died for something I wanted. I feel it is not right."

Tongda knew that the wrong perspective was poisoning Adaulah's attitude. There were things his young mind was overlooking. Even though she and Kon-Shambique had spent much time giving advice and moral support to the Aukmondi people and were quite experienced in doing so, Ramuza was the best person to advise Adaulah right now. She looked at Ramuza and stepped back.

Ramuza lifted Adaulah from the cot and stood him on his feet. He looked into the Young Creation's eyes and spoke to him firmly, but not without understanding.

"Adaulah," he said, "it is true. Those warriors died to save your life. But they did not die for you alone."

"What do you mean, Great Creation?"

"Because those warriors died, you lived. Because you live, the Chinchigwe are free. Those warriors allowed you to continue living, learning, and growing toward a time when you will be Mfalme for all the Aukmondi people. It is time that you begin to live, not for yourself, but for all the Aukmondi people and all the children of the Aukmondi people. You must begin to live for the day when a whole tribe of people will look to you, follow you, depend on you, and love you."

"Like you, Great Creation?"

Ramuza acknowledged his son with only a small smile. "It is a great responsibility – the greatest you will ever have. You must not take it lightly. From this day forward, you must understand that you are forced to live a very unnatural life, which you cannot change. There are many sacrifices you must make. For your own strength of mind, for your own sense of purpose, and most importantly, for the sake of your people, you must accept this responsibility. Embrace it. Love it. Make it your greatest passion."

"I understand, Great Creation. But … suppose I do not grow to be as worthy as you?"

Ramuza squeezed Adaulah's shoulder affectionately. "The Supreme Spirit has allowed you to be born son of the Mfalme. Know what that truly means, and you will become worthy."

"I will be worthy, Mfalme. I am your firstborn son. I will earn the name Mfalme. And I will begin by honoring those Green Warriors as I said I would."

Tongda began putting her things away. "Honor those warriors and, I am sure, the Supreme Spirit will smile at your thoughtfulness. Their untimely death is a painful experience, and we will miss them. Just remember, the pain of death is felt only by those who still live. Let us remember the great things those warriors have done and how they have touched us in their time."

"Sacred Woman," Adaulah was beginning to feel better already. "Do you think that the Great Creation Kon-Shambique, or could you help me with a small ceremony to honor the warriors? I would like to do something like carve their names for all to see on a wall in the Sacred Temple."

"If you return later today, one of us will gladly help you. I suggest you go and get some rest now. If possible, come back some time before the Daily Celebration of Life this evening, and we will see what we can do."

"Thank you, Sacred Woman." Adaulah turned to his father. "Are you going back to the Royal Kraal now, Mfalme?"

"You run ahead. I will catch up with you later. I want to talk with Tongda a moment first."

As soon as Adaulah had left, Ramuza turned his attention to the Chinchigwe. It was time to give them full consideration as he had promised.

"How are our guests?"

"They are tired and hungry. Overall, they are in very good condition considering everything they have been through. With a little food and rest, they will be fine. And the Great Creation, Ameh says that a slave merchant pursues them. Have you decided what you will do to help them?"

"No, I have not. I have been so concerned about Adaulah that I have not given them much thought. I plan to talk with them now, to find out exactly what I can do for them, if anything. I assume the Sacred Woman Rwuva has met with them?"

"Yes, she came by here earlier. It was my understanding that she had arranged to have them taken to one of the cleansing areas of the river to freshen up first. Afterwards, food would be set up for them in the Royal kraal. The Chinchigwe are probably gathering in the Royal Kraal by now."

Ramuza thanked Tongda and prepared to leave. He heard a loud sigh behind the birthing curtain as he headed for the door.

Tongda explained. "All but one of the Chinchigwe are gathering in the Royal Kraal. Only the Sacred Woman Lobarra Gendeyani is still here. Her baby is due soon. If you will excuse me, Mfalme, I must see if Kon-Shambique needs help."

"Of course, Sacred Woman."

As Ramuza exited the hut, he heard the cry of a newborn behind the birthing curtain.

— **26** —

A TRAGEDY MUST RUN ITS COURSE

In the huge celebration area in the Royal Kraal, preparations for the Aukmondi Daily Celebration of Life were well under way. The people from the Pogobi kraal had already built several large campfires throughout the area. Socializing cliques from the Pogobi and other kraals were already forming near and around these campfires. These activities represented the early phases of this evening's daily celebration.

In the back of the celebration area, at the very rear of the Royal Kraal, the four huge, mud-grass huts of Ramuza, Rwuva, Olabisi, and Kharaambi sat in a cove of trees. These huts, known throughout the valley as "the four huts of the Ncobbas", faced the celebration area and formed a huge semicircle. They were centered by the royal dais, a collection of blankets, pillows, rugs, and other decorative comforts in a canopy-covered area reserved for the royal family. The four huts and the dais represented the seat of power in the Aukmondi Valley. There was no more appropriate place for the people to come together to celebrate life and solve imminent problems.

After the Chinchigwe left Kon-Shambique's kraal, Rwuva's aides and warrior escorts took them to the Aukmondi River for their complete refreshment. This particular portion of the river itself was used for bathing and cleaning. Water from various tributaries had been extracted for drinking. These refreshments were long overdue. The Chinchigwe appreciated every moment of the experience. The people were reluctant to leave when the escorting warriors finally told the Chinchigwe it was time to move on to the Royal Kraal. The aides promised them that, if they wished, they could return after the talk with the Mfalme.

All of the Chinchigwe, except for Lobarra, sat on the ground in front of the royal dais. With the celebration area and merriment behind them, the Chinchigwe had gathered in front of Ramuza's chieftain stool, an intricately carved wooden seat which sat in the very center of the dais. Traditionally, only the Mfalme is allowed to sit upon this stool. The stool looked profoundly bare as the Chinchigwe waited for the arrival of the Mfalme.

To the immediate left of the Chinchigwe was a small and exclusive campfire. It was not as large as any of the fires burning behind them. This fire was only meant to complement the Aukmondi food dishes prepared especially for them.

As the Sacred Woman Rwuva had promised, the Chinchigwe were served an assortment of Aukmondi dishes. All were quite filling and satisfying. The most well-liked was a compatible mixture of various vegetable chunks, some boiled and some raw. Also well-liked was a couscous dish, seasoned and mixed with a powder of finely crushed nuts. Ameh, realizing his own mistake, cautioned the other Chinchigwe not to eat too much, too fast. Their stomachs still need time to heal after the tainted food provided by the slave merchant.

Now, with food before them, only two of the original requests that the Chinchigwe had asked for remained unanswered. The first was rest. The rest was forthcoming. After the Chinchigwe had eaten and talked with the Mfalme, they would be free to rest for as long as they desired.

The second unanswered request, however, was the big question on the minds of the Chinchigwe. It was the most important question of all. They sat before the seat of power in the Aukmondi Valley to learn what the Mfalme would do about their protection.

None of the Chinchigwe had any indications as to what Ramuza planned to do. The general consensus was that Mfalme did not know himself. The Chinchigwe knew that Ramuza needed much more information before making a wise decision.

This did not prevent the Chinchigwe from second-guessing the Mfalme. As they ate the food before them, they discussed the problem. They devised a few speculations based on their previous encounter with the Mfalme. Because Ramuza was adamant about protecting his own people, the Chinchigwe speculations were eventually narrowed down to two probable outcomes.

Either the Aukmondi Mfalme would treat the Chinchigwe, put them back on their feet again, and in time, release them back into the wilderness, or he would turn them back over to the slave merchant. These were essentially his only practical alternatives.

If the Chinchigwe were released into the wilderness, where would they go? Some suggested that they could try to resettle in the area where their former village had been. They were, at least, familiar with the area. That, in itself, was an advantage. The majority, however, considered their former village as just another part of the wilderness now. And the wilderness was the wilderness. Familiarity would only retard their inevitable fate.

If they were released back into the wilderness, they could be recaptured or killed. They were completely vulnerable people now. Even if Mfalme Ncobba loaned them warriors to protect their village, such a loan could not last long enough. Because the Chinchigwe were such a small number, it would take them almost forever to become independent again. The loan of warriors was impractical.

As for the other probability, the Chinchigwe feared that being returned to the slave merchant was the likelier of the two alternatives. Mfalme Ncobba did not seem so insensitive that he could truly abandon them. He would not release them into the wilderness to eventually die off. Being a tribal leader, he may feel that the most practical way to protect his people and keep the Chinchigwe alive is to stand back and let the merchant have what he wants.

At first, Ameh was the most optimistic of the group. His nature was to focus his mind and heart and move toward the best outcome. Ameh was also a realist. The more he listened to practicality and common sense, the more his optimism eroded. He was beginning to see that the best days of the Chinchigwe people had already come and gone. The bloodlines of all the Chinchigwe ancestors were nearing an end.

On the other hand, Twese's pessimism was now turning into optimism. Instead of practicality and common sense, Twese's optimism was rooted in one undeniable fact. He knew that the merchant considered Adaulah his property, too. If the merchant were willing to send slave hunters out to replace six dead people, then surely he would not let Adaulah go so easily. Twese felt stronger than ever. Mfalme Ncobba could not protect his son without providing some shelter to the Chinchigwe.

Just as the Chinchigwe were finishing their small feast, Embabi happened to look back across the celebration area. There were more and more groups of people now. All over the area, groups were gathering. Groups of children were playing; groups of men and women were talking – some laughing and joking, others apparently in more serious discussions.

In the distance, Embabi saw one of the groups slightly different from the others. It was a royal entourage working its way across the celebration area toward the Chinchigwe. Embabi recognized Adaulah, Rwuva, and Rwuva's four daughters. Six other women in the group, as well as a host of escorting warriors and aides, Embabi did not recognize.

Adaulah was the center of the group. He was not close enough to the Chinchigwe to be overheard, but he seemed to be talking nonstop. Whatever he was saying, he held everyone's undivided attention. It was understandable. The young Aukmondi had a lot to tell.

From halfway across the celebration area, Adaulah saw the Chinchigwe. When he did, he darted from the group and came running. He was obviously very happy to see them again, and his behavior showed it, like a puppy wagging its tail. Adaulah eagerly found a place to sit on the ground between Ameh and Twese. With an infectious smile on his face, he made himself comfortable.

"What happened to you after we were separated?" He asked. "I came looking for you, but I could not find you. I got lost. I made a smoke signal. Did you see it? Did you know that a Wabanga chased me? I ran from him faster than I ran from the rhinoceros. How did you find the village? I was afraid you would go back to find your village."

"When we were separated, we were separated well." Ameh finally got a word in. "A lot has happened since then. But that is all behind us now. Fate has joined us once again. We are so happy to see you are safe and well."

"I am happy you are safe and well here in the valley."

Anticipating the moment, Ameh rose to his feet. Adaulah and the rest of the Chinchigwe followed his example. With his now ever-present staff, Ameh gestured toward the approaching entourage. "Are these beautiful women the sisters that you told us about?"

"Yes, Great Creation, most of them. The two Sacred Women in front are my mothers, Rwuva Azinti and Olabisi Sheetswa. The other nine are my sisters."

Adaulah ran back out to meet the group. He positioned himself between his mothers. He took their hands and eagerly led them toward the Chinchigwe. "These are my friends that I told you about."

"Yes. I have met your friends already," said Rwuva.

"You did?" Adaulah was a little surprised at first, but then he realized that the Chinchigwe had reached the valley long before he had. He turned to Olabisi. "Have you met them too, Sacred Mother?"

"No, Little Creation. I have not." Olabisi smiled. She could tell Adaulah did not want to be left in the dark about any unfolding event. She played along with his excitement.

"This is my Sacred Mother, Olabisi Sheetswa." Adaulah addressed Ameh and Twese but spoke in general to all the Chinchigwe. "She prepared the food you are eating. I recognize her vegetables and couscous. No one makes these dishes the way she does. They are so good. Did you like them?"

"The food was delicious. I cannot remember the last time I ate so well. I may have over-eaten." Ameh addressed Olabisi directly. "I speak for all the Chinchigwe. Thank you."

"You are welcome, Great Creation."

"It is a pleasure to meet you finally," Ameh glanced at the women behind Rwuva and Olabisi, "and all the daughters of the Mfalme."

In addition to Rwuva's four daughters, whom the Chinchigwe had already met, there were five others. Among them were a set of twins slightly younger than Rwuva's daughters, one daughter who was younger still, and finally, another set of twins only slightly older than Adaulah.

"Adaulah has told us so much about you," Ameh said. "We feel as though we know you, all of you, already."

"I hope he did not talk your ears off. He is quite capable of doing so."

"He and his talk are a pleasure. He is a godsend, and we are truly grateful to him. Had it not been for him, we would probably be preparing for a long, unwanted voyage across the great waters."

"Ameh," Twese edged into the conversation, "you realize, we may still have to take that voyage."

There was an awkward moment of silence. Ameh broke the silence when he quickly introduced Twese and most of the Chinchigwe to Olabisi. He ended his introductions by qualifying Twese's last statement. "Sometimes, it seems, a tragedy must run its course. A voyage across the great waters may be inevitable."

Olabisi picked up on the seriousness of the conversation. She asked the Chinchigwe to be seated again. Adaulah assumed the original position between Ameh and Twese. Olabisi and Rwuva circled the Chinchigwe. Each settled on grass-woven pillows on either side of Ramuza's chieftain stool. The nine daughters took this opportunity to excuse themselves. They disbursed among the huts of the Ncobbas; each daughter went to the hut of their respective natural mother.

After the Chinchigwe were comfortable again, Olabisi addressed Ameh again. "Please explain, Great Creation. What do you see that is so inevitable?"

"Ameh, allow me," Twese answered instead. He and Ameh agreed. Twese, however, did not see it as something so inevitable. There was still a way out. "We intend to ask Mfalme Ncobba for protection against our enemies. It all depends on what he decides to do. If he refuses our request, we feel the voyage is inevitable."

"Who are these enemies that you speak of?"

When Twese saw the genuine concern on Olabisi's face, it occurred to him that she and Rwuva probably knew nothing about the merchant and his alliance with the slave hunters. "Please accept my apology. It seems Adaulah has not told you the whole story."

"Kon-Shambique mentioned a slave merchant," said Rwuva. "Is this the enemy?"

"Yes," Ameh spoke up. "But there is more. And I am afraid the situation is much more complicated than it sounds."

Just as the conversation was heating up, the whole atmosphere in the celebration area seemed to change instantly. A noticeable energy was moving through the people. The various noises and conversations dropped off briefly, only to be replaced by excited announcements of the Mfalme. Ramuza had entered the Royal Kraal and was working across the celebration area. His entourage flanked him – a handful of subordinated warriors and aides. Everyone, including the Chinchigwe, rose again as the Mfalme and his entourage approached.

Without a word, Ramuza walked right past the Chinchigwe. He acknowledged them with only a glance. He went directly to his hut and disappeared inside.

Word of the Mfalme's arrival somehow reached his nine daughters. While Ramuza was in his hut, all nine of his daughters came from various locations and regrouped. Dressed like true princesses, they made their way over to the royal dais and, like their mothers, each found pillows to sit on.

Attention was drawn away from the dais when Ramuza emerged from his hut a few moments later. He was now without his black cloak, spear, shield, and belted knife. The Mfalme had quickly redressed for a different occasion.

All eyes were on the Mfalme as he made his way onto the dais and stood before the Chinchigwe. Ramuza greeted Rwuva and Olabisi as his entourage joined the other warriors and aides already gathered around the dais. With everyone apparently in place, Ramuza finally sat on his chieftain's stool.

The Chinchigwe watched the Aukmondi Mfalme from the moment he emerged from his hut. All the while, they tried to sense his attitude. They still found him unreadable. It was impossible to tell if his attitude was positive or negative. Did he sympathize with the Chinchigwe?

"Mfalme, may I speak?" Ameh felt a responsibility to speak up.

"You are among the Aukmondi. Please, speak freely."

"We want to thank you for all you and your people have done for us. Please convey our gratitude to Tanake for the freedom from the shackles and chains; to Kon-Shambique and Tongda for their medical treatments and counsel; and Rwuva and Olabisi for their hospitality and food – we are truly grateful. Now we must know if you have decided what to do about us. Will you grant our final request?"

Ramuza said nothing at first, a noted characteristic. He sat back and looked thoughtfully at the pleading faces of the Chinchigwe. He looked at his son, who sat in the middle of them. It seemed so symbolic of the whole situation.

"I need to know more about this merchant who pursues you." Ramuza finally said.

"The slave merchant is accompanied by two of his aides. No doubt, they stalk the forest this very moment, hunting for us."

"Surely, there is more than the merchant and two aides."

The Chinchigwe needed Ramuza's help. They would be hopeless if they did not get that help. Ameh wanted to do everything possible to get that help. This included telling the Mfalme every helpful thing that he knew. "The merchant captured us with the help of a tribe of slave hunters. We believe that the merchant and the leader of these slave hunters already have an alliance. We feel that the hunters will return if the merchant asks."

"Great Creation," Ramuza leaned forward, "do you know who these slave hunters are? Of what tribe are they?"

"Regrettably, we are not sure."

"During your encounter with the slave hunters, did you see anything that might help to identify them?"

"I am sorry, Mfalme. I suppose all of us were in a state of panic and shock. We were too shaken to study our captors at the time. All that we can say is that the hunters all carried thunder-sticks. For this reason, many of us suspect that the hunters are from the Batushi tribe."

"The Batushi are not the only slave hunters to carry thundersticks."

"No, but they are the largest. The way our village was taken, it would have to be a very large tribe."

Ramuza sat back again. Once again, his eyes scanned the faces before him as he considered his options.

While Ramuza thought, Twese placed his hand on Ameh's arm. It was his silent way of asking to speak with the Mfalme. Ameh had strong reservations, so he reluctantly gave his permission.

"Mfalme," Twese began, "there has been talk among us. We have been wondering what you will do with us if you decide not to give us protection. Will you send us back into the wilderness? Many of us honestly feel that, without your protection, you have no choice but to hand us over to the merchant."

"As I told you before, Forcible Creation, I can not and will not jeopardize my people. I will ensure the security of this valley, even if I have to do one or the other."

"It is as we expected." Twese heard a firmness and conviction in Ramuza's voice that almost frightened him. He glanced at Adaulah before he spoke again. "Mfalme, you must know that the merchant thinks Adaulah belongs to him, too."

With this statement, all the Aukmondi who heard it rumbled. Rwuva showed the most physical reaction when she gasped and placed her hand over her mouth. Everyone, Rwuva and Olabisi, looked toward Ramuza to see his reaction.

"Then, it is clear." Ramuza leaned forward. "The Chinchigwe will, no doubt, benefit. If the merchant comes for my son, I will deal with him appropriately."

— 27 —

SUCH INNOCENCE, SUCH BRAVERY

This time, the rumble of voices came from the Chinchigwe. Ramuza's statement was a minor victory for them. It wasn't quite what they had requested, but it was a step in their favor. With Ramuza's ultimate concern for his son, the merchant would encounter a major obstacle in gaining access to the Chinchigwe.

Hearing that he was a key to the Chinchigwe problem, Adaulah stood up. He approached his father. "Great Creation, do not be concerned. If the merchant comes for me, I will get away."

"Adaulah, Little Creation." It was a gentle reprimand from his mother, Rwuva.

"I did it before, Sacred Mother. I can do it again. As the Mfalme has taught me, I live for the Aukmondi people. I must stay free. I will stay free for them."

"Such innocence. Such bravery." Ameh could only smile. "Mfalme Ncobba, you must not take the young one's words lightly. Did he tell you how he freed us from the merchant's pen?"

"No, he did not." Ramuza leaned back on his chieftain's stool. He turned to Adaulah, looking for more details.

Adaulah smiled and shrugged. "We did not belong there."

"After the slave hunters captured us," Ameh began, "we were placed in an animal pen. The slave hunters had been paid with more of those thundersticks, and it seemed their job was done. They left us alone with the merchant and his two aides.

"During that first night, three of our people died. That next morning, I learned there was an alliance between the merchant and the slave hunters. The Mfalme of the slave hunters returned to the merchant's camp. I do not know if the merchant summoned him or if he just returned because he wanted to. Whatever the reason, the hunter gave the merchant a gift to seal their alliance."

"How do you know that it was a gift?" Ramuza asked.

"They were right outside the pen. I heard them talking."

"The merchant spoke so loudly," added Twese, "we all heard them. Everyone in the camp should have heard them. But the merchant sounded angry to me."

"He was, indeed, angry," Ameh explained. "He cursed the Mfalme. Still, he called the gift a token of appreciation from the hunter. I also learned that the merchant was determined to have a certain number of captives. He ordered the Mfalme to send his hunters back out to find enough people to fill the pen, including replacements for the three of us who died. They returned the next day with Adaulah."

"My son is but one person. Was he expected to fill the merchant's pen?"

It was suddenly clear to Adaulah what had happened then. He looked up at his father. "Great Creation, the Green Warriors Thula and Lupwa, and I were all supposed to be part of the replacements."

"Then, thanks to your warriors, the merchant only got one replacement," Ameh continued. "He found it necessary to send the hunters out yet again. This time, Adaulah had slipped from his shackles before they could return. That very night, we threw him from the pen."

"I have never been thrown that high before." Adaulah demonstrated with his hands. "When I came down, I hit the ground hard. It hurt at first, but I did not care. I was so happy to get out of that pen."

"Adaulah was free to leave, but he did not. Your brave son, Mfalme, defied the merchant himself to open the gates for the rest of us."

Ramuza looked down at Adaulah. "Little Creation, you did not tell me you opened the doors for the Chinchigwe."

"You did not let me finish, Great Creation." Adaulah collected his thoughts as he returned to sit between Ameh and Twese. "I went around the front of the pen to remove the logs that barred the door. There were three of them. The first two were easy. The last one, I had to get a limb to pry it loose. I could barely move it. When the log was beginning to slide away, the merchant and his aides came running out to stop me. You should have seen the merchant. He had the eyes of a crocodile. His skin was like milk. And his hair was the color of fire. It even covered his face."

Ameh nodded his head in total agreement. "Mfalme, that description of the merchant is flawless."

"The merchant told me to stop", Adaulah continued. "I did not stop."

"The merchant held a thunderstick aimed at your son, Mfalme. Adaulah told us that he was an Honorary Black Warrior. His bravery proves it."

"I just knew that the Chinchigwe had to get out. I removed the log anyway. After that, everything began to happen so fast that I do not remember everything. The next thing I remember, the Chinchigwe and I were removing logs from the other pens."

"There were other pens?"

"Yes, Mfalme. There were four other pens. All of them were full of other people. When they were freed, they asked us to come with them. But your son was determined to find his own village. He insisted that it was not far away. The others were not as confident about the existence of their village. We chose to follow Adaulah. After what he did for us, we could not let him set out alone."

"Your thoughtfulness will not go unrewarded, Great Creation."

"We followed Adaulah until we were separated by the rhinoceros in the wilderness. We later tried to search for him but discovered that Wabanga were stalking us. That is when we thought it was best to come and find you."

28

AN ILL OMEN

At one point during the Chinchigwe audience before Mfalme Ncobba, another small but noticeable entourage entered the Royal Kraal. This group consisted of three Aukmondi Warriors. They caused the usual commotion and drew attention as they maneuvered around the campfires and the merriment and moved across the celebration area toward the four huts of the Ncobbas.

As the warriors drew nearer, the Chinchigwe recognized one of them as Quazzi Kuuza Gembali, the Brown Warrior who had been with Ramuza in the wilderness. Word had already reached the Chinchigwe that Quazzi was the warrior who had literally carried Adaulah back to safety.

On Quazzi's right was a very youthful-looking warrior. When this young warrior finally reached the royal dais and the area where the Chinchigwe were sitting, he readily gave the strangers a silent but friendly greeting. He was noticeably an easygoing individual who was respectful but relaxed in the presence of his Mfalme. His youthfulness and casual manner distracted from the fact that he wore the distinguished high rank of a Royal Warrior.

On Quazzi's left was an attractive female warrior. Alluring, long, and sturdy legs accounted for her tall stature. Her manner in the presence of her Mfalme was also respectful and very relaxed. As she walked past the Chinchigwe toward the dais, she radiated a confidence unlike anything the Chinchigwe had ever seen. She was eventually recognized as the Gray Warrior Kharaambi Nyoka Ncobba, Leader of the Aukmondi Army.

Kharaambi never took her eyes off the Chinchigwe as she circled them. She came to stand before them near Ramuza's right. Because the Chinchigwe were strangers to her, she studied them as she handed her spear and gray shield to a White Warrior. It was at this point that she noticed Adaulah sitting among them. Seeing his face was more of a surprise than seeing the twenty-three unfamiliar faces. She knew something had gone wrong during his trip to the Village of Teachers.

"Adaulah, Little Creation! What are you doing here?"

Adaulah got up again and went over to greet the Gray Warrior. He embraced her warmly, eventually forcing her to kneel to his level. "Slave hunters attacked us, Sacred Mother. All four of the Green Warriors were killed."

Kharaambi looked at Ramuza. She had selected those warriors herself and submitted them for Ramuza's approval. She seemed to take the news of their deaths personally. After Ramuza's silent acknowledgement, she took a moment to dismiss her astonishment. She mentally put the news in perspective before turning back to Adaulah. She looked at the bandage on Adaulah's head. "Are you alright?"

"I am fine, Sacred Mother. This bandage covers only a scratch I got when I fell, running from a Wabanga."

Kharaambi gently touched the bandage on Adaulah's head. The fact that Adaulah was standing before her told Kharaambi that the graces of the Supreme Spirit were at play here. She embraced Adaulah again. "I am very pleased that you could return to us."

After a thoughtful smile, Kharaambi rose to her feet again. She turned her attention back to all the strangers in front of her. "And who are these people, Great Creation?" She asked Ramuza.

"These, Sacred Woman, are the Chinchigwe. I found them during my scouting of the north region. They will be our guests for a day or two until I can decide what to do with them."

"Who speaks for the Chinchigwe?" Kharaambi addressed the group.

Ameh stood up. "I suppose that honor falls to me. I am Ameh Jobabwe."

"Ameh Jobabwe. What happened, Great Creation? Where is your village?"

"Our village is no more, Kharaambi. Slave hunters destroyed it." Ameh gestured to the people around him. "We that you see before you are all that is left of our village and our entire tribe."

Ramuza could see Kharaambi counting the people with her eyes. Her logistical mind was already at work. He volunteered the information she was looking for. "There are twenty-three here, Sacred Woman. There are two more at Kon-Shambique's kraal."

Ameh looked at Ramuza with confusion on his face. He was only aware of Lobarra at Kon-Shambique's kraal. "Two, Mfalme?"

"Yes, Great Creation." There was a gentle smile on Ramuza's face. "My apologies. I neglected to tell you that the Sacred Woman Lobarra gave birth just as I left the Favored Tribesman. You may rejoice. As far as I know, mother and child are fine. The number of Chinchigwe has grown by one."

The Chinchigwe rejoiced. Ameh returned to his seat and joined in the chatter. All the Chinchigwe felt that Lobarra's baby's birth was very special. They knew that this baby represented the rebounding of a people that was once so severely shattered.

Ramuza and Kharaambi gave the Chinchigwe time to cherish the moment. Ramuza took the opportunity to find out how Kharaambi's scouting had been. "How was the south region, Sacred Woman?"

"The same as this morning. We found nothing unusual. As I suspected, the sightings of Wabanga were concentrated in the north region. However, I am taking no risks. I have placed the Sentinels on the south rim on special alert."

"Very well. The Wabanga move like the wind. If they are in the area, they could just as well be anywhere."

"There is still a minor problem which must be resolved," said Kharaambi.

"What is that?"

Kharaambi beckoned the Royal Warrior Nionu to come closer as she answered Ramuza. "Do you remember that she-leopard that the

Great Creation Quazzi reported seeing in the south region several days ago?"

"Yes."

"Regrettably, she had to be killed. She had made a den just off the pathway, near Elephant's Ridge. I discovered it when I unknowingly came too close to the leopard's kitten. She attacked us. The Great Creation Nionu had to kill it."

The heartwarming chatter among the Chinchigwe gradually died away as the Chinchigwe began to listen to the conversation between Ramuza and Kharaambi. When Kharaambi mentioned the killing of the leopard, the Chinchigwe and Ramuza directed their attention to the Royal Warrior. Everyone noticed dried blood on the head of the warrior's spear for the first time.

"Was anyone hurt?" Ramuza asked Nionu.

"No, Mfalme, not physically."

Ramuza was fully aware that a spiritual cleansing was required because the Royal Warrior had spilled the blood of a living creation. "Have you gone to the Sacred Temple yet?"

"No, Great Creation. I will be going to the Temple directly. The Sacred Woman Kharaambi suggested that I ask your advice about something else first."

Ramuza looked briefly at Kharaambi. Her advice and leadership were second only to his. Ramuza turned back to Nionu. "You seek my advice? About what?"

Before Nionu answered, he looked around as if he was about to display something he didn't want anyone else to see. He threw back his royal cloak to reveal a large pouch that he carried. He reached into the pouch. "What do you want me to do with this?" He withdrew a tiny leopard kitten and boldly handed it to the Mfalme.

When the Brown Warrior Quazzi saw this, he walked over. "Nionu! You took a creature from the wild."

"I know, Great Creation. Under the circumstances, I had no choice. After I killed its mother, it was alone. It would have … you know, died."

Ramuza gently caressed the kitten and stroked the underside of its chin. "You did the right thing, Great Creation. So, this is why the she-leopard made her den so quickly. There should be others of her litter. Is this the only one?"

"We searched the area, but this is the only one we found."

"Then it is most unusual."

"It is more than unusual," Quazzi himself said, reaching over to stroke the mottled gray fur on the kitten's belly. "It will grow to be a rare all-black leopard."

"It is an ill omen, Mfalme." Ameh was drawn into the conversation. He spoke without seeming too convinced of his statement. "Where we come from, the presence of a black leopard means the coming of great misfortune."

"Nonsense." Ramuza was still stroking the kitten's chin.

"It is best to get rid of it."

"I have heard of that omen. I have never given it much thought."

"If you dare to taunt misfortune, you have acquired a helpless kitten. What will you do with it, Mfalme?"

Ramuza stood up. He was smiling. "Great Creation, I hear the question in your heart. You see the plight of the Chinchigwe in this kitten. Do you not?"

"No, Mfalme. The thought did not occur to me. But, now that you have mentioned it, there does seem to be a parallel. I am more curious to know your answer now. What will you do with it?"

Before Ramuza could answer, Adaulah approached his father. "Great Creation, may I keep him?"

"He is a creature of the wilderness, Adaulah. He must always remain so."

"Then, so he will remain. I promise. I will teach it to hunt and fend for itself."

"You can do that?" Nionu acted seriously surprised.

"Yes, Great Creation."

"I knew it!" Nionu, in his usual playful mood, acted as if one of his greatest suspicions had just been proven. "I thought I saw you dragging a zebra into the valley the other day. This leopard cub has nothing to worry about, Mfalme."

After the laughter died away, Adaulah defended himself. "That was not me, Great Creation. You saw someone else." Adaulah turned to his father again. "So, may I keep him?"

Ramuza looked at Kharaambi and Quazzi. Both only shrugged. When Ramuza looked at Nionu, the Royal Warrior backed away. "I have done my damage, Mfalme."

Ramuza handed the kitten to Adaulah. "He is in your care, for now. Remember, the leopard must always come and go as he pleases."

"So be it, Mfalme." Adaulah ran around to the back of the dais with the kitten embraced in his arms. He sat down and placed the kitten on the ground beside him. Adaulah thought he had found a semi-private area to get familiar with the kitten. Unfortunately, most of his sisters quickly surrounded him and the kitten. All but the three oldest siblings huddled around Adaulah and the kitten.

At that moment, everyone in front of the dais noticed the beautiful sound of an African drum. An irregular beat of hollow knocks echoed softly throughout the valley.

"What does it mean, Mfalme?" Ameh asked.

"It is the talking drum from one of the sentinels on the valley rim," Ramuza explained calmly. "Someone desires entry into the valley."

Kharaambi listened for a moment. She began to interpret the drum's hollow knocks for Ameh. "The signal you hear is directed by a Royal or Blue Warrior. The warrior finds it necessary to request special clearance for three trespassers."

After hearing this news, the Chinchigwe were alarmed. They instantly knew the trespassers' identity. Ramuza knew as well. He and Ameh looked at each other.

Ramuza got up from his chieftain's stool. "I must go up to the valley rim."

This aroused Kharaambi's attention. She knew that any Royal or Blue Warrior on the valley rim had the authority to permit or refuse entry into the valley. Under normal circumstances, there was no need for any warrior above the Royal or Blue cloak to request special clearance. Why was Ramuza going up to the north rim? "Mfalme, is there something I should know?"

Before Ramuza answered Kharaambi, he summoned a White Warrior and gave him brief, inaudible instructions. As the warrior left toward Ramuza's hut to carry out those instructions, Ramuza returned to Kharaambi. "A slave merchant is on the valley rim, Sacred Woman. It is the merchant behind the slave hunters who raided the Chinchigwe village."

"Would you like me to go up to the rim?"

"No, Sacred Woman. Stay here and acquaint yourself with the Chinchigwe." The White Warrior Ramuza, instructed earlier, returned carrying Ramuza's belted knife and spear. Ramuza took the weapons and headed out across the celebration area. "I will confront the merchant."

— 29 —

TRUST THE MFALME

When Ramuza left to go up to the north rim, all the people sitting next to him on the dais eventually disbanded. The Sacred Women, Rwuva and Olabisi, and all nine of the Mfalme's daughters left in mass to begin mingling with the people in the celebration area. The Brown Warrior Quazzi dealt with other duties beyond the Royal Kraal's entrance. The Royal Warrior Nionu also left the kraal. He crossed the Aukmondi River and headed up the south slope toward the Sacred Temple. And Adaulah began his "motherly" duties by teaching the leopard kitten to follow him. The two retreated to some remote corner in the back of the kraal.

Only Kharaambi remained with the Chinchigwe. Originally, the Sacred Woman Rwuva had planned to take the Chinchigwe to the guest kraal on the opposite side of the Aukmondi River. But Kharaambi needed to talk with them a little more. She volunteered to take responsibility for them.

Since the Gray Warrior had returned from the south region in the middle of their talk with the Mfalme, Kharaambi felt she had missed a few details. She took this opportunity to get better acquainted with them. In the beginning, Kharaambi had to take the initiative. Knowing the merchant was close, the Chinchigwe did not feel very talkative.

"Then perhaps, someone can tell me more about this merchant," Kharaambi suggested.

Ameh pushed his apprehensions aside. "You must forgive us, Kharaambi. So much has happened to us in the past few days. And we feel that it is not over yet. We are all hoping that the Mfalme will turn the merchant away. If he does not, it will mean the end for us."

"This merchant that pursues you," Kharaambi took a seat on the ground, "why is he so determined to take you?"

Ameh collected his thoughts. After a heavy sigh, he volunteered to tell Kharaambi more about who the Chinchigwe were. He told her all that had happened to them, from that tragic morning when the Chinchigwe village was raided up to the present moment. This time, as he told the tragic story, he included the deeds of Adaulah in his account. He told of the addition of Adaulah to the merchant's holding pen; their miraculous escape; their desperate flight in the darkness; the attack of the rhinoceros; Adaulah's separation from the group; and finally, their encounter with Mfalme Ncobba in the north region.

Kharaambi listened carefully, obviously concentrating on all that was said. She interrupted only occasionally to draw out more details here and there. She eventually learned as much about the situation as Ramuza had learned from all that she gathered.

"No one should ever have to endure so much." Kharaambi looked over the Chinchigwe as if seeing them for the first time. "Has the Mfalme told you what he plans to do?"

"He has not. We have asked him several times. He has told us only that he will not jeopardize this valley and his people. He was quite adamant about that. He told us that if the merchant threatened Adaulah, he would deal with him appropriately. He has not said what he will do about us." Ameh carefully considered asking Kharaambi his next question. After daring to do so, he took the time to phrase it carefully. "Kharaambi, you know the Mfalme well. Tell us his mind. What do you suppose he will do?"

"Honestly, I can not say, Great Creation."

"Honestly?" There was a slight edge in Twese's voice. "Or is it that you will not say? Please, do not spare us any bad news, Kharaambi."

Kharaambi looked at Twese with a questionable look on her face. "Great Creation, you sound as if you expect the worst."

Twese smiled. When he finally spoke again, the edge in his voice was gone. "All the Chinchigwe here will tell you, I am known to be quite the pessimist. I see the worst in most situations before the good finally falls into my lap. The truth is, we have discussed what the Mfalme will do. We suspect that he will do one or two things. He will give us just enough help to put us back on our feet and then release us into the wilderness. Or he will return us to the merchant. We think these are his only alternatives."

"Ramuza must have given you a terrible impression of himself. He is not one to create undue hope, but I am sure he will not leave you helplessly to yourselves either."

"That sounds good, Kharaambi. But do you know what that tells me? When you tell me that the Mfalme will not create undue hope, it only means the Mfalme is withholding the bad news from us."

"He is not like that, Great Creation. If there is bad news, you have a right to know it. At the proper time, the Mfalme would tell you." Kharaambi stood up. She had learned all that she needed to know for now. She felt she would only inflame the Chinchigwe speculations if the conversation continued. "I promise you, the Mfalme will do what he can for you. You must trust the Mfalme."

"So be it." Ameh sensed Kharaambi's intent to put an end to the conversation. He got to his feet, too. "We understand that Mfalme Ncobba must protect his people and his only son. We trust him to protect us too, as best he can."

— 30 —

THE AUKMONDI WARRIORS

"**N**ow, if you are ready, I will take you to the guest kraal, where you may finally rest."

As Kharaambi waited for the Chinchigwe to gather themselves up, she happened to look toward her hut. Her golden-headed spear, leaning in the doorway, caught her eye. The White Warriors, who had taken her cloak, shield, and spear upon her return from the south region, were preparing to put the items away. But something told Kharaambi to retrieve her spear.

She was only going to take the Chinchigwe to the guest kraal. There was no obvious reason for her to carry it within the valley. However, two things made her reconsider.

In the first place, only she, Ramuza, Quazzi, and the Royal and Blue Warriors can allow or refuse visitors into the Aukmondi Valley. Today was the first time in a very long time that Ramuza had stopped her form exercising that authority. That was strange.

In the second place, Ramuza went up to the valley rim wearing a knife and carrying a spear. This was very unlike Ramuza. Kharaambi knew he seldom carried a weapon, even when escorted beyond the sentry lines. Kharaambi knew that Ramuza relies mainly on his head for defense. In doing so, he has become a Master of Diplomacy and strategy. If there comes a time when he does pick up a weapon, it is a good idea for every warrior in the tribe to be on standby, with their weapon close at hand.

With only a special gesture, Kharaambi signaled to the two White Warriors. Both warriors initially hesitated before executing Kharaambi's request. It was, after all, an unusual request. But once the request was understood, one of the warriors dutifully retrieved and relayed the spear to her.

By this time, most of the Chinchigwe were on their feet. The last person to stand was Jpuma because of his injured leg. When Kharaambi saw him getting up with some difficulty, she made another silent request to the two White Warriors. With just a nod of her head toward Jpuma, the warriors understood what was necessary. They immediately went to give Jpuma the support he needed.

This spontaneous behavior of the White Warriors sparked a curiosity in Twese. He recalled how the Chinchigwe warriors had fought the slave hunters. Each of them had been trained to fight. They spent their entire careers refining the art of combat, only to be so easily defeated. Twese wondered if the Aukmondi warriors could have done any better.

As Kharaambi and the Chinchigwe started across the celebration area, Twese moved beside the Gray Warrior. "Kharaambi, it seems to me that a lot of the duties of your warriors are …," he searched his mind for the proper word, "servile. I always understood that a warrior's duties should be protection and defense."

"The Aukmondi warriors do protect and defend, Great Creation. However, our warriors are aides too. They are servants who are given the greatest of respect. Their primary duty is to help the Aukmondi people."

Twese glanced behind him where the Aukmondi White Warriors were helping Jpuma. "Help the Aukmondi people?" Twese repeated, "Like helping them to walk?"

"Yes, if necessary. It would not be uncommon to see warriors running errands for people incapable of doing it themselves or even caring for infants while their parents are away. The Aukmondi warriors are the tribe's workforce. They are our police. They are our caretakers. And they are proud of what they do. I should know because, as their leader, I am one of them."

"I meant no offense. I was only wondering if the Aukmondi warriors can fight as well as they serve."

"If given no other choice, I believe the Aukmondi warriors are the most efficient fighters and defenders you will find anywhere." Kharaambi glanced toward Twese. "Why does this concern you so?"

"It just seems strange to me for an army to be anything other than a fighting force."

"If fighting forces did nothing but fight battles, they would be a waste most of the time."

"Whose idea was it for your warriors' duties to be so servile? Surely not the Mfalme's."

"No. It was not the Mfalme's idea. The idea was born with the Aukmondi people long ago. No one, including Ramuza, has changed it. He supports it. And, as the present leader of the army, I will see to it that the idea does not die in my lifetime."

"May I ask how you became the leader of the army? Did the Mfalme give you the position because you are a warrior who is also his mate?"

"No, Great Creation. I was a ranking warrior long before I was Ramuza's mate." Kharaambi tactfully ignored Twese's insinuation. "There are only two courtesy ranks among the Aukmondi warriors, the White Warrior and the Black Warrior. One may achieve the rank of White Warrior by asking a Blue Warrior for permission to join their regiment. If you are accepted, you become a White Warrior.

"With considerably more difficulty, one becomes a Black Warrior only by inheritance, as the Young Creation Adaulah will do someday. All other ranks, including my own, are earned."

"So, as Gray Warrior, you have complete authority over the Aukmondi army?"

"Over the army and more. Among Ramuza's council of advisors I have the sole privilege of challenging his decisions. At present, the duties and responsibilities of the Gray Warrior are second only to the leadership of this tribe."

"What about the Brown Warrior Quazzi? When we met him, out in the wilderness, he was obviously in a position of leadership and authority. I was under the impression that he was second only to the Mfalme.”

“The Great Creation Quazzi is well qualified to wear the gray cloak. Fate has made him my lieutenant.”

There was a story behind what Kharaambi had just said. It also sparked Twese’s curiosity. But for now, he had heard what he wanted to hear. He had under-evaluated Kharaambi’s position. Now that he knew her importance in the Aukmondi hierarchy, there was much to consider.

THE AUKMONDI - SECRET OF THE YULULU BONE

— **31** —

TOUR THE AUKMONDI VALLEY

Just outside the entrance of the Royal Kraal, a short trail led down to the north bank of the Aukmondi River. Kharaambi led the Chinchigwe down the trail. She stopped at the foot of a well-used wooden bridge that stretched across the river. Kharaambi pointed toward the south bank with her spear.

"On the other side is the south bank pathway. The guest kraal is slightly less than a kilometer farther along that pathway." She spoke to all the Chinchigwe but looked directly at Jpuma. "As promised, it is not far."

Jpuma smiled. He leaned heavily against the White Warriors for most of his support. "I am truly grateful. I wondered if you were about to lead us on another long trek, deeper into the valley as the Mfalme had done."

"No, Great Creation. I can see that you people need your rest."

"Yes." Ameh stepped forward. "Jpuma obviously needs to rest, as do several others here. But, frankly, I do not think I can rest now. And it would probably do me little good even to try."

"What are you saying, Great Creation?"

"When the Mfalme brought us into the valley, we saw many beautiful sights on that long trek to the kraal of your Favored Tribesman. As tired as I was, I enjoyed that walk. It took my mind off many troubling things. There is no guarantee that the Mfalme will turn away the merchant and his aides. Let Jpuma and the others rest if they wish. If possible, I would like to see more of your beautiful valley as we wait for the Mfalme to return. I think that would be more relaxing to me now."

"Are you serious?" Kharaambi studied Ameh's face. "She glanced at the faces of the other Chinchigwe. "Are there others among you who feel as restless?"

The majority of the Chinchigwe preferred to rest instead. Only eight others felt as Ameh did. Among them were Embabi, Komu, Summare, and Twese. Twese did not care to see the valley anymore, but he did not feel like resting either. He reluctantly chose to be counted among the restless ones.

Kharaambi instructed the two White Warriors supporting Jpuma to finish leading the Chinchigwe across the bridge to the guest kraal. She delegated the necessary authority to the warriors so they could see to all the immediate needs and comfort of the Chinchigwe. Kharaambi could sense the pride in the young, inexperienced warriors as they set out to carry out the orders of the Gray Warrior.

Kharaambi and the nine Chinchigwe did not cross the bridge. Instead, they turned eastward, following the trail on the river's north bank *(See Appendix IV: The Aukmondi Valley (Central Portion))*.

"Despite your restlessness, I will not take you far," Kharaambi said. "We will cross the river farther down. Along the way, I will show you a few things that may interest you. We will head back this way toward the guest kraal on the other side of the river."

The trail eventually turned into a pathway. The Pathway, known by the Aukmondi as the north bank pathway, was wider and clearer. There were ample indications of a well-used thoroughfare between the Royal Kraal and places leading toward the valley depths.

Of course, the first attraction that caught the Chinchigwe's attention was the sparkling Aukmondi River. When the Chinchigwe first saw it from a distance on the north slope, its water appeared blue. But now, as the Chinchigwe walked along the north bank, the water was crystal clear. The bottom of the river could be easily seen through the sparkling water. And in it, fish were occasionally visible, lazily gliding here and there through the currents.

"The Aukmondi River," Kharaambi explained, "is one of the many tributaries of the great Mara River. Our river's source is in the mountain range south of the valley depths. Its flow is east to west.

Like the Mara, its flow is seasonal but always strong throughout Aukmondi Valley. The river finally ends its journey by merging with the Mara River on the plain of the Serengeti.

"This river segment, which flows through the Aukmondi Valley, is about thirty-four kilometers long. We use the eastern and central portions for cooking and drinking. The western portion, beginning at the Aukmondi Lake, is reserved for cleaning, swimming, and bathing."

"To have such a versatile water source running through the valley is most convenient," said Ameh. "In our village, we had to fetch all our water from a distant lake."

"I can imagine what a daily task that must have been. What about irrigation trenches? Could you not have created your waterways?"

"Yes, we could have built trenches. But they would not have worked. Water does not run too well uphill."

Kharaambi smiled at her oversight and Ameh's pleasant nature. She was learning to like this Old Creation very much. He reminded her of her father. A personal reappraisal of him was interrupted when she heard a caustic remark from one of the other Chinchigwe, Twese.

"Now, thanks to the slave hunters and the slave merchant," he said, "we will not have to worry about fetching water anymore." He looked up and down the river with a false admiration. "What else have you got to show us, Kharaambi?"

"This way, please." Kharaambi suppressed her reaction to Twese as she turned and continued up the pathway. This was the second time that she had noticed his attitude. She wondered if Twese expressed an attitude that was common among other Chinchigwe.

The next thing to catch the attention of the Chinchigwe was a colorful flower garden across the river on the south bank. Large assortments of flowers were growing in random places. Some were recognizable. Others were varieties that the Chinchigwe had never seen before. There were petunias, asters, pansies, daffodils, rhododendrons, roses, forsythias, lilacs, and sumacs, to name only a few. They gently waved in the breeze as their scents filled the air.

"How beautiful!" Embabi spoke to no one in particular. She was overwhelmed by the sight.

"That is the Katola Garden," said Kharaambi. "It stretches about 800 meters in length and about 200 meters at its widest point. It is the second largest flower garden in the valley."

"Then the largest must be the one we saw from Kon-Shambique's kraal. As I recall, it was situated on the bank of the lake that we saw."

"That is correct, Sacred Woman. That lake that you saw is the Aukmondi Lake. The garden is the Sutugusutuguvata. It is…"

"The what?"

"The Sutugusutuguvata." Kharaambi repeated the name without the slightest stutter. "It is a full 1010 meters long and 230 meters wide."

"Someone here truly has a love for flowers. Are there many more gardens like that?"

Kharaambi had to think a moment. The Sacred Woman Rwuva, the tribes Official Hostess, and the Sacred Woman Olabisi, the High Priestess, were more accustomed to giving guided tours of the valley. She was not used to doing this.

"Not counting the many personal gardens," Kharaambi finally began, "I think there are about six common gardens throughout the valley. We might see three of them from where we stand."

Kharaambi positioned herself to point out the three gardens. The first was the one the Chinchigwe were looking at across the river. Two smaller gardens, twin gardens, were barely visible through the trees, high on the south slope. They were on each side of two large golden doors built into the hillside. The Chinchigwe recognized those doors as the ones they had seen from Kon-Shambique's kraal.

"Those doors are to our Sacred Temple," Kharaambi explained. "After a good night's rest, and if circumstances permit, maybe you can get a closer look tomorrow."

Kharaambi continued to lead the group eastward along the riverbank. After several more meters, she pointed toward a large hill obscuring most of the north slope.

"Do you recognize this hill?"

The Chinchigwe studied the hill but, initially, saw nothing that looked familiar.

"If you look halfway up the hillside, on the near slope," Kharaambi pointed with her spear again, "you can see the kraal of the Favored Tribesman."

"Yes," Ameh squinted his eyes to focus his vision. "I recognize it now. And I can truly understand why the crafter Tanake objected so strongly. Were we up there earlier? That is a noticeable climb from this angle."

"Thankfully, Kon-Shambique's kraal is less than halfway up the hillside. The summit of the hill is called Nagorda Peak. It is the highest point in the valley. Some say it is also one of the most beautiful. An inspiring view of the Serengeti Plain can be seen from the summit. During the Great Migration, you can see the massive herds of gnu and zebra moving across the plains. But one of my favorite times to view the plains is during sunset. The light of the evening sun continues to brightly illuminate the plain while all around you is already dark. It is an unbelievably beautiful sight."

"I will have to take your word for it, Kharaambi. Even after a good night's rest, I know, I will not be climbing Nagorda Peak anytime soon."

"We will not be climbing any hills this evening, Great Creation. The rest of what I must show you is on the lower ground."

After a short walk farther, Kharaambi finally led the Chinchigwe across a bridge, over the river, as promised. On the opposite bank, she took a pathway that left the river and headed down a moderate incline. The meandering pathway took the Chinchigwe through a brief forest area, past a small kraal community, and across the north end of another clearing.

At the far end of the clearing, the Aukmondi Lake came into view, directly ahead. A gentle but constant roar attracted the Chinchigwe.

"What is that noise?" Asked Twese. "It sounds like running water."

Kharaambi was glad to see Twese finally taking a sincere, if not enthusiastic, interest in the tour. She had hoped he would. She was counting on the sights to temporarily take his mind away from the anxieties that he and the rest of the Chinchigwe must be experiencing.

"That, that you hear, Great Creation, is a waterfall. About two kilometers ahead, the Aukmondi River splits into two. The main portion continues westward. The smaller portion comes over the ridge, forming a waterfall and the lake you see before you. If you wish, you may see the fall. It is just ahead, around the bend in the pathway."

Sure enough, after another few meters around the bend, a very refreshing-looking waterfall on the far side of the lake came into view. It fell from a height of seven meters into the lake, which turned out to be much larger than it first appeared.

Also, across the lake, on the right bank, the Chinchigwe got their first impressive, close view of the vast Sutugusutuguvata flower garden.

Ameh stopped. He stared with amazement. No one noticed that he was also holding his breath. The collective beauty of the waterfall, the lake, and the Sutugusutuguvata flower garden seemed to pull at his spirit like an incredible vacuum. Holding his breath was useless. He could do nothing but surrender to all the beauty. It was his turn to be overwhelmed.

"I am convinced, and I must admit, that this valley is the most beautiful place I have ever seen. I am an old man. I have seen many beautiful things in my life. But I have never seen a place so akin to my vision of paradise." Ameh point out over the lake. "Just look at that."

A large, noisy flock of waterfowl gracefully glided just above the water surface. Everyone watched as most of the fowl settled into the water. It was a wondrous sight, a rolling, swirling spectacle, as the last fowl dipped down and quickly aborted their landing, causing the first ones to take flight again.

"I do no doubt that good and great spirits dwell in this place." Ameh continued.

"You have seen less than half the valley, Great Creation. About half of our kraal communities are to the west, past the Royal Kraal. Further ahead, to the east, we have food crops and fruit orchards in the valley depths. We have one of the area's coolest, vibrant, and inviting forests. Beyond the Sentinel lines, it is a little dangerous because lions, leopards, hyenas, and other wild creatures come and go as they please. But it is still so incredibly beautiful. Our…"

"Enough! Please." Ameh held up his hand. Seeing all the magnificent beauty before him seemed to magnify the memories of the recent past: the raids of the Chinchigwe village, the death of his people, the death of his mate and son, the destruction of his culture, and the seemingly profound break with all the Chinchigwe ancestors. Tears welled up in Ameh's eyes. "We have lost so much. It is not fair."

"What is not fair, Great Creation?"

"I am ashamed to admit, Kharaambi, that all that you have shown us only forces me to reflect upon the emptiness of the Chinchigwe people. Looking back over the past few days, I realize we have nothing now. Nothing!"

"Please do not think that way, Great Creation. Those of you who have survived have your memories: memories of your friends, your families, and your ancestors. That amounts to more than you seem to realize. In my opinion, it is all that matters. And you have nothing to be ashamed of."

"But I do. We have failed our friends, families, and our ancestors." Ameh believed he and most of his people had lived with only the sincerest, honest, and honorable intentions. All their deeds, great and small, were meant to ensure the worthiness of life's simple gifts. "Do not good things come to good people? We must have done something very shameful to reap so much misfortune."

"Nonsense." Kharaambi came over to stand next to Ameh. "Great Creation, good people suffer misfortunes too. Misfortunes are often life's hardest lessons. Recover and learn from those lessons. For in the end, you will be more than good people. You will be a stronger people."

"I suppose." Ameh took a deep breath. He arched his back. Using his staff, he forced himself to stand more erect. He tried to show signs of recovery. "You must forgive me. I must be much more fatigued than I originally thought."

"Shall we head back toward the guest kraal?"

"I think that we should."

Ameh's breakdown had caught Kharaambi off guard. She wished there was something more she could say to comfort him. She could think of nothing. She had no choice but to comply with the Old Creation's wishes.

Twese stood behind Ameh and Kharaambi. He shook his head as Kharaambi led the way back up the pathway. He was sensitive enough to understand what Ameh felt. He understood the losses that Ameh spoke of because he had experienced many of the same losses. He wondered if Kharaambi fully understood.

Twese maneuvered himself to walk beside the Gray Warrior. "You and your people are fortunate. The beauties of your valley have assaulted the spirit of the Chinchigwe. You must know you have something here that the Chinchigwe may never experience again."

"That is not true, Great Creation. The Chinchigwe can recover. You will recover."

"It does not seem likely. And a lot of it depends on what the Mfalme does."

"As I told you, the Mfalme will do whatever he can for you. I think you will recover, independent of what the Mfalme does."

Twese shook his head again. "You have the luxury to think that way. We do not."

"But you do, Great Creation." Kharaambi was about to say more to Twese, but the pathway on which everyone walked eventually turned, bringing the south slope into full view again. An obtuse reflection of the setting sun on the golden doors of the Sacred Temple caught Kharaambi's eye. An idea took root in her mind. She left Twese's side and maneuvered herself next to Ameh, who could best benefit from her idea.

"Great Creation," she began, "after you have rested, may I suggest that you make it a point to visit our Sacred Temple."

"Are we allowed?" Twese overheard the suggestion.

"Yes. You are more than welcome." Kharaambi turned to face all the Chinchigwe. "The invitation is open to all of you. The serenity within the Temple will help you to think thoughts of promise. The visit, I promise you, will comfort you."

"Thank you, Kharaambi." Ameh spoke for the Chinchigwe. "I intend to do so."

"There is but one thing you must remember. You, Ameh, Twese, Komu, and all the Chinchigwe Creations who wish to visit the Temple must never go into the Temple unescorted by a Sacred Woman. Any Creation alone in the Temple caverns will become lost."

"What do you mean, lost?" Twese asked.

"I mean, literally lost! Due to the nature of the Temple, the sensitive nature of a Sacred Woman is necessary to walk the network of caverns within the Temple."

— **32** —

NINE DAUGHTERS

When the evening sun disappeared below the horizon and darkness filled the valley, Kharaambi had led the touring Chinchigwe to the guest kraal. Seeing that all the other Chinchigwe had been comfortably accommodated, she dismissed the two White Warriors initially tasked with caring for them. As the warriors left, she asked them to summon her immediately upon Ramuza's return.

In the meantime, she would personally help the final few Chinchigwe to settle into the kraal. Unlike most of the other Chinchigwe who were already asleep in the various huts, the restless nine still refused to retire in anticipation of the Mfalme's return from the north rim. Instead of bedding down, they preferred to wait. Kharaambi waited with them. They gathered together in the center of the kraal. All but one of them sat around a crackling campfire.

"What is taking the Mfalme so long?" Twese, the lone one, paced. He took a few steps toward the entrance of the kraal, hoping to see the Mfalme coming. His restlessness was becoming more obvious.

Kharaambi looked past Twese, beyond the kraal entrance, and across the river toward the Royal Kraal. All that she could see through the darkness and trees was a few of the daily celebration campfires over a kilometer away. She saw no sign of the Mfalme. "I do not know, Great Creation."

"Do you suppose anything is wrong?"

"No. The sentinels on the valley rim would warn us if there was anything wrong. The time seems to suggest that the merchant is a Formidable Creation."

"I do not know how formidable he is, but he seems very determined."

"Then if I know Ramuza, the Mfalme, he is standing his ground. He can be quite headstrong, too."

"Just how well do you know the Mfalme?" Embabi asked. "How long have you known him?"

"I have known Ramuza for almost as long as I can remember. He, the Sacred Women Rwuva and Olabisi, and I were all childhood friends. We grew up together."

"You are his third mate?"

"Yes. I have been mate number three now for over twelve harvests."

The shy Summare squirmed. She was happy to hear questions she had long wanted to ask herself. "Kharaambi, you are a warrior. May I ask how you became the Mfalme's third mate?"

"That is a long story, Sacred Woman." Kharaambi made a thoughtful glance toward Ameh, Twese, and Komu. "It is a story that the Creations here may not want to hear."

"Nonsense," Ameh made himself more comfortable. He stretched out, almost reclining, to rest on his elbow. "Tell your story, Kharaambi. Summarwe wants to hear it. Fatigue will let me know when to stop listening."

Kharaambi had been tending the campfire with a small branch. She broke the branch in half and tossed it into the campfire as she gathered her thoughts. "The union between Ramuza and me was born of love, but I believe the Mfalme was also desperately looking for a mate to bear him a son. I tried but was unsuccessful."

"What are you saying? You have given the Mfalme children?"

Kharaambi smiled. "Yes, one of the Ncobba daughters is my contribution. She is called Zindzhi Nyoka. She was the one who was sitting at the Mfalme's immediate right on the royal dais."

"Yes, I remember her," Embabi said. "She was the talkative one."

"She does draw her share of attention. She is somewhat opinionated, but in a gentle way. She won't hesitate to speak her mind. I am quite proud of her. She is not the son the Mfalme wanted, but she came close."

"You have reasons to be proud of her," Ameh added. "From what I have seen, she seems to take after her mother."

"I hope that is a compliment."

"It is, Kharaambi. You are one of the most admirable women I have ever known."

"Thank you, Great Creation."

"Will you try again to bear the Mfalme another son?"

"In all honesty, I would love to. But I am leaving that up to the Mflame and the Supreme Spirit. I do not know what the Mfalme's intentions are. He seemed so satisfied after Adaulah was born; in no hurry to try again. As for the Supreme Spirit, it was Her design in the first place to give the Mfalme nine daughters and only one son. We are all subject to Her will."

"But the Mfalme has but one son. That is the most unusual." Ameh sat up again. His interest was still intact.

"Yes, it is unusual. And it was not a concern until after Rwuva's fourth daughter, Audi Azinti, was born."

"Then, the Mfalme's first four daughters are Rwuva's?"

"Yes. It all started with Omari Azinti, the oldest of the Ncobba daughters. Shortly after the union between Ramuza and Rwuva, Omari was born. That was nineteen harvests ago. It was a joyous occasion, celebrated by the entire Aukmondi tribe. If there was any disappointment that the firstborn was a female, no one showed it, least of all Ramuza. To this day, I believe that the Sacred Woman Omari is the warmest and one of the most beloved of all Ramuza's daughters.

"She appears to be a strikingly responsible woman," Embabi recalled the regal young woman who sat on the dais at Rwuva's side.

"She also takes after her mother in more ways than one. Omari is very protective and nurturing. She is like a mother to Adaulah and all the other daughters.

"Shortly after Ramuza became Mfalme, the second daughter, Yejide Azinti, was born. So far, she is the only Ncobba offspring who has visited the Village of World Teachers. She was the most educated and probably the smartest of all the daughters. Currently, she is the only offspring to hold a position on the Mfalme's council of advisors. The Mfalme will often seek her advice on all matters that concern him.

"Then, one harvest after Yejide was born, Rwuva gave birth to the third daughter, Kunto Azinti. And the harvest after that, Audi Azinti was born. That was four daughters in four harvests."

"They are all daughters one could be very proud of."

"Unquestionably. However, a harvest apart, Kunto and Audi were two of the most thoughtful people in the tribe. They are unquestionably the most sociable. They are always out helping someone do one thing or another.

"But it wasn't until after the birth of Audi, the fourth daughter, that the need for a male heir became a serious concern. As mentioned, Ramuza, Rwuva, Olabisi, and I grew up together. The bonds among all of us lasted even through the union of Ramuza and Rwuva, and the birth of their four daughters. We continued to share most of our thoughts and our concerns.

"Even before Ramuza showed any concern, Rwuva and Olabisi were already addressing the matter."

"I have tried," Rwuva said to Olabisi one day in confidence. "The Supreme Spirit has blessed me with four daughters. For some reason, She refused to bless me with a son. The Mfalme needs a son."

"You must keep trying," Olabisi responded. "You have no other choice."

"I know." Rwuva took a deep breath and tried to hide her feelings. "Ramuza is becoming impatient. He has said nothing, but I know what he feels."

"Yes, I can sense impatience from both of you."

******

"That very evening, Rwuva took Ramuza in confidence. She said she introduced Ramuza to taking Olabisi as his second mate. Ramuza objected at first. Rwuva argued that the bond between Ramuza and Olabisi was already there. The two had been close since childhood. Love between the two stood on solid ground, and there was no denying it. Rwuva drove her idea home when she told Ramuza a most intimate secret: Olabisi was one of the most fertile women in the Aukmondi tribe. If anyone could give him a son, Olabisi could."

"That was a very noble thing, Rwuva did." Twese had come back to his seat. Kharaambi's story had captured his interest.

"Yes, it was," Kharaambi continued. "If Olabisi bared Ramuza a son, then the Sacred Woman Rwuva would have given up her chance of becoming Principal Mate. That is just the kind of woman that Rwuva is. She was willing to sacrifice for Ramuza and the Aukmondi people.

"Ramuza eventually took Olabisi into the union with him and Rwuva. That was about fifteen harvests ago. It was also a festive occasion, celebrated throughout the valley. Ramuza and Olabisi wasted no time. Before the next harvest, Olabisi was pregnant. And she did prove to be very fertile. But as life would have it sometimes, things did not go as anticipated. Olabisi gave birth to twin girls, Akwate and Akuato Sheetswa."

"That is six daughters in five harvests now." The shy Summare could not help but smile at the joke life was playing.

"Akwate and Akuato won Ramuza's heart, probably the only thing that kept the Mfalme from losing his mind. He adored those girls, spending more time with them than the other daughters. It was probably his way of hiding his impatience. But he was beyond impatience. I would say he was officially desperate now."

"So, what did he do?"

"It is not so much what he did. It is what I did." Kharaambi paused momentarily, wondering if she should reveal such a personal side of herself. "I was already a Royal Warrior when the twins were born. Even though I had spent much time away from Ramuza, Rwuva, and Olabisi, initially training as a warrior and eventually performing my duties as commander of two armies, I was still strongly bonded with them. As the closest people in my life, I could sense their desperation. I took it upon myself to solve their problem."

"How?"

"I came to Ramuza. In his weakness, I convinced him to impregnate me. I loved my calling as a warrior, but I loved Ramuza too. I was more determined to give Ramuza the son that he wanted. I do not know what made me think I could easily give him a son. I suppose my determination just blinded me.

"Neither of us said anything to Rwuva or Olabisi. For a full cycle of the moon, I carried Ramuza's child, and no one knew it but Ramuza and me. It was wrong. Consequently, it began to affect both of us. Day after day, Ramuza never left the Royal Kraal. He sat in his hut, or on the royal dais, lost in his thoughts. As for me, I took it out on my armies. My Blue Warriors knew something was wrong, but respectfully did not challenge me.

"Then, one day, I was sitting alone by the lake, deep in thought. The Favored Tribesman, Kon-Shambique, came to me. He said, 'Come, walk with me.'

"I did as he asked. As we walked, I could tell he was trying to get me to tell him what was wrong. Kon-Shambique is the most Trusted Creation in our tribe, and yet, I could not reveal the secret that Ramuza and I held.

"I walked with Kon-Shambique clear across the valley. I was so busy guarding my words and the secret that it did not occur to me where Kon-Shambique was leading me. It did not occur to me until we walked into the Royal Kraal. The next thing I knew, the Favored Tribesman and I were seated before the Mfalme.

******

"Great Creation, why have you come?" Ramuza asked Kon-Shambique.

"I have come to serve my Mflame."

"Serve me? How?"

Kon-Shambique held up three fingers. "The Supreme Spirit gave all of us three guiding lights. She gave us a head to think with. She gave us a heart to love with. And She gave us an intuitive ember that seems to burn deep in our stomachs. Keep these three guiding lights synchronized, and you can never go wrong."

"What are you saying, Kon-Shambique?"

"All three guiding lights are burning erratically, in both of you, because of the secret that you and the Sacred Woman Kharaambi hold."

Ramuza and I reacted with looks of surprise at Kon-Shambique. We looked at each other as we realized that Kon-Shambique knew our secret.

"It is a complicated matter," Ramuza finally confessed.

"Yes, Mfalme. I am sure that it is. And with each passing day, it becomes more and more complicated."

Ramuza stood up. He introduced a factor that neither Kon-Shambique nor I knew. The Great Creation Zobulabe, who was the Gray Warrior at the time, had recently come to Ramuza.

"Because of his age," Ramuza said, "he wishes to step down. He has recommended Kharaambi as his replacement." It caught me totally by surprise.

"But Mfalme," I protested, "the Royal Warrior Quazzi is the reasonable choice. Zobulabe knows it as well as I. Why has he recommended me?"

"Quazzi does not want the position."

"That is no excuse. If you appoint him, he has no choice."

"I am his Mfalme. But Quazzi is my friend. He is my best friend. He is like an older brother to me. And I owe him more than my life. The least that I can do is honor his wish."

"Why does Quazzi not want to wear the cloak of the Gray Warrior?" Kon-Shambique was curious.

Ramuza smiled as he recalled his friend's career. "In his heart, Quazzi is an eternal sentinel. He was happiest when he was a Green Warrior. I think that he longs for those serene days. He would still be a Green Warrior if duty and responsibility did not force him higher through the ranks."

"Duty and responsibility are still at work here, Great Creation." I tried to reason with the Mfalme.

"No, Sacred Woman. I will honor my friend."

"But Ramuza," I placed my hand on my stomach, unaware that I had done so, "what if I cannot wear the gray cloak either?"

Kon-Shambique also quickly realized that if I bore Ramuza a son, I would automatically become the Principal Mate. I could not be the Gray Warrior, either. Kon-Shambique could only smile at the situation. "I would say, the matter is indeed more complicated."

"What must we do, Mfalme?" I asked.

"Allow me to make a recommendation." Kon-Shambique stood up. He was preparing to leave the Royal Kraal. As far as he was concerned, he had done all he could for Ramuza and me. "The two of you must visit the Sacred Temple and get those guiding lights synchronized."

******

"Ramuza and I immediately climbed the south slope up to the Sacred Temple. Once inside, I led the Mfalme directly to the central chamber. We knelt before the altar there. Together, we addressed the Supreme Spirit, asking for Her guidance. We waited for Her answer."

Twese was on his feet again, pacing. When he heard Kharaambi mention a verbal address to their Supreme Spirit and that she and the Mfalme waited for a response, he stopped pacing and reclaimed his seat next to Ameh. "You can talk with the Supreme Spirit in your Temple? She talks back to you?"

"In a way. It is probably better to say that visitors to the Sacred Temple communicate with the Supreme Spirit. Words need never be spoken. But when you leave the Temple, you feel as if you have talked with the Mother of All Creation one-on-one."

"What did She say to you?"

"Ramuza and I entered the Temple feeling that we had done something wrong. And the consequences and complications were beyond our control."

******

"Ramuza," The Supreme Spirit said, "your unending love for Kharaambi has grown since childhood. And Kharaambi, your love for Ramuza is proven by your willingness to mother his child. A child born of such love is never wrong."

"Then why do we feel as we do?" Ramuza asked.

"You have hidden that love from others who love the two of you just as strongly. Love is meant to be shared. Go and share your love."

Ramuza and Kharaambi got up from their kneeling positions to leave the central chamber. But then Ramuza hesitated and turned back to the altar.

"Sacred Woman, what about a son?"

"What about a son, Great Creation?"

"The Aukmondi tribe needs a male heir."

"The Aukmondi tribe will have a male heir in due time."

Ramuza glanced at Kharaambi. He said nothing, but he was wondering if the child in her womb was male.

"You are asking for divine intervention, Great Creation?"

Ramuza kneeled again. "Forgive me, Sacred Woman. I surrender to your will. I was only wondering…"

"I know what you were wondering. I will tell you this, and you must understand. There are many lights born into this world each day. These lights come with their purpose and in their own time. If one light precedes the purpose of another, that light's purpose must come first. You must respect that and accept each light as it comes, when it comes."

"It will be done, Sacred Woman." As Ramuza rose again to leave, the Supreme Spirit spoke to him again.

"Ramuza," She said, "Your mate will give you a son."

******

"Ramuza and I left the Temple. We called Rwuva and Olabisi together and confessed our secret to them. To our surprise, Olabisi showed complete understanding and acceptance. Rwuva was a little angry, but not because of the secret pregnancy. She was angry because Ramuza and I were afraid to come forward initially.

"And, once again, Rwuva suggested that Ramuza take me as his third mate. She reminded us of what the Supreme Spirit had said as we left the Temple's central chamber. 'Your mate will give you a son.' Rwuva explained, if there was any hope that the child I carried would be born male, there had to be a union between Ramuza and me."

"You became the Gray Warrior. How did the Mfalme decide between Quazzi and you?" Ameh asked.

"After we confessed to Rwuva and Olabisi, we let circumstances decide. The Mfalme and I agreed that if my child were born male, I would become the Principal Mate, and Quazzi would have no choice but to wear the gray cloak. If my child were born female, I would accept the position of Gray Warrior."

Summare giggled again. "The Mfalme got his seventh daughter."

"Yes. I gave birth to Zindzhi Nyoka. She is only two harvests older than Adaulah, and I suppose she strongly takes after me. For a while, she seemed to be the son that Ramuza was looking for. She has a warrior's heart. Even at her age, she has a mind for truth and fairness and will challenge you immediately.

"As Ramuza had promised the Supreme Spirit, he accepted Zindzhi completely. With the self-discipline that Ramuza is known for, he changed his attitude. He surrendered completely to the will of the Supreme Spirit. It was almost as if he had stopped looking for a son. And it was a good thing, too. One harvest later, Olabisi became pregnant again."

"The other set of twin girls were born," Summare spoke up, her shyness gone.

"Yes, Baako and Alaba Sheetswa. Those two are the quick-witted comedians of the family. They are relentless pranksters too, which is only made worse by the fact that there are two of them."

"Then came Adaulah."

"Yes. After the next harvest, Rwuva finally gave birth to him, a son."

"I am sure the Mfalme was quite pleased." Ameh smiled at the joyous end of Kharaambi's story.

"Ramuza was elated. Adaulah's birth caused a celebration that lasted several days. Now you understand why the Little Creation is a special jewel among the Aukmondi."

— 33 —

THE SACRED TEMPLE

When Ameh looked around, most of the restless nine Chinchigwe had made themselves very comfortable around the campfire as they listened to Kharaambi's story. Only Komu and two others had fallen asleep. Their fatigue had won out. Twese, who had been the most restless one of all, was nowhere to be seen.

"Twese?" Ameh turned in one direction, trying to survey the clearing in the center of the kraal. He turned in the opposite direction, straining his eyes in search of Twese. "Where is he?"

Kharaambi got up. Her quick mind at once told her where Twese had gone. She turned and took a few steps toward the entrance of the guest kraal, as if to catch him before he had gone too far. Then, she noticed the two White Warriors coming up the pathway toward the kraal. Their pace was strong.

Kharaambi met them at the entrance. She addressed the female warrior. "What is it, Upenda? Has the Mfalme returned?"

"He is on his way, Sacred Woman. We just received word that he has just started down the north slope."

"Well, it is about time," Kharaambi responded to Upenda, but her eye still searched the pathway for Twese.

Upenda noticed her distraction. "Sacred Woman, is there something wrong?"

"It is one of the Chinchigwe. He has wandered off."

"We just saw him. Just after we crossed the bridge, we noticed him heading up the south slope."

"As I suspected. He is headed toward the Sacred Temple. Once he goes inside, he will never find his way out. Do me a favor, Sacred Woman. Retrieve him for me, please. When you find him, if he is amid some meditation or offering, do not disturb him until he has finished. But bring him back to the guest kraal as soon as possible."

"It will be done." Upenda turned and left immediately.

Kharaambi turned to the other White Warrior. "Dzhangu, Great Creation, I want you to return to the Royal Kraal. Upon the Mfalme's arrival, ask him to come to the guest kraal with his news regarding the Chinchigwe."

"It will be done, Sacred Woman." Like Upenda, he turned and left obediently.

******

Long before Kharaambi had finished her story, the idea to sneak away took root in Twese's head. The idea came when he heard Kharaambi say that visitors always came out of the Temple feeling as if they had communicated with the Supreme Spirit on a verbal level. He had many questions that he wanted answers to. When the opportunity came to steal away to the Temple, Twese did not hesitate to take it.

Twese was not familiar with the south slope. The thought had occurred to him that he might lose his way in the darkness. Thankfully, the meandering pathway up the slope was clear. He had no trouble at all. Although he lost sight of the Temple only once, he stayed with the pathway. The closer he got to the Temple doors, the torch lights in the Temple gardens were like beacons.

When Twese reached the Temple gardens, he saw two men and a woman lingering about. They were wrapped up in their talkative affair and did not notice Twese. Still, Twese did not want to draw any attention. He turned his back on the trio and developed a mock interest in the flowers at his feet. His full attention was always on the trio who stood between him and the Temple doors.

Twese was startled when the trio began to move slowly in his direction. In an instant, he was ready to abandon his quest and leave.

But, to his relief, the trio still did not notice him. They walked directly past him without incident.

Twese darted for one of the huge Temple doors with no one else around. He pulled at the door handle. At first, the gigantic door seemed heavy and immovable. It seemed to be locked. But then, as if his efforts had some delayed, magical effect, the door swung open, as if by its own will. Twese felt a cool breeze from inside rush out to greet him. He quickly slipped inside and closed the door behind him.

A frightening, endless void of darkness swallowed Twese. Absolutely nothing was visible, and he felt completely paralyzed with fear. He deliberately stepped back, falling against the door. The door against his back reassured him and gave him some sense of security.

The fear that Twese felt did not go away completely. It subsided just a bit, only to come back with a vengeance when he began to discern vague shapes in the darkness. Strange figures began to take shape before him from out of the void. 'Any Creation alone in the Temple caverns will become lost.' The words of Kharaambi echoed in his mind.

Twese began to panic again until he realized his eyes were slowly adjusting to the darkness. With growing relief, he realized that the strange figures before him were only the stalagmites and stalactites, randomly scattered throughout the cavern. His sense of being in control was gradually returning. He sighed and smiled at his melting fear.

Twese's eyes were functioning almost normally again in a relatively short time. He was not in total darkness after all. The walls of the cavern glowed with a soft, velvety fluorescence. It was the only light source, but more than enough to see by. Twese held his hands up in front of his face, pleased that he could see the lines in the palms of his hands.

Twese's first legible sights in the Temple were overwhelming. For the moment, he forgot about the problems of the Chinchigwe. He forgot about the whole outside world. The Temple's interior demanded all his attention. He had never seen anything like it before in his life.

The cavern's main passageway stretched before him endlessly, disappearing into the distant darkness. The visible part included walls lined with manufactured and natural designs. All of it was extremely pleasing to the eye. Twese stood momentarily, studying the passageway and designs, trying to decide how much the Aukmondi people had changed and how much was naturally beautiful.

At one point, the curious Chinchigwe followed a particular mural resembling a parade of stick figures. The figures were dancing toward another design that he could not recognize. Twese assumed the figures represented people, but the unrecognized design was beyond his comprehension.

The Chinchigwe abandoned his attempt to interpret the mural. He continued his slow walk along the passageway, deeper into the cavern. Occasionally, he felt a very gentle air flow current pass him, first in one direction and then in another. It carried a subtle scent that he could not identify. It was aromatic and slightly spicy. Twese concluded that it was either incense burning deeper in the cavern or a lingering essence of the flower gardens outside the Temple. Like the mural, its source and identity were beyond his mental reach.

Now and again, a stronger, warmer current of air would rush past Twese's ears. It felt as if someone was deliberately toying with him. It was such a deliberate sensation that Twese turned several times to try and catch the culprit. Each of his attempts, of course, was fruitless.

This repeated sequence of actions and reactions sent a chill down Twese's back. Once again, he wondered if he had committed a sacrilege by entering the Aukmondi Sacred Temple. Once again, he began to fear that his well-being was jeopardized. For his good, he decided to leave the Temple before it was too late.

Just as he turned to leave, he noticed a strangely attractive sound. It sounded like a chorus of women, chanting some unintelligible but melodious tune, far away, somewhere deeper within the cavern's interior. And true to the many legends of beckoning sirens, Twese surrendered to their call. He was irresistibly curious.

Twese continued his slow walk along the passageway with just a little more caution. Despite carefully placed steps, he stumbled on a small stone in the pathway. His ankle turned so violently that he lost his balance and fell.

Twese recovered his pride, picked himself up, and brushed the dust and dirt from his hands. He glanced down at the stone that tripped him. The fist-sized stone lay in the center of the pathway. Twese thoughtfully kicked the stone to the side of the pathway so that no one else would trip.

Twese turned and continued his way along the pathway. He looked back several times to get his bearings, then descended a small incline and around a bend to the right. Everything was going smoothly until Twese stumbled again on another obstruction. He did not fall this time. But the jolt was enough to make him break his focus and take note of the obstruction in the pathway. At first, it appeared to be another small stone. But a closer look revealed that it was not another stone. It was the very same stone he had tripped over earlier. Somehow, it had rolled back into the center of the pathway.

"This can not be!" Twese said to himself. He studied the stone a little closer. He studied his unfamiliar surroundings. He focused back on the stone. "This cannot be!"

There had to be a reasonable explanation. Maybe he had been focusing too hard on the chorus of women. He had not paid enough attention to where he was going or his surroundings. On the other hand, the designs on the cavern wall were unforgettable. Twese felt that he would have remembered them had he seen them before.

There were more dancing figures on the walls in this place, predominantly women. They were dancing in circles around the men. Each figure was linked, hand in hand. Each figure had what appeared to be a glowing orb of light on its chest.

Over the heads of the figures was another orb of light, much larger than the others. Twese wasn't sure whether it stood for the sun, a star, or a huge and remote heart hanging in the heavens.

If there was one thing Twese was sure about, it was the stone which lay at his feet. It was the same one. The Chinchigwe concluded that he had gone in a circle, returning to where he had first stumbled.

He picked up the stone and carefully placed it out of the way, on a flat stony ledge on his right.

"So, this cavern is tricky," he told himself again. "No real damage done. I will have to be more alert from now on."

Twese focused on the enchanting chorus again. He was determined to find those elusive sirens. He walked, studied his surroundings, and walked some more. He walked until he realized the chanting was not getting any closer. The melodious tune sounded as far away as ever before. Despite his alertness and caution, he had gotten nowhere.

The thought finally occurred to him that if he went any farther, he might be unable to find his way out of this maze. He made the wise and mature decision to forget the sirens and ensure his chances of finding his way back out of the Temple.

Twese turned around. He carefully retraced the several meters he had come. As alert and as cautious as before, he looked for the 'stumbling stone' where he had placed it on the ledge. It was now a point of reference.

The several meters brought Twese back to the dancing figures on the wall. The several meters brought him back to that flat, stony ledge where he had placed the stone – but his 'stumbling stone' was gone.

"This is impossible!" Twese was now in a place where his voice reverberated off the cavern walls, mocking him. 'This is impossible … is impossible … impossible … impossible.'

A parade of thoughts began to fill the Chinchigwe's head. Some tribal magic was at work here. After all, he had committed a sacrilege and was slowly being punished for it. He had angered the Aukmondi Sacred Spirit and could die for his transgression. 'You must never go into the Temple unescorted by a Sacred Woman,' Twese heard Kharaambi's voice again. 'Or you will certainly die,' his mind filled in.

Twese panicked again, unable to decide how much of his thoughts were factual. He was confused and disoriented, and his reasoning was faltering. He desperately wanted out of the Temple. All his instincts forced him to seek the Temple's exit, but which way was it?

"No! No. Just wait a minute! I must get control of myself." Twese stopped his desperate movements. As calmly as possible, he walked another several meters, hoping that by sheer luck, he was going in the right direction, hoping that he would come upon something that would give him some perspective. He eventually came to a small embankment on his left and a dead end of the pathway.

Twese looked all around, to the left and the right. He even looked up, refusing to accept this dead end and the wall before him. "This is just great!"

To keep his calmness, Twese stepped back. He calmly sat down on the embankment and forced himself to relax. He deliberately tried to recall the cavern's layout for the first time. He found his memory jumbled, confusing, and frustrating. He could not recall a single, useful memory of twists and turns he had made.

Just as Twese prepared to get up, his eyes locked onto an object on the opposite side of the pathway. He jumped up, startled. On the ground in front of him lay his 'stumbling stone', untouched.

Twese backed away from the stone as if it had physically attacked him. He turned to run. A few panicky steps back up the pathway brought him to another dead end. He was cornered in a cove with only one way in and one way out. On the wall at the back of the cove was a majestic drawing of a woman looking down on him.

"This is madness!" Twese turned to exit the cove. He managed to find a pathway again, but it was unfamiliar. He tried to run up the pathway. It was too narrow to keep his pace. He stopped, helpless, wondering if falling off a cliff here or down into an unseen crevasse was possible. He wondered if he could become forever lost here and die before anyone ever found him.

"Can anyone hear me?" Twese called out desperately. He was hoping the chorus of women was nearby. "Can someone help me?"

At first, his anxious voice came back to him, giving him a fleeting moment of hope. He was so desperate that he almost did not recognize his own echo. Just as he was about to call out again, a different voice reached his ears, the voice of a distant female.

"Hello? Did someone call?" The faint voice called back.

"Yes! Yes! I … I don't know where I am. I am lost. Can you help me?" Twese ran three or four steps toward the welcoming voice but thought better of it. He stopped.

"Stay where you are," the voice said. "We will come to you."

We? Maybe there was a chorus of women wandering about in here after all, Twese thought. He took a deep breath, relieved that help was on the way. He forced himself to relax again.

He turned around slowly, studying his surroundings with considerably more respect now. Even though he did not understand it, he was convinced he could become hopelessly lost with a single step. He realized he was probably lost when the Temple door closed behind him.

Within minutes, Twese heard footsteps approaching. It wasn't a chorus of women. The footsteps belonged to a young man – a boy who walked with his arm lovingly embracing a young female about his same age. The two stopped their confidential chatter and laughter when they saw Twese.

"Great Creation!" The young man began. He was almost as speechless as Twese. "You … you are one of the Chinchigwe."

"Yes, I am."

"Please, forgive me for staring. I am surprised to see you here." The young man produced a friendly smile. "I am called Ntubi. And this is my friend, Rhama."

"I am very glad to see you, Ntubi. And you, too, Rhama. I am called Twese."

"Twese, Great Creation, what are you doing here … alone?"

"Kharaambi said I was welcome to visit. I suppose curiosity got the best of me. I could not wait. I entered and became lost. Now, all I want is to find my way out. Will you help me?"

Ntubi looked at his friend Rhama.

Rhama, in turn, looked at Twese and offered her hand. "Come. I will gladly help. The Temple doors are this way."

Twese was a little hesitant to take Rhama's hand. He started to ask if it was necessary but quickly stifled the thought. He took her hand. He was willing to do almost anything to get out of the Temple.

— **34** —

ELEDAH

Twese allowed Rhama and Ntubi to lead him along the pathway. After only a few meters, they came to a fork in the pathway. Rhama and Ntubi led Twese down the left branch. Twese was grateful. He had glanced down the right branch. It did not look very inviting at all. It stretched as far as he could see into a void of darkness. He saw a white, formless, floating apparition in the middle of that void.

"What is that thing?" Despite his present company, Twese was still easily frightened. He tried not to show it.

Both Rhama and Ntubi turned to see what Twese had seen. They examined the apparition as it moved toward them slowly. Rhama could feel a slight tug from Twese as he tried to keep her moving.

"It is alright, Great Creation," Rhama finally said. "That thing is someone coming."

Twese looked at the figure again. He tried to accept Rhama's words. Despite the figure's closer proximity and the bright velvety glow from the cavern walls, he still could not recognize the figure as an approaching person.

Twese watched the figure grow closer. Fortunately, the longer he watched it, the more it appeared to take a solid form. Twese eventually began to recognize it as a person dressed in white.

"I thought I heard voices over here." The figure spoke. The voice belonged to a female – a White Warrior who finally walked into clear view.

Twese was instantly impressed by the warrior's appearance. He remembered seeing her when the Chinchigwe were found, north of the valley. But this was the first time he had seen her close. Without realizing it, he studied her from head to toe. Her face, bare arms, and shapely legs had the smoothest dark complexion he had ever seen. He found her astonishing. Rhama and Ntubi greeted her as the Sacred Woman, Upenda.

"And you found the Chinchigwe for me."

"Yes, Sacred Woman. He is called Twese. Ntubi and I were escorting him toward the Temple doors. He was lost."

"Of course, he was." There was a twinkle of mischief in Upenda's eyes as she looked Twese up and down. She said nothing to him. Her eyes said everything.

Twese felt excited. He was almost disappointed when Upenda turned away from him and moved toward Rhama and Ntubi.

"So, what were you two doing?" Upenda asked. "No. Wait. On second thought, do not tell me. I do not think I want to know."

Twese listened to Upenda, Rhama, and Ntubi's conversation, feeling like an outsider. Judging by how the three talked, they were very well acquainted. Their conversation covered a subject Twese felt he should not be hearing. Yet, they made no attempt to speak privately.

"Please." Twese felt that he had heard enough. "I do not wish to intrude, but I would like, very much, to get out of here."

Again, without acknowledging Twese, Upenda politely ended the conversation with Rhama and Ntubi. "We will finish this later. Do not worry about the Chinchigwe. I will escort him out. You two go and finish whatever you were doing."

Twese watched Rhama and Ntubi depart until they disappeared in the darkness. He assumed that Upenda was watching them, too, but when he turned to face the White Warrior, she watched him.

"What are you doing in here alone, Great Creation?"

"Why does everyone keep asking me that? Have I committed some sacrilege by coming in here alone?"

"You tell me. Is foolhardiness a sacrilege?"

Twese did not know how to answer that. "I must apologize. You must know, I meant no harm."

"You don't have to apologize. You have committed no sacrilege. And you have caused no harm."

"I was only curious. Kharaambi said that we were welcome to visit. And when I heard her discuss the wonders of your Temple, I had to see for myself."

"Was it all that you expected?"

"To be honest, it is nothing like I expected. I must admit, I have walked into something I am not quite ready for here."

"Great Creation, every time you walk in here without the guidance of a Sacred Woman, you will not be ready."

"My lesson has been learned."

Like Rhama had done, Upenda held out her hand. "Come, Chinchigwe. The exit is this way."

Twese took the White Warrior's hand. The two started in a direction opposite the way Rhama had been going, down the right pathway. Twese was acutely aware of it.

"Wait. Where are we going? Where are you taking me?"

"Out of the Temple."

"Yes, but Rhama was taking me back the other way." Twese pointed over his shoulder.

"The Sacred Woman Rhama goes her way. I will go my way. Trust me."

Twese stopped his protest. He did not have a choice. He allowed Upenda to take him … wherever.

For several meters, Twese and Upenda walked in silence. As Twese relaxed, he became more aware of Upenda's hand in his. It pleased him. He found himself studying her. He was experiencing a tremendously strong attraction to her without rational grounds and much too rapidly. Some force within him was taking control of his common sense, making him feel and behave unlike himself.

"You came looking for me." Twese tried to sabotage his runaway feelings. "How did you know I was in here?"

"The Sacred Woman Kharaambi sent me to find you. The Mfalme is returning from the north rim. Kharaambi wants me to return you to the guest kraal as soon as possible."

"Do you know if the Mfalme turned the merchant away?"

"No. I do not know."

"I suppose we will soon find out."

Again, there was an awkward silence between Twese and Upenda. Twese's thoughts and feelings continued to be out of his control, and he made another attempt to suppress what he was experiencing.

"I recognize you," he began. "You were with the Mfalme when he found us in the wilderness, north of your valley."

"Yes, I was there."

"Then, you are one of the warriors who rescued Adaulah."

"One of them."

"The Mfalme is probably very grateful to you."

"I am sure that he is. But I cannot claim all of the credit. I can claim very little. If you will remember, I was only one in 170 warriors who brought Adaulah back."

"Was it that many out there? I remember seeing a few warriors. I remember the Mfalme. I remember Quazzi. And I remember you." Twese was desperately trying to keep a casual conversation with this woman. It was his only defense against her mystical effect on him. His efforts were not very good.

Upenda noticed. "What is wrong, Great Creation? You look uncomfortable."

"I am fine." Twese lied. The shape of her lips was perfect. The magic in her eyes was divine. The very smoothness of Upenda's dark skin excited him.

"Are you sure? You do not look well."

"I assure you. I am fine. It is only this, … this Temple. Things are very different in here."

Upenda pointed to another embankment nearby. "Here. Why not sit and rest a while?"

Twese started to protest. It had been long since a woman had affected him this way. This woman was special. He could not protest. "Maybe, just for a moment."

Twese sat on the embankment next to Upenda with a respectable distance between them. Helplessly, his eyes trailed over Upenda's shoulders and muscularly toned arms. Even her legs did not escape her integral beauty.

This is wrong. Twese tried to force his ethics and morality to the forefront. He was being disrespectful. A man should not hunger for a woman like this, especially a woman he did not know. Twese forced his attention toward other things.

"Listen. Do you hear that?"

"Hear what?"

"The chanting. Since I have been here, I have been trying to find those chanters. But, like everything else in here, they elude me."

Upenda openly laughed at Twese. She did it without seeming rude. "You will not find them, Great Creation. In the first place, very few Creations can navigate the Temple's passageways without getting hopelessly lost, as you did. And in the second place, the chanters you hear do not exist."

"What do you mean, they do not exist? I hear them."

"You hear only the currents of air that flow through the Temple's coves and caverns."

Twese listened again. He still heard people singing, not the currents of air. He had to take Upenda's word. He turned his attention to the other statement she made.

"So, why can men, Creations as you call them, not navigate your Temple passages? Is your Sacred Spirit partial to women? In the short time that I have been here, I have had a very frightening time. I would be reluctant to call a place like this 'Sacred'."

"Nevertheless, it is our Sacred Temple. The Aukmondi worship the Mother of All Existence, who, of course, is female. Just as the huts of the valley are our homes, these caverns are Her home in our valley. We hold the caverns as sacred to welcome Her."

"That still does not explain why men become lost here and women do not."

"Well, that is a long story you do not have time to hear. The Sacred Woman Kharaambi asked me to retrieve you. Unless you were meditating, or making and offering, I am to return you to the guest kraal as soon as possible."

"Then let us continue. I am anxious to learn what the Mfalme has done anyway." Twese got up. He followed Upenda along the pathway, careful not to let the distance between them grow. "Kharaambi mentioned a central chamber in her story to us. Is that chamber near here?"

Upenda surveyed her surroundings as if she were lost. But then she responded confidently: "It is not far from here. And it is between here and the exit. If you like, I will show it to you as we pass."

Twese and Upenda walked in silence. Once again, Twese noticed his attraction to this woman intensifying. Once again, he deliberately suppressed his feelings. "So, you still have not told me why men cannot navigate these passages?"

Upenda glanced at Twese and smiled. She did not want to tell him the story simply because she would have to give him a shortened version. She felt that such a beautiful story should never be abridged, especially when told to someone who had never heard it before.

"All that I will tell you now," she began, "is that Creations, men as you call them, are Her most precious creations. The pure and noble spirit of man is Her greatest love.

"Initially, She created his spirit to walk this land alone. And She marveled at him from afar. During that time, there was no other creation like Her Great Creation. Over time, the Supreme Spirit became so impressed and attracted to Her Great Creation that She wanted to be closer to him. She decided to live, learn, and grow at his side.

"The Supreme Spirit set Her great forces aside, to act independently as nature. Then She stepped down from Her great and lonely reign to be forever with Her Great Creation.

"Women can navigate these passages simply because in Her home, we are most like Her. As sisters and daughters of Her Spirit, we have an intuitive sense that is merely a lingering spiritual link between who we were long ago and who we are now.

"A few Rare and Sensitive Creations can move about here, like the Favored Tribesman, the Great Creation Kon-Shambique. He can navigate these passageways almost as well as any woman. And likewise, there have been a few insensitive women who have become completely disoriented, in here, unable to move a few meters without getting lost."

"Have you ever gotten lost?"

"No. Not yet. Sometimes, when I come here, I might see a drawing, cove, or passageway I have never seen before. But I always know where I am."

At this point, Twese happened to look ahead. To his surprise, he saw other people. A small group of people was moving along the pathway up ahead. "People! Where were they when I needed them?"

Upenda understood Twese's question to be rhetorical. She did not answer him. Instead, she signaled him to keep his voice down. She spoke in a whisper. "They are going to the central chamber. It is just ahead, over that embankment. This is the heart of the Temple. This is where most of us come to commune with the Supreme Spirit. Please be as quiet as possible so we do not disturb anyone in worship."

Twese acknowledged Upenda but eagerly took the lead on the pathway. He followed the group of people up a small incline toward the embankment. The group eventually disappeared on the other side. Twese stopped at the top of the embankment and turned toward the White Warrior.

"There is a cove over here," he whispered.

"It is the entrance to the chamber."

"May I see inside?"

Upenda rushed up the incline to Twese's side. She took his hand again and went ahead over the embankment into the cove. The cove turned out to be a prelude to a huge chamber. Upenda allowed Twese to enter the chamber first.

The chamber was the largest Twese had seen so far. The walls and ceiling were visible, but their distances were illusions. He could not figure out how far away they were.

The velvety glow in the chamber was much richer, caused by concentrated mineral deposits. Twese could see irregular orbs and inanimate streams of deposits embedded in huge stalactites and stalagmites. The deposits glowed so intensely that their shapes appeared to alter before his eyes.

Several piles of creative artifacts stood throughout the chamber among the stalactites and stalagmites. Piles of pottery, jewelry, sculptures, and weavings reached heights above Twese's head. Twese did not have to be told that these artifacts were gifts given by the Aukmondi people to their Supreme Spirit.

Twese attempted to get a closer look at one of the piles. Upenda tugged his hand hard as he did, trying to pull him back. It was too late. Twese accidentally nudged something with his foot. It moved upon contact, startling Twese. He looked down to see an elderly woman looking up at him.

"I am sorry," Twese said as apologetically as possible in a whisper. "I did not see you. Please forgive me."

"You are forgiven, Great Creation." The elderly woman whispered back and then smiled. "Enjoy your visit."

"Thank you." Twese respectfully returned the woman's friendly smile. He moved away, changing his mind about getting a closer look at the pile of artifacts. In doing so, he noticed other people in the chamber, quietly meditating here and there. In the darkness, he had not seen them at first.

Responding to his better judgment, the Chinchigwe decided to leave the chamber. That was his intention, until he caught sight of the altar on the far side of the chamber. Instead of leaving, Twese carefully worked toward the altar, pulling Upenda behind him.

On top of the altar, the Chinchigwe saw a life-size statue of a beautiful woman sitting on a rock formation. The statue seemed to stare directly at Twese, almost as if it knew he was there. The craftsmanship was so perfect, refined, and full of feeling that it appeared to possess living features. The shimmering effect of the velvety light made Twese question whether the statue sat perfectly still. Twese was almost sure he was looking at a real person.

Twese went closer. He began to return the statue's constant stare. He studied it and realized, with every passing second, that it resembled Upenda.

"It is you!" Twese's excited whisper was almost vocal.

Upenda placed her hand over Twese's mouth. Then she led him quickly back across the chamber and out the exit. She turned to face him. "Great Creation, you must keep your voice down. People are meditating in there."

"But the statue!" Twese felt excited again. "It is a statue of you."

"I am truly flattered, Great Creation. But it is not a statue of me. It is only the lighting in the chamber and your mind."

"What are you saying? The features of the statue were yours, Upenda."

"Have I had that much of an effect on you?" Upenda smiled at Twese's excitement. After a thoughtful moment, she turned Twese around to face the chamber's entrance. "Go back. Take another look. Look closer this time."

Upenda allowed Twese to reenter the chamber alone. She knew there was only one way in and out, and the Chinchigwe could not get lost.

Twese walked into the chamber. He stayed a few minutes longer than Upenda's patience. He came back out just as she was about to go in and get him. She noticed confusion and disappointment on his face.

"Well? Whose features did you see this time?"

"I do not know. Just as you said, the features were different this time. They were unfamiliar."

"Eledah," said Upenda. "When the Supreme Spirit takes human form and walks among us unrecognized, we call Her 'Eledah'."

"That is a beautiful name."

"It is Her name."

"But I was so sure; the statue looked like you the first time."

"I do not doubt you. It is possible."

"The lighting in the chamber makes such changes?"

"Yes, and your heart and your mind."

Twese wondered if he was the only one victimized by illusions. "Whose features did you see when you looked at the statue?"

"As I told you, Eledah," Upenda repeated.

"I think I have seen Eledah before," Twese said as he focused on a recent memory.

"Of course you have. Everyone has."

"No. I meant just recently. During our flight to escape the slave merchant, we were charged by an angry rhinoceros. Adaulah, the only one among us not bound by the merchant's chains, was free to challenge the rhinoceros. He did it, saving the Chinchigwe. I am unsure what happened then, but I saw a woman standing beside the docile beast when it was all over. She was too far away to see her features clearly, but I think it was Eledah."

Upenda smiled. "I'm sure that it was."

"What sort of magic is this?"

"It is no magic, Great Creation. It is a natural illusion, a characteristic of the Sacred Temple. If there is magic, it is only the magic of the heart. The whole experience is just an example of Her love."

"An example of Her love." Twese glanced back at the central chamber. "Why do you suppose I saw your features on the statue?"

"Only you can answer that, Great Creation."

Twese searched his mind, but he had no good answer for Upenda. When he finally spoke, he spoke his mind: "I do not know. Just being in your presence seems to put a lot of things into perspective for me. It is a wonderful feeling."

Upenda smiled again. "Come. We had better get you to the guest kraal."

Upenda took Twese's hand and continued along the pathway. After only two small turns, Upenda led Twese into a small cove. Twese recognized it as one he had been in before.

"Upenda, this is a dead end." He remembered the majestic image of a woman looking down on him. "Why have we come in here?"

Upend said nothing. She led Twese to a corner of the cover and turned toward the confused Chinchigwe. Her back was against the wall, and she smiled as she leaned heavily against it. Like magic, light from the torches in the Temple gardens poured into the doorway as the Temple door opened.

— 35 —

MISTAKES AND MISUNDERSTANDINGS

Twese and Upenda came down from the Sacred Temple just in time to see a parade of people crossing the bridge from the north to the south slope. At the head of this parade were two Blue Warriors who had turned to take the south bank pathway toward the guest kraal.

The Mfalme Ramuza Ncobba and the Brown Warrior Quazzi were just a few meters behind the Blue Warriors. Both walked steadily and with determination, appearing eager to reach the guest kraal.

Three white men, the slave merchant and his two aides, walked behind the Mfalme and Quazzi. There was an arrogant confidence in the merchant's walk. By contrast, his aides showed signs of nervousness as they stared at all the African faces staring back at them. All three men looked out of place in this parade. They were bracketed by four Green Warriors – two in front, and two behind.

Twese and Upenda reached the bottom of the south slope just as the merchant and his aides came off the bridge and turned up the pathway. As if Upenda couldn't tell, Twese pointed the merchant out to her. The merchant walked with a crooked smile on his face. As usual, he chewed on his tobacco, his beard bobbing wildly up and down.

"The hair on his face," Upenda gasped, "it is on fire!"

"If that frightens you, then wait until you hear him talk." Twese led Upenda onto the south bank pathway. They joined the parade of people behind the Green Warriors. "His speech is venomous. And he spits bile behind his words."

Some distance behind Twese and Upenda was the bulk of the parade of people. A large group from the Royal Kraal had momentarily abandoned the evening's Daily Celebration of Life to follow the Mfalme to the guest kraal. Everyone was curious to learn what the Mfalme had done about the merchant. Why had the Mfalme not turned the merchant away? Why did he bring the merchant down into the valley?

The Sacred Women Rwuva, Olabisi, and most of their daughters led the majority of people. Adaulah, almost hidden from view, walked in the middle of his sisters. His obscurity did not hide his curiosity, or the tiny leopard kitten cradled in his arms.

******

Kharaambi and the restless nine Chinchigwe continued to wait for the Mfalme in the guest kraal. With words that the Mfalme was on the way, all nine were on their feet, and more restless than ever. Ameh was the first to see the crowd coming up the pathway. When he spotted the three white men, the expression on his face turned grim. It was not what he expected.

The Blue Warriors at the head of the group stopped at the entrance of the guest kraal. They respectfully allowed the Mfalme and Quazzi to enter the kraal first. The Green Warriors escorting the merchant and his aides also stepped aside at the kraal entrance. They allowed the white men to enter the kraal behind the Mfalme.

From this point, the merchant took the initiative. He quickened his pace. He had spotted and recognized the restless nine standing in the center of the kraal. He rushed around Ramuza and Quazzi, pointing. "Why, there they be!" The smile on his face broadened. "That's them alright."

The merchant's aides, Sam and Pete, gathered at the merchant's side. They also smiled, but their nervousness was clear.

McIntyre leaned over and spat out the old wad of tobacco in his mouth. He wiped his mouth with his sleeve and turned to Ramuza. "You trying to hoodwink me, chief? This here ain't all of 'em. Where's the rest of 'em?"

"They are probably resting, merchant."

"Well, good. I really do appreciate you atakin' such good care of 'em for me like this. I really do."

The merchant walked over to stand directly in front of the restless nine. Ameh, Embabi, Summare, Komu, and others huddled in his presence. The merchant pulled out a fresh twist of tobacco from his pocket, unwrapped it, and bit off a huge piece. He wildly moved the tobacco around in his mouth, then chewed loudly to loosen it up. He seemed to be prolonging time itself as he performed this strange ritual. With one final glance back at Ramuza, his cheeks bulging, he addressed the Chinchigwe.

"You know, you people done a terrible thing, arunnin' off like you did. You caused a lot o' trouble and you wasted a hell of a lot o' precious time. I want you to know I don't appreciate it one bit. Now, I know you don't know no better. I can understand that. But you see, that sort o' thing just can't be tolerated. Not even once. What you folks need is to be taught some discipline. I mean, some good, long-lastin' discipline."

There was a rumble of voices from the people gathered at the kraal entrance. The merchant's words were unexpected. Even Ramuza had a look of confusion on his face as the merchant continued to talk.

"Now, it will probably hurt me more than you. That is why, for this one time, I'm awillin' to make an exception. I've thought about it, and I've decided to punish only one o' you. But I assure you, it's meant to be an example to you all. I promised me boys, Sam and Pete, here, that if I ever get me hands on that little bastard-boy that turned you folks loose, I was agonna teach him a lesson right here on the spot. And, hell's fire, I still aim to do it. You see, by doing that right now, I can kill two birds with one stone, iffin' you know what I mean. Now, if one o' you folks will be kind enough to tell me where he is, I'd appreciate it."

McIntyre searched the group of restless people who stood speechlessly before him. Since his trek past the Royal kraal, he was not aware that Adaulah was only a few meters behind him all the while. He turned to Ramuza.

"Chief, I'm agonna need you to roust up the rest of these folks so they can see this here important lesson. And if that little bastard-boy is arestin' with 'em, make sure you bring him out too. Now, I know he's here. Me boy Sam saw you bring him toward the valley, not more than two 'r three hours ago."

"Merchant," Ramuza spoke. His voice was calm but full of warning. "I suggest that you forget your vengefulness. It is not what we agreed upon on the valley rim. Or, is there some misunderstanding on your part?"

"Misunderstanding? After that long-winded talk we had? Of course not. I don't see no cause for it all, but me and me boys, we left all our guns and things up yonder on the rim, like you told us to do. And we come down into your valley, all peaceful-like, to settle things, like you said we could. No sir. There ain't no misunderstanding, chief. I was just ahopin' to let these people know that I don't intend to tolerate no nonsense."

"Then, merchant, please be aware of what you do. You have been warned."

"Of course, chief. Me 'n you, we seem to be on friendly terms. I certainly don't want to make no mistakes 'n jeopardize all o' that."

Sam was the first to spot Adaulah. He happened to look back toward the entrance of the kraal. He saw Adaulah standing between Rwuva and Olabisi. Like Captain McIntyre and Pete, Sam was very relieved that this tribal chief was being much more cooperative than expected. And not realizing the gravity of Ramuza's warning, Sam thoughtlessly walked over to get Adaulah.

"Here's the boy, Capt'n McIntyre. If he was a snake, he would've bit you." Sam tried to grab Adaulah. Adaulah eluded him and ran to seek refuge behind Ramuza. Sam made the awful mistake of chasing after him.

Suddenly, and completely unexpectedly, Sam received a blow to the face. Ramuza had made a powerful, backhand swing, striking Sam across the mouth. The impact sounded like dry wood snapping in two. The force behind the blow lifted Sam off the ground. He fell flat on his back. His head was suddenly pounding, compounding the injuries the Wabanga had caused him. All of it made his split and bleeding lip seem insignificant.

They were reluctant when McIntyre and his aides were told to leave their weapons on the valley rim. But Ramuza insisted; otherwise, the merchant and his aides would not have been allowed into the valley. The merchant ordered his aides to comply. They did so, but not completely.

Pete never trusted these people. There was no telling what they were capable of. He was not going to be caught unprepared. Pete had surrendered his musket, flintlock, and knife to one of the warriors. But unseen by everyone, he had kept his pistol hidden in his belt, near the small of his back. The moment that Ramuza hit Sam, the usually level-headed Pete panicked. His mistrust paid off. These people were hostile after all, and, in his opinion, things were suddenly out of control. He unwisely drew his hidden pistol and aimed it. His target was that dangerously irate chief.

Before he could fire, Kharaambi aimed and launched her spear. With the grace and agility of a career warrior, she sent the spear flying over five meters. As intended, Pete's pistol was dislodged from his hand. Pete's jacket sleeve was ripped open. Blood began to flow from Pete's arm. Pete bent to his knees in pain. He held the wound tightly in a desperate attempt to stop the bleeding.

Ramuza walked over to the merchant and grabbed him by his lapel. Even though the merchant was a large man, Ramuza had him on his toes. That calmness in Ramuza's voice was gone. He was showing controlled anger.

All this caught McIntyre by surprise. He futilely tried to remove the chief's hands from his lapel, but the chief's grip was too strong. He tried to avert any harm to himself by pointing at Sam and Pete. Sam was still on the ground, just learning that his lip was split. Pete was struggling to stand up again as he gripped his wrist, blood still oozing through his fingers.

"What did you do that for, chief? Spare me hell's fire! None of this is called for!"

"It is called discipline, merchant. It is crude, primitive, and the only kind Creations like you seem to understand. As long as you and your Disrespectful Creations are in my valley, you will show self-discipline and respect to every living creature here, including my son."

"What?" There was a true look of surprise on McIntyre's face. "Your son? You mean ... that there boy is your son? Why, hell's fire chief, we didn't know. It never occurred to us that ... "

Ramuza was not listening to the merchant. "If you cannot pay us the homage of respect, then leave this valley at once, and never return. Is that clear?"

"Now just wait a minute. Calm down, chief. I told you, we didn't know."

With a jerk, Ramuza's grip tightened. "Is what I say to you clear, merchant?"

"Yes. Whatever you say." The smile returned to the merchant's face as Ramuza released him. "Seems, there was some sort of misunderstanding on me part after all. I'm real sorry. Hell, you didn't expect we meant your boy no harm, did you?"

"I only expect you and the Chinchigwe to resolve your differences."

"Differences?" The merchant chuckled. "You got us all wrong, chief. We don't have no differences. Why, these folks here; what was it you called 'em?"

"They are the very last of the Chinchigwe people."

"Yes, the Chinchi... ah, whatever. They mean a lot to us. They do. We don't intend to hurt a hair on their heads. The truth of the matter is, we come all the way over 'ere to help 'em." The merchant readjusted his clothes. Trying to smooth away new wrinkles in his jacket, he walked over and stood in front of the Chinchigwe again. He spoke to them noticeably softer, trying to be polite and respectful.

"Listen up. As I just told the chief here, there has been a couple o' minor mistakes 'n misunderstandings. And I'm real sorry. You must believe me when I say, we didn't come 'ere to hurt you in any sort of way. We might act a little rough sometimes but, hell's fire, that don't mean nothing."

The merchant paused a moment to spit another spurt of tobacco juice. "Now, the truth is, we heard that your huts and village were destroyed a few days ago. That there is terribly unfortunate. We think such a thing ought not to happen to nobody. So, I'll tell you what we're agonna do. Sometimes tomorrow, me and me boys, we're agonna take you away from this hostile place. We will take you to a new land, a new world, where things are much better. And all that we ask in return is just a little cooperation. That's all. Iffin' you do, I promise you, you'll start to live like real human beings. You'll be cared for. You'll be protected. You won't go hungry another day in your lives. Why, you'll even be trained to do decent, useful, civil jobs where…"

"No, slave merchant!" Twese had been standing at the entrance of the guest kraal. He had heard enough. He boldly cut the merchant off. He worked his way among the people, past the Green and Blue Warriors, past the Ncobba daughters, and past Rwuva and Olabisi. He walked directly toward the merchant. "We will not go with you."

After the little incidents with the chief, McIntyre thought things had recovered. But when Twese suddenly rejected his offer, he began to sense trouble again. He suppressed his anger and held a finger up in Twese's face.

"Now you listen to me, boy! Don't you dare start nothing with me. You just shut that kind o' talk up this minute. Enough has happened already without your interference. I'll not tolerate any more trouble. I got too much time and money invested in your black hides already. You understand me?" The merchant glanced at Ramuza. He forced himself to calm down. With a fake smile on his face, he turned to Twese again. "Now behave yourself. Cooperate with me, alright? We can get our differences resolved in no time."

Twese stood his ground. He was not going to be swayed by the merchant's gracious behavior. "You have wasted your time and your money, merchant. We did not ask for your help. We will not accept it."

The merchant clenched his fist at his side. He wanted very much to hit this troublemaker. The terrible vision of losing his entire investment flashed through his head. He could not afford that under any circumstances. He held his rising temper in check and turned to Ramuza.

"Chief, what did you do to these folks? They weren't like this before."

"I have done only what I could for them."

"What did you do to make 'em so god-awful rebellious like this?" He pointed at Twese.

Ramuza glanced at Twese. The Chinchigwe was showing a combative nature that he had not seen before. He wondered where it had come from. He almost smiled. He was personally glad to see it.

"Merchant," Ramuza finally said, "please do not delay this any longer. Is it your intention to resolve this conflict, or has there been a mistake on my part?"

"Frankly, chief, I beginnin' to suspect that maybe you have. For your sake, I truly hope you haven't done anything to cause me no trouble. 'Cause iffin you have; if you told these folks some cock 'n bull story 'bout not havin' to come with me…"

Ramuza turned his back on the merchant. He walked a few steps away. His patience with the merchant was gone. "Merchant, I have told you what I expect of you. The problem between you and the Chinchigwe must be resolved. The two of you must come to an agreement so that you can go your separate ways."

"Separate ways? What in hell's fire are you atalkin' about? These folks are acomin' with me."

"We will not be coming with you, merchant." Twese was as bold as ever before. He stood defiantly with his arms folded across his chest.

The merchant pointed angrily at Twese. "Damn you, boy! What did I tell you? You just keep out of this. What do you plan to do 'bout it? You can't do nothing and you ain't got nothing to say."

"You are right, merchant." Ramuza faced the merchant again. "I have made a mistake. I went against my judgment when I allowed you into the valley. I felt it was necessary so that you and the Chinchigwe could work things out. But I see now, you have deceived me. Under The circumstances, I must ask you to leave. You may return when you are more willing to resolve this conflict peacefully."

"You must be jokin', chief. Why, this here is 'bout as peaceful as it's ever gonna be."

"Must you be taken out of the valley?"

The merchant smiled. Whether he was adopting a friendly attitude or simply laughing at Ramuza's threat wasn't certain. He boldly put his hand on Ramuza's shoulder. "Come 'ere, chief."

Ramuza looked down at the merchant's hand. The look suggested to the merchant that he should remove it. The merchant took his hand away as if realizing he had overstepped a boundary. "Come on over 'ere so we can talk in private."

"Why must there be secrecy among Honest Creations?"

"Say what?"

"Say what you have to say," rephrased Ramuza, "so that all of us can hear it."

"Tell me. Why are you backin' these people, chief? What have you got to gain? This business is betwixt me 'n them. Hell's fire, the way I see it, you don't owe them nothing."

"The Chinchigwe need help, merchant. The way I see it, if I can help them, I will."

"I might warn you, chief. You're aputtin' yourself in a mighty bad position. Mighty bad! But, I'll tell you what. Iffin' you just give this situation a blind eye; let me take me property, excluding your son of course, and I promise you, me 'n these folk will be out of your valley for good, all trouble avoided."

"We must avoid trouble some other way. I cannot do as you ask."

"Then that's a real pity. I had hoped I wouldn't 'ave to do this, but I see, I got no choice." The merchant chewed loudly on his tobacco as he fished around in his pockets. He eventually pulled out the Yululu

Bone. He held it up like a precious jewel. "Look 'ere, chief. Do you know what I got 'ere?"

For the first time since the merchant showed intent to harm Adaulah, the Mfalme expressed alarm. He recognized the trinket and stepped back.

The merchant smiled. "You surprise me. By the look on that ugly face of yours, you do know what this is."

"Foolish Creations have died by that bone." Ramuza had regained his composure.

"Yes, I know. And iffin' you don't get on me good side, you could be next."

"Merchant, the possessor of the bone dies as well."

"In most cases. Not if the possessor knows the secret to staying alive. I mean, look at me. Do I look like some kind o' fool to you? Would I be fool enough to carry this thing around knowing it was agonna kill me? No sir. There's a secret and I know it. Do you?"

Ramuza did not answer the merchant. He had occasionally heard stories and was vaguely familiar with the bone. He did not know its secret. He was not even aware that there was a secret that would ensure the possessor's life. Of course, the merchant could be lying. The bone, as he knew it, was deadly. It was nothing to be played with, even by Fool-hearted Creations.

"Where did you get it?" Ramuza asked.

"I don't suppose there's any harm in tellin' you. I got it from a group of amiable slave hunters who call themselves the Batushi. Why? Do you know 'em? Are they friends o' yours?"

Again, Ramuza did not answer the merchant. He had a suspicion and was concentrating on deciding the facts.

The last time Ramuza heard of a Yululu Bone was several harvests ago. He recalled that a visitor from Ratshuru, Zaire had come into this vicinity of Africa. For some unknown reason, the visitor was given a Yululu Bone by an unknown tribe. The visitor knew enough about the bone to know that his life was in danger. He fled at once, back to his homeland. He successfully crossed Lake Victoria and the country of Rwanda. But instead of returning to Ratshuru, the visitor made an impulsive, desperate, and evasive decision to go to Angumu for refuge.

The visitor's strategy was to no avail. A few days later, the visitor was found dead. Everyone, including Ramuza, thought it was strange that the visitor had been killed by a Batushi warrior so far away from Batushi territory. Now, the circumstance here just proved to Ramuza that the killing was not so strange after all. The Batushi tribe was the evil force behind the deadly bone.

Twese unfolded his arms. His defiance was undermined by the mysterious unknown and by the Mfalme's hesitant behavior. He came over to where the merchant and Ramuza stood. "What is that? What can he do with that bone, Mfalme?"

The merchant answered instead. "Why, I can bring the whole Batushi tribe down on this valley iffin' I want to. And everybody in these parts of Africa knows, the Batushi ain't nothing to mess around with.

"I'll do it too, chief. I don't know what you told these folks, but if you don't motivate 'em into acomin' with me, I swear to you, I'll decree that this whole valley look like a damned monsoon hit it."

Ramuza has past all phases of alarm now. After seeing the dreaded Yululu Bone and realizing who stood behind it, nothing could be more alarming. Ramuza calmly looked the merchant in the eyes. "You will leave now. Get out of my valley."

"What?" The merchant chuckled and looked at his two shaken aides. "What did he say to me? Did I hear right?"

"Leave, while you still can."

"Is that a threat, chief? We both know better, now don't we? When one chief threatens another, one or the other dies. And all hell breaks loose. To be quite honest with you, you don't stand a chance against me and the Batushi. How many warriors you got? Seven or eight thousand, maybe? The Batushi number five times that many. Do you still intend to keep your threat?"

Ramuza made a beckoning gesture. Kharaambi, Quazzi, and every warrior around responded. In an instant, they converged, surrounding the merchant and his aides.

"I didn't take you for a fool, chief. I guess I was wrong. My mistake. But alright. Iffin' that's the way you want it, you can consider this whole valley doomed to God-damned hell." The merchant stuffed the Yululu Bone back in his pocket. He went over to pick Pete's pistol off the ground. A Green Warrior stopped him by placing his foot on the pistol.

"You will not be needing that," said Ramuza.

"Fine. I reckon I won't. The Batushi has got all the guns I need."

After a gesture from Kharaambi this time, the four Green Warriors responded by ushering the merchant and his aide out of the guest kraal. The crowd of onlookers parted as the merchant and his aide were escorted back up the pathway toward the bridge.

"I'll be back, chief." The merchant yelled back. "And when I do, I won't be acomin' alone."

"Mfalme Ncobba," Twese stepped forward. "Is it wise to let him leave? Why not stop him before he reaches the Batushi?"

"It will do no good, Brave Creation."

"What do you mean? He and his aides can do nothing now. Let us stop him now, while we have the advantage."

"No, Twese. Because of the Yululu Bone, the merchant is called Mfalme by the Batushi. To do him harm would be to offend the Batushi. Even if we only held him prisoner, the Batushi will come for him if not, but to carry out the ultimate meaning of the bone."

"Can that be so bad?"

"Yes, it can. In the first place, the Aukmondi believe that killing another, for whatever reason, is barbaric. As long as you are among my people, we ask that you respect our belief."

"And in the second place?"

"In the second place, if we hold the merchant, the Batushi will come without fail. While they wait for the moment to kill him, the moment known only to them, they will carry out every order that he gives them."

"And to make the situation worse," Kharaambi added, "the merchant claims to know a secret to preventing his death. If this is true, it can only mean endless misfortunes for all of us."

"Then, what do you intend to do, Mfalme?"

"I do not know. We must learn to fight the merchant some other way while still having the time."

"But there is no other way. The next time we see the merchant, we must confront him and the Batushi."

"So, it would seem, Great Creation. In truth, since the moment he made known his possession of the Yululu Bone, that has been our destiny."

36

BIRTH TO A BATTLE STRATEGY

A heavy silence hung in the air until the Green Warriors had finally escorted the merchant and his aides from sight. Then the whispers began and grew to a full cascade of voices as news of the incident at the guest kraal traveled throughout the valley. The Chinchigwe people were not the only ones who stood to be victimized by the merchant's quest. The Aukmondi had been drawn into the crisis. And there was no way out – except one.

Ameh reconsidered the whole situation. He could see the predicament that the Aukmondi tribe had been drawn into. He understood the uncomfortable pressures that Mfalme Ncobba must be experiencing. From an unselfish perspective, Ameh could see that none was necessary. He gave Twese a quick and guilty glance before doing what he knew had to be done. He approached Ramuza.

"Mfalme," he began thoughtfully, "Kharaambi has shown us many beautiful things in your valley. We have met many of your wonderful people. We have seen, firsthand, what you have tried so hard to protect. I understand why it was such a difficult decision to decide whether to offer Chinchigwe protection or not. You are a wise man to choose your enemies."

"Ameh!" The perceptive Twese could tell what the old man was about to say. He could not believe it. "What are you doing?"

"Please, Twese! Allow me to finish. We cannot allow destruction to come to the Aukmondi because of us."

"But Ameh, please!"

"Twese! We do not have the right. I am very proud of what you have done. All of us, as well as our ancestors, are very proud of you.

It took courage to stand up to the merchant the way you did. It takes the determination that you have shown to try to save a lost cause. Let us not drag the Aukmondi down with us."

"You forget, Ameh, I am the pessimist. What happened to all that optimism that you once had?"

"It was confronted by the truth, Twese, as all things must." Ameh turned to Ramuza again. "We will give ourselves up to the merchant. No harm will come to your people."

Ramuza shook his head. "No, Great Creation. This peace cannot be bought with lives. Your intent is honorable, but I can not allow you to do it."

"We asked for your protection when you found us in the wilderness. Now, we have a means to protect you. The tragedy that has already come to our people must end. The Chinchigwe can end it here and now. We are grateful for what you and your people have done for us. And, as great as we respect you, Mfalme, you do not have the authority to prevent this sacrifice."

"Ameh, the slave merchant is a Creation of Greed. To give yourselves up to him now will do no good. He will take you, and then he will take the Aukmondi. He will do it because he has the power to do it and knows it."

"I think it is worth a try."

"No, Ameh. I will not allow you to throw your lives away. Our only alternative seems to be to defend the Chinchigwe and the Aukmondi in some other way."

"But you know, and I know, there is no other way. If the merchant returns with the Batushi, there will be bloodshed."

Ramuza untied the belt that held his knife. He drew the knife and looked at the blade. "There must be a better way. It is senseless for the Supreme Spirit's most Noble Creation to disagree violently."

"Then whatever happens, Mfalme, you have the complete support of the Chinchigwe, even if blood must be shed. It seems we now have a common enemy and," Ameh looked at Twese, "a common will to survive."

The Favored Tribesman, Kon-Shambique, had come down from his kraal on the north slope just in time to see the incident with the slave merchant. He had stood silently among the other on-lookers until now. After a brief word with Kharaambi, he and the Gray Warrior approached the Mfalme.

Kharaambi got the Mfalme's attention. "Great Creation, if the merchant returns with the Batushi, must there be bloodshed?"

Ramuza glanced at Kharaambi and the Favored Tribesman. He could tell that the two of them had already put their heads together and were giving birth to a battle strategy. "The only way to prevent bloodshed, Sacred Woman, is to give ourselves to the merchant. As long as I am Mfalme, that is not going to happen. Why do you ask?"

"The Favored Tribesman has an idea. I think it has strategic value."

"Yes, Great Creation?"

"Like most people, concerning the Yululu Bone, I know only a few stories and legends. I am afraid I may not know anything significantly useful. But the merchant said that he knows a secret to prevent his death. If there is such a secret, then that is what we must learn."

"How will that help?"

"There is a chance we may be able to use it against the merchant. If we can learn the secret and keep the merchant from doing whatever is necessary, then maybe the merchant will be too busy safeguarding his own life."

"Hopefully," Kharaambi added, "if he is busy safeguarding his own life, then the Chinchigwe and the Aukmondi will be the least of his concerns."

"What if the merchant has already done what is necessary to exercise that secret? It may be, already, too late."

"It is a chance we must take. We must learn that secret."

Ramuza nodded in agreement, but he had his doubts. "We must depend on too many chances and rely on too much hope. It is not a sound strategy."

"We must sometimes take our chances," Kon-Shambique said. "And sometimes, hope is the best strategy. It may be all we need to keep trying. Otherwise, we must accept the consequences."

37

TO THE POSSESSOR, POWER AND DEATH

The stillness and quiet of the night came early in the Aukmondi valley. Under the brilliant glow of a waxing moon, the only movements were made by a few nocturnal animals or vigilant warriors on night patrol. The only sounds came from the continuous chirps of crickets or the periodic hoots of an owl. From somewhere on the Serengeti Plain, the occasional cackles of hunting hyenas and the bellowing of a restless lion echoed through the valley.

Every evening, when all the daily chores and routines were done, it was the custom of the Aukmondi people to gather in the celebration area to pass the time. These free-spirited evenings were called their Daily Celebration of Life. This past evening, however, was an exception. The Celebration ended early. The Aukmondi people retired to their kraals and the solitude of their huts. There was very little desire to socialize publicly, and it was understandable. The news of that unscrupulous slave merchant had spread across the valley like a creeping fog. As it did, it left a dismal mood in people's hearts and caused them to have no desire to celebrate life.

******

Eventually, during the late-night hours, most people managed to calm their minds and fall asleep. Only a few were still failing at the effort. Ramuza was one of them.

Of all the people with the slave merchant on their minds, Ramuza was probably the most concerned. As the Aukmondi Mfalme, the bulk of the crisis rested heavily on his shoulders. Ultimately, finding a solution was his responsibility. He had the final word on what was or was not to be done.

Ramuza lay fully awake on his cot. He stared at the tightly thatched grass ceiling over his head, thinking. A battle with the slave merchant and the Batushi seemed inevitable. If it happens, there would be bloodshed. Close friends and loved ones would be killed. Property would be looted and vandalized. The valley would be destroyed. So far, there seemed no way to prevent any of it.

Frustrated with his unproductive thoughts, Ramuza set up. He knew harboring such a pessimistic view of the situation would not solve anything. He had to concentrate on a solution. Every problem has an acceptable solution. There has to be one for this problem. After all, would the Supreme Spirit allow Her people to suffer such a tragedy?

Ramuza had thought of asking Rwuva, Olabisi, or Kharaambi to escort him into the Sacred Temple to meditate. In the past, meditation in the Temple chambers had given him many insightful answers. But then, as soon as thoughts of visiting the Temple occurred, Ramuza dismissed them. He realized what the result of this meditation would be.

The Supreme Spirit was a hard and strict teacher in all Her mercifulness and compassion. We live to learn and grow. We must learn and grow, or we will struggle in ignorance to survive. Tragedy usually comes on the heels of ignorance, when our hearts and minds do not prepare us for what we must face. This is her natural law, which all creatures must live by. No creature is exempt.

If the Supreme Spirit did anything at all, it would only be to touch the minds and hearts of the Aukmondi so that they found their inspiration and will to keep living, learning, and growing. Only the strongest, most determined hearts and minds can withstand tragedies.

All evening long, since the slave merchant left the valley, Ramuza was aware of others going to the Sacred Temple to meditate. As a minimum, these anxious visitors had hoped to gain some peace of mind and relief from their worries. Ultimately, they had hoped to evoke divine intervention; to make the problems with the merchant and the Batushi as past problems. Regardless of their wishes when they entered the Temple, Ramuza already knew they would come out wanting one common thing – the desire to be closer to friends, family, and loved ones. Bonded by love, it seemed to be the answer to everything.

Ramuza looked across the main chamber of the hut where Adaulah slept when he visited his father's hut. The Aukmondi prince slept soundly, the tiny leopard kitten curled beside him. Would circumstance even allow him ever to be called Mfalme? Ramuza wondered what kind of valley this Innocent Creation would inherit.

Ramuza realized that he was failing badly to quell his restlessness. So as not to disturb Adaulah, he got up. He quietly crossed the main chamber and stepped outside the hut into the warm African night. A White Warrior stood guard outside the hut. The Mfalme and the warrior greeted each other with silent but respectful nods.

The Mfalme looked to his left. White Warriors stood guard outside the huts of Rwuva and Olabisi. No torchlight from inside their huts could be seen, which suggested that Rwuva and her daughters, and Olabisi and her daughters were all sleeping peacefully.

To the right, at Kharaambi's hut, a White Warrior also stood guard. But a torchlight emanated from inside, unlike Rwuva's and Olabisi's huts. Someone, Kharaambi, her daughter, or both were still awake. Ramuza began walking toward Kharaambi's hut but changed his mind. Instead, he turned toward the royal dais. Rather than add to their disturbance, he chose to sit outside for a moment to take in the night's tranquility.

Notwithstanding the anxieties and worries of the Aukmondi people, the night was filled with the quiet beauties of the tribe at rest. The bluish glow of the waxing moon mystically tinted the usual blackness of the night. The whole celebration area was visible. A barking dog, somewhere on the south slope, joined in with the chorus of crickets, the owl, the hyenas, and the bellowing lion on the Serengeti.

This beautiful peace had to be preserved, Ramuza thought. He knew he had to do whatever it took to preserve this peace. But how? Somehow, as the Favored Tribesman had insisted, the answer ironically seemed related to the Yululu Bone. Every alternative that

Ramuza had considered led him back to that bone. The Yululu Bone was the key.

What was its secret? So far, Ramuza had no idea. All he knew was that the bone was once a highly honored tribal trinket of a tribe he had just learned to be the Batushi tribe. At one time, the Batushi only gave the bone to people considered to be trustworthy friends. When the bone is given, the Batushi Mfalme shares his tribe and people.

Or was this the case? Has the legend been distorted as it has been passed from one fascinated storyteller to the next? Everyone who is given the bone eventually ends up dead, killed by the Batushi themselves. Was this a coincidence or design? Suppose the bone was meant to be a token of death in the first place? Did the Batushi give the bone to the slave merchant because he was a trustworthy friend? Or did the Batushi want the merchant dead?

Ramuza recalled how the merchant negotiated with pretenses to get into the valley and lied about his reasons for wanting to recover the Chinchigwe. It is very doubtful that anyone could consider the merchant trustworthy. A fool could see the selfishness and deceit in his heart. No. It was easier to conclude that the merchant was marked for death. It was only a matter of time.

But time was one thing Ramuza did not have. The merchant could return with the Batushi as early as tomorrow. To make matters worse, the merchant claims to know a secret to staying alive. If this is true, how long would he remain alive? How long will he be called Mfalme by the Batushi? Even after Ramuza learns the secret, could he use it against the merchant? Would he have any new options to save the Chinchigwe and the Aukmondi from the horrors of a senseless and bloody war?

Ramuza's barrage of questions was interrupted by a noise behind him. He turned to see Kharaambi standing in the doorway of her hut. Even without any of her warrior's garments, and silhouetted by the torchlight behind her, she was an impressive, statuesque woman.

"Why are you up so late, Great Creation?" She asked as she walked out to the royal dais.

"I could ask you the same question."

Kharaambi took a seat at Ramuza's side. She made herself comfortable on a woven rug beside Ramuza's chieftain's stool. "I could not sleep."

"Neither could I. I have been thinking about the suggestion you and the Favored Tribesman made concerning the Yululu Bone and its secret."

"Do you think we can use it against the merchant?"

"I do not know. We must first learn what that secret is."

Kharaambi searched her memory one more time. One more time, she drew a blank. "Suppose we do not learn the bone's secret? What will be our defense, other than the obvious?"

"I do not know. Let us begin by learning all that we can about the Yululu Bone. We will appeal to anyone who knows anything, truth or legend, to come forth and make their knowledge of the bone known. Hopefully, something useful will be learned."

"Very few people know what a Yululu Bone is, Great Creation. Even Kon-Shambique, one of the Wisest Creation among us, has confessed that he knows only very little, only a few stories and fewer facts."

"It is not how much anyone knows. The smallest bit of new information may be all that we need." Ramuza stretched and wiped his face as if to wipe away fatigue. "I have been thinking about the bone most of the night. My thoughts have already begun to repeat themselves."

Kharaambi studied her mate. She could tell he had devoted much time to this matter, possibly too much. She tactfully told him so. "Mfalme, I think you should try to get some rest. Fatigue and worry could prevent you from seeing even the most obvious answer."

"I do not dispute that. The truth is, I cannot afford to rest at this point. Rest loss is a small sacrifice compared to what we stand to lose. If there is something about the Yululu Bone that I can use against the merchant or the Batushi, I must learn it as soon as possible."

Kharaambi's tactical mind was still at work and about to pay off. "Everyone who owns a Yululu Bone is killed. What if we begin with the simple fact of 'possession'?"

"Possession?"

"Yes. Think about it. It is a common thread. Possession of the trinket seems to have some significance."

Ramuza considered the idea. Possession gave foundation to many of the thoughts he had already entertained. The possessor of the bone carried the unquestionable power and authority of the Batushi Mfalme. Yet, the possessor is always killed. Ramuza nodded his head in total agreement. "To the possessor comes power and death."

The faint trace of a smile on Ramuza's face gave Kharaambi the gratitude she was due. But she wasn't finished yet. She had been Ramuza's tactical advisor for eleven harvests. She knew how to support the Mfalme and then push him one step farther. "And now, assuming this is true, how will we use it?"

Ramuza's smile broadened. He was used to Kharaambi's technique. "We will build on it as we learn more."

Kharaambi sat up with Ramuza a little while longer. The two briefly discussed the Gray Warrior's plans for tomorrow, to drill all her armies and to fortify the sentinel lines in preparation for the worst. Ramuza showed no concern about the military defense of the valley. He had total confidence in Kharaambi. He had only one minor suggestion.

"We have visitors among us from neighboring tribes. We must see to their safety as well."

"That is taken care, Great Creation. I will sacrifice the regiments of the Kdedi Army to provide escorts wherever our visitors need to go."

"So be it." Ramuza stood up. He took Kharaambi's advice and suggested they both try to sleep before dawn. Both of them had a lot to do tomorrow. A restful mind was important. They returned to their respective huts.

— 38 —

A BLESSING AND A CURSE

Ramuza was still dressing when he came from his hut during early dawn the next morning. He stood in the doorway surveying the Royal Kraal with his sandals in his hand. Unlike the stillness and quiet of last night, there was noticeably more activity this morning. In addition to the White Warriors who continued to stand guard outside the Ncobbas' huts, several other people were moving about.

Five of his daughters, Yejide, Kunto, the twins Akwate and Akuato, and Zindzhi, were busying themselves between Rwuva's and Olabisi's huts. At this time of the morning, they were probably attending to their usual morning routine: boiling water, preparing various foods, or doing some other chores. The Sacred Woman, Rwuva, was usually involved in this routine, but Ramuza did not see her this morning. He assumed that she was simply out of view, inside her hut.

A few people from various kraal communities were scattered throughout the celebration area. Ramuza recognized most of them as the volunteers from the Pogobi kraal who had come back down from the north slope to help clean up the area after last night's abbreviated celebration. Since the celebration ended early, there was not much to clean. At this early hour, the volunteers were practically finished.

To the right, Ramuza saw a group of warriors congregating in front of Kharaambi's hut. Most of them were Royal and Blue Warriors, which was typical. Many warriors came every morning to receive their daily assignments or special instructions. This morning, Ramuza noticed, the group was unusually large.

The Gray Warrior stood in the center of the group of warriors. She had gotten her day started early. Ramuza knew that, throughout the day, Kharaambi had planned to call out all her armies. Somewhere, in the valley depths, the Gray Warrior intended to drill each army through exercise after exercise, mock battle after mock battle, until near perfection. Kharaambi's day would probably not end until she was satisfied with the performance of her warriors.

Even the sentinel armies would not be exempt from intense training. Kharaambi intended to see them go through their special drills, too. All the sentinel armies' performance needed to be flawless. Up there on the valley rim, the Green Warriors of the sentinel armies were the valley's first line of defense. An aggressor must defeat these elite warriors to get into the valley. Kharaambi intended to have them prepared for every contention.

Ramuza dropped his sandals to the ground to slip them on. Before he could slide both feet in, the tiny leopard kitten suddenly darted from the hut and swiped at one of the sandals, sending it sliding across the ground. The kitten playfully pounced on the sandal as if to kill it. With the sandal held tightly by its fore-paws and clawed at by its hind-paws, the kitten rolled over on its back and began gnawing on the toe of the sandal.

Just as suddenly, Adaulah darted from the hut to rescue his father's sandal. "Good morning, Great Creation. I will get it for you."

Adaulah pulled the sandal from the kitten's grip. But the kitten was still in a playful mood. As Adaulah lifted the sandal away, the leopard kitten pounced again. Half a meter off the ground, it hung onto the sandal to recover its "kill". Adaulah had to use both hands to separate the sandal from the kitten. Triumphantly, he handed the freed sandal to his father. "He was only playing."

"Yes, I can see." Ramuza took the sandal and slipped it on. "Have you named him yet?"

"Yes, Great Creation. He is called Sharikumba. The Sacred Woman Yejide helped me name him."

Ramuza glanced over at his daughters. Yejide, his second daughter, was sorting garments that had just been washed. "Why Sharikumba, Little Creation?"

"Yejide said he will grow up to destroy the evils among us. After the merchant came into our valley last night, I thought it was a good name."

"It is a very good name." Ramuza smiled. "Yejide must know that you will train him well."

"I have only just begun to train him, Great Creation. I am not his mother. And I do not care what the Royal Warrior Nionu said about me. I am not a leopard who drags dead zebras into the valley. I am not sure what I must teach him first."

Ramuza kneeled to stroke the kitten's furry chin. "Teach him to find whatever he needs. With that one lesson, he can take care of himself in most cases."

"It will be done."

"Does he know how to find food yet?"

"I do not know." Adaulah thought for a moment. He gently lifted the kitten and held it up to his face. "Are you hungry, Sharikumba?"

Ramuza did not hear an answer, but Adaulah did.

"He wants milk, Great Creation." Adaulah turned to reenter the hut. "I must hide a bowl of milk to see if he can find it."

Ramuza wished that his plans for the day were as simple and clear. He savored the brief moment with his son but at once returned to a more serious matter, to see if he could find what he needed.

Ramuza intended to spend his day searching for the secret of the Yululu Bone. It was a task that was not so clearly mapped out, but it was clearly the key to this crisis. Ramuza knew that, if he did nothing else all day, his ultimate goal was to find some information that he could use to defeat, or at least stop, the merchant and the Batushi without bloodshed.

Ramuza walked over to where his daughters were working. Respectfully, all five stopped what they were doing when they saw him coming. Yejide, the eldest among them, spoke for the group.

"Good morning, Great Creation."

Ramuza greeted his daughters with a smile. "I noticed you have already begun your chores this morning. Why is everyone up so early?"

"There is much more to do today." Yejide moved a stack of folded garments to one side and offered her father a place to sit. "And not all of us are here to do it."

Ramuza accepted the offer. "Where are the Sacred Women, Rwuva, and Omari?"

"Rwuva and Omari got up early this morning. They had planned to visit the guest kraal to check on the Chinchigwe. The Sacred Woman, Olabisi, had also planned to pay an early morning visit to the Sacred Temple. She wants to make a special offer. Since the three of them were going in the same direction, at the same time, they decided to do it all together. They just left a short while ago. That left me to supervise the morning chores."

Ramuza glanced at his other four daughters, who had diligently resumed work. "I can see you have everything under control."

"Thank you." Yejide already knew why her father was up and about so early. She pressed for the details. "How may I serve you, Mfalme?"

"I am on a quest today. I must discover the secret of the Yululu Bone."

"That trinket that the merchant brought into the valley."

"Yes. It is a very powerful and dangerous trinket. The Favored Tribesman has suggested that if we can discover its secret, we may be able to use that knowledge against the merchant and prevent him from harming the Chinchigwe and the Aukmondi."

Yejide stopped working and sat on the ground in front of her father. "Great Creation, I am not aware of any secret. I have never heard of a Yululu Bone until last night."

"It seems knowledge of the bone is as much a secret as the secret itself."

"Have you learned anything useful about it yet?"

"The Sacred Woman Kharaambi and I discussed it last night. We think that possession of the bone has some significance. The possessor holds the power of the Batushi Mfalme. Yet, the possessor always dies – killed by the Batushi."

"A blessing and a curse in one trinket."

"Yes. The merchant is the possessor of that blessing and that curse. Our problem is that the merchant claims to know a secret to prevent his death. That secret is what I must learn."

"I am afraid I can offer no insight, Mfalme."

"That is basically what Kharaambi said until we realized the significance of possession. I intend to speak with all my other advisors to discover other such hidden significances."

Yejide thought for a moment. "You must speak with the Craftsman Tanake, too."

"Why Tanake?"

"He is an artist, with knowledge of such trinkets. He can surely give you valuable guidance if he cannot tell you what to look for."

"There, you see." Ramuza smiled at his daughter as he got up to leave. He gently kissed her on her forehead. "You could not offer me insight into the secret, but you have helped me focus my search."

"I serve my Mfalme."

"Thank you. I must begin my day."

39

A SERPENT'S BITES

By the time the first golden rays of the morning sun streamed into the valley, Ramuza had left the Royal Kraal and was walking along the north bank pathway, which paralleled the river. He was not in a big hurry, but his pace was strong. He walked with his head down, deep in thought.

During his journey toward Kon-Shambique's kraal, Ramuza wondered what the day's end would bring. Would he succeed in learning the secret of the Yululu Bone? And if he did, would it make any difference? Would he be able to use the secret against the merchant? The thought occurred to Ramuza that, when this day was done, the secret of the bone may be worthless to him. That thought disturbed him. He forced it and that line of thinking out of his head. He deliberately adopted a more positive frame of mind. Nothing would distract him.

Ramuza was so concerned about his mission and the dreaded act of climbing the steep hillside of Nagorda Peak that he did not see a large dog coming rapidly down the pathway. This section of the pathway on which Ramuza and the dog traveled was narrow, and a collision between the two was inevitable.

No collision occurred, however. The dog's powerful sprint was only an expression of its cherished freedom. Even though Ramuza did not see the dog, the dog saw Ramuza. When it reached the Mfalme, it stopped running. It circled Ramuza several times, wagging its tail frantically and sniffing at Ramuza's hand.

"Where did you come from?" Asked Ramuza, as if he expected an answer. "What are you running from?"

Ramuza kneeled to pet the dog, which was exceptionally friendly. It seemed happy to see Ramuza, lapping at the Mfalme's face and pawing at him.

Not far behind the dog, a young woman came running into view from around a bend in the pathway. She struggled to carry a large bundle under one arm. She held up the hem of her ankle-length dress with her free hand so as not to trip.

"Benai! Benai! Stop!" She called after the dog. The moment she recognized the Mfalme, she also stopped running. She dropped the hem of her dress and tried to regain her composure. She adjusted the bundle under her arm and adopted a brisk but more respectful walk.

"Good morning, Mfalme Ncobba," she said through an embarrassed smile. "The animal will not listen to me. Would you be so kind as to hold him for me, please?"

It wasn't necessary, but Ramuza ensured the dog could not go anywhere. Then he stood to greet the woman. "Good morning to you, Sacred Woman. Is he a pet of yours?"

"No. He is cared for by my brother, but I have been asked to keep him for a while."

"He is a lively animal. He seems to be getting the best of you. Will you be able to manage him?"

"I think so. I only wish he would listen to me."

Ramuza looked down at the dog, marveling at the dog's energy. "He only wants to play. And he is exceptionally friendly."

"Yes, he is." The woman placed the bundle she carried on the ground to catch her breath and rearrange her ruffled clothing. "He is sometimes a little too friendly. I have to watch him closely for his own sake."

"How bad can such friendliness be?"

"Do you wish to know? Only recently, his friendliness and curiosity had him playing with a viper, of all things. That is how bad. He was bitten."

Ramuza looked at the dog again. He kneeled to resume petting it. "He seems to be doing well now. It was not serious."

"It was serious enough. He became quite ill. He almost died. But once he began to heal, he recovered quickly."

"That is not so unusual. If an animal survives the first bite, it will recover quickly. A serpent's bite is not always as harmful to an animal as to you or me."

"Oh? Is that so?"

"It is as I understand it. I do not know for sure. I believe it has much to do with how the animal reacts," Ramuza explained. "But have no undue confidence. The venom of such a serpent is often fatal. It seems the dangerous effect can be lessened if the animal stays calm when bitten. The venom does not travel to the heart as fast. Your brother's dog took the bite without fear or panic."

"So, it would seem. When I was a little girl, my grandfather used to drink an elixir made from the venom of serpents."

"Great Sacred Spirit! For what purpose?" Ramuza glanced up at the woman.

"He was a fisherman. Every day, he fished in waters where poisonous serpents were abundant. Since he was a child, he drank the elixir regularly. He believed that if he were ever bitten, the poison would not kill him."

"Was he ever bitten?"

"Yes, many times. Many times, he survived the bite."

"Then, like your brother's dog, your grandfather was also quite lucky."

"Not entirely, Mfalme. The last time he was bitten, he died."

"I am sorry, Sacred Woman."

"It is alright, Mfalme. He lived a full life, and he lives on in our memories. To this day, he is still a cornerstone in our family."

The young woman's behavior was distracting. In addition to holding Mfalme's attention with her fascinating story, she also showed a nervous and candid admiration for the man kneeling before her. It was the first time she had ever been so close to the Aukmondi

Mfalme. As Ramuza continued to pet the dog, the woman studied Ramuza.

Ramuza did not notice her distraction until he glanced at her face again. When he did, he stood up and smiled. Her behavior was not so unusual. Ramuza had seen it often. Many women admired the Mfalme, for one reason or another. What was unusual was the fact that this young woman was not an Aukmondi.

Ramuza had seen her once or twice recently. The designs in her clothing and the way she wore them suggested to him that she was a visitor from one of the neighboring tribes.

"You are from the Kiwane or the Rimoza tribe?"

"Rimoza, Mfalme."

Ramuza maturely dismissed her admiration of him, concentrating on a more important matter. He wondered if she was preparing to leave the valley, as all capable visitors had been instructed to do.

"How are you called, Sacred Woman?"

"My name is Andallah Gallagana."

"Has your visit to our valley been a complete one?"

"Not as complete as I would have liked. I did not expect to leave so soon. Last night, one of your warriors came by the Ptompa kraal, where I am staying. He said all visitors must leave the valley."

"Yes. I am sorry you had to cut your visit short, but it was for your safety."

"It does not matter. It was only a social visit with a friend. Although my visit was cut short, I must say it has been …," Andallah carefully chose the perfect word, "interesting. I was in your celebration area last night when you returned from the north rim. My friend and I followed you and that slave merchant to the guest kraal. We saw the whole incident. That slave merchant was truly frightening."

"Then I am also sorry that you had to experience such a hostile moment. As it turned out, that confrontation with the merchant was unavoidable. I hope it did not spoil your visit."

"It was disturbing, but I will survive."

Ramuza wished he could speak confidently about the Aukmondi. "The crisis is not over yet. There may be other incidents to come, far worse incidents. I am still trying to avoiding them, but ..."

"Do you think that you will succeed?"

"I cannot say. If I do not, all visitors must return to the safety of their villages as soon as possible. It could get very unpleasant here within the next few days. The Aukmondi Gray Warrior has arranged escorts through the wilderness if you have none of your own."

"Thank you for your concern, Mfalme Ncobba. Your escorts will not be necessary. I have summoned my escorts. They are expected to be here by nightfall. Also, I have some garments here that I must clean first. I think I will be ready to leave by tomorrow morning."

"Tomorrow morning may be too late, Sacred Woman. My warriors can escort you as soon as you are ready today."

"Please. I do not want to take any of your warriors at a time like this. From what I have heard, that slave merchant has threatened to bring back an army of slave hunters. You may need every warrior that you have."

"Is that so?" Ramuza was surprised to hear this news from Andallah, a visitor. He hoped such a frightening fact was not so clear, even among his people.

"You are the thoughtful one," said Ramuza. "But even if I must provide every visitor here with an escort, everyone who does not belong here must leave as soon as possible. The longer there is a delay, the more dangerous it may be. If I must battle an army of slave hunters, I can not guarantee your safety."

"I understand. Please, allow me to finish my preparations. I promise, by tomorrow morning, I will be gone."

The woman's safety was one of many concerns of the Mfalme. It was a concern he could take care of right now, if he wanted to. He could order her to leave at once. There was no reason to grant her request except in consideration of her wishes. As strict as he was, Ramuza was not a Difficult Creation.

"So be it. I expect you to be gone by tomorrow morning. Not a moment later."

"Not a moment later." Andallah smiled to show her gratitude.

"It has been pleasing talking with you, Sacred Woman, but I must be on my way. There is much I have yet to do."

"Thank you, Mfalme, for your kindness. I hope everything turns out well for you and your people, and the Chinchigwe."

— 40 —

BEHIND ITS HONOR

Upon reaching Kon-Shambique's kraal, Ramuza learned that the Favored Tribesman was not there. Only Tongda Sameah Leng was there. Ramuza found her out in front of the hut, preparing for the day's schooling of some of the Aukmondi children. She was selecting small writing slates from a pile of various sizes.

When Ramuza asked for the Favored Tribesman, he was told that Kon-Shambique had been called to one of the nearby kraals to attend to an acute illness. That call was earlier this morning. According to Tongda, he was expected to return shortly.

Since Ramuza's mission was so important, he decided to wait. He hoped that the wait would not be long. He could feel in the pit of his stomach that time was a valuable resource he could not afford to waste.

Ramuza offered to help Tongda lay out some of the writing slates to make himself useful while he waited.

"Thank you, Mfalme." Tongda passed Ramuza an armload of the slates. "Do you remember how to place them?"

"It has been a while since I have attended such a class as this. I think I remember." Ramuza allowed Tongda to begin placing the slates on the ground. She was forming a huge semicircle. Ramuza followed her example and began to place a concentric semicircle behind hers.

As Ramuza worked, he watched the Sacred Woman. He saw in her yet another uniquely beautiful woman and one more reason why this valley was such a pleasant place to live. Tongda was another example of why this valley must be secured from all destructive forces.

Tongda Sameah Leng was Upenda Sameah Mushwala's cousin. Like the Sacred Woman Upenda, Tongda was easily considered one of the most physically beautiful women in the Aukmondi Valley. Physical beauty seemed to run in the Sameah family. Both Upenda and Tongda had the most impressive, unforgettable features.

But the physical beauty between Upenda and Tongda was as different as night and day. While Upenda's skin was like smooth, rich ebony, Tongda's skin was like honey and cream, a gift from her paternal grandfather, Leng Chou-Li, from China. Her Asian ancestry influenced her raven black hair and other features.

Tongda's most striking feature, however, was her eyes. They were uncommonly brown and clear. They were pools of sparkling dark amber that held more fascination than the eyes of any hawk or wildcat. And even the lineage of Tongda's Asian ancestry could not account for the magic they reflected. Looking into her eyes was to behold something completely unexplainable.

This did not mean that there wasn't an explanation. Tongda was so attractive in her way that all types of rumors were used to explain her beauty. The most popular, of course, was that Tongda was the incarnated Supreme Spirit. A single look into her eyes was often enough to confirm that rumor.

Tongda lived with Kon-Shambique in an unofficial union. Although their union was never officially declared, it was probably one of the valley's most popular and natural. Stories of their love were common throughout the valley.

Their relationship was based on a deep concern they shared in the personal growth and development of each individual they knew. No two people in the valley were alike in heart and mind than Kon-Shambique and Tongda. Love has grown out of that relationship. It was only coincidental and ironic that the very woman so often suspected of being the incarnated Supreme Spirit was also the woman who enjoyed this uniquely close relationship with the Favored Tribesman.

Tongda had assisted Kon-Shambique for so long and closely that she was often capable of helping in his absence. She placed the last of her writing slates and looked up at Ramuza. "Mfalme, may I ask why you wish to see Kon-Shambique? Is there something I can do?"

Ramuza was several meters away from Tongda when she spoke to him. Even at that distance, he could see the magical influences that sparkled in her eyes.

"It is possible, Sacred Woman." Ramuza put the last of his slates in place and then approached Tongda. "Do you know anything about the Yululu Bone?"

Tongda smiled with embarrassment. "On the other hand, maybe you had better wait for Kon-Shambique. Yesterday was the very first time I had ever heard of one. Last night, Kon-Shambique and I discussed it. Regrettably, I do not think I learned anything that may be useful to you."

"Anything at all could be helpful. I must learn all that I can about it. There is a secret about it that I must learn."

"A secret?"

"Yes. It is a powerful trinket that is quite deadly to the one who possesses it. Yet, according to the slave merchant, there is a secret for preventing the death of the possessor."

"I am sorry, Mfalme. I am aware of no such secret." Tongda recalled the talk that she and Kon-Shambique had last night. "The Favored Tribesman and I did not discuss the bone itself very much. He only told me how highly the Batushi honor it."

"What did he say?"

"He described an incident when a British hunter was given the bone. The hunter had come to Africa to harvest what he called 'rare game'. When he was given the bone, he was completely ignorant of the bone's true meaning. And he learned of the bone's value by accident. He eventually realized that he could give the Batushi any command. The Batushi would execute it without question.

"Needless to say, the hunter made the best of his newly discovered power. Every day, he commanded the Batushi to bring him the head of some new animal. Every day, the Batushi complied faithfully until one evening.

"The hunter gave the Batushi a relatively simple command, but the Batushi refused to respond. Instead, several Batushi surrounded the hunter. They began to approach him with the obvious intent to kill him.

"The hunter took out one of his guns and warned the approaching Batushi to stay back. They did not. Their approach was not swayed by the hunter's commands or the gun he held. The hunter shot one of the Batushi dead. The others continued to approach him. One by one, five more of the Batushi were shot to death before the hunter himself was finally killed.

"Both Kon-Shambique and I thought it was strange how the Batushi honor that bone to every extent and then suddenly kill despite it."

"It is strange, indeed." Ramuza was thoughtful, reflecting on the story Tongda had just told him.

"So, what do you suppose provokes the Batushi to kill like that, Great Creation? Is there a limit on the number of commands that can be given? Or, is it the nature of a particular command that triggers such a response?"

"No. I do not think so. I suspect neither of those reasons. I know of another incident myself. It was such a case where no request was ever given. The possessor proudly wore the bone about his neck as a decorative ornament. He did not know the bone's power or purpose. He never used it. Yet, he was also killed. No. The Batushi are prompted to kill by something else."

"I am sorry I could not be of any help to you, Mfalme."

"Do not apologize. I have learned something here that I did not realize before."

"What is that?"

"The Batushi are extremely faithful toward the Yululu Bone. Their lives are placed behind its honor. That, Sacred Woman, is also information that I can use."

"Maybe Kon-Shambique can tell you more. He should be back by now." When Tongda mentioned the Favored Tribesman, she saw him in the distance, coming up the pathway.

41

THE OLD TRIBE

Kon-Shambique, the Aukmondi tribe's healer, philosopher, and spiritual teacher, climbed the hill on the eastern slope of Nagorda Peak with strong youthful strides. He moved with the appearance of being much younger than he was. Looking at him, one would never suspect that he had the insightful wisdom of a Wise Old Creation in his head.

The reasons why he was known among the Aukmondi people as "a genius in the ways of life" are endless. He constantly amazed people with his common sense. He often expressed simple truths that only a long and heavily experienced life could teach.

As if naturally ordained, Kon-Shambique began to show his remarkable wisdom at the age of ten. Without much prompting from the teachers of that time, he naturally adopted the Aukmondi philosophy. He showed a great respect and compassion toward all living things, especially people. When interacting with people, he always managed to touch their hearts. He never failed to display true concern for the freedom and natural development of the human spirit.

By age 15, Kon-Shambique was the closest assistant to the tribe's aged Healer, Tamu Lodalgwa Emoke. At that time, he was already a highly preferred Spiritual Teacher. He had learned all the basic knowledge he could from Tamu and the other healers, but he continued developing his knowledge. And he never hesitated to apply it in his quick-witted style. By age 18, he was the tribe's senior Healer and Spiritual Teacher.

At this hour of the morning, Kon-Shambique had already made a medical errand to one of the kraals in the western half of the valley and was now returning to his kraal. Walking through the kraal entrance, he saw Mfalme Ncobba talking with Tongda. He did not expect to see a visitor to his kraal so early. Tongda took Kon-Shambique's medical pouch. She entered the hut to put the pouch away for him. Kon-Shambique approached Ramuza and greeted him respectfully.

"Good morning, Great Creation, Mfalme Ncobba," Kon-Shambique spoke formally. His relationship with Ramuza was close enough that he usually skipped all formalities.

"Good morning to you, Great Creation. Why so formal?"

"Because I know that your visit here is an official one." Truthfully, Kon-Shambique could sense Ramuza's serious frame of mind. He was trying to put the Mfalme's mind at ease. "No one climbs halfway up the Nagorda Peak for pleasure. The pleasure of Nagorda Peak is farther up, on its summit."

That insight brought a smile to Ramuza's face. "Who was it that required medical attention so early this morning?"

"The Sacred Woman Wensetti. At her age, she is so frail."

Tongda returned from the hut in time to hear the Favored Tribesman's comment. "I hope it was nothing serious."

"No, Sacred Woman. She suffers from exhaustion, agitated by anxiety. She was so worried after the news of the slave merchant that she got no sleep last night. In the middle of her morning chores, she collapsed. With rest, her illness will pass." Kon-Shambique took a deep breath and exhaled. The slope he had just climbed had affected him after all. He turned to Ramuza. "And you, Great Creation, have come to relieve Wensetti's anxiety. Have you not?"

"I have come to try."

"How may I serve you?"

"As usual, I wish to talk with you briefly."

"Of course. Let us sit and be comfortable." Kon-Shambique led the Mfalme to a grassy clearing near the entrance of his kraal. The clearing had a magnificent view of the south slope of the valley and the river below.

Kon-Shambique respectfully allowed Ramuza to be comfortably seated first. Then he sat to his left. "I see the Sacred Woman Kharaambi is preparing her warriors for war. Army after army is headed for the valley depths to train."

"At this point, it is only a precaution."

"Do you expect an armed conflict?"

"If the merchant returns with the Batushi, it may be our fate."

Kon-Shambique looked down into the valley. From his vantage point, he could see several kraal communities, the lake below, and the Sacred Temple doors on the south slope. He wondered what effect a war would have on the beautiful sights and the people who lived there. He imagined what the Great Creation Ba-Ogu would feel if he knew the fate of the Aukmondi people.

******

Ba-Ogu, a great ancestor of Ramuza, was the founder of the Aukmondi Valley and its people. He was the father of the high respect for life that the present-day Aukmondi people live by.

Many harvests ago, Ba-Ogu broke away from his original tribe, which historians nowadays call the 'Old Tribe'. Due to circumstances beyond his control, Ba-Ogu was forced to realize that he lived in a community that suppressed evolutionary thoughts and feelings. He was forced to realize that humankind was preserving its immaturity.

This attitude of Ba-Ogu developed when, during his life, he began to feel the natural attraction for a woman whose name was Chumoramae Hendezzi. Ba-Ogu had grown up to be a very Well-like, Young Creation. He had been very helpful throughout his village. He was thoughtful and considerate of everyone he met. There was nothing significantly controversial or disagreeable about Ba-Ogu until he made known his love for the woman Chumoramae.

Chumoramae was twice Ba-Ogu's age. She already had a son who was only a harvest younger than Ba-Ogu. In the hearts and minds of the villagers, Chumoramae was not a proper match for a Young and Promising Creation like Ba-Ogu. Chumoramae lacked youth and fertility. In both subtle and blatantly inconsiderate ways, the people of the Old Tribe made their thoughts and feelings known.

Eventually, Chumoramae could not take the ridicule or negative popularity anymore. Twice, she tried to sever the relationship between herself and Ba-Ogu. Twice, she succeeded. But she could not deny her love for Ba-Ogu each time.

Ba-Ogu began to react. In his heart, he knew that what he and Chumoramae were doing was not wrong. The more the people tried to discourage his relationship with Chumoramae, the more outspoken and rebellious Ba-Ogu became.

Fortified by the anger he had been suppressing, Ba-Ogu began to challenge all the immature traditions that his people had lived by for years. Each day, he pointed out more and more of the nonsense that did nothing for his people except retard their emotional growth.

"We dearly love our ancestors," Ba-Ogu had said. "We always will. But why must we hang on to their ways when we have long ago outgrown the benefits of such ways? Why must we continue to hide new feelings? Why must we deny the existence of these feelings when, in truth, such feelings are quite common among us? Why are we so afraid to grow into a culturally new people?

"Like a child that outgrows old garments and must put on new ones, we must discard the traditions and beliefs that have not grown with us. We must abandon or alter all those old attitudes that hold us back. We must be eager to learn newer and better attitudes; to build on the foundations our ancestors so lovingly gave us.

"My people, do you realize that we still have unchanged beliefs and attitudes since the day we were first born? In our efforts to keep our ancestors alive, we still think and feel with the same hearts and minds as our ancestors. Such an act would seem to honor them highly. But you shame them. I believe they will be the first to tell you that it is not wrong to admit you have hearts and minds of your own.

"If a neighbor steals from us, as barbaric as it sounds to our mature hearts and minds, we still cut off our neighbor's hand. Why? Our ancestors wrote that such a response was the proper punishment. Can we not think and feel for ourselves now? I challenge you. The next time someone steals from you, inflict the proper punishment yourself. Cut off your neighbor's hand and live with what you have done.

"If it is discovered that a young maiden is not a virgin, though she may be a very warm and loving human being, she is considered an outcast. Why? Because our ancestors have said that such a woman is no longer pure. She is not worth the attention of a mate. But have you stopped to think what has made her so impure and unworthy? If you have an answer, you condemn anyone who has ever experienced a cherished moment of intimacy.

"If your mate is found to be an adulterer, they are hated and stoned. Our ancestors say that we must reject that mate completely. It does not matter that the rejection of that mate may include a priceless human closeness you may never find again. Such a rejection may include someone still fully capable of understanding and loving you like no one else."

Ba-Ogu continued with similar arguments. He became a crusader for change, fighting against humanity's stagnation.

Unfortunately, most of the people of the Old Tribe were too set in their ways to listen to Ba-Ogu. Others were truly fearful of offending their ancestors and the written laws. It was easier to consider Ba-Ogu a troublemaker, a social agitator, and a disrupter. He tampered with traditions and violated sacred areas of life. He was trying to instigate too many changes, too fast.

The day when Ba-Ogu announced that he was taking Chumoramae as his mate, he went directly against the Mfalme's permission. The act was a direct insult to the Mfalme. As a result, Ba-Ogu and his new mate were exiled from the Old Tribe.

Ba-Ogu gave up trying to promote the emotional maturity of his people. It was the first time and the last time that he had ever given up on anything that he felt was so important. He and Chumoramae left the Old Tribe, never to return.

But Ba-Ogu's efforts were not completely ineffective. A few people seemed to hear more than Ba-Ogu's words. They understood and felt the spirit of human growth that Ba-Ogu was trying to inspire.

These few people voluntarily exiled themselves and followed Ba-Ogu. They became the seed of what are now the Aukmondi people. With Ba-Ogu and Chumoramae, they roamed like nomads for several harvests, until they found and settled in this beautiful valley, southeast of the Serengeti Plain.

In their new home, instead of desperately and fearfully creating tribal laws to suppress and control the human spirit, the Aukmondi people began to cultivate their emotional growth. They developed a special conscience that fortified their survival through unity, enriched their lives through trust, and gave them the attitude to fulfill their most personal dreams. And, since the day Ba-Ogu and Chumoramae were exiled from the Old Tribe, the Aukmondi people have known nothing other than peace.

— 42 —

BEYOND THE SECRET

"We have no attitude for war," said Kon-Shambique thoughtfully. "It will be the first time the Aukmondi has lifted a spear for such a purpose."

"Yes, I know. And I hope to prevent it with your help." Ramuza shifted himself to a more comfortable position. "Last night, you mentioned to Kharaambi that we might foil the merchant's plans if we learned the secret of the Yululu Bone."

"Yes. We know that the Batushi intend to end the merchant. If the merchant were preoccupied with preventing his death, it would shift his focus. He would not be so intent on harming the Chinchigwe or us."

"The merchant did not seem too concerned about his own life. And his threats were clear. I must assume that he is confident about what he is doing. He knows a secret to prevent his death. And I must learn that secret."

"Like many people, Mfalme, I do not know its secret. And I do not know any real facts about the bone either. I only know a couple of stories and fragments of stories."

"I hope to piece together something useful from those bits and pieces. As Kharaambi and I discussed the bone last night, from the fragments of information that we knew, we agreed that the secret may have something to do with the possession of the bone. Possession is a common thread."

"A common thread," Kon-Shambique repeated. "I like that approach."

"In every story, the possessor is always killed."

Kon-Shambique thought about the stories that he had heard. He focused on anything else that might be common in all the stories. The Favored Tribesman was known for his amazingly faithful and methodical mind. After turning several thoughts repeatedly in his head, he finally latched onto a new common thread. It was a thread accompanied by an irrefutable positive feeling, meaning it was probably useful.

"As I said, Mfalme, most of the stories I know are fragments, rumors, legends, and tales I have heard. Of all the stories I can recall, I know only three complete stories about the bone. And in these three stories, I think I see another common thread."

"Which is?"

"The moon. I do not know exactly how it relates, but if I am correct, the possession of the bone, the secret you look for, and the moon are all related."

"How does the moon fit into all of this?"

"Of those three complete stories that I know, the moon is always mentioned prominently at one point or another. For example, a Young Creation was given the Yululu Bone in one story. One of the Batushi, said to be the Young Creation's friend, told him he would be safe if he could hide from the moonlight. Of course, he could not, and the Young Creation was killed.

"In another story, it was just the opposite. A Kikuyu warrior was given the bone. He was told by the very Batushi who gave him the bone that he would be safe as long as the moon smiled upon him. Night after night, the moon smiled at him. But the moon stopped smiling one night, and the Kikuyu warrior was killed.

"And in yet another tragic story, a Sacred Woman was given possession of the bone. She suffered from such greed that one Batushi finally came to her and told her she could have almost anything she wanted, but she would never see the moon again. Like the rest, she was killed.

"I think the moon has some ritualistic significance."

"It certainly seems so." Ramuza thought with considerable concentration. When he spoke again, it was mainly to himself. "Could something about the moon prompt the Batushi to kill?"

"What do you mean?"

"The Sacred Woman Tongda and I were talking just before you returned. We were wondering what prompts the Batushi to kill when they do. If what you say is true, then I suspect something about the moon signals them."

"It makes sense. But we could be in error here, Great Creation. Whether or not the moon has such an effect, I can neither confirm nor deny."

Ramuza did not acknowledge Kon-Shambique's statement. He had lapsed into another moment of concentration. It lasted until he began to shake his head negatively.

"What is wrong, Great Creation?"

"I do not know. On the one hand, it makes sense. But on the other hand, something is wrong."

"Do you doubt that possession of the bone, the secret, and the moon are interrelated?"

"No, it is not that at all. All of that is good and valuable information."

"Then, what is it?"

"I have this feeling. There is something beyond the secret that I look for."

"Beyond the secret?"

"Yes. It is a feeling I cannot explain. And it is the second time I have experienced it. I feel that I am wasting my time. The more I learn about the secret of the Yululu Bone, the more I feel that the secret is not all that I should know to prevent this crisis."

"Pay attention to such feelings, Great Creation. They are, what I like to call, divine nudges."

43

PROTOCOL AND PRIORITIES

Despite that baseless feeling, Ramuza knew that the talk with Kon-Shambique was not wasted. If Kon-Shambique was right, and the moon held some ritual significance, he had learned another piece of the puzzle. Although everything he knew about the Yululu Bone was virtually useless, Ramuza took some comfort that it was still early. The day was fresh. There was plenty of time to learn more.

When Ramuza told Kon-Shambique that he would be spending the day trying to uncover the secret of the Yululu Bone, the Favored Tribesman eagerly asked to join him. Ramuza welcomed his company.

"So, where do we go from here, Mfalme?"

Ramuza reviewed his plan of action. He intended to talk with every skilled and knowledgeable person in the valley; anyone who might know anything about the Yululu Bone. Ramuza got up from where he sat. "First, we will go to the south slope, to the Chemzoli kraal. We will pay a visit to the Great Creation Tanake."

"Of course, the master artisan. He should be able to tell you something from a completely different perspective."

"It was the Sacred Woman Yejide's idea." The slight smile on Ramuza's face showed the pride in his daughter.

"It is no wonder she is among your valued advisors."

With a firm sense of direction and purpose in his mission, Ramuza wasted no time. He gave a courtesy nod to Tongda and turned to leave the kraal.

Kon-Shambique took a moment to tell Tongda about his plans to help the Mfalme. He explained to her where he was going, just in case he was needed. Then he darted from the kraal and down the hillside to catch up the Ramuza, who had already gained a substantial lead on him.

******

When Kon-Shambique finally caught up with Ramuza, he again found the Mfalme deep in thought. Ramuza's face looked concerned. Kon-Shambique thought Ramuza was concentrating on some aspects of the Yululu Bone mystery and chose not to interrupt him. He kept his silence down the hillside of Nagorda Peak. A conversation with the Mfalme was out of the question anyway. Even on a downward incline, matching the Mfalme's strong stride was hard.

By the time the two reached the foot of the peak, Kon-Shambique realized that the frown on Ramuza's face was a little too uncommon. The Favored Tribesman knew Ramuza well enough to know that something was troubling him. He knew when to keep quiet about it and when to speak up.

"Mfalme," he began, "tell me what is on your mind. The look on your face is noticeable. And you have said nothing since we left my kraal."

"It is nothing. I was only thinking about the Yululu Bone, Great Creation."

"I have known your face for as long as I can remember. I have occasionally seen you worry, but only after you have done all that you can do. To this very day, I have yet to see you worry before you have done anything at all. Something troubles you, and it is not just the bone."

"Even a half-truth can not get past you, can it?" Ramuza smiled, fascinated by the Favored Tribesman's gift of insight. "You are right. I was wondering about the bone, but there is something else."

"What is it?"

"It is that feeling that I told you about."

"The feeling that the secret of the bone is not what you should be trying to discover."

"Exactly. It is a feeling that comes and goes. I cannot dismiss it. It keeps coming back to haunt me, distract me."

"Very often, Mfalme, our mind knows much more than we allow it to tell us. Do you think such a feeling deserves no attention?"

"That is part of my difficulty, Great Creation. I cannot confidently make that decision."

"You cannot make a decision?" Kon-Shambique almost laughed. "You? Tell me about wingless birds that fill the sky, and I will believe it. Tell me about fish that swim in the desert sand, and I will believe it. But do not tell me, you cannot make a decision. You are known throughout the tribe for your decisiveness, Mfalme."

"Decisive people often make difficult decisions too."

"Then what is difficult in this case?"

"On the one hand, there is the haunting feeling. I cannot deny it. On the other hand, if I give this feeling the attention it seems to demand, it means I must make the secret of the Yululu Bone a lesser priority."

"What is so difficult about that?"

"Using the secret of that bone against the merchant is the only way I know to prevent this crisis."

"It is the only way that you are aware of. There may be other ways to stop the merchant and the Batushi; ways that you know nothing at all about now."

Ramuza was about to ask the Favored Tribesman if he had any suggestions. But they had come to the bottom of the pathway and one of the bridges that crossed the Aukmondi River. They were distracted by a Red Warrior who was seen trotting toward them, across the bridge from the south slope. He had come from the valley depths on a mission. When he came off the bridge, he stopped and greeted his Mfalme and the Favored Tribesman.

"Good morning, Mfalme. Good morning to you, Great Creation Kon-Shambique." The warrior did not seem winded even though he had been traveling at a slow run.

Kon-Shambique nodded while Ramuza responded for both. Ramuza recognized the warrior as Dahannah Fopolozzi, from the Nobuli Zekele regiment of the Gazimba Kdedi Army. "Good morning, Great Creation. Is the Zekele regiment finished with its exercises already?"

"No, Mfalme. I was sent from the valley depths to deliver a message from the Sacred Woman Kharaambi. Contrary to what she told you last night, she says that only one warrior regiment will be sacrificed to provide visitor escorts through the wilderness."

"One regiment?" Ramuza did not know if he should be surprised by Kharaambi's judgment or impressed by her management. "Will one regiment be sufficient?"

"She believes that it will, Mfalme. There are few visitors to escort, and final arrangements have already been made. Most of the visitors will leave the valley by late evening. There is but one exception."

"Which is?"

"There is the Sacred Woman Andallah Gallagana of the Rimoza tribe. She is visiting a friend in the Ptompa kraal. She refuses escorts, claiming to have talked with you about it already."

"Yes, she has. Andallah told me that she will be gone with her escorts by morning. I have allowed her to stay until then."

The Red Warrior only nodded to show his understanding of the situation. He opened his mouth to speak again but changed his mind. Both Ramuza and Kon-Shambique noticed the warrior's hesitancy.

"Was there anything else, Great Creation?" Ramuza asked.

"No, Mfalme."

Ramuza was about to dismiss Dahannah until Kon-Shambique responded in his way to the warrior's hesitancy.

"Dahannah, please speak your mind. You have a personal question to ask the Mfalme?"

"Yes, Great Creation." The Red Warrior spoke nervously. He turned from the Favored Tribesman to the Mfalme. "With your permission? I speak on behalf of the Blue Warrior Nobuli, not as my regiment commander, but as my friend."

Ramuza nodded to show that he was listening.

"Nobuli is disappointed about having to provide escorts from his regiment. Like everyone else, he prefers to stay and help defend the valley."

Ramuza thought about the matter briefly. "Has Nobuli approached the Royal Warrior Gazimba about this?"

"No, Mfalme. I do not think that he will."

"You think correctly, Great Creation. He will not. Have you spoken with your friend directly about this?"

"No, Mfalme. But I know him well."

"Dahannah, Great Creation, the Blue Warrior Nobuli is a Blessed Creation to have a friend who shows concern about his feelings. When you find the time, go and talk with your friend. He will teach you why he is a Blue Warrior."

"Mfalme?"

"Return to your regiment, Dahannah."

"Yes, Mfalme." The Red Warrior obediently turned and trotted back across the bridge.

After Dahannah had gone, Kon-Shambique and Ramuza resumed their walk. As they began to cross the same bridge, Kon-Shambique addressed the Mfalme. "So, what was that all about?"

"That was a Red Warrior's lesson in protocol and priorities, Great Creation. If the Blue Warrior Nobuli had said nothing to anyone about his disappointment, Dahannah should not have approached me. The first person Dahannah should have visited was his friend, Nobuli."

"That is the lesson in protocol. Where is the lesson in priorities?"

"Dahannah will learn that lesson when he speaks with his friend. Nobuli is a Blue Warrior who did not achieve that rank by accident. He has earned it through self-discipline and a sense of responsibility.

These qualities clearly explain why he has said nothing about his disappointment."

"Nobuli's disappointment is understandable, Great Creation. To give up your regiment to escort visitors through the wilderness, when your people may so desperately need them, is a very undesirable situation."

"I am sure that Nobuli's feelings about providing escorts are personal. They are probably feelings known to only a few friends, such as Dahannah. Nobuli understands that his warriors are needed to see that no harm comes to innocent people who have nothing to do with the Chinchigwe and Aukmondi predicament. It is his way of helping his people. And helping his people has priority over his feelings."

"Interesting. That brings us back to you, Great Creation."

"What do you mean?"

"What protocol must you follow? What are your priorities?"

"You are, indeed, a Wise Creation, Kon-Shambique." After a moment's thought, Ramuza gave the Favored Tribesman a decisive answer. "I cannot risk the lives of the Aukmondi by devoting my time to the pursuit of uncertain feelings. As you have suggested, I will pay attention to my feelings. I will not ignore them. They are, as you call them, divine nudges. But, until I am convinced of another, more reliable way to stop the merchant, I must devote my time to learning the secret of the Yululu Bone."

"Now you sound like the Ramuza, I know. Based on what you told me, I suspect this divine nudge will become clear and useful in its own time."

— 44 —

TALES THAT WE TELL OUR CHILDREN

The Great Creation Tanake lived at the foot of the south slope, just past the Aukmondi Lake, in the huge Chemzoli kraal. The kraal was a place of constant activity. It was the third-largest kraal in the Aukmondi Valley, where most artists and crafters worked and lived. Since Tanake was the senior crafter, he spent most of his time in the heart of the kraal, teaching, advising, or working himself. This is where Ramuza and Kon-Shambique found him, walking back toward his hut from the work area.

"Tanake, Great Creation," Ramuza called out to him.

Tanake, in his slightly bent posture, stopped his slow pace. He turned to see who had called his name. Ramuza and Kon-Shambique approached him with cordial greetings. Tanake said nothing to them. A respectful smile and a nod were his only acknowledgement.

"May we walk with you?" Ramuza asked.

"Of course you may, Mfalme. You know I always welcome your company."

Since the time when Ramuza was a small child, he had known the Old Creation and had grown accustomed to many of his ways. He knew the Old Creation's statement was not entirely true. "Except when you are working."

"Except, sometimes, when I am working. The Favored Tribesman will tell you that we all have our flaws."

"Why are you leaving the work area anyway, Great Creation?" Asked Kon-Shambique. "Have you finished work for today? I was told that you seldom stopped until your craft is completed, or the day has ended."

"There was a time, young one, when such a statement was true. I am not as youthful as I used to be. Come mid-morning, I cherish a few moments of rest."

Both Ramuza and Kon-Shambique knew Tanake was being modest. It was his custom to get up long before sunrise and return to work in the work area. The Old and Skilled Creation would do almost a day's work before the younger artists and crafters showed up.

"How may I serve you?" Tanake asked the two.

"We wish to talk with you a moment," said Ramuza. "We will not be long."

"Please, come into my hut. Stay as long as is necessary. At my age, I care little for time. As a result, there is always time to do as I please." Tanake led the way through the doorway of his hut. "Sit down. May I get you anything? Something to eat? Something to drink?"

Both visitors sat down comfortably on mats on the ground. Kon-Shambique accepted a small gourd of water that Tanake offered. Ramuza only apologized for interrupting Tanake's mid-morning rest.

"My rest begins when I lay my tools down. My rest ends when I pick them up again. Relax and be welcome. I am truly glad to have your company." Tanake sat on a small stool like Ramuza's chieftain's stool. His old body complained when he sat on the ground like most. "What is it you wish to talk with me about?"

"The Yululu Bone."

"Yes, the Yululu Bone - that troublesome trinket the slave merchant brought into the valley yesterday."

"The merchant claims to know a secret to prevent his death. We wish to learn about the bone and discover that secret. We were hoping you could tell us something useful, Great Creation."

At first, it seemed Tanake did not hear Ramuza. He sat staring down at his hands. He chuckled softly, masking an almost sad expression on his wrinkled face. "I do not know what I would have given to have seen that thing. All my life, I have considered a Yululu

Bone to be only legendary. Then yesterday, I heard that a real one was here in the valley. I wish I could have seen it."

Kon-Shambique took a sip of his water. "Do not languish, Great Creation. The sight of one is not as impressive as the real effect one has. Knowing those bones exist should be all anyone should wish to experience."

"That is where you are wrong, young one. To learn that a legendary thing is real would interest practically anyone. I was in the middle of a smelting process in the work area when I heard that a Yululu Bone was in the valley. I did not want to believe it at first. Once I learned it was true, it was curiosity at its strongest. I had to see it for myself. I at once stopped what I was doing and hurried over to the guest kraal. But, by the time I got there, this young ram here," Tanake nodded toward Ramuza, "had thrown the merchant and the bone out of the valley."

"The merchant and his bone are coming back," said Ramuza. "Only, you still may not be able to see it. We fear he will bring the Batushi Army with him when he returns. Seeing the bone will be the least of your concerns."

Like everyone else, Tanake had heard the rumors of a coming battle with the Batushi. Hearing it again directly from Ramuza made it sound much worse. A rare expression of seriousness covered Tanake's face.

"Mfalme, you cannot let that happen. A battle with the Batushi will destroy so much. I am an Old Creation. My life has been full, and I truly long for nothing. But for the young ones, it is not fair to them. There is so much of life they have not seen."

"Those thoughts and feelings may be premature, Great Creation." Kon-Shambique was trying to console Tanake. "Our fate is known to no one. The Supreme Spirit has blessed us with the gift of influence. With the right heart, mind, and information, we can sometimes alter our fate."

"Again, you are right, young one. I stand corrected. It would not do me or anyone any good to entertain such thoughts." Tanake dismissed his serious frame of mind and returned the smile to his face. "I will only say this then. In my body flows the blood of an artist. I hope you can understand it when I say, from my point of view, not seeing the Yululu Bone was truly unfortunate."

"It is understood, Great Creation, for we value your point of view now. We would appreciate it if you could tell us what you know."

Again, Tanake stared down at his hands, thinking. He shook his head negatively. "I do not think I can tell you anything that you don't already know. I see the bone as an artistic creation. Unfortunately, my understanding of the art is just as incomplete as that of the bone's legend. I had hoped to see the bone for myself. I had hoped to study it, for studying the art helps to explain the legend."

"I would think that knowing the legend also explains some of the art."

"They go hand in hand, young one. And since I have never seen a Yululu Bone, I can only repeat the legend as I have heard it."

"But, you hesitate to tell us the legend?"

"I would rather not, Mfalme. My knowledge of the bone is one-sided. It is so full of rumors and distortions. My version of the legend would be like telling you one of the many fairy tales we tell our children. Such stories and tales are nice and entertaining to hear. But they are told for a child's ears. Many of them hold hidden truths or other events that are quite serious. These hidden truths and events are masked because they are often frightening and not meant for a child to hear."

"You think the legend of the Yululu Bone contains hidden truths and events?"

"There is no doubt about it. That is why you must hear the legend told in its purest form."

"How do we do that?"

"Bakha!" Kon-Shambique suddenly realized where Tanake was leading them. His quick and sharp mind brought a smile to Tanake's face.

"Bakha? The Historian?" Ramuza asked. "Do you think the Great Creation Bakha would know such a legendary thing?"

"Well, the bone is a trinket. A trinket such as that is not without its history. If nothing else, Bakha should be able to tell you an undistorted account of the legend. You need to hear that if you intend to learn the bone's secret."

"We have nothing to lose by consulting Bakha." Ramuza thought for a moment. With a new sense of direction, he stood up. "Thank you, Great Creation."

"I could have told you the legend, Mfalme. But I know what you want, and Bakha is the Best Creation to give it to you."

"I appreciate your thoughtful guidance."

As Kon-Shambique and Ramuza followed Tanake toward the doorway of his hut, Kon-Shambique nudged a large cloth-tarpaulin with his foot. Because it was cloth, the Favored Tribesman expected the tarpaulin to move. It didn't. Kon-Shambique stumbled and almost fell.

"Are you alright, Great Creation?" Asked Tanake.

"Yes. I am fine."

"Please forgive me for having that in such a well-used walkway. I intend to move, but I have not had the opportunity."

"What is under the tarpaulin, if I may ask?"

"Well, if you two Strong Creations will be kind enough to move it for me, over here, out of the way, you will see."

Ramuza knelt to throw back the edge of the tarpaulin. "It is the chain that you took from the Chinchigwe arms."

"Yes, Great Creation, every link and shackle."

Tanake stepped back as Ramuza and Kon-Shambique struggled to move the chain out of the way. Because there were only the two of them, the chain was very heavy and difficult to move. Instead of lifting and carrying it, they had to practically "drag and roll" it out of the way.

"You mean this was on the arms of the Chinchigwe?" Kon-Shambique looked at the chain in a different light. "I had no idea it was so heavy."

"It has lain there since I brought it down from your kraal, Kon-Shambique. I could not move it myself. The only thing I could do now was cover it with the tarpaulin."

"What do you plan to do with it anyway?"

"I do not know right now. I thought of offering it to the Great Creation Ameh as a keepsake. If he or any other Chinchigwe does not want it, I may melt it down and forge it into something useful or, at least, pleasing."

"Then, good luck with it."

"Thank you. And good luck to you, Mfalme."

Ramuza and Kon-Shambique filed out of Tanake's hut.

******

It was already midday in the valley, and only minor progress had been made in discovering the secret of the Yululu Bone. Ramuza and Kon-Shambique left the Chemzoli kraal and headed for the valley depths in hopes that the Great Creation Bakha could tell them something helpful.

They were stopped only a few meters along the pathway, and it was long before the two made any significant ground toward Bakha's hut. A Young Creation ran behind them to catch them.

He was a pupil from Tongda's class because that is where a Young Creation his age should be now. As he caught up to Ramuza and Kon-Shambique, he breathlessly but formally greeted the two.

"What are you doing away from your studies, Young Creation?" Ramuza asked.

"The Sacred Woman Tongda sent me to summon the Favored Tribesman, Mfalme."

Kon-Shambique wanted very much to accompany Ramuza to Bakha's hut. Tanake had inflamed his curiosity. He managed to suppress his desire and pay more attention to his responsibilities. "Is this an urgent summons, Little Creation?"

"I do not know, Great Creation. The Sacred Woman Tongda had to stop class to deal with a visitor to your kraal. After examining the visitor, she thought it was best to send for you."

"Thank you for your service, Little Creation. I would appreciate it if you would please run ahead and tell Tongda that I am on my way."

The Young Creation quickly showed respect to the Mfalme and ran off as instructed.

Kon-Shambique turned to Ramuza. "It would seem we have another illness in the valley."

"As before, I hope it is nothing serious."

"It is probably not. It is common for minor illnesses to develop among people when great uncertainties are upon us like this." Kon-Shambique sighed. "Mfalme, after you have talked with the Great Creation Bakha, and if time is not limited, would you mind coming by my kraal and telling me what he said? I am helplessly curious."

"I will make no promises, Great Creation. But if Bakha tells me something significant, regardless of limited time, there is no doubt that I will seek your opinion."

$$— 45 —$$

THE ORAL TRADITION

The hut of the Great Creation Bakha was in a wooded area in the valley depths. It was not in a kraal and was one of only a few huts in the area. Bakha was a private person and enjoyed the seclusion that the woods provided.

There was only one thing that Bakha Otumu Bele liked better than the wood's seclusion and natural beauty. That one thing was the immense pleasure he got from passing down history, including little-known facts of history, all in the 'oral tradition'.

Just as Tanake had dedicated his life to the arts and crafts, Bakha lived for tribal history. He was the tribe's Senior Historian. In his head was an archive of fascinating incidents, dating back to the days before the "Old Tribe".

There was no major incident in history that Bakha did not know about. And when he spoke about any incident, he provided a very humanistic point of view, as if he had been an eyewitness. Bakha could relate the motives, the passions, and the fears that usually go unmentioned in most historical accounts. To listen to him speak was always a spellbinding experience.

When Ramuza arrived at Bakha's hut, the Old Creation led a discussion among fellow historians and students. Ramuza was reluctant to interrupt. He knew the great importance that Bakha placed on these discussions. Despite all that historians put down in print, Ramuza understood Bakha's belief that these discussions and the oral tradition were the only way to keep history tangible.

All eyes turned toward the Mfalme as he waited on the area's fringe. Bakha respectfully struggled to stand as he welcomed him. "Mfalme, come closer. How may we serve you?"

"Please excuse me for interrupting," said Ramuza, gesturing to Bakha to stay seated.

"You are excused, Great Creation. I know you would not do it if it were not important."

"It is very important. I must take a few moments of your time to talk with you, if I may."

"Of course you may. Here, have a seat and be comfortable." Bakha gestured toward the other historians and students. "Do you wish the others to leave before we begin?"

"No. It is not necessary. I wish to learn about the Yululu Bone, the trinket the slave merchant brought into the valley yesterday. If you can tell me anything about the bone, it will also give the others here an opportunity to learn."

"The Yululu Bone," Bakha repeated.

"Please do not tell me you have never heard of such a thing."

Bakha poked at a small campfire with a stick to rekindle the flame. Pine nuts, in a small pan, were roasting over the flame. Their aroma filled the air. "I have heard of the Yululu Bone, Mfalme. But I am not sure that I can help you. What is it you wish to know about it?"

"There is supposed to be a secret associated with the Yululu Bone. I am trying to learn that secret. I have already talked with the Sacred Women Kharaambi, Yejide, and Tongda. I have talked with the Great Creations Kon-Shambique and Tanake. Through them, I have learned that the Batushi, the force behind the bone, are quite faithful toward the bone and every wish of its possessor. They also, just as faithfully, eventually kill the possessor. I have learned that the moon may have some significance, but I do not know exactly what. Just a while ago, the Great Creation Tanake told me that he bone is a trinket with a legendary history. I was hoping you could tell me something about that history."

As Bakha thought about the Mfalme's request, he carefully raked a few hot pine huts from the pan and set them aside to cool. "You know, Mfalme, a good historian will always try to keep myths and legends far apart from true history. Myths, legends, and half-truths are like poison to true history."

"That is understandable."

"Besides that, the Yululu Bone was born in Batushi's history. It has nothing to do with the history of the Aukmondi or the Old Tribe."

"I was afraid you would tell me something like that. In other words, there is little or nothing you can tell me?"

"I can tell you no truths, Mfalme. And I am not certain that my knowledge of the bone will reveal the secret that you look for. I can only tell you the bone's legend and my opinion of that legend."

"To my knowledge, the secret of the Yululu Bone is my only peaceful hope of preventing the aggression of the slave merchant. I must say, I am desperate. I am willing to learn all that I can. Please tell me the legend. And as always, I do value your opinion."

Again, Bakha gave the matter some thought. He picked up some cooled pine nuts and offered some to Ramuza. The Mfalme politely refused.

Ramuza, the other historians, and students could see the Old Creation's eyes reflecting far back over long forgotten incidents, recalling all that he knew. He was about to relate a mythical story, a radical departure from his usual dedication.

"How shall I begin?" Bakha shelled a nut, put it into his mouth, and began to chew on it. With that, he began to say what everyone was waiting to hear.

— 46 —

A MARK OF OMANINAH'S LOVE

Many, many forgotten harvests ago, when the Batushi tribe was young, the Batushi people worshipped several gods and goddesses, both good and evil. There were good and evil deities who ruled the sky, the land, and the waters. There were deities of fate, of knowledge, and of time. There were even deities who ruled over families and kindred. The Batushi had gods and goddesses for practically everything and every purpose.

One of the benevolent goddesses; one of the most praised and beloved was Omaninah, the goddess of contentment and good fortune.

Worshippers thought highly of Omaninah because it was Omaninah who generously gave rewards for thoughts and deeds that pleased her. The Batushi worshippers knew that if they wanted anything, all they had to do was please Omaninah accordingly and their desires would be granted, be they material gains or personal gratifications.

According to the legend, Omaninah once came among the Batushi people and fell deeply in love with a mortal, a brave and charismatic Batushi warrior. His name was Gamin Yululu. When Omaninah saw how Gamin Yululu challenged all his fears, though she was a goddess, she was astonished. No mortal had ever impressed her so.

Omaninah was so drawn to Yululu that her attraction quickly developed into love. She eventually promised him happiness forever. She promised him that if he achieved only partial success in anything that he tried to do, she would guarantee him the rewards of complete success.

Of course, news of this relationship between Omaninah and Yululu eventually reached the attention of others, both mortal and immortal. There were those who were pleased and rejoiced in Omaninah's happiness. And then, there were others who were not so pleased; their displeasure being born out of jealousy and envy. Many felt that Omaninah was being much too partial toward Gamin Yululu and was neglecting everyone else.

Among those displeased by the relationship between Omaninah and Yululu was the Batushi witch doctor, a mortal named Mbonutu. Like everyone else, Mbonutu loved and praised Omaninah. He desired Omaninah's love and blessings, but in a considerably more selfish way. When he heard of the relationship between Omaninah and Yululu, he could not accept it. He felt that it was unfair. He strongly felt he deserved to be Omaninah's lover. No one else loved her, or so he thought, more than he did.

Mbonutu spent many days trying to come to terms with the relationship. He eventually managed to hide his true feelings from the Batushi people. In truth, his envy grew stronger and stronger every day. Mbonutu was polite and cordial in Gamin Yululu's presence, showing no malcontent. In truth, he hated the young warrior and longed for his death.

One day, as Mbonutu watched Gamin Yululu in battle, an idea came to him. If he could arrange for Yululu's death, half of his problem would be solved. Omaninah would have to find another lover. With just a little extra effort, Mbonutu was sure he could make himself that new lover.

It was an idea worth pursuing. Mbonutu took the time to perfect the idea carefully. He spent several more days pondering every aspect of the idea until he thought he had a foolproof plan. Masked in dishonesty, he went to see the goddess Omaninah.

******

"What is it you wish to see me about?" Asked Omaninah, suspecting nothing.

"It is your lover, Gamin Yululu."

"What about him?"

"I was watching him in battle a few days ago. It occurred to me, with great horror, if he were cut down in battle, you would be without a lover."

"Yes, Mbonutu, I have often thought of it, and it also terrifies me. But what is there to do about it? Gamin Yululu is a great warrior. His bravery blinds him to such dangers."

"Omaninah, my Beloved Goddess, would not it be a wise idea to mark him?"

"Mark him? What do you mean?"

"Place upon Gamin Yululu a distinguishing mark; one so unmistakable that all who confront him will recognize him and know that he is your lover."

"Do you think a marking of my lover is necessary?"

"Oh, most certainly, Omaninah. There are no sons and daughters in the heat and fury of battle. There are no mothers and fathers. There are no loves and lovers. There are no faces, only companions who fight at your side, or enemies who must be killed. Personal identities are lost."

"Yes, Mbonutu. I must agree."

"And, if that is not reason enough alone, all who still want your precious blessings, though they may confront Yululu in battle, will take heed. If they are wise, no harm will come to your lover."

Omaninah considered the proposal for a moment. It was thoughtful and worth considering. A sparkle of happiness came to her eyes, and she nodded with acceptance.

"It is a wonderful idea, Mbonutu. But how do you suggest Yululu be marked?"

"I am a powerful witch doctor, Omaninah. I have magic powers that rival some of the lesser gods and goddesses. Please, allow me the great honor to mark him for you."

"You will do this for me?"

"There is nothing that I will not do for you."

"Then do it, Mbonutu. Do this for me and you will reap a reward greater than your greatest dream."

Mbonutu bowed to Omaninah, concealing a broad triumphant smile. Omaninah had fallen into his trap. Now, he was ready for the second step in his villainous plan.

******

Mbonutu's mark would require much more than his tainted magic could produce. He had in mind something much more horrifying than he could ever conjure up himself. Mbonutu intended to ask for the aid of the evil and bloodthirsty god, Abezzin.

It is said that the god Abezzin is grotesquely ugly, even unto himself. It is said that it takes the moon's fullness to conceal his ugliness. Abezzin knows this, and to mask his ugliness, he hides from himself and everyone on the other side of the full moon. Whenever the moon is full, Abezzin is apt to come out from hiding and viciously, fatally attack anyone whose features are better than his own. The legend is that no one has ever seen Abezzin's face and lived.

Of course, Mbonutu was not about to face Abezzin himself. No. The evil witch doctor called in his servant-boy, Gonjewebo.

The meek and innocent Gonjewebo had just seen his twelfth harvest when Mbonutu called him in. The boy dutifully approached his master. "Yes, praised Mbonutu?"

"Here. Drink this." Mbonutu handed Gonjewebo a small gourd filled with a concoction he had prepared.

Gonjewebo hesitated, but then he obediently drank the liquid. He gave Mbonutu an empty gourd back. Within seconds, all expressions left Gonjewebo's face.

"Now," said Mbonutu, "I have very important instructions for you, Gonjewebo. You will obey them without question."

"Yes, of course, praised Mbonutu. You have instructions for me. I will obey them. I will have no questions." Gonjewebo spoke with Mbonutu as if in a casual conversation. His attitude was most eerie and submissive. He listened to his master very intently.

"Tonight, you will climb the Sanegeze Peak, the altar of Kilimanjaro, the top of the world, and wait. You will wait for the moon to rise to its summit. Do you understand me, Gonjewebo?"

"Yes. Tonight, I must climb Sanegeze Peak, the altar of Kilimanjaro, the top of the world. I have to wait there until the moon rises to its summit."

"When this is done, you will call upon the god Abezzin without fear. When he comes, look upon him. Tell him that I, Mbonutu, master of potions and cures, will make a very special trinket soon. Tell him that I will correct all his grotesqueness, the cause of all his miseries, if he promises to kill the possessor of the trinket that I shall make. Tell him, Gonjewebo, that if he sanctions my request, give me a positive sign by allowing you to return to this village, to me, alive."

Without the slightest reaction to this deadly task, the poor and unfortunate Gonjewebo nodded and paraphrased his master's instructions. He spoke as if explaining to the evil Mbonutu what must be done. "I will call upon Abezzin and look upon him. I will not be afraid. I will tell him that you, the master of potions and cures, will make a trinket. You will correct Abezzin's grotesqueness if he kills the possessor of the trinket. And if Abezzin sanctions this request, I will return to you, alive."

Mbonutu smiled.

Poor Gonjewebo responded with his innocent smile. Still in his submissive trance, he left at once for the Sanegeze Peak.

Mbonutu waited almost impatiently for Gonjewebo's return. For fifteen days and fourteen full nights, he waited. Each night, he sat out under the stars, watching the crescent moon grow broader and broader, knowing what was to come.

On the evening of that fifteenth day, a very different Gonjewebo was finally seen walking aimlessly, mindlessly, through the Batushi village. The Young Creation was crying uncontrollably. He trembled so badly that he could barely walk; his knees buckled after every few steps. He periodically rubbed his eyes with madness because of what he had seen on Sanegeze Peak. The Poor Creation suffered an irreversible mental and emotional trauma.

A crowd of villagers gathered around Gonjewebo. They tried to question him, wanting to know what was wrong. They asked him where he had been for fifteen days, why he was behaving the way he was, and why he continued to rub his eyes so vehemently. They asked, but they got no intelligible answers.

"Take him to the witch doctor!" Someone shouted. "We must take him to Mbonutu. Mbonutu can cure him."

Gonjewebo screamed and fought when the villagers caught him. He struggled harder than ever against the terror that lingered in his memory. As young and frail as he was, two Strong Creations held him. It took two more to carry him to the witch doctor.

He calmed down only when Gonjewebo was finally placed in Mbonutu's arms. His madness subsided to the point that he recognized Mbonutu's face. The Young Creation embraced the witch doctor as if finding some comfort at last. His crying gradually faded. He became peacefully silent. He never said a word. In Mbonutu's arms, and before a crowd of onlookers, Gonjewebo died.

The whole village mourned Gonjewebo's death, everyone except Mbonutu. The fact that Gonjewebo had returned to him and had not died at the hands of Abezzin was a joy. It was a sign that Abezzin had agreed to his proposal. That was all that he wanted. He was ready for the next step in his plan to win the love of Omaninah.

Mbonutu at once went to make the trinket. As a false tribute to Gamin Yululu, he chose to use the proudest materials to work with; hair from the majestic main of a lion; teeth that slay the lion's food; lion's claws that can rip the belly of a zebra open in a single stroke; and most important, the bones that cages the lion's heart. In tribute to Omaninah, he adorned the trinket with tiny nuggets of pure gold.

With great care, he worked continuously for one day and one night. When he finished, he was truly proud of his craftsmanship and flawless execution of his plan. The next morning, he rushed the trinket to the goddess Omaninah.

******

"It is beautiful, Mbonutu! And you made it as a necklace, to hang over the heart." Omaninah held the trinket up, studying its detail in the morning sunlight.

"It pleases me that you like it."

"This is deserving of a great reward. Tell me, Mbonutu, have you been blessed with contentment and good fortune?"

"In all humbleness, my beloved Omaninah, I am satisfied with all I have."

"Nonsense, Mbonutu. I am sure there is something else in all the creations that you would like. Name it and it is yours."

"If you are pleased, Omaninah, there is nothing else I desire in all creation." Mbonutu lied.

"How would you like to be my lover, Mbonutu?"

"Me?" Mbonutu had overplayed his modesty.

"Yes."

"But, what about Gamin Yululu? He is your lover."

"You have won my love. You have more pleasing qualities. Gamin Yululu is too focused on being a great warrior. He has only blind bravery. He is a hero without a heart. You, Mbonutu, have devotion to me. You give me the attention that I like. Be my lover and wear the mark of it."

Mbonutu looked at the trinket in Omaninah's hand. He knew its true significance and could not accept it. "No, Omaninah. I live with no dangers that threaten my life. It is not necessary to mark me. The trinket was made for Gamin Yululu. It belongs to Gamin."

"It belongs to my lover. And I have chosen you. I want all mortal and immortal eyes to see who my lover is. Please, do not make me beg you. Wear the mark of my love."

Mbonutu reluctantly took the trinket into his hands, his false smile quivering. Omaninah noticed his apprehension and hesitancy.

"What is wrong, Mbonutu? Do you not want to be my lover?"

"Yes, but…"

"But what? Please. I promise you all the contentment and good fortune any mortal could want, for as long as you live. If, in the future, for whatever reason, you should grow tired of my love or if being my lover is too great a commitment, then discard the trinket. It will break my heart, but because I love the attention and devotion you give, you will continue to reap contentment and good fortune until my heart heals."

"Omaninah, I would never want to break your heart," Mbonutu spoke softly and without conviction. His quick and evil mind was already focusing on a flaw in what he knew was Omaninah's revenge.

Knowing he could discard the trinket any time, Mbonutu realized he had a way out. And knowing that he had a way out, he also realized it would be foolish not to accept the trinket and Omaninah's promise of contentment and good fortune until the next full moon. Mbonutu slipped the trinket over his head and pretended to wear it proudly.

******

For the next month, all mortals and immortals saw the mark of Omaninah's love around Mbonutu's neck. For the next month, Mbonutu's life changed dramatically. He was treated with more respect than ever before. In all his encounters, people went out of their way to please him. Villagers spoke to him unnecessarily. Strangers took pleasure in saying his name. All his patients persisted in overpaying him. People who never liked him before began to show unusual friendliness. No one wanted to bring him any dissatisfaction and thus, indirectly, dissatisfy Omaninah.

Mbonutu was so inebriated by the tributes that he was getting that he foolishly began to discount the sinister significance of the trinket. He began to believe, with confidence, that he was an exception; that the evil Abezzin would surely spare him. After all, if Abezzin came after him, who would find a cure for the god's ugly malady? Besides, the rewards of Omaninah's love were worth much more than he imagined. No threat of Abezzin was enough to make him give up that love.

For several days, when Mbonutu realized he had received a blessing from Omaninah, he stroked the necklace around his neck.

When the people praised him, Mbonutu stroked the necklace. It became a habit. When he felt particularly favored for whatever reason, he stroked the necklace.

Each night, so that no one would steal the necklace while he slept, he would remove it from his neck. He carefully secured the necklace in a box and placed the box under the cot where he slept. But each morning, the first thing he did was retrieve the box under his cot, pull out the necklace, and place it back around his neck again.

One night, Mbonutu secured the necklace under his cot as always. He went to sleep as routinely as any other night. He had forgotten that this was the night when the full moon was due to rise.

Mbonutu fell asleep peacefully, but was soon awakened by a powerful, sour stench that filled his hut. Thick, foul currents of air enveloped him. Somewhere in the darkness, he heard an animal's heavily congested breathing. He opened his eyes and searched the darkness. In the corner of the hut stood the most horrible beast he had ever seen.

It was neither an ape, wild boar, nor a man. Yet, it was all three. Its body was as massive and as hairy as a great mountain gorilla. Its head was elongated with huge wart-like protuberances. From both sides of its mouth came two huge, upturned tusks, stained with deposits of decayed matter. It stood erect like a man. Long, powerful, disproportionate arms hung at its sides. White foam and spittle dripped from its mouth and pooled on the ground at its talon-like feet. Tears of blood ran from its eyes; huge sunken eyes that were as black as the deepest abyss. The beast was unmistakably the god Abezzin.

Mbonutu sat upright. His first impulse was to retrieve the box under his cot and the precious necklace inside. Despite the imminent danger, Mbonutu carefully slipped the necklace around his neck. Even now, he was not giving up Omaninah's love and blessings. As he stroked the necklace, his next impulse was to try to reason with Abezzin.

"Abezzin, wait! Just wait one moment, please! Listen to me! I can cure you!"

Abezzin continued to stand in the corner, staring at Mbonutu. He began to moan as if in tremendous pain. The moans gradually turned into laughter, then crying, then horrifying moans again. A more intense concentration of stench rose from the sour belly of the beast and rolled across the chamber toward Mbonutu.

"Abezzin! Abezzin! Look. You are making a mistake!" Mbonutu held out his hands, as if the gesture would show his sincerity and calm the beast. "You must listen to me. I am the creator of the trinket. Its effect was not meant for me. Do you think that I am such a fool to pattern my death?"

Abezzin said nothing. Before Mbonutu's eyes, Abezzin's expression made a mercurial change. The laughter, crying, and moans became deep, guttural growls, like a vicious dog about to attack. Black lips were slowly drawn back to reveal sharp, carnivorous teeth. And then, for the first time, Abezzin moved. He took one thunderous step towards Mbonutu.

"Abezzin! You fool!" Mbonutu made a feeble attempt to evade the beast. He ran to the other side of a table, as if the table would protect him. "Do you know who I am? I am Mbonutu, lover of the goddess Omaninah. Does that not mean anything to you?"

With one powerful arm, Abezzin swept the table away as if it were made of paper.

Mbonutu realized that his words of reason were useless. They did not affect the evil god. He knew he was marked for death. His only choice now was to run for his life. He darted for the doorway of the hut.

Mbonutu ran from the Batushi village toward the nearby forest in the full moon's bright light. As he ran, he occasionally looked back to see if Abezzin was following him. He was. To Mbonutu's horror, the beast moved much like the knuckle-vaulting sprint of a mountain gorilla. His speed was surprisingly fast.

Mbonutu was lucky enough to reach the forest ahead of Abezzin. He knew this forest well. He hoped to seek refuge in the forest's darkness among the trees. After only a few meters, the forest became thick with trees. Most of the moonlight was blocked out.

When Mbonutu thought he had gone deep enough, he stopped to find a reliable hiding place. To throw Abezzin off his trail, Mbonutu impulsively decided to hide at the top of one of the huge trees.

Mbonutu selected a suitable tree, filled with branches but with few obstructions. With the agility of a Creation half his age, Mbonutu quickly climbed from limb to limb. Fear was driving him. He reached the top of the tree with enough time to get comfortable on one of the limbs and catch his breath. Best of all, there was no sign of Abezzin.

With his eyes closed, his breathing subsiding, Mbonutu stroked the necklace and silently appealed to Omaninah. Why had she abandoned him? If she had abandoned him, was the trinket worth holding on to? He held the end of the necklace up to look at it in the moonlight, wondering if he should discard it after all.

Then the stench of Abezzin assaulted his nose. The unmistakable smell told Mbonutu that Abezzin was near. From his perch on the limb, he looked down. Standing at the base of the tree, Abezzin was looking back at him. Mbonutu panicked. He struggled to climb higher in the tree.

Before Mbonutu could progress, Abezzin threw his powerful arms around the tree trunk. Abezzin uprooted the whole tree with a bone-chilling roar and toppled it over. Mbonutu was sent flying as if he were one of the dead leaves. He screamed, hitting the ground hard. Fortunately, other branches of the tree cushioned his fall. He was not hurt. Was this a blessing from Omaninah?

Mbonutu struggled to his feet. He turned in a circle, figuring out which way to go. He had to keep moving. The only thing between him and Abezzin was the tree the beast had toppled over. Since the forest was not providing the refuge that Mbonutu expected, he desperately decided to run back toward the Batushi village. There was no place else to go; no place he could hide. Maybe there was someone in the village who could help him.

Mbonutu ran as fast as he could. Again, he managed to put some distance between himself and Abezzin. Along the pathway into the village, he looked back several times. He did not see the evil god in pursuit. Was Omaninah protecting him after all? Maybe he shouldn't discard the trinket.

Then the evil mind of Mbonutu latched on to a brilliant compromise. Long before he reached the outskirts of the village, he recalled that there were several huts along the pathway into the village. He recalled the first hut that he would reach. It just happened to be the hut of Bopah, the melon-grower. With one last look behind him, Mbonutu resumed his run into the village and directly to Bopah's hut.

"Bopah! Bopah!" Mbonutu called out as he left the pathway toward Bopah's hut. He smiled when he saw a torchlight ignited inside the hut, and Bopah stuck his head out the doorway.

"Who calls my name at this hour?" There was an edge in Bopah's voice.

"Bopah, it is only me, Mbonutu."

Bopah's attitude changes when he recognizes the witch doctor and the current lover of Omaninah. "Praised Mbonutu! Come closer and be welcome."

"Thank you, Bopah."

"Why are you out and about at this hour?"

"I had a nightmare," Mbonutu lied. "I thought the fresh air would help."

"Is there anything I can do, Praised Mbonutu?"

"There is." Mbonutu pretended to think for a minute. He reached up and slipped the trinket from around his neck. He forced it into Bopah's hand. "This is the mark of Omaninah's love. Please hold it for me, but only for a day. Tomorrow I will return for it. Will you do this for me?"

"For you and the Blessed Omaninah, I will gladly do it," Bopah said without asking questions. He simply accepted the trinket as asked. He was dumbfounded when Mbonutu turned and ran back toward the pathway without saying anything.

When Mbonutu reached the pathway, he looked back toward the forest and smiled at his brilliance. He had discarded the trinket in a way that would allow him to retrieve it when the danger had passed.

His brisk walk up the pathway toward his own hut turned into a leisurely pace.

At that moment, the goddess Omaninah appeared to him. She stood, waiting for him in the middle of the pathway ahead. Mbonutu smiled, ran toward her, and dropped to his knees.

"Praised Omaninah," he said. "You must forgive me. Blessed one, I had to discard the trinket."

"There is powerful magic in that trinket, Mbonutu. I am impressed. Unfortunately, you have discarded it too late."

"What?" Mbonutu looked up into Omaninah's face. "What are you saying?"

"The moon has risen. Abezzin still comes for you. My broken heart has already healed, and I cannot stop him."

"But you are the goddess of contentment and good fortune."

"I cannot stop him, Mbonutu."

Mbonutu looked back toward the forest. Abezzin, in his knuckle-vaulting sprint was approaching fast.

There was a terrible screaming in the Batushi village that night. It is said that Abezzin, like a rabid animal, chased a frightened Mbonutu the whole night long, tearing patches of hair from the witch doctor's head, ripping flesh from his bones, breaking fingers from his hands.

Mbonutu was found the next morning far from the village, near death, and mutilated almost beyond recognition. The Pathetic Creation was madly stroking the trinket that he no longer wore.

Before Mbonutu died, he confessed everything. With his last breaths, he made plain that the trinket meant for Gamin Yululu was, indeed, a mark of Omaninah's love. But it was also a token of death for anyone who owned it.

******

"And that, Mfalme, is the legend of the Yululu Bone."

Like everyone else in the area, Ramuza was spellbound. It surprised him to realize he had been listening to Bakha so intently.

"That is quite a story, Great Creation."

"A legendary story. I hope it has helped you."

Ramuza took a deep breath as he digested everything he had just heard. "Tell me, Bakha, according to the legend, what ever happened to Gamin Yululu and Omaninah? The trinket? Abezzin and his cure? And poor Bopah?"

"The Innocent Creation Bopah; for thirty days and nights, he received the love and the blessings of contentment and good fortune from Omaninah. When the full moon rose on that thirtieth evening, Abezzin came for Bopah. He was killed just as mercilessly as Mbonutu.

"It is said, with each full moon, Abezzin still comes out from hiding, ignorantly trying to fulfill his part of the agreement that he and Mbonutu made. Supposedly, many people continue to die from Abezzin's attacks.

"The trinket, now called the Yululu Bone by the Batushi, is a death sentence. It is given by the Batushi to those who have wronged them. It is accepted only by the foolish, like Mbonutu, or the ignorant, like Bopah.

"As for Gamin Yululu and Omaninah, Yululu is considered a lesser god now, sharing the powers of contentment and good fortune with Omaninah. Omaninah rewarded him with such fortunes for understanding, all along, that a mark of her love was never necessary between them. When Omaninah gave Mbonutu the trinket, neither she nor Yululu had any more to do with it."

— **47** —

THE URGE TO ACT

The hut where Ameh and Twese stayed was situated in the rear of the guest kraal. It faced north, offering a broad view of the rest of the kraal, part of the Katola flower garden across the river, and the north slope of the valley.

Ameh stood in the doorway of the hut looking out. He was passing the time by taking in the beautiful scenery and watching some of the other Chinchigwe in the kraal and Aukmondi people who walked by on the pathway past the kraal's entrance. Twese stood behind him, doing the same. The two had spent most of the day talking with the other Chinchigwe, trying to calm their ever-growing restless attitudes. Ameh and Twese had learned that many of the others felt as they did. All were experiencing the very same desire to do something helpful.

"There has to be something we can do," Twese repeated. "To wait like this, sitting idly by, is not right."

"We have gone over this already, Twese. Kharaambi was quite insistent yesterday. Mfalme Ncobba and the rest of the Aukmondi are doing all that can be done. We would only be in their way."

"That is nonsense. You know it and I know it."

"We can not underestimate these people, Twese. They have already amazed me time and time again. If Kharaambi says we will be in the way, although I do not agree, I must take her word for it."

"What about the Mfalme? He has said nothing about being in the way."

"Twese, when Kharaambi speaks, the words might as well be the words of the Mflame."

"Who are they to decide our fate? This crisis is not solely theirs. It is our crisis too. Just because the Aukmondi seem more capable of handling it does not mean we must withdraw and be idle."

"Then what do you suggest?"

"I do not know. Maybe, go and appeal directly to the Mfalme." Twese came away from the doorway. He sat on the edge of the cot where he slept last night. The cot reminded him of the restless night he had.

"Ameh," he began, "did you sleep well last night?"

It was an unusual change of subject. Ameh turned from the doorway to study Twese. "I slept soundly, in the beginning. But I awoke early this morning and could not go back to sleep. I think I was a little too tense to relax and sleep. How about you?"

"Like you and everyone else, I could not relax enough to sleep. I cannot say that tension kept me from sleeping soundly. I was just restless."

"Our nights will probably be filled with restlessness as long as we continue to worry about the insecurities that we are experiencing."

"Insecurities? I will admit that I suffer from insecurities, but my restlessness was not from being insecure. My restlessness was due to flights of fantasy and unrealistic thoughts of freedom and peace. Can you believe that?"

"Yes. Yes, I can believe that."

Twese stretched out on his cot and sighed heavily. "As I lay here, turning from one side to the other, I imagined a day that will probably never come. It was as if my battered spirit had given up on the harshness of reality and created within my head a time of peace. Despite all the misfortunes that have befallen the Chinchigwe, I imagined a time when the rest of us are happy."

"And thoughts like that disturbed you?"

"It was only an escape, Ameh. None of it is true. None of it could ever be true. Those thoughts did nothing to help the situation. They only aggravated me. That is why they disturbed me." Twese paused a moment. There was silence as he reviewed another part of his fantasy, his thoughts of Upenda. "None of it could ever be true."

Ameh smiled at Twese. "It seems you have been touched by that strange Aukmondi spirit that we have heard so much about. Do not feel bad. I have had thoughts of peace, too; my flights of fantasy. You are not alone. There will come a day when we can live those fantasies."

"It is out of our hands. Our fate depends on the Mfalme and the Aukmondi. There is nothing the Chinchigwe can do about it."

Ameh could not respond. Twese was right. The old man returned to the doorway again. He saw people going about their business despite the pending tragedies that involved them all. He had no other choice but to accept fate and live as best he could.

Of the people that Ameh watched, he noticed more and more warriors among them. "It seems the Aukmondi warriors have finished with their exercises. I think they are returning from the depths of the valley."

Twese set up. He quickly got up from the cot and came to stand behind Ameh again. Just outside the kraal, he saw a part of the Bendabe regiment walking along the pathway.

"I must admit, they are some very capable-looking warriors," Ameh said with true admiration.

"Capable looking, indeed. But rumor has it, the Batushi will easily overwhelm them."

Among the warriors Ameh and Twese watched, Twese just happened to focus on one of the White Warriors, Upenda. The very real sight of her was more stimulating than his thoughts of her last night. There was a magic about her that excited him. He could not ignore it.

Twese came away from the doorway and began to pace. Adrenalin seemed to fortify the urge to act. "Ameh, with your permission, I would like to go and speak with the Mfalme."

"Twese." Ameh sounded exasperated.

"I know what you are about to say but listen. We spent the day talking with our people. We want to do more than huddle with the women and children. None of us are warriors, but at least ten are willing and capable of fighting on the side of the Aukmondi warriors. It is the least we can do."

"Foolishness! The Mfalme would not hear of it. Kharaambi, I know, will have no part of it."

"They cannot stop us. They do not have the right. It is our fight too. The least we can do is tell them what we intend to do."

"Twese, the closest one to a warrior among us is Komu. As big and strong as he is, he is a boy. The ten who take up arms in battle will be the first to die."

"It is inevitable. We will die anyway."

"What about getting in the way of the Aukmondi warriors? The Mfalme and Kharaambi certainly will not tolerate it."

"I do not care. If they are so organized, I am sure they can find a useful function for ten inexperienced but very willing warriors."

Ameh considered the matter. The effort to aid the Aukmondi was full of good intentions, and it could not make things any worse. He looked at Twese and reluctantly nodded his permission. "Go."

— 48 —

WHERE DO WE BEGIN

Like a fleeting gazelle, Twese bolted from the hut, across the kraal, and out of the kraal entrance. It was not that he was so eager to talk with the Mfalme. He was trying to catch up with Upenda. Among other things, he intended to ask the White Warrior where he might find the Mfalme. In his rush to catch Upenda, Twese passed several other people he could have asked. But he wanted to ask Upenda.

Twese caught up with Upenda just after she stepped off the south bank pathway onto a smaller pathway leading up the south slope. She was headed toward the Motobo kraal where she lived. Twese trailed behind her for several minutes. He did not call her until he started up the south slope himself. At that time, he savored the simple act of watching her struggle against the slope's incline.

A closer look at the White Warrior revealed she had been working hard. The white of her garments and shield were dirty. Her hair was in a minor state of disarray. The beautiful dark skin of her neck, arms, and legs glistened with sweat. But even with these conditions, she radiated an intense magnetic attraction.

"Upenda," he finally called her name, coming up behind her, "you look as though you have been in a battle already."

Upenda turned. She brushed a trail of sweat from her forehead and smiled. She was both surprised and pleased to see Twese. "Looks are deceiving, Great Creation. If you must know, I feel invigorated. If I look neglected, please excuse me."

"I think I understand what you have been doing all day. Believe me, your appearance is very admirable."

Upenda was sensitive enough to pick up on more than Twese's admiration. She understood Twese was attracted to her. She liked him too. She wanted his company. She looked forward to a strong, positive relationship with him. Her only concern was whether her natural amorous attitude would still be attractive to him. Since he was not an Aukmondi, there was a lot he had to learn about her, a little at a time.

"Where are you on your way to, Great Creation?" She asked without acknowledging his compliment.

"I am looking for the Mfalme."

"Here? On the south slope?"

"Well, I was hoping you could tell me where he might be."

"I do not know where he might be, Great Creation. At this time of the day, the Mfalme could be anywhere."

"I must talk with him. It is important."

Upenda took a moment to think about Twese's request. She brushed another trickle of sweat from her forehead. "May I suggest an agreement between us?"

"Of course."

"I am quite hungry. The Bendabe regiment has been exercising since early this morning, and I have not eaten all day. And because of the situation here, it looks as though our Daily Celebration of Life will be cancelled again. I will help you find the Mfalme if you agree to share an evening meal with me."

"I would love that. I agree. Where do we begin?"

"When looking for the Mfalme, it is always best to start looking in the Royal Kraal."

— **49** —

ON THIS VERY EVENING

The information that Ramuza received from the Great Creation Bakha had his mind racing. Truths, myths, and legends associated with the Yululu Bone were merging, falling into place, and forming one revealing picture. Ramuza felt he had what he was looking for: the Yululu Bone's secret. In a somewhat crude form, the secret was in his head. He knew that the secret could be considered firmly known if the Great Creation Kon-Shambique reached the same conclusion from the same information.

Ramuza was so elated over the progress that he had made that he forgot about the strange feeling he had had earlier. There was nothing else to look for now. The secret of the Yululu Bone was still the obvious key to this crisis. And now that the secret was in hand, Ramuza could concentrate on nothing else.

With leaps and bounds, Ramuza climbed the slope of Nagorda toward the Favored Tribesman's kraal. When he reached the kraal, somewhat winded, he found Kon-Shambique, Tongda, and an elderly woman, Kwana Enkedi, laughing and talking. Kwana looked exceptionally well for someone who had needed urgent medical attention only a short while ago. Kon-Shambique had succeeded again in his noted ability to heal the infirm.

Kon-Shambique left Tongda and Kwana when he saw Ramuza enter the kraal. Evidently, he was eager to learn what the Mfalme had found out. Ramuza was just as eager to tell him. The two settled on the same grassy clearing near the entrance of his kraal where they had sat earlier.

In the next few minutes, Ramuza carefully told Kon-Shambique the legend of the Yululu Bone. Using many of Bakha's words, Ramuza told the legend from beginning to end. He went so far as to include Bakha's belief in how the Batushi use the legend and the bone to fit their purpose. Ramuza left nothing unsaid. When he finished, he sat quietly, allowing Kon-Shambique to draw his conclusion. He hoped it was the same as his.

Ramuza attempted to wait patiently while the Favored Tribesman analyzed the legend. The Mfalme knew that Kon-Shambique was considering almost every possibility, almost systematically. But the process was taking too long. Ramuza finally had to ask Kon-Shambique to share his thoughts.

"What do you think, Great Creation?"

"It is almost too simple, Mfalme. It is so simple that it disturbs me." Kon-Shambique quoted a part of the legend as told to him. Said Omaninah to Mbonutu, 'If, in the future, you should find that being my lover a commitment too great, simply discard the trinket'. As simple as it sounds, that must be the answer that you look for."

"That is my opinion as well. Few people will willingly give up a promise of contentment and good fortune. Such a promise would discourage any desire to discard the bone."

"Let us not be too hasty, Mfalme. We must consider that the Batushi may have changed the legend. They may tend to use the bone as they please."

"I have considered that too. The Batushi have proven extremely faithful toward the bone and its legend. If they honor the countless wishes of an enemy with their lives, then I believe they will also honor the significance of discarding it."

"Probably. The Batushi give the bone primarily as a death sentence. To meet this end, suppose the Batushi will kill the possessor even if the bone is discarded."

"If that is the case, then why give the bone in the first place? No. Unlike the killer Wabanga, the Batushi are executing an elaborate ritual. The bone is part of that ritual."

Kon-Shambique thought a moment. It made sense. He finally nodded his head in total agreement. "So, it is clear then. For the Aukmondi and the Chinchigwe to survive the merchant and the

Batushi, we must somehow force the merchant to keep the Yululu Bone in his possession."

"Exactly."

"That task may not be an easy one. Do you know how you will force the merchant to do this?"

"Please, Great Creation. Let us take one step at a time. We have only just learned the secret."

"Mfalme, you must recall, Omaninah did promise Mbonutu that, once he discards the trinket, she would continue to bestow contentment and good fortune upon him until her heart heals."

"For someone as dishonest, deceitful, and selfish as Mbonutu, how long can that be?"

"And the slave merchant?"

"If the Batushi gave him the bone, I would say he is just as dishonest, deceitful, and selfish. He will not keep the influences of Omaninah for long."

"Then the merchant must discard the bone to be still alive. And yet, he must keep the bone or have not long ago discarded it to command the Batushi upon us."

"That sums it all up."

Kon-Shambique bit his lip. He was beginning to show signs of concern, an uncommon trait for the Favored Tribesman. Ramuza was acutely aware of it.

"What is wrong, Great Creation? Have we overlooked something?"

"It is possible, Mfalme. Are we certain the evil god Abezzin only strikes when the moon is full?"

"The full moon is when Abezzin attacks. The full moon prompts the Batushi to kill the bone's possessor."

"Then, if it is not too late already, you must decide quickly how to force the merchant to keep the bone. On this very evening, Mfalme, the full moon rises."

Ramuza stood up. This fact occurred to him just seconds before Kon-Shambique said it.

"This evening," continued Kon-Shambique, "the Batushi will kill the possessor of the Yululu Bone. This means the merchant is playing games with us, never intending to attack with the Batushi, or he intends to attack us between now and this evening."

Ramuza could not gamble that the merchant was bluffing. For his people's sake, and the sake of the Chinchigwe, he had to assume the worst. There was not a moment to lose. Without a word, Ramuza left the kraal. With the speed of an impala, Ramuza ran down the hillside of Nagorda Peak. He had to get to the Royal Kraal. Kharaambi and the Aukmondi Army had to be alerted at once.

— 50 —

THE NORTH BANK PATHWAY

After reaching the foot of Nagorda Peak, Ramuza took the north bank pathway paralleling the Aukmondi River. He had sprinted down the Nagorda hillside. Once he reached the pathway, his momentum slowed to an intense pace as he continued westward toward the Royal Kraal.

Most of the journey along the pathway was uninterrupted. Ramuza made it as far as the Katola Garden before he met the first encounter. He was so wrapped up in the thought of being attacked by the Batushi that he did not see the Brown Warrior Quazzi coming toward him.

"Mfalme," Quazzi called out to him. "I was just looking for you."

Ramuza continued his pace. He did not acknowledge the Brown Warrior. His mood was calm, but there was an alarming tone of urgency in his voice when he finally spoke to Quazzi. "Great Creation, how soon can the Aukmondi Army be ready for battle?"

"That is exactly why I was looking for you. Training is complete. The warriors are somewhat tired, but they are battle-ready. Why?"

"I have reason to believe the slave merchant will attack with the Batushi between now and this evening."

"Sacred Spirit, be with us! We knew this moment was coming. We did not know it was coming so soon."

Ramuza slowed, but he never stopped walking. He began to walk backwards as he rushed past Quazzi. "Where is the Sacred Woman Kharaambi?"

"I just left her, Great Creation. She is in the Royal Kraal."

"Gather the Royal Warriors, Quazzi. Then meet Kharaambi and me there."

Ramuza did not wait for Quazzi's acknowledgement. He turned to resume his strong pace along the pathway. Deep in thought, he bumped into his second encounter.

The visitor, Andallah Gallagana, walked along the pathway. The dog that she cared for energetically ran about at her feet. Andallah carried her freshly washed bundle of garments on top of her head. She and Ramuza were on a collation course. The sudden impact with the Mfalme sent the bundle flying. The bundle came loose, and the garments were scattered on the ground.

"Excuse me, Sacred Woman." Ramuza held Andallah's shoulders to secure her. "Are you alright?"

"I am fine, Mfalme. It is my fault. I saw you coming. I should have said something."

"Nonsense. I accept total blame. I did not see you. I am truly sorry." Out of kindness or respect, Ramuza thought it was only right to sacrifice a few moments to help Andallah retrieve her garments. He kneeled to begin gathering up the garments. But as he grabbed some scattered pieces, his full attention returned to the crucial issue – getting to the Royal Kraal to prepare for war.

Lost in thought, Ramuza collected the garments, two and three at a time. He couldn't seem to get them up fast enough. He tossed the bunch he had gathered onto a pile and quickly gathered more.

The dog that accompanied Andallah did not help matters. He was a hindrance. He playfully grabbed at some of the same pieces of garments that Ramuza reached for. Ramuza was often caught in an unwanted game of tug. He tempered his frustration by conceding the disputed pieces to the dog.

Andallah noticed Ramuza's behavior. "Mfalme, I apologize for the dog?"

"He is but a playful dog, Sacred Woman. It is not necessary to apologize."

"I can tell that you are in a hurry. Your time is important. Do not worry about the garments. Go. I will gather the rest."

Without a word, Ramuza tossed another bunch onto the pile. Almost rudely, he turned to continue along the pathway. One last piece of garment, which the dog had carried away, lay on the ground before him. Ramuza grabbed it up. But he was in such a hurry now that he did not bother to return it to Andallah and the rest of the pile. He continued toward the Royal kraal with the garment still in his hand.

As life will have it sometimes, especially when focused on one goal, interruptions and distractions seem to come simultaneously as if deliberately. He had yet another unexpected encounter just before he entered the Royal Kraal. This time, it was Twese and Upenda. They had come looking for the Mfalme in the Royal Kraal. They were coming out of the kraal when they finally found him coming off the pathway.

At about the same time, Ramuza saw them coming. There was no doubt that they were coming to address him. His first impulse was to wave them aside, but he thought better.

"What is it?" He asked sharply.

"Mfalme Ncobba," said Twese. "I wish to talk with you for a moment."

"Great Creation, I do not have a moment. Can it not wait?"

Twese was about to answer, but Upenda, who knew Ramuza much better, took Twese firmly by the arm. She understood that the Mfalme's question was not just a question. "I think we had better talk with the Mfalme later, Great Creation."

"But it is very important." Twese persisted. "Mfalme Ncobba, the Chinchigwe have…"

"It must wait, Great Creation," Ramuza spoke in no uncertain terms. He turned to Upenda. "Sacred Woman, we may battle with the Batushi this evening. Please join your regiment and await instructions from your Blue Warrior."

"At once, Mfalme."

At this point, Ramuza seemed to realize for the first time that he still held a piece of Andallah's garments in his hand. He was at a loss for a moment as to what to do with it. He resisted the impulse to toss it aside. He finally forced it into Upenda's hand and walked away.

Twese and Upenda were left standing there. Neither of them realized, until this moment, the gravity of the situation in the valley. With astonishment, they watched the Mfalme enter the Royal Kraal.

"Great Creation," Upenda was the first to speak. "I am sorry. The Mfalme is quite busy."

"It is alright, Upenda. The Mfalme is right. Under the circumstances, it is a matter that must wait."

"I have been instructed to join my regiment on the south slope. I must go now."

"Yes, I understand." There was no place else to go but back to the guest kraal. Coincidentally, it was also on the south slope. "May I walk with you across the bridge?"

"Of course."

"Upenda, I want to thank you for the help you have given me."

"It was my pleasure, Great Creation."

Twese and Upenda did not say anything until they were halfway across the bridge. Both were too absorbed in their thoughts to talk.

As they walked, Twese looked back over his left shoulder. He saw more people on the north bank pathway, coming and going. Among the people, he noticed Andallah. She was finally tying off her bundle of garments and was struggling to lift it atop her head.

Twese stopped. He turned and stared. He walked to the edge of the bridge. "Upenda!" He called for the White Warrior, never taking his eyes off Andallah.

"Yes, Great Creation?"

"Do you see that woman with the bundle on her head?"

"Yes. What about her?"

"Who is she?

"I do not recognize her from this distance. Looking at her clothing, I would say she is a visitor from, maybe, the Kiwane or the Rimoza tribe. Why?"

"I have seen her before." There was growing excitement in Twese's voice. "She is the woman, Upenda! She is the one that I saw in the wilderness. She was standing next to the rhinoceros!"

"What are you saying, Great Creation?"

"She is the woman who made the rhinoceros docile. She stopped it from charging us in the wilderness!"

Upenda looked at the woman again. Suddenly, she knew the woman's true identity. "Eledah!"

Twese also knew there was more going on here than meets the eye. "So, what does this mean? What do we do?"

Upenda thought a moment, then looked down at the piece of garment in her hand. It did not take a genius to realize where the garment had come from. Understanding the seemingly minor events that placed it in her hands wasn't necessary. Upenda at once started back across the bridge to the north slope. "Come with me, Great Creation. We must talk with the Mfalme."

51

THE FISHERMAN OF RIMOZA

The entire royal family sat around the dais in front of the four huts of the Ncobbas. Rwuva, Olabisi, and all nine of the Ncobba daughters sat quietly, intently listening to the conversation between Ramuza and Kharaambi.

Adaulah was there as well, listening in his way. While most of his attention was on the conversation, he was busy trying to retrieve Sharikumba. The leopard kitten had climbed up one of the wooden poles that held the canopy over the royal dais. The kitten was well over Adaulah's head. Adaulah started up the pole himself to rescue the kitten.

"What about the armies?" Ramuza was asking. Just moments ago, he had told the Gray Warrior about the imminent return of the slave merchant and the Batushi. He was now reviewing some of the final preparations. "Are they in position?"

"The armies are in complete readiness, Mfalme. I have divided them into specialized units and instructed them on how to reinforce each other. The armies are in position to engage, regroup, and recover in overlapping sequences."

"And the sentinels?"

Kharaambi had just spent the entire day drilling her armies. She had returned to the Royal Kraal, removed most of her warrior-gear, and was preparing to recover from her grueling day when Ramuza told her the news. Now, she was putting her warrior gear back on. She answered Ramuza's question as a Red Warrior handed her a fresh spear and shield. "I have converted eight of the strongest warrior regiments into sentinel regiments for twenty. If nothing else, our sentry line must not be penetrated. It is our first line of defense. I have given the sentinels priority."

"Good." Ramuza had total approval and confidence in Kharaambi's combat strategy. He did, however, expect and override her next move. "There is no need to summon the Royal Warriors, Sacred Woman. I spoke with the Great Creation Quazzi already. He should be returning with them shortly."

At this point, Sharikumba jumped from the pole to the ground. Like the wildcat that he was, he flew over Adaulah's head as if determined not to be caught. He landed in front of the royal dais, almost at Ramuza's feet. Adaulah scurried down the pole and went to retrieve the kitten. He came to stand in front of his father.

"Mfalme, I am an Honorary Black Warrior," he said as he lifted the kitten into his arms. "What do you need me to do?"

Ramuza smiled at this son. He gestured toward Rwuva, Olabisi, and the Ncobba daughters. "Little Creation, do you see these Sacred women?"

"Yes, Mfalme. I see them."

"When the slave merchant returns, I will need you to keep them from being afraid. They need to know that everything will be all right when it is all over. Can you do that?"

"I do not know. How do I keep them from being afraid?"

"You and Sharikumba must stay close to them. You will figure out a way."

******

Down by the river bank, the Brown Warrior Quazzi and most of the Royal Warriors stepped off the north bank pathway onto the trail leading up to the Royal Kraal. Twese and Upenda had just come off the bridge to the north slope at about that same time. Everyone was converging on the kraal entrance.

When Quazzi saw Upenda, he instantly knew she was out of place. He reacted. "Sacred Woman, you must go and find your regiment, now."

Upenda hesitated for only an instant. "Great Creation, with all due respect, I must speak with the Mfalme."

"Now is not the time."

Upenda held up the garment in her hand. "It is from the Sacred Woman Eledah."

Quazzi looked at the garment only briefly. However, if the garment was from the Sacred Woman Eledah, then instantly, there was no more to be said, and Upenda was no longer out of place. "Come. Walk with me."

Quazzi, Upenda, and Twese entered the Royal kraal. Walking three abreast, they led the pack of Royal Warriors that followed behind them. In mass, they began the short trek across the celebration area to the four huts of the Ncobbas.

One of the Royal Warriors walking behind Upenda was Nionu. Despite the situation, his good-natured mood still showed. In words just loud enough for everyone to hear, he jokingly commented. "Give some people a little training, and they will think they can wear a Royal cloak."

Upenda knew he was talking about her. She turned and smiled.

******

When the group finally reached the four huts of the Ncobbas, Kharaambi was the first to address them. She expected to see Quazzi and her Royal Warriors. She did not expect to see Upenda and Twese.

"Upenda, Sacred Woman, why are you not with your regiment? And why is the Chinchigwe here?"

"Sacred Woman," Quazzi spoke, "she and the Chinchigwe are here with my permission."

Twese stepped forward and addressed Ramuza. "Mfalme, I must speak with you."

"It does seem to be unavoidable. Great Creation, did we not go through this already?"

"Please. This is different. It is about a woman I just saw, down on the bank of the river. I have seen her before."

"I believe you just spoke with Her, Great Creation," Upenda added, "down on the north bank pathway."

"What woman?" Ramuza instantly recalled the woman he had recently spoken with. "The Sacred Woman Andallah Gallagana?"

"If that is her name, Mfalme."

Somewhat confused, Ramuza turned to Twese. "You have seen her before? When?"

"I saw her during our trek in the wilderness, Mfalme. A rhinoceros charged the Chinchigwe and Adaulah. At a crucial moment, when all seemed hopeless, she appeared. She stood within arm's length of the rhinoceros. Her very presence seemed to make the beast docile."

"Eledah?"

"Eledah," Upenda repeated. She handed the garment that she still held in her hand back to the Mfalme.

Ramuza took the garment. He recognized it as belonging to Andallah but did not look at it. He was overwhelmed by the sudden new and very important change of circumstances. "What is happening here? What does this all mean?"

Just then, the Favored Tribesman broke through the sea of Royal Warriors. He had arrived in the Royal Kraal just behind the Royal Warriors. He had heard most of Twese's confession and the Mfalme's questions. "Mfalme, the question you should ask yourself is 'why did the Sacred Woman Eledah came to you in the guise of Andallah Gallagana'."

"I have no idea, Great Creation." Ramuza tried to focus on what he knew about the Sacred Woman Andallah. "I barely know her. I have seen her only once or twice before."

"Great Creation," Quazzi stepped in to jog the Mfalme's memory. "The Sacred Woman Andallah was but a baby in our time. You probably do not remember her, but you do know her. We grew up with her father. You and I, as children, used to play with her father quite often. And her grandfather was the infamous fisherman of Rimoza. Surely, you remember him?"

Ramuza suddenly recalled a true legend from his childhood. The fisherman of Rimoza bravely waded into snake-infested waters just to catch a day's fish meal for family and friends. The memory, long forgotten, came back with crystal clarity. "Yes. Yes, I remember now. He was the only one who would fish in those waters. Most people thought he was insane because of the deadly snakes."

"He is the one. There was an affectionate term that everyone in the Rimoza village called him. We got into the habit of calling him by that name ourselves. What was it we called him?" Quazzi closed his eyes, concentrating, trying to recall the name. "We called him, Baba something, Baba Bopah."

"Bopah!" Ramuza looked at Kon-Shambique.

"The name 'Bopah' is part of the legend of the Yululu Bone, Mflame," Kon-Shambique said. "Do you remember?"

Ramuza finally unfurled the garment that he held in his hand. He held it up to study it closely. It was a beautiful pink scarf, with prints of cassava, papaya, guava, passion fruit, and various other melons. "Yes, I remember. Bopah, the melon-grower."

"Now, Great Creation. Now, it is proper to ask, what does this all mean?"

52

SURRENDER TO THE BATUSHI

Like thunder, sentry warning drums suddenly rumbled through the valley. The sound and the rumble grew louder and louder as other drums on the valley rim joined in. It was a truly frightening noise.

Ramuza was the first to react. He calmly turned to Kharaambi. "Sacred Woman, deploy your armies."

Kharaambi huddled with the Royal Warriors. After only a few seconds of instructions, the Royal Warriors scrambled across the celebration area and out of the Royal Kraal to take charge of their armies. Only a few Orange, Red, and White Warriors were left in the kraal to care for the Royal family and other immediate needs.

Upenda was one of the few White Warriors still in the kraal. She knew her assigned duties were with the Bendabe regiment of Nionu's army. She started across the celebration area to join the regiment, but Ramuza called her back.

"Yes, Mfalme?"

"Sacred Woman, I have a very important task for you." Ramuza scanned the western half of the Royal Kraal, looking for something. "I need you to find high ground somewhere. Whatever happens this evening, I do not want you to lose sight of me. I want you to watch the rising moon. Let me know the moment you see it rising. Is that clear?"

"Yes, Great Creation." Because the moon rises in the east, Upenda began searching the western half of the kraal herself. She at once selected a large tree on the hillside behind Kharaambi's hut.

As strange as her instructions were, Upenda did not question them. Dutifully, she ran toward the hillside to take her position in the tree.

"Mfalme," Quazzi appeared at Ramuza's side. "The villagers will, no doubt, be curious about what is happening. We can expect a huge convergence on the Royal Kraal. Would you like it closed off?"

"No, Great Creation. It may get crowded here, and we may need a little crowd control, but do not close the kraal."

Sure enough, curious villagers could already be seen pouring into the Royal Kraal from across the celebration area. In the far distance, they could be seen coming off the north bank pathway onto the trail toward the kraal. Others could be seen coming across the bridge from the south slope. Many of them were frightened. But because they already expected something like this, no one was panicking.

As the sentry warning drums continued to rumble, seemingly from every point of the valley's north rim, people poured into the kraal to learn what was happening. None of them had ever heard so many drums at once.

At the entrance of the Royal Kraal, most of the Chinchigwe could also be seen among the crowd of people coming in, including Ameh, Embabi, Komu, Summare, Jpuma, and several others. They were visitors to the Aukmondi Valley but knew where all the answers could be found.

The celebration area was about half-filled with people when the sentry warning drums finally stopped. The rumbling was replaced by a moment of silence and the sounds of another set of drums. The crowd of restless people fell silent as they listened. The new set of drums had a distinctly different sound. It was an irregular series of hollow knocks from some obscure sentry post on the north rim.

"Talking drums, Mfalme?" Ameh, who had made his way to the front of the crowd, recognized the drums. "What do they say?"

"It is the slave merchant," Kharaambi interpreted the hollow knocks. "He has returned…with the Batushi. They are armed…with guns…approaching…in battle formation."

Kharaambi paused as the faint knocks continued. Suddenly, the messages of the talking drums made Ramuza, Kharaambi, and Quazzi look at each other with expressions of unmistakable alarm.

"Sacred Spirit, be with us!" Quazzi could not contain himself.

"What is it?" Ameh wanted to know. "What is happening?"

"There are hundreds of them. Hundreds, spanning across the entire north region!" Quazzi turned to Ramuza. "Great Creation, we will have to act soon. The Royal Warriors need your instructions."

Once again, everyone's attention was on the Mfalme. This time, many of the villagers and many of the Chinchigwe were waiting for his response.

"First," Ramuza finally began. His manner was calm, but there was no doubt he was still putting his strategy together as he went. "I will need my set of talking drums."

With just a gesture, Kharaambi sent a Red and White Warrior to retrieve a set of drums from Ramuza's hut.

"Three hundred meters," Kharaambi continued, interpreting the talking drum from the valley rim. "They are getting closer."

Ramuza only nodded.

After a few seconds, the Red and White Warriors returned from Ramuza's hut with three large, barrel-size drums and two batons. Quazzi took the batons as the warriors set the drums before him.

"What will you have me say, Mfalme?"

"Listen carefully, Quazzi." Ramuza paused, only to mentally refine the instructions he was about to give. "My first instructions are to the sentinels nearest to the slave merchant. Determine if the slave merchant still has the Yululu Bone."

With powerful strokes, Quazzi began his series of irregular knocks. When he finished, there was silence as everyone waited for the response. Finally, after an indefinite time, a short series of knocks were heard from the valley rim.

"He has the Yululu Bone, Mfalme." Quazzi interpreted.

"Good. Now tell the commanders of the sentinel armies … not to resist the merchant. Tell them … to allow the slave merchant and as many Batushi warriors as he thinks are necessary … to enter the valley."

Quazzi was poised, ready to send the next message until he heard what it was. He looked at Kharaambi with disbelief.

"Great Creation," Kharaambi had to raise her voice slightly over the rumble of voices. "Mfalme, what are you doing? The sentry line must not be broken. If the Batushi get into the valley, we …"

"I understand this, Sacred Woman. It is necessary." Ramuza turned to Quazzi. "Please, send the message."

Quazzi still hesitated. "Mfalme, the warriors on the sentry line will not accept such a message. It is contrary to all their training."

"I know that, Great Creation. You must make it clear that I gave the instructions. Do whatever you must but send the message … before it is too late."

Quazzi had never disobeyed instructions from his Mfalme, but it was one of the most difficult things he had ever done. He could not bring himself to begin the message; it was just wrong.

"Must I do it myself?"

"Ramuza, Great Creation," Kharaambi supported the Brown Warrior. "Such instructions are madness. We might as well surrender to the Batushi."

"Kharaambi!" Ameh stepped forward to interrupt. He could see things were not going smoothly. It was time for him to react. The least he could do was offer some advice. "I am only a visitor here. But I can see this valley has been led and protected for a very long time by a wise and thoughtful man. As you told me just yesterday, we must trust the Mfalme."

Kharaambi recalled the conversation. Her own words came back to her. She turned to the Brown Warrior. "Send the message, Quazzi."

"I beg your forgiveness, Mfalme." After a silent nod from Ramuza, Quazzi began another series of powerful strokes on the talking drums. Because of the nature of the message, he had to repeat it three times. He sighed with relief after the third attempt when the message was finally acknowledged.

"Tell the Sentinels to do nothing that might antagonize the merchant or the Batushi. Tell the ranking Royal Warrior on the sentry line to escort the merchant directly here, to me."

53

THE TRINKET IS DEADLY

Here were the beginnings of some very tense moments as everyone waited to see if Ramuza's strange instructions were being carried out. The situation was extremely delicate.

Contrary to the Mfalme's instructions, many things could have gone wrong. Some warrior, either Aukmondi or Batushi, could have become overly anxious and struck at the opponent. There would be retaliation, and the unwanted battle would have begun. It would be too late to stop it.

Or, it could have been the merchant's plan to forgo negotiations. The merchant could have come with the Batushi, attacked, and harvested the helpless spoils. He could have done it. He had the power.

But no. Ramuza had something else in mind. It was his way of exploiting the secret of the Yululu Bone against the merchant. For the moment, he still had control of the situation. For the moment, he was giving all the instructions. It was his decisions and directions as to what was or was not to be done. How long this would last was anybody's guess.

There was a constant chatter of disturbed voices as the people in the celebration area discussed the strange way the Mfalme handled this. No one understood it. It was a development that no one expected. Whatever the Mfalme had in mind, if nothing else, it had not caused any bloodshed yet. So far, there was still the approximation of peace.

Walking between the valley's north rim and the Royal Kraal normally takes nearly two hours. It was an excruciatingly long time to wait and finally see a massive group of people coming through the trees and down the valley's north slope. An Aukmondi Royal Warrior, commander of one of the sentinel armies, led the way. Behind him came three unmistakable white men: the slave merchant and his aides. They were followed by the massive bulk of the group – the Batushi warriors. Like a trail of ants, they formed an endless procession along the winding pathway from the valley rim, down the slope, and into the Royal Kraal. Even as the beginning of this group finally gathered in the celebration area, the end was still nowhere in sight.

The crowd of Aukmondi villagers and Chinchigwe who were already in the area slowly parted as the merchant and his aides triumphantly walked across the celebration area. The Royal Warrior in the lead stepped aside and allowed the white men to finish the last few meters up the royal dais themselves.

The merchant walked boldly and calmly as if this overly dramatic return was nothing unusual. He stopped directly before Ramuza, showing no sign of respect toward the Mfalme.

As usual, the merchant chewed loudly on his tobacco. He removed his oversized sunhat, pulled a bandana from his pocket, and dabbed the sweat from his forehead. Feeling that he was the master of the moment, he took his time to thoroughly wipe the sweat from the inner band of his hat. Then he calmly replaced the hat neatly on his head and the bandana back into his pocket. He made one sweeping glance behind him at all the Batushi warriors before finally smiling at Ramuza.

"Well, chief? Have you come to your fool senses yet?"

Ramuza looked into the merchant's eyes just as calmly. "Yes, I have. We will settle our dispute without war."

"Well, good. You are amakin' this real easy for the both of us. I do appreciate that."

Ramuza turned away from the merchant. He searched the crowd of onlookers until he located Ameh, Twese, and most of the other Chinchigwe standing together. He gestured toward them. "There are the Chinchigwe, merchant. You may take them."

Voices erupted, protesting Ramuza's statement. There was a particular objection, of course, from the Chinchigwe. Twese became so vocal and rebellious that Ameh and Komu had to restrain him physically.

The merchant had to wait until Twese was subdued before responding to Ramuza's generous offer. "I thank you kindly, chief. But, hell's fire man, I don't reckon they're yours to give."

"You may have the Aukmondi as well." Ramuza turned to face the merchant again. There were more voices of protest.

"The point I was atryin' to make, chief, is you don't 'ave to give me what I already got." The merchant paused long enough to spit. He eyed the Aukmondi chief suspiciously. He was acutely aware that the chief was behaving unexpectedly. This was much too easy. "Why 're you bein' so damned cooperative, anyhow? What, exactly, 're you up to?"

"I would like to request a favor of you, merchant."

"A favor? After all the trouble you caused me? You don't deserve no favors from me."

"Grant this favor, merchant, and I believe you will make a small profit."

The merchant chuckled. He turned to his aides. "Would you listen to this? This big ignorant buck is atalkin' business. I do believe he's trying to get on me good side. You know. I kinda like that."

"Well, merchant?"

"Never let it be said that I don't 'ave the heart to make a profit. Go ahead. Let's hear what you got to say."

"I am under the impression that you have a particular vengeance for my son, the Young Creation, who freed the Chinchigwe from your animal pen."

The merchant glanced at Adaulah, who sat proudly between Rwuva and Olabisi. "That's right. That there boy, he's a bad apple. It's best we weed 'im out afore he spoils the whole lot. Why do you ask?"

Ramuza was amazed that the merchant could be heartless enough to ask such a question. It was no wonder the Batushi gave him the Yululu Bone. "I wish to die in his place."

"What? Now just how, in hell's fire, am I supposed to make a profit by lettin' you die in his place?"

"As I understand your business, he is worth more than I because he is younger. Am I not correct?"

"You are correct, chief. He's worth a tad bit more, providin', he can be trained. But, hell's fire man, as rich as I am now, it really won't make much difference whether I kill you or him. No sir. The boy dies. I 'ave to teach him a lesson. It's a personal thing, iffin' you know what I mean."

"The lesson will be no good to him if he is dead."

The slave merchant pretended to think about the request again. He gave the matter no serious thought, however. His mind was already made up. What he did think about was why this particular request. The more he listened, the more it did not sound right. What could be the chief's motive? Of all the things he could have asked for, he only asked to die in his son's place. There was something about the request that rubbed McIntyre the wrong way.

"No! "I'm real sorry, chief. I'm agonna 'ave to reject your request. The boy dies. If it wasn't for him, none o' this would be happening in the first place. I just can 'ave 'im causing no more trouble. And since we're on the subject, why don't we just go ahead and get this nasty little business over with?" The merchant pointed at Adaulah. "You. Come on down 'ere, boy!"

Adaulah sat unmoved, his arms folded defiantly across his chest. "I am not afraid of you, merchant."

"Merchant," Ramuza caught McIntyre's arm and held it tightly. He pointed at Twese, whom Ameh and Komu were still holding. "Look. How do you know there are not others like him? Place no restraints on him, and I am sure he will willingly give his life to end yours for his people's sake."

McIntyre remembered Twese from yesterday's incident. He knew that Twese was bad merchandise, too. If all precautions were properly taken, troublemaking Chinchigwe like him would be put to death, too. But he couldn't set a precedent of killing all his merchandise. There might not be anything left.

"No. Killing the one boy will teach him and everybody else a lesson."

"If you must teach a lesson and make an example of someone, then I am the one, merchant. Allow my son to live. If you do, I will ensure that you do not experience resistance here. And, as a final tribute to me, I will ask that you get no resistance throughout your entire journey back across the great waters."

McIntyre broke free of Ramuza's grip and massaged the spot where he was held. He spat out the massive wad of old tobacco in his mouth. He smiled and turned to Ramuza. "You know something, chief? I always figured you to be sort o' intelligent for an African native. Of course, I can't see why you're so damned anxious to die. But, iffin' that is what you really want, then I guess I'm awillin to oblige you this one time."

The merchant was considerably more stubborn than Ramuza had expected. Finally achieving his goal, the Mfalme sighed with relief. The difficult part of his strategy was over.

Ramuza glanced over at the hillside behind Kharaambi's hut. He made eye contact with Upenda, who stood comfortably on one of the limbs in the tree. Then he turned back to the merchant. "There is one other thing before I die, merchant."

"What now? I thought I said I'd oblige you only once. Don't get into the habit o' asking too many favors."

"Give me the Yululu Bone."

"Say what?" The request caught the merchant by surprise. He stared at the chief. He turned and looked at Sam and Pete. Initially, with creeping chuckles, the merchant and his aides eventually surrendered to hardy belly laughs. The fact that the Aukmondi chief didn't know what he was asking for was funny to them.

The merchant turned back to Ramuza, still laughing, tears of hysteria in his eyes. He could barely talk. "Is that all you want, chief?"

"Why do you find that so amusing?"

"Have you learned the secret of the bone since my last visit?"

"Yes, but…"

"I mean, the whole secret?"

"I think I know what you know."

"And you still want the bone? Are you aware that the full moon will rise in about fifteen or twenty minutes?"

Ramuza glanced at Upenda again. "Yes, I know."

McIntyre was surprised but not disappointed. "You're a smart boy, chief. You do fast work, and I'm truly impressed. Some folks can search Africa for a lifetime and still don't learn the secret of this here bone."

"I had help."

"If you know the whole secret, then it seems to me, it would be in your best interest if I was forced to keep this damned thing. You must know I 'ave to get rid of it before the moon comes up. If I don't, I'm a dead man."

"Yes, I know this."

"And you must also know that these heathens behind me here will kill whoever has this bone when the moon comes up."

"That is part of the bone's legend."

McIntyre reached into his pocket and pulled out the Yululu Bone. On its long string of beads, bones, teeth, and nuggets of gold, he began twirling it around his fingers. "And you still want it?"

"It is my way of dying."

McIntyre stopped twirling the bone. He held it high so everyone, particularly the Batushi, could see it. Then he tossed it at Ramuza's feet. He glanced over his shoulder to see if the Batushi knew he had discarded it. McIntyre was pleased to see a small amount of restlessness, confusion, and even disappointment among the Batushi.

Ramuza looked down at the discarded trinket. He glanced over at the hillside and Upenda in the tree. She gave him no sign that the moon was visible yet. Ramuza looked back down at the trinket again as if he was about to pick it up.

"Now, I know what you 're athinkin'," the merchant said. "I'm no fool. I'm a whole step ahead o' you. If you touch that bone before the moon comes up, you can give these Batushi heathens all kinds o' troublesome orders before they finally kill you. I cain't 'ave that, now can I? Now that I've gotten rid of the bone, me authority will last just long enough for me to issue one or two of me own final orders. I aim to use that authority smartly, with no trouble from you."

"I was only concerned about my people."

"A chief to the very end. Looks to me like I just took away your last chance to help your people. I really wouldn't worry none about their condition, chief. It's completely out of your hands now. The truth o' the matter is, their condition is about to get much worse. These darkies are agonna wish they were dead before they get across the ocean. I got a pretty good size ship called the 'Maiden's Hand' awaitin' on the coast. With this here big haul though, I'll probably 'ave to buy two 'r three more ships to haul 'em. But hell's fire, anyway you look at it, it's agonna be a mighty crowded trip. Them that don't manage to cut their own throats or jump overboard, will go through a livin' hell. But don't you worry none. Them that survive the trip, it'll all be good for 'em. In the end, they'll be what you might call real obligin' human beings."

"I suppose, conditions could be worse," Ramuza said, sounding very unlike himself.

There was that wave of disturbed voices again as the people reacted to Ramuza's statement. Even Sam and Pete looked at each other, perplexed by the chief's complacency.

"Say, Capt'n McIntyre," Pete approached the merchant. He spoke just above a whisper. "I don't know about you, but I don't like how this fool sounds. I think he's up to something."

"He is actin' rather strangely, ain't he?"

During another glance toward Upenda, Ramuza saw the Great Creation Tanake standing in the crowd of onlookers. He smiled and beckoned the Old Creation to come closer.

Tanake shuffled his way to the front of the crowd. After he broke through, he obediently approached Ramuza. "How may I serve you, Mfalme?"

"You wanted to see a Yululu Bone, Great Creation. Here is your chance. Take a good look."

Tanake looked down at the bone. He began to kneel, to pick it up. Ramuza caught his shoulder and stopped him.

"No, Great Creation, the trinket is deadly. Touch it and you will be killed when the moon rises."

"Kon-Shambique was right, Mfalme. The sight of the trinket is not as impressive as its influence. For now, I think I have seen everything I want of it."

Ramuza put his arm around Tanake's shoulder. "Great Creation, with your permission, I would like to send someone to your hut to retrieve the chain you took from the arm of the Chinchigwe."

A perplexed expression appeared on Tanake's face, but it quickly disappeared. "It is still lying where you and the Favored Tribesman moved it. No one else seems to want it. It is yours, Mfalme."

"Thank you." Ramuza gestured toward Kharaambi. She, in turn, dispatched four warriors to Tanake's hut.

"What, in hell's fire, are you up to, chief? What's this nonsense about a chain?"

"The chain that you had on the arms of the Chinchigwe," Ramuza explained, "I want to give it back to you."

"That won't be necessary. I don't need no damned chain. With this big catch, I intend to shoot any fool that steps out o' line." The merchant lied.

"I want to give it to you anyway. Think of it as a gift from me to you."

"Alright, chief, if you want to return it to me, I reckon I'll take it. It might come in handy during another trip betwixt here and the homeland."

Suddenly, Sharikumba, the leopard kitten, came trotting out from behind the royal dais. His sudden appearance caught the eye of everyone in the area. Completely oblivious to the current events, the kitten playfully pranced out to a spot directly between Ramuza and the merchant.

Ramuza bent down to pick it up. He smiled as he put his finger against the kitten's wet nose.

"His name is Sharikumba," Ramuza said to the merchant.

"Is that s'posed to mean something to me?"

"It means 'destroyer of evil'." Ramuza set the kitten down. Everyone watched it as it began chasing an unseen prey again.

Sharikumba darted here and there at the feet of the merchant and his aides. In its play, the kitten found the massive wad of tobacco the merchant had spat out earlier. After one cautious sniff, the kitten forgot about playing. He turned as his instincts took over. With diligent sweeping strokes, the kitten began to throw dirt on the tobacco wad in an attempt to bury it.

Even the merchant took a moment to laugh before he turned his attention back to Ramuza. "I reckon you think I'm evil. Chief, you don't know evil. It will take more 'n a damned wildcat to get rid of the evil that's astandin' behind me."

Ramuza stepped forward, standing almost face to face with the merchant. "Would you like me to save your worthless life, merchant?"

"What, the hell?" The merchant stepped back. Surprised by the chief's suddenly aggressive posture, he spoke primarily to himself. He turned to face Sam and Pete again. "Did I just miss somethin' here?"

Ramuza continued speaking to the merchant. "The Batushi Mfalme gave you the Yululu Bone right after you paid him with guns. Am I correct, merchant?"

"How do you know about me business with the Batushi?"

"The Chinchigwe overheard some of it. They told me most of what they heard."

"Me and Jagotta, we had a deal. So, what about it?"

"What did you do, merchant? I am curious. You must have given him less than he expected. Or was it bad merchandise that you gave him?"

"I gave 'im what he wanted." The merchant was defending himself in the presence of the Batushi. Then he seemed to realize that the Aukmondi chief was turning this conversation in a direction he did not want. "Anyways, that there is water under the bridge and none o' your business."

"In retaliation," Ramuza continued, "he gave you the Yululu Bone. He wants you dead, merchant."

There was a rumble of voices as the majority of everyone present learned, for the first time, why the merchant was given the deadly trinket.

"You don't always get what you want."

"That sounds like a lesson that the Batushi Mflame learned the hard way."

The merchant tried to appear calm rather than defend himself and risk admitting his crime. He reached into his pocket and pulled out a fresh twist of tobacco. Before he finished unwrapping it, he lost the taste for it. He rewrapped it and stuffed it back in his pocket.

"Chief, the fact o' the matter is you don't know what you're talking about. I recommend you keep your mouth shut afore it gets you into more trouble than you're already in."

"Once I pick up the Yululu Bone, I am doomed to die. What more trouble can there be?" Ramuza smiled at the merchant's confusion. "You are a Very Crafty Creation. The Batushi Mfalme underestimated you. He did not think you knew the secret of the Yululu Bone. Now, you have wisely gotten rid of it. You have saved your life. Would it surprise you that the Batushi would still like to see you dead?"

The merchant forced a smile on his face. The Aukmondi chief was trying to intimidate him. For a brief moment, he was succeeding. The merchant bolstered his shaken confidence and walked away from Ramuza.

He approached one of his aides. "Tell me something, Pete. You reckon I ought just to shoot this poor soul, right now, 'n put 'im out of his miseries?"

Pete could tell that Captain McIntyre was being condescending toward the Aukmondi chief. When the question was asked, Pete could not play along. He gave his blatantly direct answer in whispered confidence.

"Capt'n, this so-called poor soul is scaring the living hell out of me. You ought to do something. Either make him pick up that damned bone or shoot him. Just shut him, the hell, up!"

The merchant turned from Pete. He pulled out his pistol and walked back toward the Aukmondi chief. "Now, I've got three choices here, chief. I can let you die by the Yululu Bone. I can order the Batushi to just run you through right now. Or I can shoot you meself. As I think about it, shooting you meself sounds like a little pleasure I just might enjoy."

The merchant checked the powder pan on his pistol. Pulling the hammer back to lock it, he suddenly heard a female voice coming from the hillside.

Everyone in the area heard the voice. It was Upenda, standing in the tree behind Kharaambi's hut. She was pointing to the east with her spear.

"Mfalme!" She called out. "The moon!"

The commotion of voices that followed was quieted again when Ramuza addressed the merchant.

"Put your gun away, merchant." He walked back over to where the Yululu Bone lay. He picked it up without the slightest reservation. "The Batushi will take care of things now."

"Well, it's about damned time." The merchant stepped back. With his pistol still in hand, he motioned toward the apparent leader of the Batushi warriors. "Kill that son of a bitch!"

The Batushi warrior did not move. He just stood there as if he had never heard the merchant.

"I will ask you once again," Ramuza ceremoniously hung the Yululu Bone around his neck. Faking pride in his new adornment, he approached the merchant. "Would you like me to save your worthless life?"

The merchant ignored the Aukmondi chief. He stormed over to a large group of Batushi warriors. "Did you hear what I said? I ordered him dead. The moon is up. He's got the damned bone. Kill 'im!"

Again, the Batushi gave the merchant a deaf ear. The merchant angrily cursed the warriors under his breath. He turned and aimed his pistol at Ramuza. Like well-trained reflex responses, several of the Batushi and Aukmondi warriors, in unison, aimed their spears at the merchant.

"What, in hell's fire, is agoin' on here?" The merchant was stunned by the sudden and imminent threat to his life. He quickly threw his pistol to the ground and stepped back.

Kharaambi walked over and picked up the pistol. She also took the merchant's knife and other weapons. Quazzi and two Aukmondi warriors disarmed Sam and Pete.

When Ramuza saw the four Aukmondi warriors sent to Tanake's hut coming with the chain, he told the Batushi warriors to take it and chain the merchant and his aides together. The Batushi responded immediately and respectfully.

The slave merchant began to express his rage verbally. He cursed the Batushi and struggled against their restraint of him. "Get your damned hands off me! He's got the bone, not me! Let me go and kill that heathen bastard!"

"I have offered to save your life, merchant. Yet, you refuse to even listen to me."

"I don't know how you did this, chief. But you can go to hell!"

With this, Ramuza felt he had agitated the merchant enough. He approached the apparent Batushi leader. "Take them to your Mfalme. They are his to do as he pleases."

"Now just wait! Wait a minute!" The merchant protested. "You can't do this. Jagotta will kill me."

Ramuza smiled again. "I'm sure he will. And this time, I do not believe his attempt will be by any tribal ritual."

"Alright, chief. Alright! You win. I'd be much obliged if you saved me worthless life."

"Me too!" Sam quickly added. "I mean, us. Me 'n Mr. Rexley. Save us too!"

Ramuza did not acknowledge any of the pleas. He turned his back on the merchants and his aides as he addressed the leader of the Batushi warriors. "I am told there is a slave ship on the coast. It is identified as the 'Maiden's Hand'. Find it, dismiss the rest of its crew, and destroy it. The merchant will no longer need it."

"Wait! Wait! You can't do this!" The merchant had overheard the instructions. He was both fearful and angry. "That ship is all I got now! Damn your hide, chief! I'll get you for this! I promise you, before I die, if it's the last thing I ever do, you 're agonna pay for this. Mark me word. "You'll pay!"

"Take them out of my valley." Ramuza watched as the merchant and his aides were led away, dragging the unused part of the heavy chain behind them. As he did, he held the Batushi leader back. When he felt the merchant had been taken far enough away, he spoke to the Batushi leader again.

"I am an Aukmondi and can not sanction the death of the merchant and his aides. Tell your Mfalme not to kill them. I realize that he would like nothing better than to put them to death. But it is my decree as the possessor of the Yululu Bone that the merchant and his aides stay alive and learn to regret their shallow hearts and minds."

The Batushi leader acknowledged the request and started to walk away. Ramuza caught his arm.

"It is also my decree that your Batushi Mfalme provide for his people by some way other than slave hunting. Free all other captives that you may be holding for the merchant. From this day forward, no more people will be caught and sold for any reason. I decree that, however possible, your Mfalme make amends to every tribe he has ever raided."

The Batushi leader hesitated, but only briefly. He nodded his acceptance of Ramuza's decrees. To honor the Yululu Bone, he had no choice. He turned and signaled for the rest of his fellow tribe members to leave.

As peacefully as they had come in, the Batushi began to file out of the celebration area. Smoothly and quietly, they began to climb the north slope, escorting a frantic slave merchant and two dumbfounded aides with them.

The crisis was over.

54

BOPAH'S SECRET

Before the Batushi warriors finished filing out of the Royal Kraal, the cheers of joy and dancing began in the celebration area. The Aukmondi and Chinchigwe peoples could not wait to begin celebrating the miraculous end to their terrible ordeal. The joyous people credited Ramuza for the peaceful end. Kharaambi, Kon-Shambique, Ameh, Twese, and everyone gave Ramuza endless compliments and praises.

Above the noise, Ramuza explained that he was not due all the credit and only used the help and knowledge others had given him. Still, the praise came.

Underneath all the joy, praises, and compliments, there was one major thing on everyone's mind. A miracle like this is seldom seen these days. The people were overwhelmingly curious as to how the miracle was done. How did the Mfalme know how to prevent such an inevitable tragedy?

"To begin with," explained Ramuza, "this was no miracle. As the Great Creation Kon-Shambique will tell you, to call it a miracle is a serious distortion of the truth and a thoughtless misguidance for others who may later learn of the story. The Supreme Spirit ordained long ago that our lives be our responsibilities. We set our destinies long before we are born. With free will, we decide to follow the destinies we have set."

"But Mfalme," Twese objected. "There was help from your Supreme Being. I saw Her myself. You cannot say that this end did not come without divine intervention."

Kon-Shambique smiled at Twese's confusion. "Great Creation, if the Sacred Woman Eledah walks among us every day; if She interacts in our lives every day, then there is no such thing as divine intervention. The Sacred Woman Eledah, in the guise of Andallah Gallagana, did nothing unusual. She only gave us insight and inspiration. They are insights and inspirations that we may act upon, or we may not. They are," Kon-Shambique glanced at Ramuza, "divine nudges."

"What are you saying?"

"When you saw Her, on the pathway, you could have easily dismissed Her features altogether. You could have assumed that She only looked familiar. You could have done nothing at all. Because you acted the way you chose to react, we are not at war with the Batushi."

Ramuza added, "I could have given no interest in Her seemingly talkative conversation when I spoke to Her earlier today. I could have dismissed all that She said to me. I almost did just that. It was not until after the Great Creation, Quazzi, reminded me of a childhood memory that I realized the significance of Her conversation."

"What childhood memory was that, Great Creation?" Kharaambi asked.

"The Sacred Woman Andallah and I were talking about Her brother's dog; how he had been bitten by a viper and recovered. One thing led to another, and she eventually mentioned her grandfather, a fisherman whom poisonous snakes often bit. I remember her grandfather. I did not recall who he was until Quazzi reminded me."

"Who was her grandfather?"

"He was a Rimoza fisherman, infamously known for fishing in snake-infested waters. He did it because he had learned to build an immunity to snake bites by drinking the venom of snakes.

"The significance of all this is twofold. Not only did he accept the deadly venom, but his name was Bopah Gallagana. Coincidentally, 'Bopah' was also the name of a minor character in the legend of the Yululu Bone. In the legend, Bopah was given the deadly Yululu Bone when the moon was full. He accepted it willingly during the very time when the possessor of the bone was due to die."

"You acted like Bopah to save us," Twese smiled.

"Yes, Great Creation. The secret of the Yululu Bone was to get rid of it before the full moon rose. The merchant knew this secret and used it to stay alive. The secret I learned was to accept the Yululu Bone when it was most deadly. I used it to save us."

"Bopah's Secret."

"For history's sake, we may call it 'Bopah's Secret', Great Creation."

"Tell me, Great Creation," Kharaambi wanted to know, "does using Bopah's secret make the Yululu Bone completely harmless?"

"No, Sacred Woman. Bopah, the grandfather of the Sacred Woman Andallah, eventually died of a severe snake bite, though he lived much longer than he normally would have. Bopah, in the Yululu Bone legend, lived until the next full moon. He died because he did not know to discard it. The Yululu Bone is harmless only until the next full moon."

"Then, when do you intend to get rid of it? Or are there more wishes that you would like to make first?"

"No. I have made my wishes. I intend to get rid of the bone as soon as I know the Batushi are watching. And believe me, I will be watched. When it comes to executing their justice with the Yululu Bone, the Batushi are as sly and crafty as the Wabanga."

"I overheard you tell the Batushi not to kill the merchant and his aides, Mfalme. And the merchant has vowed to return. By securing his life, you may have helped him to do just that. He has the potential to be a determined threat."

"That is possible. We still have to see what the Batushi can do with him."

"If he does return," Kharaambi added, "let us hope he finds no more Yululu Bones to fortify his threats. I think we can manage him any other way."

"I agree." Ramuza raised his hands. "No more questions, please. Now that this crisis is over, there is much to do. If there are more questions, I will answer them later. For now, let us prepare for a great celebration that will last the whole night long."

Most of the people around Ramuza began to disperse. Before the Chinchigwe could get too far away, Ramuza caught the attention of Ameh, Twese, Embabi, and several others.

"Ameh, Great Creation," Ramuza said, "you and your people, please remain. I wish to speak with you for a moment."

"But of course, Mfalme."

— **55** —

THE LARGEST CLAN

After Ramuza had gathered most of the Chinchigwe together again, he led them past the royal dais. He took them into the large work area between the huts of Rwuva and Olabisi. The area was not meant to be a meeting place. But it was a large area, large enough to accommodate all the people gathered there. It could also be blocked off from the usual crowd in the celebration area. Two White Warriors stood guard outside the area as Ameh, Twese, Embabi, Komu, and Summarwe were led in.

Ramuza's mates, Rwuva and Olabisi, were already seated in the area. Ramuza's oldest daughter, Omari, was also there. Kharaambi and the Brown Warrior Quazzi walked in behind the Chinchigwe. Ramuza invited the Chinchigwe to sit comfortably, and he took a central seat on the ground before them.

Ameh and Twese looked at each other, wondering why this private gathering had occurred. Twese thought he knew. He was bold enough to address the Mfalme in his usual direct manner.

"Mfalme Ncobba," he began, "now that the merchant and the Batushi have been taken care of, I suppose you are preparing to return the Chinchigwe to the wilderness?"

"If that is your wish, Great Creation. Are you ready to return to the wilderness?"

Twese did not expect a question to be volleyed back to him. His mouth opened to answer, but no words came out. All eyes were on Twese for a moment as everyone waited for his response.

"Twese, the Mfalme asked you a question." It was a subtle reprimand by Ameh.

Twese seemed to realize what he had done. "My apologies, Mfalme."

"Why did you wish to speak with us, Mfalme?" Ameh asked.

"Now that the merchant and the Batushi have been taken care of," Ramuza repeated, using Twese's words, "the Aukmondi hope to have a very special Celebration of Life this evening. It will be very special because, during the celebration, the Sacred Women Rwuva, Olabisi, and Omari have suggested that I invite the Chinchigwe to join the Aukmondi tribe as the Chinchigwe Clan."

The Chinchigwe, including Twese, were all speechless. They looked at one another as joyful smiles overtook their faces.

"Since the time the Chinchigwe arrived in the Aukmondi Valley," Olabisi spoke, "since we learned of your terrible ordeal, the Sacred Women Rwuva and Omari, and I have felt that this invitation was the proper thing to do. We spoke with the Mfalme and convinced him that, if all went well, he should extend an invitation before all eyes and ears of history."

Ameh finally found words. "Rwuva, Olabisi, and Omari, thank you for your concern. Thank you for speaking on our behalf."

"It was our way of helping," added Rwuva.

"Thank you." Ameh turned to Ramuza. He spoke in broken phrases. "Mfalme Ncobba…we will be…we are forever in debt to you and your people. I can tell you now that…"

"No, Great Creation." Ramuza held up his hand to stop the Old Creation from talking. "Tell me nothing now. I only wanted to tell you my intention to extend the invitation during our Celebration of Life. I want to give you time to think about the invitation and make a proper decision, for there is much to consider first."

"Understood, Mfalme."

Ramuza looked at Twese. "If you should choose to return to the wilderness, the Chinchigwe will need time to reestablish their autonomy. Only you and your people can say how much time you will need."

"However long it takes," Kharaambi entered the conversation, "you are welcome to stay within the Aukmondi domain for your protection and complete support until then."

"Mfalme Ncobba," Twese was not about to let this chance of survival slip away. The Chinchigwe can never set up the autonomy that we once had. Even if we could, the process would take generations. We will discuss your invitation, but I can tell you we will be staying now."

"Then consider these things as well," Ramuza continued. "If you choose to stay with the Aukmondi, then one among you must be chosen and recognized as the Mfalme of your people. This individual must be willing to live for the good of all the Chinchigwe and the Aukmondi."

"The Aukmondi?"

"Yes." Kharaambi began to explain. "If the Chinchigwe should stay among the Aukmondi, you will be the largest sovereign clan because of your number. You will be known as the Chinchigwe Clan of the Aukmondi. By Aukmondi law, the Mfalme of the largest sovereign clan must also serve as one of Mfalme Ncobba's closest councilors. By Aukmondi law, and third only to Ramuza and me, the Mfalme of the largest sovereign clan has final authority over the army's Brown Warrior."

All of the Chinchigwe turned to look at Quazzi. Quazzi smiled back at them. "I am prepared to accept all consequences of your decision."

"What do you mean by all consequences?" Twese was curious.

Quazzi, standing off to one side, moved around to the front of the group. "The Mfalme of the largest sovereign clan has the right to abolish the position of Brown Warrior altogether. The Mfalme of the largest sovereign clan may serve as the Brown Warrior. Or, without challenge, the Mfalme of the largest sovereign clan may choose anyone and appoint that choice as Brown Warrior. If the Mfalme of the largest sovereign clan takes neither of these actions, then the status of Brown Warrior falls back to the Sacred Woman Kharaambi. Those are the consequences."

Ameh sighed heavily. "That is, indeed, much to consider."

"But we need no time to think, Mfalme." Twese took the initiative when he saw Ameh wrestling with the offer and all its consequences. "Extend your invitation. The major decisions by the Chinchigwe have already been made. We wish to stay with the Aukmondi. As for selecting one among us as Mfalme, since the raid on our village and when Mfalme Lomani Usai was killed, Ameh Jobabwe has spoken for the Chinchigwe. If the Aukmondi are willing to adopt the Chinchigwe, then we all will agree that Ameh is naturally the one to be called Mfalme."

"Twese, no!" Ameh protested. "This can not be decided like this. I cannot…"

Before Ameh could say another word, Ramuza spoke, as if supporting Ameh's protest. "Mfalme is not just a name. It is an honored position, passed down from father to son. It is an unbroken bloodline. But even then, it is a name that is never given until it is earned. Understandably, the Chinchigwe Mfalme bloodline has been broken. So, it must begin anew with the one from among you who has earned the name. All the Chinchigwe must make that decision."

"It has already been decided," repeated Twese. "I can tell you now that there is no lack of support from the Chinchigwe. Ameh has led us, scolded us; he has comforted us. He has been like a father to all of us. All the Chinchigwe will agree that Ameh Jobabwe was born for this very day and this moment."

"No, Twese." Ameh continued his protest. "In the past few days, I have only done what I could, as all of you have done. I do not think I can fulfill all an Mfalme must do."

Ameh spoke from his heart. He was positive that he could not fulfill all that he must do. He had the love and the respect of his people. He had an old man's wisdom and a presence of mind. Most of all, he could lead with the best intentions for the future of the Chinchigwe.

If it was true that he had earned the right to be called Mfalme, then he should be ready to begin a royal bloodline. Ameh knew that he couldn't. If he were Mfalme, the bloodline would begin and end with him. His only son was dead. The Chinchigwe had already lost their Mfalme bloodline once. Ameh thought too much of his people to cause them to experience that loss again.

Ameh looked at Mfalme Ncobba. He smiled almost apologetically. "As you know by now, Twese Merende is an impetuous young man. He is gifted with a keen mind, often attuned to situations as they ought to be. The fundamental question, whether the Chinchigwe should accept your invitation to stay, still must be officially decided. And yet, Twese has already appointed me Mfalme. In this case, he is wrong."

"But Ameh…"

"Twese!" The sharp intonation of Twese's name was enough to discipline the young Chinchigwe. Ameh continued to address Ramuza. "Thank you for giving us the time to think about this matter. Twese, the rest of the Chinchigwe, and I will discuss what must be done. I will let you know what we have decided during your Daily Celebration of Life this evening. The decisions cannot be made lightly."

"Take your time, Great Creation." Ramuza stood up, bringing an end to the gathering. Everyone else followed his queue. They also stood up and began filing out of the area.

Ramuza and Ameh were the last two people in the area. Once again, Ramuza caught Ameh's attention and held him back.

"Yes, Mfalme?"

"Please stay."

"Is there something else, Mfalme?"

"Honestly, Great Creation, I do not know." With this, the Aukmondi Mfalme walked past Ameh and left the area behind the other people. He left Ameh standing alone.

56

THIS SECRET NEED NEVER HAVE BEEN KNOWN

It was an awkward moment for Ameh, but it did not last long. Shortly after the Mfalme left, Ameh saw Kon-Shambique enter the area. Behind him was Lobarra Gendeyani. It was the first time he had seen her since the Chinchigwe left Kon-Shambique's kraal. He had not seen her at all since her baby was born. Ameh rushed over to greet her.

"Lobarra, you have come down from Nagorda. I am so very glad to see you."

Lobarra lifted her bowed head only long enough to smile back at Ameh.

"May we talk with you a moment, Great Creation?" Kon-Shambique asked.

"Yes. Of course." Ameh suddenly realized he was in a position to be the gracious host. "Come, please be seated."

Ameh waited until Kon-Shambique and Lobarra were seated in the exact same spot where he and Twese had sat moments ago. Then, he took a seat where Ramuza had sat.

"Lobarra, I must apologize for not coming to see you. There has been so much happening. And the hillside of Nagorda is very discouraging. How have you been? You look strong."

Lobarra lifted her head again. The gentle smile on her face was gone. "I am well, Ameh."

"How is your baby? Mfalme Ncobba told us you had a little boy."

Lobarra wore a small blanket over her left shoulder the whole time. She gently removed the blanket, revealing a baby nursing at her breast. "My baby is doing well too, Ameh."

"He is a beautiful child." Ameh could barely resist the impulse to touch the infant. He raised his hand to do so. But because the infant was nursing, he respectfully put his hand back in his lap. It was at this point that he noticed Lobarra had been crying recently. "Lobarra, what is wrong? Is there something I can do?"

Lobarra only bowed her head again and pulled the blanket back over the baby and her shoulder.

"It is the reason we have come, Great Creation," Kon-Shambique said. He turned to Lobarra. "Sacred Woman now is the proper time."

Lobarra raised her head. There were fresh tears streaming down her face. With her free hand, she tried to wipe the tears away. She only managed to streak the tears across her cheek. She looked Ameh in the eye for the first time.

"Ameh Jobabwe, I have come to beg your forgiveness."

"Forgiveness? For what?"

"Kon-Shambique has told me that the Mfalme intends to ask the Chinchigwe to join the Aukmondi this evening," Lobarra spoke through sobs, unable to hold back her crying. "It will be a wonderful moment. It will be what the Chinchigwe have needed. There will be much joy and happiness. But, for you, I will spoil it all."

"What are you talking about? How can you spoil such a moment?"

Ameh waited for the answers to his questions, but Lobarra had bowed her head and fallen silent again. He looked at Kon-Shambique for an explanation.

When Kon-Shambique realized Lobarra did not want to continue her confession, he gently pulled the blanket back on her shoulder. With loving care, he separated the infant from his mother's breast. He handled the baby with such gentleness that it showed no frustration when taken from the cradle of its mother's comfort and nourishment.

No words were ever spoken when the full essence of Lobarra's confession was finally revealed. Kon-Shambique handed the infant to Ameh.

"What is expected of me now?"

"Take the infant, please." Kon-Shambique insisted. "Hold it."

Ameh slowly took the naked infant. Rather awkwardly, he held it up by its shoulders as if examining a piece of clothing. As he studied the features of the satiated infant, Ameh saw more than just a healthy baby boy. He saw a revelation. He saw the physical features of someone he knew quite well, the shape of the infant's nose, the bow of its tiny lips.

"Mahjani?" He whispered. A coarseness in his voice hid his sudden embarrassment. He lowered the infant into his arms to shield it from view. Ameh found himself too ashamed to raise his head.

When he finally forced himself to look up, he slowly raised his eyes to Lobarra. He found her silently crying, hiding her face in her hands. Ameh realized that she was experiencing considerably more shame than he was. "Is this true, Lobarra? Did my son father this child?"

Lobarra acknowledged without removing her hands. It wasn't until Kon-Shambique gently touched her shoulder that she finally took her hands away and looked into Ameh's face again. She forced herself to speak.

"Mahjani and I, we meant to hurt no one," she said. "We were friends, drawn close by so many little things. I could tell Mahjani things that I could tell no one else. And Mahjani would always listen to me. Mahjani shared many of his hopes and dreams with me. I always seemed to understand what he felt in his heart. We had a closeness that was natural and good. Both of us felt good about our relationship. But because of what we knew people would think or what people would say, our closeness had to be kept a secret. It had to be hidden. It had to be protected."

"What about your mate, Whanu? How could you have done this to him?"

Lobarra wiped tears from her face again. "I loved Whanu. I always have. And although I do not expect you to believe me, I still do, to this very day. But my cherished relationship with Whanu had little to do with how Mahjani and I felt. The things Mahjani and I shared were also special, in their way. They had to be protected even from my own mate.

"I had no intention of ever hurting Whanu or anyone. What happened between Mahjani and me was a development that neither of us anticipated. It was a closeness that grew stronger each day. Eventually, it went beyond our control. I am sorry, Ameh, if we have brought you shame."

Oddly enough, Ameh was not thinking about his shame now. He was thinking about Lobarra. His knitted brow did not completely express the concern he felt. What would force her to confess this secret now?

"Both Whanu and Mahjani are dead. You did not have to tell me. You did not have to tell anyone. This secret need never have been known."

"Yes. I tried to keep it to myself." Lobarra looked at Kon-Shambique. She grew strength from the talk that the two of them had over the past two days. "After the infant was born, I too was ashamed. I tried to hide my shame, but I could not. Kon-Shambique knew something was wrong long before I ever said a word. He talked with me until I finally told him everything. In time, he convinced me that you have a right to know and that I must accept and bear the consequences."

Ameh looked accusingly at Kon-Shambique. "You knew? Why did you not tell me?"

"As Lobarra explained, Great Creation, I learned the truth soon after the baby was born. You have every right to know because he is your flesh and blood. But it was never my place to tell you. It took me until this evening to convince the Sacred Woman to do what must be done."

Ameh sighed. He allowed his knitted brow to dissolve as he looked down at the infant in his arms. Under normal circumstances,

Ameh would have thrust the infant back into Lobarra's arms. Under normal circumstances, Ameh would have been extremely angry. He knew that both Mahjani and Lobarra would have been disgraced and would have no chance of receiving forgiveness from him or anyone else.

Instead, there was none of that. The innocent infant in his arms seemed to change all of that. Ameh suddenly understood what prompted such a rage in his son that night, when he was killed. Instead of shame, love was taking root here; a bond developing from grandfather to grandson.

"Lobarra Gendeyani," Ameh said softly, "do not be ashamed. For all that it is worth, I will always stand proudly by your side. By what name shall we call the infant?"

Lobarra looked up at Kon-Shambique. The Favored Tribesman had said that Ameh was a Forgiving Creation and that, given time, he would understand. She stopped crying and sat up straight. As she wiped away her last unhappy tear, a look of redemption was on her face. A smile seemed to force its way through. She could feel tremendous relief as the tension melted away.

She turned back to Ameh. "You…you are not angry with me?"

"I loved my son very much. Though he saw fit to take another man's mate, I know he was not evil. And I have known you, Lobarra, since you were a baby girl. You have always been a thoughtful and kind person. I cannot fully accept what the two of you have done," Ameh looked down at the infant, "but I cannot condemn the result. No, Lobarra. I am not angry with you."

Lobarra's intense and chaotic feelings, which had developed over the past nine months, suddenly burst into a hysterical cry of relief. She sobbed tears of happiness.

"If I may," she began slowly, between sobs, "I would like to call him Tutapona."

"Tutapona?" Ameh repeated. "It is a good name."

"We will recover," Kon-Shambique translated. "It is an appropriate name."

Ameh gave Tutapona back to his mother. "You are the mother of my grandson. Although you carry the name Gendeyani, lovingly given to you by your mate, Tutapona will rightfully carry the name of his father, Jobabwe. Tutapona Jobabwe."

57

UNANIMOUS MANDATE

A meh needed time to think. Mfalme Ncobba had intended to invite the Chinchigwe into the Aukmondi tribe. Lobarra had confessed that her baby was fathered by his son. So much was happening so fast. Ameh left the Royal Kraal and headed straight for the solitude of his hut in the guest kraal. He wanted to get his thoughts together.

Before that private session with Kon-Shambique and Lobarra, Ameh had expected to wrestle with explaining why he could not be the Chinchigwe Mfalme. He felt he would have to refuse the honored position, even with a mandate from his people, for the simple reason that his bloodline ended with him.

All of that has changed now. There was a Jobabwe bloodline after all.

******

After Mfalme Ncobba had made known his intention to invite the Chinchigwe into the Aukmondi tribe, Twese, on the other hand, took the bold initiative to quickly and personally visit each of his fellow Chinchigwe: Embabi, Komu, Lobarra, Summarwe, Jpuma, and all the others. He explained to them the situation as he saw it. He also gave each of them two tiny stones, a white one and a black one.

Before Twese finished each visit, he asked that one of the imparted stones be dropped into the pouch he carried. He did not care about knowing which stone; his only request was that a choice be made. The white stone would signify a desire to have Ameh as the Chinchigwe Mfalme, while the black stone signified a rejection.

Twese visited Ameh last. He found the old man at the entrance of the guest kraal. Ameh had been drawn out of the hut by the beauty of the full moon. He was sitting alone, enjoying the serenity as he organized his thoughts.

Twese placed the two stones into Ameh's right hand. Unlike the others before Ameh, Twese placed the entire pouch into Ameh's left hand.

"What is this, Twese?" Ameh glanced at the pouch and the stones.

"Ameh, may our ancestors bear witness to what I have done. I have asked each of our people to accept or reject you as Mfalme. The pouch contains their answers. I have not counted the stones. I do not know their answers, but I can make a pretty sound guess."

Ameh held the pouch up as if to weigh its contents. Then he looked at the two stones in his right hand. "Then, what are these?"

"Just in case our people are divided, you still have a choice. Who knows? Your stone, be it black or white, may make a difference. But I doubt it." Twese smiled and walked away.

******

Moments later, Ameh sat alone in his hut, mentally preparing to serve his people as best he could. He sat on the ground with the contents of the small pouch poured out on a mat before him – twenty-four white stones, his mandate. It was unanimous.

He placed the stones back into the pouch when he heard a noise at the hut's entrance. He looked up to see an Aukmondi Red Warrior peeping in.

"Great Creation," the warrior said, "Please excuse my intrusion."

"You are not intruding."

"The Mfalme awaits your arrival in the Royal Kraal."

"Thank you. You may tell the Mfalme that I am on my way." Ameh tied the pouch to the belt at his waist and got to his feet.

When Ameh stepped outside the hut, he immediately noticed how quiet the area was. Everyone was already in the Royal Kraal's celebration area, about a kilometer away. However, he could still hear the faint sounds of singing, drums, and music as the people celebrated.

The full moon, climbing higher in the night sky, brightly illuminated the clearing in the guest kraal. Even with an old man's eyes, he could see clearly across the clearing to the kraal entrance. He saw the Red Warrior that had just summoned him to leave the Kraal. Surprisingly, he also saw Summarwe Bata leaving one of the nearby guest huts. She walked briskly and carried a large blanket under her arms.

Ameh rushed out into the clearing to intercept her. "Summarwe, is that you?"

"Yes, Ameh. It is me."

"I thought everyone had gone to the Royal Kraal by now. What are you still doing here?"

"I had to come back on an errand. As you may know, Lobarra Gendeyani moved down from Nagorda Peak, Kon-Shambique's kraal. She has come to stay with the rest of us, here in the guest kraal."

"Yes, I heard."

"She is waiting for you in the celebration area with everyone else. I returned here to get an extra blanket for her and Tutapona." Summarwe held up the blanket as if to show proof.

Ameh only smiled. The shy Summarwe seldom talked. But when she does, it is always a delight to hear. "If you are on your way back to the Royal Kraal and the celebration area, I will walk with you."

"Thank you. I would like that."

Ameh and Summarwe walked silently until just after exiting the guest kraal, they began walking up the south bank pathway. Ameh was about to ask Summarwe about her brother, Jpuma, when Summarwe herself broke the silence.

"Ameh, should we start calling you Mfalme yet?" she asked. "Will you accept the position?"

Ameh touched the pouch of white stone at his waist. "I seem to have no choice. There were twenty-four white stones in the pouch, a unanimous mandate. Officially, I suppose I am the Chinchigwe Mfalme."

"Then I am glad. It is as it should be."

"You think so?"

"Yes. Yes, I do."

Ameh and Summarwe walked a few more meters in silence, listening to the singing, drums, and music from the Royal Kraal. They were closer now, and they could hear voices and laughter.

Ameh and Summarwe were almost at the bridge crossing over to the north bank before either spoke again. This time, it was Ameh who finally broke the silence. "How is your brother's leg?"

"It is better. He still walks with a limp. But he doesn't need assistance anymore."

"Good. In time, even his limp will be gone."

"Mfalme," Summarwe giggled. She enjoyed saying the name. "There is a rumor that Tutapona was your grandson."

Ameh stopped walking for a second. He glanced down at the young woman. "Where did you hear that from?"

"Jpuma told me. Is it true?"

"Rumors and wildfires," Ameh said to himself. "Nothing travels faster. Yes, Summarwe. Tutapona is my grandson."

"I knew it!" Summarwe's giggle was much stronger. "I knew it!"

"What do you mean, you knew? Am I the last to know?"

"If you are the last to know, then I am, most certainly, the first."

"Summarwe, young woman, you must explain yourself." Ameh feigned anger, although he wasn't.

"Earlier today, I visited Kon-Shambique's kraal to visit Lobarra. I wanted to see how she and the baby were doing. I was concerned about her. I wondered why she had not moved down into the guest kraal with the rest of us."

"That was very thoughtful of you," Ameh said. "You have cared for Lobarra since the hunters raided our village. She probably would not have made it without you."

Only a shy smile on Summarwe's face acknowledged Ameh's compliment as she explained. "After Kon-Shambique and Tongda welcomed me in, Lobarra showed me the baby. Lobarra and I sat and talked for a little while. Most of the time during our talk, I could hardly take my eyes off of Tutapona."

"Why was that?"

"I wasn't sure at the time. But there was something about him that I kept looking at. I kept looking and staring. Lobarra noticed me staring with such curiosity that she finally asked me what was wrong."

"And, was there anything wrong?"

"No. I told her, honestly, there was nothing wrong."

"So what were you looking at?"

"The infant looked so familiar. I did not realize it then, but I was looking at your son, Mahjani. All that I could say to Lobarra, at that time, was that you, Ameh, should see the baby. That is when Lobarra started crying. She cried so hard that Kon-Shambique finally asked me to leave and let Lobarra rest."

Ameh chuckled at Summarwe's revelation. "You were staring at a secret. It was a secret that Lobarra was not quite ready to reveal."

"I did not mean to upset her. I may have started the rumor. But she seems to be alright now. When I left Lobarra in the celebration area just now, she proudly showed everybody Tutapona, your grandson."

"You were right, Summarwe. I guess you were the first to know."

Ameh and Summarwe crossed the bridge from the south to the north bank. They began walking up the small trail toward the entrance to the Royal Kraal.

— **58** —

THE DAILY CELEBRATION OF LIFE

As the name implies, the Daily Celebration of Life usually occurs once a day in the Aukmondi Valley. It is a very casual and free-spirited event. The only formal aspect is its commencement, the few moments when Mfalme Ncobba stands before the people and summarizes why each day is being celebrated.

On this day, there were several reasons to celebrate life. In the first place, yesterday's Celebration of Life was postponed. The Aukmondi were overdue for one. Secondly, the Aukmondi had just gone through a tremendous life-threatening crisis. That crisis was over now. There was a more intense appreciation for being alive. And finally, a special ceremony was to be held during this celebration. Ramuza and the Great Creation Ameh were due to unite the Chinchigwe and Aukmondi tribes formally. From this day forward, the two tribes were to experience a common future, a merging of cultures, and a sharing of ancestors.

No time had been wasted in preparing the celebration. Not long after the slave merchant was taken out of the valley, the people, in a great community spirit, immediately went to work. Campfires for socializing were set up throughout the celebration area. Various foods and beverages from the postponed Celebration were brought down from the Pogobi kraal and set up randomly in the celebration area.

The musicians brought out their marimbas, drums, and other instruments. Singing, dancing, and other forms of impromptu entertainment began to occur, one behind the other, and sometimes simultaneously. Nothing was lacking at this Celebration; this very special Celebration, which began long before Ramuza announced its official beginning.

Three hours after sunset, Ramuza received word that the Great Creation Ameh was going to the Royal Kraal. Only three hours later than usual, Ramuza stood on the royal dais. He proudly got the attention of the people before him.

"Let us not forget the experiences of today and yesterday," he began. He spoke with the same mind and heart as his great ancestor, Ba-Ogu. "Our lives can be greatly enriched if we apply our lessons. All of us can benefit greatly.

"Shallow and Desperate Creations came into our lives recently. They were driven by one of the worst types of greed: the type of greed that consumes the lives of others. Their Ignorance and selfishness closed their eyes to the harm they were creating for themselves and us. For themselves, those Shallow and Desperate Creations eventually became victims of the Batushi. Their inevitable fall was a result of their own doing.

"As for their attempt to consume our lives, we have survived. Why? We have survived because we have embraced the love of the Supreme Spirit of Life. Her love is the key. Her love guides us toward all secrets of survival. Because we have embraced Her love, She speaks to us. When She speaks to us, all we must do is pay attention to survive."

Ramuza spoke much longer than usual. He had a lot to say. He knew that the Aukmondi had heard this wisdom's essence before and understood. It was the Chinchigwe that he spoke mainly to. They were hearing this perspective for the first time.

"This is the wisdom," he said, "that the Supreme Spirit has been forcing on us since our earliest beginnings. We have no choice but to embrace this wisdom and live by it. If we don't, we fall like the merchant and his aides. There is no other way. The merchant and his aides are learning this the hard way."

With this, Ramuza ended the main part of his commencement. With only a brief pause in his momentum, before the eyes and ears of history, he officially asked Ameh and his people to join the Aukmondi Tribe. He asked the Chinchigwe to become a newfound part of the Aukmondi spirit, to share cultures, accomplishments, and all other human life pursuits.

For the Chinchigwe, Ameh officially accepted Ramuza's invitation. By word, the union was sealed. For all eyes and ears of humankind to come, the Chinchigwe became a full clan of the Aukmondi, and Ameh Jobabwe, its Mfalme.

******

When Mfalme Jobabwe accepted the tribal union, he had to make his first official decree. He stepped up to stand beside Ramuza and turned to face the crowd.

The Gray Warrior Kharaambi came and stood ceremoniously before Ameh. To her left was Quazzi, dressed not as a warrior but as a tribe member. Quazzi carried his brown cloak and shield, which he gave just as ceremoniously to Kharaambi. Kharaambi, in turn, handed them to the new Mfalme.

"Mfalme Jobabwe," she began, "by right, I surrender to you what are yours, the cloak and shield of the Brown Warrior."

Ameh accepted the cloak and shield. Both Ramuza and Kharaambi had explained to him that this moment would come. During those moments of solitude just before walking over, Ameh had carefully considered how he would respond.

As the leader of the Aukmondi's largest clan, Ameh had to choose among three options. He could accept the brown cloak and shield and legally retire them. The Aukmondi would be without a Brown Warrior. The fact that Kharaambi had a Brown Warrior in the first place showed to Ameh that a Brown Warrior was needed. So, this choice was eliminated.

Ameh could legally become the Brown Warrior by wearing the brown cloak and carrying the brown shield. But this was ridiculous. Ameh felt he had leadership abilities but was a farmer, not a warrior. Consequently, this choice was eliminated, too.

Ameh exercised his final choice: appointing a Brown Warrior, preferably someone with proven qualities as both a leader and a warrior. Ameh knew that this disqualified anyone from among the Chinchigwe. Though good people, they were only crafters and farmers like him. To Ameh, there was but one reasonable and practical choice. Ameh turned to Quazzi.

"Great Creation Quazzi Kuuza Gembali, the Gray Warrior, Kharaambi, needs a Brown Warrior. I choose you to serve us in that capacity. Will you accept this appointment?"

Quazzi smiled. "Great Creation, Mfalme Jobabwe, I will be honored."

Quazzi took the brown cloak and shield. Once again, he was the tribe's Brown Warrior. The only difference was that his appointment came from Ameh rather than Kharaambi.

There arose a joyous cheer from all around.

Ramuza finally ended the formal commencement. He spoke the words that the Aukmondi were accustomed to hearing every evening. "Enjoy your evening."

Rhythmic music suddenly filled the air. The singing and dancing resumed. Already, it was a celebration that no one would soon forget.

EPILOGUE

Later that evening, after most everyone was somewhat exhausted from the dancing and singing, people began to coalesce into several socializing groups throughout the celebration area. The brief moments of rest were filled with lively conversations and laughter. One of the largest groups included Rwuva, Olabisi, Kharaambi, Kon-Shambique, Tongda, Adaulah, Ameh, Twese, and others. All of them were sitting around Ramuza.

"Mfalme Ncobba, since earlier this evening, I have been wondering about something." Twese had discovered a whole new perspective about people, women in particular. He was still trying to learn all that he could. "How often does the Supreme Spirit assume human form and walk among us?"

"I am told, much more often than we are ever aware, Great Creation. We can easily assume every day. But that is a question you should ask the Favored Tribesman."

"No one knows," Kon-Shambique responded as everyone turned to him. "I can only say that each day, we see Her at least once a day without realizing it. She assumes the features of various Sacred Women as She mingles here and there."

"The Sacred Woman Andallah is a perfect example," added Ramuza. "I saw her early in the morning. But I did not realize that Andallah was the guise of the Sacred Woman Eledah until this evening. She often comes and goes without ever being discovered."

"Is She here, among us now?" Twese scanned the people around him as if to locate Her.

"As a matter of fact," Ramuza sat forward. He just remembered part of the conversation he had with Andallah. "When I talked with the Sacred Woman, down on the north bank pathway this morning, She promised me that She would be gone from the valley by early morning. Of course, always being true to Her word, this would imply that She is still here."

"I would like to know when I am talking with Her. How can She be recognized if She changes Her identity?"

Kon-Shambique laughed at Twese's concerns. "She does not hide from you, Great Creation. She never has. She never will. You don't recognize Her simply because you don't realize who you are looking at. It is said that only infants are sensitive enough to recognize Her on sight."

Until then, Adaulah sat quietly, listening to the conversation around him. When the subject of recognizing the Sacred Woman Eledah came up, he had to speak up. An untruth was being told to Twese. He had to correct it.

"I am no infant," he said, "and I can recognize Her when I see Her."

"Oh? Since when?" Kharaambi asked teasingly.

"I think, since always, Sacred Mother."

"How come you never told anyone about this ability?" Olabisi asked.

Adaulah shrugged. "I don't know. I thought everyone could do it."

"Is She among us now, Little Creation?" Twese anxiously wanted to know.

Adaulah quickly searched the faces around him. He even stood up to check the faces in other nearby groups. Sitting back down, he pointed to a young woman sitting in a group to his right. "There. Do you see the Sacred Woman in the flowered garment? She is the Sacred Woman Eledah."

"And how do you know this?" Ramuza asked.

"I do not know, Great Creation. I just know."

The Great Creation Ameh attempted to see where Adaulah had pointed. His eyes were not so great after all. Because of the glare of the campfire around which he sat, he could barely recognize anyone in the nearby group. He certainly did not see a woman in a flowered garment. Ameh gave up and turned his attention back to the people and conversation in his group.

"Little Creation," Twese said to Adaulah, "the young woman you indicate is a Chinchigwe. I have known her since she was an infant. Her name is Summarwe."

Hearing this, Ameh recalled the talkative walk with Summarwe from the guest kraal. The more he thought about their conversation, the more curious he became. Ameh quickly forced his old man's body to stand. With the glare of the campfire gone from his eye, he could see the nearby group.

Embabi, Lobarra, her baby, and Summarwe were among the people in the group. Summarwe looked up at Ameh with a knowing smile on her face.

APPENDIX I

Aukmondi Family Names

Each individual of the Aukmondi tribe has two family names, an immediate and an ancestral. In their own respect, both reveal a very important family lineage.

The most important is the ancestral family name. This is an individual's middle name. It is passed on to a child by his or her natural mother. It is this name which determines an individual's family lineage. In some cases, the ancestral family name is traceable back to one of the 59 Sacred Tribal Mothers, women who were born in the "Old Tribe".

The immediate family name, an individual's last name, is given to a child by his or her natural father and to a female by her mate after an official union (marriage). In the very rare cases of multiple unions, where there is more than one male, the female takes all the last names, hyphenated in union order.

The immediate family name is used to determine the lineage of material property inheritance. In the case of the Ncobbas, the immediate family name also helps to determine the lineage of the Mfalme, from father to oldest son.

APPENDIX II
Echelons of the Aukmondi Army

Black Warrior
Military Rank of the Mfalme
|
Gray Warrior
Leader of the Aukmondi Army
|
Brown Warrior
Foremost Lieutenant of the Aukmondi Army
Senior Mfalme of all clans or his designate
|
Royal Warrior
Leader of one of the twenty independent Aukmondi Armies
(Each army consists of approximately 350 warriors in two regiments)
|
Blue Warrior
Leader of one of the forty army regiments
(Each regiment consists of 175 warriors; There are two types of regiments)

12 Sentinel Regiments	28 Warrior Regiments
(Each consisting of	(Each consisting of
175 Green Warriors	**10 Green Warriors**
Sentinels	Special Tasks : Intelligence, Scouts

60 Gold Warriors
Independent/Master Warrior: Trainer,
Police
|
50 Orange Warriors
Semi-independent Warrior: Police,
Tribal Caretaker
|

<u>40 Red Warriors</u>
Dependent Warrior: Tribal Caretaker,
Guard, Trainee, Aide
|
<u>15 White Warriors</u>
Dependent Warrior: Guard, Trainee,
Aide, Recruit

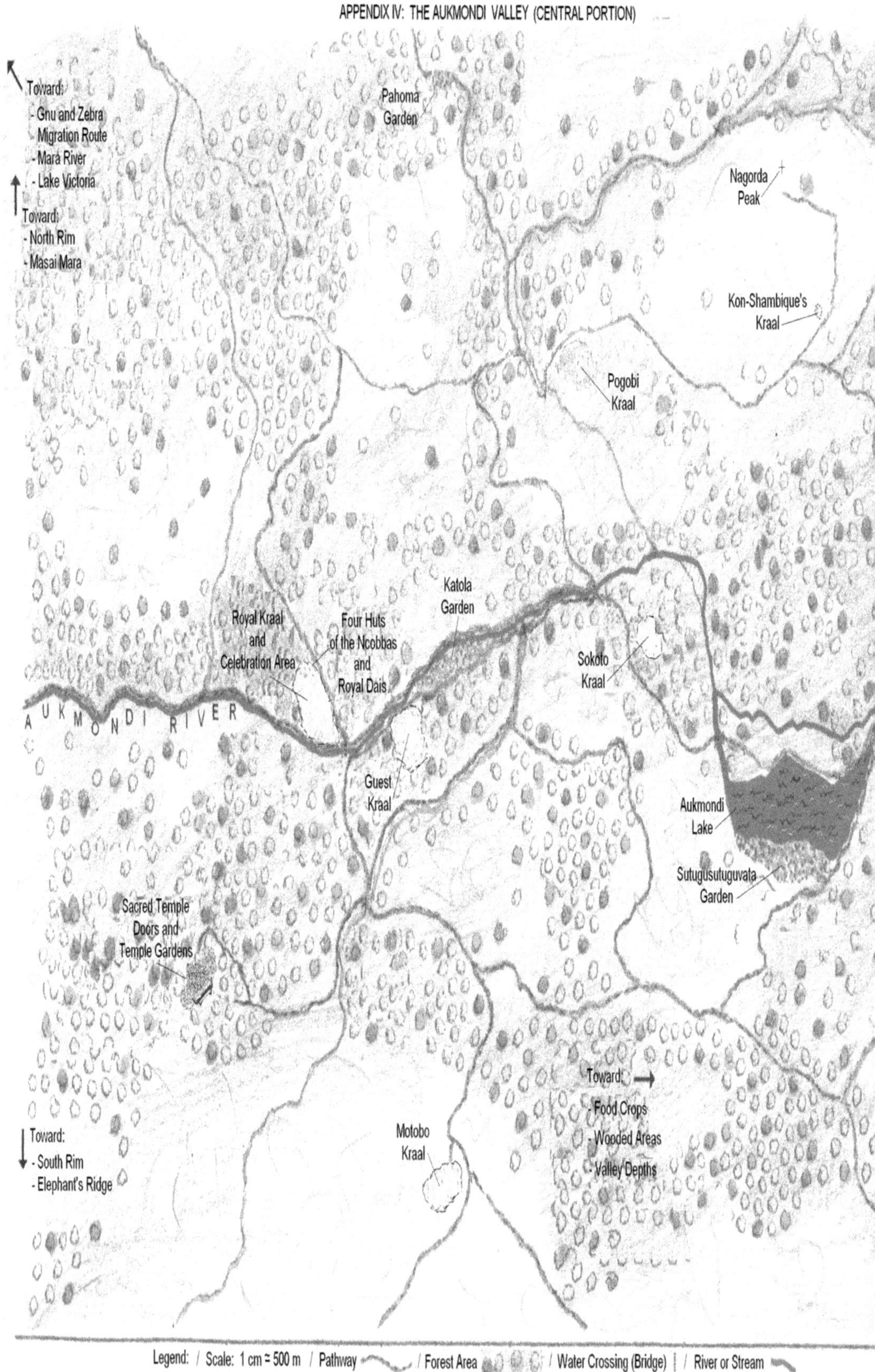
Toward:
- Gnu and Zebra
  Migration Route
- Mara River
- Lake Victoria
Toward:
- North Rim
- Masai Mara
Pahoma
Garden
Nagorda
Peak
Kon-Shambique's
Kraal
Pogobi
Kraal
Katola
Garden
Royal Kraal
and
Celebration Area
Four Huts
of the Ncobbas
and
Royal Dais
Sokoto
Kraal
Guest
Kraal
AUKMONDI RIVER
Aukmondi
Lake
Sutugusutuguvata
Garden
Sacred Temple
Doors and
Temple Gardens
Toward:
- South Rim
- Elephant's Ridge
Toward:
Motobo
Kraal
Toward:
- Food Crops
- Wooded Areas
- Valley Depths
Legend: / Scale: 1 cm ≈ 500 m / Pathway / Forest Area / Water Crossing (Bridge) / River or Stream

APPENDIX IV: AUKMONDI VALLEY